Summer at Rose Island

HOLLY MARTIN

bookouture

Published by Bookouture

An imprint of StoryFire Ltd.
23 Sussex Road, Ickenham, UB10 8PN
ited Kingdom

bookouture.com

To all the wonderful bloggers, for your tweets, retweets,
Facebook posts, tireless promotions, support,
encouragement and endless enthusiasm.
You guys are amazing. I couldn't make this
journey without you.

CHAPTER 1

An endless world of blue stretched out below Darcy. The sandy seabed lay about ten metres beneath her and she smiled as she saw fish of every colour and size swimming lazily between the rocks and seaweed. Starfish and sunstars littered the seabed, and with the sun's rays penetrating the water and gently caressing their outstretched arms, it was as if they were sunbathing on a tourist-filled beach. Giant stalks of seaweed moved and swayed gently as if they were trees caught in a breeze rather than the constant roll of the waves and the tide. There was something so tranquil and serene about this underwater vista, she could look at it for hours and never get bored.

The fish didn't have jobs to worry about or bills to pay and she was pretty sure that the starfish didn't have parents to try to please – or, as in her case, constantly disappoint. Life continued here as it always did, an almost worry-free existence where the only dark cloud was when something bigger than you was looking for something to eat.

As she bobbed on top of the waves, her head face down in the water, Darcy could pretend, just for a minute or two, that she was part of this world. A tiny fish in a big pond.

She rolled onto her back and took a deep breath of salty, tangy sea air. The sun shone down on her, glinting off the droplets on her goggles. As the waves lapped over her fingers, she felt a sense of contentment fill her almost like a great sigh of relief. Although she had been in the town only a few hours, she knew that moving from London to White Cliff Bay was the best decision she had ever made.

Her love for the sea had been with her as far back as she could remember, but it was here in White Cliff Bay on many childhood holidays staying with her aunt that her love had blossomed. Swimming in the sea every day, she spent her evenings reading every non-fiction book about the water and its wildlife she could get her hands on. Her aunt had taken her scuba diving when she was twelve, opening up a whole other world she had never known before. The sea was in her blood. Coming back here felt like coming home.

A bark nearby disturbed her tranquil reverie and she moved so she was treading water, rather than floating, and looked around.

Her beautiful black Labrador, Ben, had come back for her, clearly wondering why she was just floating there, staring at the sky rather than swimming. He shoved his wet nose in her face and, happy that she was OK, he turned and swam off in the direction of the island. Darcy laughed and swam after him.

As Darcy reached the rocks surrounding Rose Island Lighthouse, Ben swam on ahead. He pulled himself out of the water, turned round and started barking at Darcy to hurry up. The sea birds nestled on the rocks took off in a grey cloud, squawking their annoyance at the evil, black dog. Ben clambered over the rocks, wagging his tail as he chased the last few birds away.

'Leave them be,' Darcy laughed as she climbed out onto the rocks beside him; she pulled him towards her and tugged playfully on his silky ears. He sat down on her so she could continue her stroking more thoroughly.

'Oof! Ben, you are not a lap-sized dog. You do not fit on my lap. Do you think you're a Chihuahua or something? You're a Labrador and a fat one at that, get off,' Darcy moaned, halfheartedly trying to push Ben off her. He continued to sit on her lap, wagging his tail in her face.

Darcy pulled her goggles onto her forehead and looked over the golden-crested waves at the tiny town of White Cliff Bay. The late afternoon sun was just starting to make its descent, painting the sky a candyfloss pink. From her position on Rose Island, about three hundred yards out into the bay, she could see almost the whole town in all its glory. The quieter part of Silver Cove, where she now lived, the main shops and the hodgepodge of cute little houses that cascaded down the steep hills of the main town centre. She smiled. She knew she was going to be happy here. Despite her parents' misgivings and looks of disapproval when she told them she was packing up all her worldly goods and travelling hundreds of miles from her home to take up a new job, she knew she had made the right decision. It didn't matter that she didn't completely know what her new job entailed or that she knew no one down here, this gorgeous little town was going to be a great new chapter in her life.

Everything seemed slower here, more laid-back and relaxed; it felt cleaner, safer, but despite this her parents couldn't understand why Darcy had wanted to leave London, with its high-powered jobs, multi-billion-pound companies, and the prestige of living and working in the capital. She didn't want restaurants that stayed open until after midnight or the constant hum of traffic and voices that never seemed to stop, no matter what time of day it was. Since she had lost her perfect job a few years before, and moved back to London with her dreams in tatters, she had felt almost claustrophobic, as if the buildings were too close. She had been a face in the crowd that no one cared about. The city had slowly chipped away at her soul until she was no more than another suited drone heading off to work every day. Here it felt like she could finally breathe again.

Part of the problem with her relocation had been her choice of White Cliff Bay itself. A place that was entirely to blame, at least as far as her parents were concerned, for her aunt's spectacular drop-out from society. Aunt Ginny had been a highly paid solicitor in the City until she had sold her house, bought an old-fashioned horse-drawn gypsy caravan to live in, and spent the rest of her life living off the sale of the odd painting and homemade jars of jam and apple sauce. She had always been spoken about in hushed tones, if she was spoken about at all, and Darcy strongly suspected she was going to end up that way too. She couldn't help smiling at the thought.

She leaned back to look at the lighthouse, the sun glinting off the glass at the top. It was a beautiful, old building, painted in traditional red and white colours, with the multi-faceted lantern at the top. She had always enjoyed swimming in the sea, but this had to be the most picturesque swim she had done in a long time. The lighthouse had been deserted for many years; certainly when she had swum round the island as a child no one had ever lived there. New-fangled technology meant the days of the lighthouse keeper were a thing of the past. So her heart leapt from shock when her eyes cast down the tall tower and she saw a man standing at one of the windows watching her and Ben.

He was wearing a faded blue crumpled shirt hanging loose over dark jeans. His black hair was equally messy in an un-kempt just-got-out-bed look. The man's tanned arms were folded angrily over his chest. Easily reaching the top of the leaded windows that were flung open either side, the man's height seemed to add to the anger he was projecting. She supposed he was quite good looking, if you liked the tall, dark, mean and moody type.

Darcy suddenly became aware of the first impression she was making on him. In her skin-tight, show-every-lump-and-bump wetsuit, with her long red hair matted against her head and to-day's make-up smeared across her face like a Picasso painting gone wrong, she was a sight to behold. She stood up, tipping Ben off her lap as she did so, then belatedly realised she was showing her body in its full glory; at least sitting down Ben had been covering her modesty.

'Great. What a brilliant view of my wobbly bits he's getting right now,' Darcy muttered, sucking in her belly and wringing out her hair.

The man started shouting at her. Gesturing with his hands, he pointed at the sea, then her and then Ben. Whatever he was yelling – furiously, it would seem – was lost in the sound of the wind and the waves crashing against the rocks.

'Hi, nice to meet you, would you like to come in for a cup of hot chocolate and some great sex?' Darcy mumbled under her breath. 'I'm sure that's what he's saying. That and: Great body, by the way. No one looks good in a wetsuit but somehow you manage to pull it off. How about that great sex?'

Mystery Man continued to shout and then, getting frustrated at not being heard, he left the window, no doubt on his way downstairs to yell at her face to face.

'Time to go, Ben,' Darcy said, climbing down the rocks. She turned to make sure Ben got down OK. As Ben drew level with her, she took one last look at the lighthouse to see that Mystery Man had arrived at the door, still shouting. She pulled her goggles over her eyes and dived into the sea. The water closed in over her head and seconds later she felt Ben beside her. Darcy surfaced about ten metres from the rocks and looked back at Mystery Man, who was continuing to yell at her from the shore.

'Sorry, can't hear you,' Darcy shouted and then, confident he couldn't possibly hear her, she added, 'But I'll be back soon for that great sex.'

Mystery Man looked momentarily confused and stopped shouting for a second before continuing his tirade. Darcy turned and swam back to the shore.

As she clambered out onto the beach, she looked back across the bay to the lighthouse. He was still standing there watching her. She grabbed the bag she had left by some rocks, pulled out a towel, patted herself dry. Dragging her T-shirt over her wetsuit, she then pulled another towel out to dry Ben. As she flipped Ben over onto his back to dry his belly, Ben's favourite bit to have dried, she could still feel Mystery Man's eyes on her. She stood up and, sure enough, he was still standing there, as the waves crashed theatrically onto the rocks around him.

She turned away and looked down at her wetsuit and sighed. It wasn't the greatest first impression. She had inadvertently done something to upset him too, and that certainly hadn't been her intention.

She walked back to Sea View Court, the old house at the end of the beach that had been converted into four flats.

She let herself in and Ben ran on ahead of her, but she stopped suddenly when she heard a noise from the flat opposite hers.

She had briefly seen her new neighbours when she'd been unpacking the last of her belongings from her car earlier that day. A young married couple, they had introduced themselves as Libby and George, but Libby had seemed so tearful that George had quickly ushered her into their flat and closed the door behind them.

She listened now and heard a crash, as if something had been thrown and smashed. It was quickly followed by a loud thud and a cry of pain. She heard George shout something and then another thud, and another moan from Libby that made Darcy's heart crash into her stomach.

God, he was beating her up. She felt sick. As another wail of pain resounded from the flat, she marched straight up to the door and banged on it with her fist. The door flew open under her weight and she stormed in.

She froze at what she saw. Libby and George were stark naked and she was clinging to him, her arms and legs wrapped around him as he made love to her against the wall of their flat. Her head was thrown back in obvious ecstasy as he kissed her breasts.

Shit. She couldn't have got it more wrong.

They hadn't noticed her yet, too wrapped up in each other to be aware of anything else. She could just sneak out and they would be none the wiser. But, as she took a step back towards the door, Ben burst in and before she could grab him he launched himself at George's bare backside, shoving his wet, cold nose up where the sun didn't shine.

George let out a scream of shock and looked around to see what it was that had attacked him so inappropriately. If Darcy had thought she could get away without being seen, she'd been sorely mistaken, as first George's eyes then Libby's found hers.

For the longest moment, nobody moved or said anything, George still pinning Libby to the wall with his weight. There was only one way to get out of this with any shred of dignity left intact. Darcy was going to have to brazen this out.

'I just came round to borrow some sugar. I probably have some somewhere in one of the many boxes but I thought you might have some . . . I can see this isn't the best time.' This was a terrible excuse and they all knew it. Libby stifled a giggle as she buried her face in her husband's neck. 'The door just came open when I knocked on it. I'm not a pervert or anything.' Her feet frozen to the ground seemed to contradict that statement, as she continued to stare at them in horror. Oh God, what was she doing? She should have just apologised and left, grabbing her perverted dog on the way out.

George didn't say anything. Probably wondering why she was still standing there. She was wondering that herself.

'Erm . . . There's sugar in the kitchen if you want to help yourself. I, erm . . . have my hands full or I'd get it for you myself,' George said, as Libby's giggling went up an octave.

'Right, well. Maybe I'll pop by later and get it if I don't find my own before then. Carry on. I mean . . .' She gestured lamely to the door and George nodded numbly.

She grabbed Ben by the collar and walked out, quickly closing the door on Libby's laughter a moment later.

Wow. She was really going all out to make a good impression on the residents of White Cliff Bay today.

She scurried back to her own flat, to see she had a text from her best friend Carmel.

How's it going? You unpacked yet? Have you found the kettle? Are there any hot single men?

Darcy smiled. Carmel had married her childhood sweetheart and though she was blissfully happy she always said she'd missed out on the dating scene and had to live her life vicariously through Darcy.

She considered carefully how to answer. Was Mystery Man hot? Of course he was, anyone could see that, but he certainly wasn't worth mentioning when he was obviously a grumpy hermit.

She opened up a new text to reply.

Haven't found the kettle, though I haven't looked. Just been for a swim. It's so pretty here. No hot single men. Though I did just see a man naked.

The reply was instant.

WHAT?? Was he fit? Did you see his willy? Why was he naked? Have you moved to a nudist beach? I want pictures!!

Darcy laughed.

Sadly it's not a nudist beach. I just walked in on my neighbours having sex. Very embarrassing.

The phone beeped back at her almost immediately.

Hahahaha, only you Darcy, only you.

She smiled and put the phone down. She had some unpacking to do.

There was a knock on her door a while later, just as Darcy was hanging a large photo of a beautiful hammerhead shark on her wall.

She went to answer it, only to find Libby standing on her doorstep with a bunch of flowers in one hand and a bag of sugar in the other.

Darcy blushed and laughed, stepping back to let her in. 'Can I get you a . . . tea?' She looked around hopelessly at all the boxes, one of which housed the kettle and another that probably held the coffee and teabags. 'Or a glass of juice?'

Libby smiled. 'Juice would be great.'

Darcy moved to the kitchen and Libby followed her. Darcy really did owe her an explanation for earlier.

'I'm so sorry about before. I thought George was beating you up. I heard thuds and groans and, coupled with seeing you so upset earlier, I jumped to the wrong conclusion.'

Libby's eyebrows shot up in surprise. 'Is that why you came bursting in? Ha. George hasn't got a mean bone in his body. I was upset before because . . . Well, I'm pregnant and everything is making me cry lately. Yesterday George bought some fresh bread from the shops because I wanted beans on toast and I wailed for over half an hour because he'd brought the wrong type of bread.'

Darcy laughed. 'Oh no. How does George cope with all the tears?'

'He's amazing. I married my best friend and when I cry he just holds me until the tears pass. I'm sure the tears must be so frustrating for him, but he seems to have endless patience for it all. I really am incredibly lucky. Do you have a boyfriend, Darcy?'

Darcy shook her head. 'No, the last few men I dated were from work, and when the jobs came to an end, the relationships seemed to as well.'

'Well, there are lots of lovely men who live in White Cliff Bay. Are you staying here long?'

Darcy noticed Libby looking hungrily at a packet of doughnuts she had bought from the shops that morning. She offered her the packet and Libby gratefully took one.

'I have a new job down here, so I hope I'll be staying for a long time.'

'Oh how lovely, what is it you'll be doing?' Libby asked, through a mouthful of doughnut.

'I'll be working for the local council. The office is in Apple Hill but it covers the areas of White Cliff Bay and Port Cardinal too. You're looking at the new Community Development Liaison Manager,' Darcy said, proudly.

'Ooh, that sounds like a fancy title, what does that involve?'

Darcy hesitated for a moment. 'Honestly, I have no idea. The job description was very woolly. I somehow bluffed my way through the whole interview and miraculously got offered the job. I know it's something about working with the community on new local projects. I'm very excited. I love meeting new people, so it sounded right up my street.'

She'd told anyone who would listen how excited she was about her new job. It wasn't true, but if she kept repeating it then she hoped she would start to believe it.

'Sounds fab. When do you start?'

'Ten days. A week on Monday.' Darcy poured out two glasses of juice.

'And was it just the job that brought you to White Cliff Bay or do you have friends down here?'

Darcy paused as she thought about how to answer that. She could at least partly tell the truth.

'It was the sea, mainly. I love it. I used to be a marine biologist and though that chapter of my life is over, I still want to be by the sea. I used to holiday in White Cliff Bay as a child and

I always wanted to live down here. Life seems to have held me back from fulfilling my dreams, but I'm here now.'

Libby cocked her head slightly as if she knew Darcy wasn't telling the whole story.

Darcy sighed. 'My parents are . . . difficult. When I lost my last job, I ended up living with them while I was searching for a new job. It was hell. The looks of disappointment, the little comments about how I'd let them down. I couldn't bear it. They've been like it all my life but I've always put up with it before. My aunt Ginny died recently and I came down here to sort out her stuff.' She paused, not sure why she was telling Libby all of this when they'd only just met, but the story was half out now. She pulled the locket she was wearing over her head. It was antique silver and the front was decorated with beads of sea glass. 'This was in a box with my name on it.'

She passed it to Libby and watched as she opened it and read the inscription that she knew off by heart:

Don't let anyone tell you your dreams aren't good enough.

Libby smiled and passed it back.

'I don't know whether she had it specially made for me or just found it and thought of me, but I knew she was right. I'd been letting my parents dictate my life for far too long. Living down here had always been a dream that I'd convinced myself would never happen. So I made sure it did. I found a job and . . . here I am.'

'Well, the people of the town are very friendly, I'm sure they will make you very welcome,' Libby said, finishing off the doughnut and licking her fingers. 'We'll take you to the pub tonight, introduce you to some of the locals.'

'That would be great, thank you. I've only met a few people so far and I didn't exactly make the greatest impression on the lighthouse keeper.'

'Riley Eddison? You met him?' Libby took the proffered juice and followed Darcy into the lounge. Darcy threw herself down on the sofa and tiny motes of dust flew up and sparkled in the light of the late evening sun.

'I swam out to Rose Island. I had no idea anyone lived in the lighthouse. Let's say the welcome was not a warm one.'

Libby sat next to her, resting her hand protectively over her tiny bump. 'Riley's a funny one. He's been here about six months, moved into the lighthouse just after Christmas. He's American and the women seem to love his accent. Whenever Riley comes into town he's like the Pied Piper with the women that follow him around, though none of them get anywhere with him. He's terribly polite, has gorgeous manners, but keeps himself to himself. He comes to the Bubble and Froth some-times, sits in the corner with his dog and doesn't really talk to anyone. He's never rude but not exactly friendly either. George rescued Riley earlier this year when he slipped on the rocks around the lighthouse, knocked himself unconscious and fell into the sea.'

'Oh God,' Darcy gasped.

'He was fine. Luckily the lifeboat crew were nearby on a training exercise and George saw the whole thing happen and they were able to get to him in record time. He gave a hefty do-nation to the lifeboat station after that. He is Suzanna's grand-son, the lady from the chemist. She's fab but she tells it like it is, no beating around the bush, though she keeps her cards very close to her chest about Riley. He was in the local paper a month or so ago after he rescued a stray puppy from the sea, who he then adopted. You could tell from the photo that the last thing he wanted was the attention, whereas Suzanna couldn't have been prouder.'

'So he has a soft side?'

Libby pulled a face as she sipped her juice. 'I wouldn't say soft, but some of his edges are perhaps not as hard as he would like people to believe. So you two didn't hit it off?'

'Well, he came out of his lighthouse and started shouting at me, so . . .'

'I've never seen him lose his temper before. He may be very quiet, but he's definitely not the angry, nasty type. What on earth did you do?'

That didn't fill Darcy with a good feeling. Five minutes in the town and she had pissed off a man who never got angry. 'I don't know. I just swam out to the lighthouse, climbed up on the rocks for a rest and the next thing he appears, waving his arms in the air like a madman.'

'Oh, I wonder if he was scared you might hurt yourself on the rocks. After his fall, he had steps built into the rocks round the back where he keeps his boat so it's safer for him and any visitors to traverse the rocks to the door.'

Had that been it? He was concerned for her safety?

'I feel really sorry for him, actually. He must have spent thousands doing up the inside of the lighthouse with all the new furniture I've seen being delivered over there. There were build-ers and decorators coming and going for months when he first moved in. Anyway rumour has it, two days after the final lick of paint had dried, he was served with some kind of compulsory eviction notice. Rose Island Lighthouse is to be pulled down – a new, more modern lighthouse has just been built a few hundred yards up the coast on Dagger's Point. At the moment he is refus-ing to leave, but he has very little choice.'

'That's terrible, they can't kick him out of his home.'

'Apparently, they can. I don't know all the ins and outs of it, but he has been told he has to leave. Oh, maybe he thought you were one of the people trying to evict him.'

'Unlikely when I turned up in a wetsuit and with a fat dog in tow.'

Libby nodded to concede this, as she glanced over at Ben ly-ing upside down and snoring loudly on the opposite sofa.

'Well, you'll just have to go back and ask him,' Libby smiled, mischievously.

'Maybe I should just leave him be. If me being there upsets him so much, then maybe I should just find somewhere else to swim.'

'Maybe you should go back and show him that he can't boss you around.'

Darcy laughed. 'Are you trying to set me up with him?'

Libby shrugged as she stood up. 'I'm a romance writer. I want everyone to find their happy-ever-afters, just like me and George. Anyway, I'll leave you to unpack. We'll pick you up at seven and take you to the pub then.'

Darcy nodded.

As the door closed behind Libby, Darcy glanced over Silver Cove to Rose Island Lighthouse.

Maybe she would go back and apologise for any misunderstanding. Then she shook her head. Maybe she really should just leave well alone.

CHAPTER 2

There was a knock on her door later that night. Darcy blushed again when she opened it and saw George on the other side, knowing the last time she had seen him, he'd been stark naked.

'I'm sorry about earlier . . .'

'Ah, don't worry about it, Libby told me why you burst in. It's nice to know you were looking out for her. We'll just pretend it never happened and we'll say no more about it. I certainly don't want you to feel embarrassed or awkward every time you see me when you were just doing the right thing.'

'OK, thanks.' Darcy smiled with relief at how well he seemed to be taking it. She had spent her whole life trying to do the right thing and ended up careening from one disaster to the next.

Just then Libby came running out of their flat. 'Sorry, needed to pee. This baby spends most of his time leaning on my bladder.'

If George was embarrassed by his wife talking about her toilet issues, he didn't show it. Instead he took her in his arms and kissed her forehead as if he had missed her in the five minutes she had been gone.

Libby linked arms with Darcy and, taking George in her other hand, escorted her down the stairs that led from the flats out onto the street.

'You'll love the Bubble and Froth. It's quiz night tonight, so you can be on our team. What's your area of expertise?' Libby said, as they walked like characters in the *Wizard of Oz*, arm in arm towards the pub.

'Erm . . . I'm not really good at anything.'

'Everyone has something they are good at. George loves silly facts about the Second World War and he is really good at capital cities. He also has a love of musicals and old films, and I'm good at books and authors. You must be the fount of knowledge in at least one area.'

'Sharks.'

'Sharks?' Libby stared at her incredulously.

Darcy shrugged. 'Yeah. It turns out I'm quite the expert.'

'Well, normally the questions are about films or TV or music. Not so much about sharks. There's some general knowledge mixed in there, too. We might get lucky with a question about sharks that no one else will know the answer to.'

'There was that question about crustaceans last week, do you know anything about them?' George asked, encouragingly.

'I know quite a bit about all sea life, actually. I used to be a marine biologist, so maybe I might be of some use to you after all.'

'There you go, you'll be our secret weapon,' George said.

Darcy looked out over the sea at Rose Island Lighthouse, as the beam lit up the early evening sky. 'Does Riley take part in the pub quiz?'

'Ah, you have a little soft spot for our American friend, do you?' George said. 'I wouldn't get your hopes up, he doesn't seem to be interested in any of the women in the town. And no, he's not really the taking part sort. He just sits there and reads his book. There was once a question about American presidents and he whispered the answer to me, but other than that he's definitely not a team player. He probably won't even be there tonight. He does tend to avoid quiz night or karaoke nights. They're not really his scene.'

Darcy felt her heart sink a little bit and she didn't know why. He was nice looking but quite angry and she didn't really go for the strong, silent type. She was more interested in fun-loving types. But there was something about Riley that intrigued her; she was mostly wondering what he was doing living out in the lighthouse all alone and why he was so against visitors.

Libby pushed the door open, and the warmth and bustle of the pub greeted them.

Darcy held her breath, waiting for the curious or hostile looks from the locals, who might wonder who the stranger was that was trying to breach their midst. But although a few people glanced her way, they were all friendly and smiley.

'What would you like to drink, Darcy?' George asked.

'Oh no, let me buy you guys a drink to apologise for . . .' She trailed off as George shook his head.

'We said we weren't going to mention that again. We have to buy you a drink to welcome you to the town.'

'Oh, OK, I'll have a cider, please.'

George disappeared into the crowd.

Libby watched him go with a smile and then turned back to face her. 'I'll introduce you to Amy when she appears, you'll like her. Oh, look who's here!' Libby nodded over her head as the door opened up behind Darcy.

Darcy turned round. As Riley stepped into the pub, Libby gave Darcy a firm shove from behind, propelling her straight into Riley's hard chest.

He steadied her with a hand to her waist. Up close, he was tall. At five foot eight, she always towered over everyone else but he was several inches taller than her. He had the most amazing smell, sort of sweet like toffee apples, but there was a dark smoky scent to him too. She looked up into the greenest eyes she had ever seen, shadowed by the black cowboy hat he was wearing.

He touched the rim of his hat, as he looked down at her with concern. 'Ma'am, are you OK?'

She straightened. 'I'm so sorry. I . . . lost my balance.'

His eyes didn't leave her face, studying her as if trying to place who she was. She quickly looked down before he recognised her.

Tucked under one arm was a small dog that was all straggly fur and seemingly no eyes, the fur was so long. Its whole body shook, as its oversized tail wagged furiously. Darcy smiled and reached out a hand to stroke its head. The wagging increased significantly.

'What's his name?'

'It's a girl. Her name is Kelpie.'

He had the most incredible southern American accent, soft but raspy. No wonder the women of the town went mad for it. It was sexy as hell.

She looked back up at him. 'A water spirit?'

'It seemed fitting, though I did wonder whether the woman who turned up on my island today might also be a kelpie.'

Darcy blushed. He did recognise her.

'Kelpies are Scottish and there aren't many female kelpies in folklore. They tend to be men or horses. Maybe she was a mermaid.'

His mouth tugged up into a half smile. 'Or a siren.'

Darcy didn't know whether to be flattered by the association with the incredibly beautiful women or hurt by the fact that sirens were known to lure men to their deaths. Riley knew nothing about her and had already decided she was a woman to be avoided at all costs.

But then she had been shouting about great sex when she last saw him which, knowing her luck, he'd probably heard, and she had just thrown herself at him, albeit inadvertently, within seconds of him walking into the pub. He was probably lumping her in with all the other women in the town that followed him around and came up to him to stroke his cute puppy. She was a walking cliché.

She stepped back, suddenly embarrassed, but he gently snagged her arm as she moved to walk away.

'Ma'am, I'm going to have to ask you not to swim out to my island again.'

God, he really didn't want to see her again.

As the locket moved around her neck, she suddenly felt angry that her first day of following her dreams was ending on a sour note, thanks to him. Everything was supposed to be perfect and he was ruining that.

'I don't think you have any right to stop me swimming out to a bunch of rocks. If I want to keep swimming out there, I will,' she snapped.

She knew she was being belligerent, and for no real reason except Libby was right: she wasn't going to be bossed around.

His eyes hardened. That clearly wasn't the response he was expecting.

'The island is private property and if you go there after I have explicitly told you not to that would be trespassing and as such would be illegal,' Riley said, his voice low and angry.

She didn't know whether he was telling the truth or not about the island, but she knew she had to find out before she argued her case any more.

'We'll see,' Darcy muttered, keen to get away from him now.

He let her arm go but continued to stare at her as she moved quickly to the table where George and Libby were sitting, both smiling inanely at her.

'Please don't do that again,' Darcy said to Libby as she sat down and took a big glug of cider.

'What happened?' Libby said, unable to suppress her smile at her little bit of matchmaking.

'Well, they say first impressions last. Mine was obviously a startling one.' She watched Riley as he moved to get a drink. 'He told me in no uncertain terms that I'm not to go out to *his* island again. Pompous ass. He thinks I'm some sort of femme fatale ready to pounce on unsuspecting men . . .' She trailed off as he sat down in a nearby booth, preventing any more discussion of him.

After a few minutes Libby whispered in her ear. 'Well, you've certainly made some kind of impression, he hasn't taken his eyes off you.'

The pub quiz started, but Darcy couldn't concentrate. Although she refused to look at him, she could feel him staring at her. And, despite his request, she found herself plotting reasons to go out to the lighthouse again the next day.

The pub was slowly emptying and Darcy couldn't help but smile as several people came over to say goodbye to her. It had been a great night and she had made some lovely friends. On their team had been George's friend Big Dave and his wife Kat, Giselle who lived above George's flat and her boyfriend Noah, and Amy, Libby's friend who worked in the pub. Darcy hadn't stopped laughing all night, as she chatted to them all.

As luck would have it, the pub quiz that night was raising money for the new aquarium that was opening in the town and as such there had been two sea-themed rounds which Darcy had sailed through with flying colours. It had piqued people's attention when Libby had cheered after getting each question right and after the quiz had finished several people had come to talk to Darcy to find out why she knew so much about the sea. She felt a real sense of contentment here; all the worries and doubts she'd had before she arrived had just gone away.

Although the evening hadn't been all sunshine and roses. Riley hadn't stopped looking over at her. Every single time she looked in his direction, her eyes met his. It was unnerving but oddly thrilling at the same time. She glanced over at him now and he looked up from his book almost as if he could feel her stare. There was something so enticing about him: his unwavering, calm green eyes framed with dark, long lashes. He had removed his cowboy hat and his black hair still retained that messy unkempt look. Darcy found herself wanting to run her fingers through it. His arms were strong, muscular under his crumpled shirt. Her eyes cast down to his lap where he was stroking a sleeping Kelpie, who was curled up on his large thighs with a smug smile on her face. Was it wrong that she suddenly wanted to trade places with that puppy? But despite the fact that she was attracted to him, she was annoyed by him and didn't know why. His staring rattled her and he hadn't said a single word to her for the rest of the evening.

Maggie, one of the women she had chatted to that night, came over to say goodbye and Darcy dragged her eyes away from Riley.

'Darcy, it was lovely meeting you. You'll have to come over for dinner one night. My son, Ryan, would talk to you all night about sharks. It's the only thing he is interested in. He is such a closed-off child, doesn't play with other children, has no idea how to engage with them, he doesn't really talk to anyone unless it's about sharks. He follows me around the house telling me all the shark facts. It would be lovely for him to talk to someone who has the same passion as him.'

'I'd love that. Once I get talking about sharks, I can't stop either. Here, let me give you my number, let's make a date. We could do next week sometime. I don't start work until the week after so I have some time on my hands. Once I've finished all my unpacking, that is.'

Riley stood up, scooped a sleepy Kelpie into his arms and put his hat back on. As Darcy put her number into Maggie's phone, he walked past them without giving her another glance. While Maggie tried to work out how to save Darcy's number, Darcy looked over her shoulder to watch Riley leave. He opened the door and glanced over at her just for a second and she felt a kick of desire slam into her stomach, something she had never felt before with the men she had dated.

A second later he was gone and the warm sea air surrounded her, mingled with his sweet, smoky scent.

She turned back to Maggie, who was smiling at her mischievously. 'He is easy on the eye, isn't he? But I'd try to forget about him, if I were you. He isn't interested in any women from the town. From what I can gather, he was hurt in the past and he doesn't want to risk his heart again.'

Darcy glanced out the window as he walked away along the beach. Forgetting him was not going to be easy.

CHAPTER 3

Saturday morning arrived, promising another hot day. The night had been hot too, and Darcy had found herself sleeping naked for the first time that year. The morning was already warm and muggy. They needed a good storm to freshen the place up, but as the cornflower-blue sky was cloudless, it didn't look like that would happen any time soon.

Darcy washed and dressed and decided a walk into town was in order. She needed to get to know more people. In her job as Community Development Liaison Manager she would be working alongside these wonderful people and she wanted to know what made them tick, their loves and hates, things that could possibly improve the town. She had no idea what her job would entail but surely more knowledge of the town and its people would only be a good thing. With just over a week to go until she started her job, now seemed the perfect time to get to know the residents of the town.

She stepped out onto the street and looked down the beach. She knew the main part of the town was to the left and over the headland, but she wondered if there was anything to the right. Past the rocky outcrop that jutted out into the sea was a large, mostly glass building that looked almost alien, as it nestled into the hillside. Large peaks rose and fell around the building, which looked like an oversized glass crown. Whoever had designed it had decided that trying to create a building in keeping with the landscape was not something worth doing. It looked new but not yet in use, as there were a few JCBs and other heavy construction machinery parked outside.

As there didn't seem to be any other building or any life at all down that side of the beach, she turned and walked over the headland towards the main town.

She recognised Seb, the landlord of the pub, walking on the beach with his dog Jack and she waved at him. There was no sign of Riley and Kelpie, and Darcy didn't know whether to be relieved or secretly disappointed by that fact.

As shops and pubs started appearing and more people were lining the streets, Darcy couldn't help but smile at the cute little town, where everyone seemed to know everyone else. There were no chain stores here, every shop seemed to be individual – privately owned places with quirky names like Emily's Emporium, which seemed to be the local supermarket, and Iced Dreams, which sold ice cream in every flavour. Sugar and Spice was the local bakery.

There was a wooden furniture shop that proudly boasted in gold curly writing on a huge polished piece of wood that it was the White Cliff Bay Furniture Company. She knew this company, knew they had a big factory in the town and that their pieces were much sought after the world over.

Darcy loved handmade pieces of furniture, even though she doubted she could afford the high price tag that came with them, but there was something so charming about seeing the finished pieces. Pushing open the door to the small shop and stepping inside, she inhaled the rich smells of wood and varnish. The shop had two other customers browsing, but it was mostly empty.

There were chairs, chests, drawers, tables and even a wonderful love seat – two chairs curving beautifully round each other in an 'S' shape, as it stood gleaming in the window. She laid her hand on the smooth wood and ran it over the curves of the chair.

'Darcy, hello.'

Darcy turned round and realised that Maggie was working behind the counter.

'Hello, I didn't know you worked here.'

'Just two days a week. I had a baby in January, so I'm just dipping my toe back into the working world again. It's nice to get out of the house sometimes, though I do miss the little tyke.'

'This place is beautiful. I'd buy everything in the shop, if I could.'

'Well, then, you'd certainly be Edward Stratton's favourite person. He's the CEO of the White Cliff Bay Furniture Company. Is there anything in particular I can help you with?'

'To be honest, I don't think I can afford any of this, almost every penny I had was spent on the rent and deposit for my flat. I have enough left over for food and bills for the next few weeks but certainly not enough money for any of these wonderful pieces. I just came in to be nosy.'

Maggie grinned. 'That's no problem. Most people do that. I see you're admiring the love seat.'

Darcy turned to look at it again. 'It's beautiful.'

'That's one of Henry's pieces. He's new to the town and has brought a whole load of imagination and skill with him. He's dating Penny, one of my best friends, and she couldn't be prouder of him. Why don't you sit down in it, give it a go?'

Darcy did as she was told. The seat had cushions wrapped around the back and it was big enough to curl up in. It was incredibly comfortable and she knew she could spend hours sitting in it. She stretched her hand over to the chair that was facing her. She imagined doing that with her husband one day, both of them holding hands over the divide as they read their own books.

'You look right at home there,' Maggie laughed. 'It's funny, but your friend Riley Eddison was just in here admiring that love seat too. Though he sat in the other half.'

Darcy found herself snatching back her hand from the other side and Maggie laughed.

'Hardly my friend. Grumpy sod made it very clear that I wasn't welcome on his island. Obviously thinks I'm going to damage his precious lighthouse. It's not like I pitched up there yesterday with a wrecking ball ready to pull the place down myself.'

'Oh, that poor man,' said a nearby lady, her silver hair in a neat bob. She looked to be in her mid-sixties and had obviously been listening in to their conversation. 'I can't imagine how heartbreaking it must be for him to lose his home like that. Especially when it has belonged to his family for over a hundred years.'

Darcy immediately felt guilty for her offhand comment.

Maggie smiled. 'This is Verity Donaldson, George's mum. Verity, this is Darcy, she just moved to the town yesterday.'

'I know all about you. I used to be friends with your aunt Ginny.'

'You knew her?'

Verity plonked herself down in the opposite half of the love seat as Maggie walked back behind the counter. 'Oh, yes. In fact, there were quite a few times that you and my George played together on the beach when you were very little. Small world how you've ended up living next to him now – it's funny how things turn out.'

'Seriously? I used to play with George when I was a child? How funny. I don't remember that at all. I remember playing on the beach and swimming in the sea, but no curly-haired little boys. And you and Ginny were friends?'

'Well, sort of. She liked to keep to herself. I know several of the other ladies used to invite her out or round for dinner, myself included, and she always declined. I used to go round to her caravan for tea and cake. She made the most amazing chocolate brownies. But our conversations never really ran deep. I do know she adored you and your brother.'

Darcy winced. 'We were so close when I was growing up. I stayed in touch with her, phoned her once a month, visited when I could, but life just got in the way. I regret that I didn't see her as much as I should have over the last few years.'

'You had your own life to lead and Ginny would have wanted that for you. You were studying marine biology at the University of Edinburgh for several years. It's a long way to come for a visit. But she couldn't have been prouder of you for following your dreams.'

Darcy sighed. Look how that had turned out.

Verity looked out the front window and Darcy followed her gaze to the Rose Island Lighthouse peeping between the shops and houses.

'Ginny loved the lighthouse. Every single one of her paintings had the lighthouse in it. Big, almost cartoon-like paintings with bright colours. She must have done a hundred or more of the town, with the tiny shops and houses, the bright blue sea and golden sands, and right smack bang in the middle was the red-and-white-striped lighthouse. The tourists loved them. The town even commissioned several of them to be postcards. Ginny would be so upset to see the lighthouse pulled down after all these years. I think we will all be sad to see it go. My Bill proposed to me out there. After Riley's dad left, the key to the lighthouse was left under a big rock right outside the door. No one was supposed to know but most of the town did. Bill rowed me out there one moonlit night, took me inside and in one of the rooms he'd lit hundreds of candles. Of course back then the place was no more than a shell. All of Riley's family's possessions had been stripped out by then. But it didn't matter. Looking out the windows at the moonlight and the sea, stretching out for miles in all directions, in that room filled with hundreds of flickering candles, Bill asked me to marry him, and of course I said yes. It kind of became the place where everyone proposed to their girlfriends. I imagine those walls have seen more than a hundred proposals over the years. The lighthouse is a part of the town, in more ways than anyone can imagine.'

'Then we have to do something to save it,' Darcy said, suddenly galvanised into action.

'We're trying,' Verity said.

'There must be appeals we can make. They can't just pull it down.'

'As far as I know, Riley has tried all of that.'

'A petition, then. Would people in the town sign one?'

'You'd get the signature of every single person in the town, but I can't see it doing any good.'

'Well, we can apply for the lighthouse to be listed; no one can touch it if it's protected.'

'It's not old enough for that, surely,' Maggie said, re-joining them with a tray filled with three mugs of tea. Darcy took two, and handed one to Verity. Maggie grabbed a rocking chair and pulled it up to join the impromptu meeting. 'Aren't listed buildings normally hundreds of years old?' She looked over at a tiny old man who was admiring a rocking horse. 'Charles, how old is the lighthouse?'

'A hundred and forty-one years old,' Charles said, and Darcy smiled as he ambled over to them. He almost looked old enough to remember the lighthouse being built.

Darcy stood up to allow the man to sit down and grabbed a stool for herself.

'Exactly,' Maggie said. 'That's not old enough.'

'That's not true,' Darcy said. 'Age plays a big part in whether a building gets listed, but there are lots of other factors too. Whether there is something special and unique about the building, especially with regards to how it was built. Historic importance or significance, for example if it played a part in the war somehow – that might help our case. I can look into it. It's very simple to apply for a building to be listed. And we should hear back very quickly too. What else have you guys tried doing?'

'There's a meeting next weekend. I know Suzanna is in charge of it. She's trying to raise money to hire a solicitor, I think, someone who will fight our case for us.'

'That's good. What about press attention?' Darcy asked.

'There have been several stories in the local papers about it,' Charles said.

'What about the national press? They would love a story like this to get behind. Especially with all the proposals that have been made there. We could bill it as the most romantic place in England. The papers would lap it up. I have a friend who works for one of the big papers in London. I could see if she would be interested in running the story.'

They all nodded keenly.

There was the beginning of a plan. If the lighthouse had meant so much to Aunt Ginny, then Darcy wanted to do everything she could to save it.

Darcy walked back along the beach towards the block of flats. She'd popped into a few other shops and got a few things to eat, but she wanted to get back and carry on with the unpacking.

She felt positive about her first trip into town, meeting some more locals but also contributing to the fight to save the lighthouse. Her phone rang in her bag and she dug it out, smiling when she saw it was her brother, Toby.

'Hey, Cheese Feet!' Darcy answered the phone, falling into their normal pattern of conversation, trying to find unusual ways to insult each other.

'Hey, Fart Breath!'

'Fart Breath?' Darcy laughed. That one was a new low. 'I think you win that round. Saved anyone's life today?'

'I've just come out of a very important surgery, actually.'

'What was it, heart bypass, brain surgery?'

'Close. I was removing a mole on someone's bum.'

Darcy laughed again. Speaking to Toby always made her feel happier. 'Well, that sounds like a very noble operation, thank goodness you were there to help with that.'

'And, of course, by the time I tell Tabitha tonight about my day, I will have embellished it to sound a lot more vital and heroic.'

Darcy rolled her eyes. Tabitha was Toby's newest girlfriend, the latest in a long line.

'Not sure you can make the removal of a mole from someone's bum sound remotely heroic, not unless the mole was particularly large and hairy. Maybe then you could dress it up as saving someone from a yeti-type monster,' Darcy said.

'Yes, maybe I'll give that a go. How you settling in?'

'Good, not finished unpacking yet but I've met some lovely people.'

'How were Mum and Dad when you left?'

'As you would expect. As far as they're concerned, I'm obviously making the worst mistake of my life and they took great pleasure in telling me that.'

Toby sighed. 'Did they at least wish you luck?'

'Of course not. They told me they thought I'd cock this job up like I've cocked up all the rest. They even had a bet between them about how long I would last. Dad thinks it'll be six weeks before I come back to their house with my tail between my legs, Mum thinks four.'

She tried to laugh off their lack of support. They had been the same her entire life, but it still hurt.

'I think moving down there will be the best thing you've ever done,' Toby said, seriously, and Darcy stopped walking. 'You can start living your own life again without them looking over your shoulder the whole time. You should never have moved back to London in the first place. I know financially you were stuck, but I would have helped you out, I've always said that.'

'I know, but I don't want to take your money. You work hard for that – removing moles, for one.'

Toby laughed. 'Listen, I know you'll miss Carmel and obviously you'll miss me, I mean who wouldn't, but promise me you won't come back. I love Mum and Dad but they are poison to you. I've watched you fade away over the last few years as they knocked your confidence. I've told them time and time again to leave you alone, but they're never going to change. If you need money to stay down there, I'll lend it to you.'

'Thank you, but it won't come to that. Aunt Ginny's caravan is going spare. If the worst comes to the worst, I can live in that and make jars of jam.'

Toby laughed. 'That's the spirit. Look, I'd better go. I need to have some lunch before the next surgery.'

'What's this one?'

'Probably an ingrown toenail, knowing my luck.'

Darcy laughed and said goodbye before running back up the steps to the main front door of the flats.

Ben greeted her as if she had been gone weeks instead of an hour or two, howling and jumping up at her, trampling over boxes in his excitement at having her home. She made a sandwich for lunch and ate it as she unpacked a few more boxes into the kitchen cupboards.

She wandered into the lounge and stared out over the sea. Her brother was right: she could never go back to London or to her parents' house. Looking out on that view of the sea, she knew she belonged here. Her eyes wandered over to the lighthouse. Helping to fight to save it felt like she was already becoming a part of the town and she liked that. She felt sorry for

Riley, with the threat of losing his home hanging over his head. Knowing she had got off to a bad start with him, she decided to go back over to the lighthouse later and tell him how she and the town were going to try to help him.

She opened up another box and on the top was a photo of her and Ginny a few years earlier, when she had visited her aunt in White Cliff Bay. It was funny to think, after all those years, playing here on the beach, that she was living here now. Although it probably wasn't that strange. Her love of the sea had been fostered here. She wished she had photos of herself from that time, to see that little girl fall in love with the sea for the first time.

Suddenly, she had an idea. Stepping over some boxes, she left the flat and knocked on George and Libby's door. A few moments later, George answered just wearing a pair of shorts.

'Hello, decided to knock this time instead of letting yourself in?'

Darcy laughed. 'You promised you wouldn't mention it again.'

'Ah, I did, didn't I? OK, that was the last time, I promise.' George smirked and Darcy guessed that it probably wouldn't be. He stepped back to let her in. As she squeezed past him into the lounge, she spotted a laptop open on the coffee table. There looked to be a script of some sort on the screen. She knew George worked from home and she didn't want to disturb him.

'Are you busy? I can come back later.'

'No, not at all. I've just finished a new advert actually, so I was going to take a break. Libby's gone into town. She didn't want me to come with her, so I suspect she's gone to get my birthday present. Did you want some more sugar?'

She laughed again. 'No, I met your mum earlier. She used to know my aunt Ginny – did you know her, too?'

'Yes, sort of. We used to visit her quite often when I was growing up, but she lived on the outskirts of town, so once I was older I didn't really see her. I'm sorry to hear she died.'

'Thank you. It was a shock, she was still so young and I miss talking to her so much. We didn't speak as often as we should have, but she was always so supportive.'

George nodded, 'Would you like a drink?'

'No, I'm fine, thank you.'

George gestured for her to sit down on the sofa, and when she did he sat on the recliner opposite.

'Do you remember us playing together on the beach when we were little?'

George's eyes widened. 'No, is that what Mum said?'

'Yes, apparently we went to the beach together a lot. I was down here almost every school holiday, in my younger years, sometimes with my brother, sometimes not. I guess we must have played together at some point. I don't really remember a lot of it. I just remember playing and swimming in the sea. I stopped coming so frequently when I was ten; well, my mum stopped sending me so often. I think she thought Ginny was corrupting me. But I was wondering if you have any photos of you on the beach as a kid – it would be wonderful to see Ginny and maybe I'm in them, too.'

George stood up. 'I have a couple of albums, Mum has a ton. I've not looked at them for years. Mum made me take them when I got married to Libby, as she said Libby might want to see them. We've not looked at them yet, though.'

He moved to a bookcase, shifted a few DVDs and books off a pile on the bottom and grabbed three large photo albums. He sat down next to her and opened up one between them.

'So, we're looking for a little red-headed girl?'

'Yes, fifty per cent legs and fifty per cent red curly hair, think Orphan Annie with giraffe legs. I was not a pretty child.'

George laughed.

'And Ginny, too. I really want to see her.'

He turned the page and there was a tiny curly-haired baby, probably George on the day he had been born, all red and wrinkly and screaming loudly in his mum's arms.

'Ah, I can see this is going to be embarrassing.'

'Is this you? You had a full head of hair when you were born!'

George fingered his curls awkwardly. 'Yes, it's always been curly and out of control.'

He turned the page and laughed when he spotted a photo of a chubby curly-haired naked George in the bath. He quickly turned the page again.

Darcy laughed. 'That's the second time I've got to see you naked.'

'Hey, we promised never to mention it again!'

Just then Libby walked in. 'Hey, honey, I'm home,' she called. 'Oh hello, Darcy.'

Libby looked from one to the other, and Darcy suddenly panicked that this looked bad. Her and George sitting next to each other, laughing over childhood photos. George wasn't wearing a top. It looked too cosy.

George wasn't bothered at all, though, about Libby finding them together. 'Darcy is laughing at photos of me as a baby,' he said, by way of explanation.

'I want to see,' Libby said, dumping her bags and sitting next to Darcy.

Darcy moved the album more fully onto her lap, so Libby could see too. But she felt like she should explain her presence more.

'Apparently, George and I used to play together when we were kids, though neither of us remember. We were just looking for proof.'

'Oh, wow, small world!' Libby said, flicking back to the first page, seeming unperturbed to find her husband home alone with another woman. 'Oh, George, look at you as a baby . . .' She trailed off as tears filled her eyes. George smiled and reached across Darcy to hold Libby's hand. 'Our baby might look like you.'

Darcy felt suddenly in the way; they should be alone to look back at old photos, and if Libby got emotional George could hug her properly, not just hold her hand.

'Look, I should go, why don't you two look at the photos and if you find any of a ginger giraffe or Ginny, you could bring them over to show me.'

'No, don't be silly. Stay, we can laugh at George together,' Libby said, smiling fondly at her husband.

'Are you sure? These photo are very personal.' Darcy blushed as Libby turned to the naked bath picture again.

Libby giggled. 'Look at your little willy!'

'Oi!' George laughed.

They turned the pages together and, as they laughed at George at various stages of his childhood, the initial awkwardness Darcy felt at being the third wheel faded away. They genuinely liked having her there and talking to her and sharing these memories with her. They reached the end of the first album and George grabbed the second one. There were a few pages of Christmas photos with George as a young boy, maybe six or seven years old, in bright purple corduroy trousers and a badly hand-knitted top. Then, when they turned the page, there was a load of George on the beach wearing a floppy hat and a pair of bright yellow swim shorts.

Darcy leaned in closer, looking in the background for any sign of Ginny or herself.

'Is that you?' George said, suddenly pointing at a photo of his younger self eating an ice cream, the sticky white cream all round his face. In the background was a girl in a red swimsuit with a mass of red curls; surprisingly, she was scowling at George.

Darcy laughed. 'Yes, that's me. I wonder why I'm scowling at you.' She looked more closely and saw the younger Darcy was clutching a book on mermaids tight to her chest. 'Oh God, I remember this. You kept telling me that mermaids didn't exist and I decided I hated you for it.'

George laughed. 'You're the mermaid girl.' He turned to Libby. 'She was utterly obsessed by mermaids.'

'I wasn't obsessed.' She chuckled. 'OK, I was.'

'She even thought she might be one herself.'

'George told me I was being ridiculous, so I stuck chewing gum in his hair.'

George gasped. 'That was you? I had to cut it out, I looked a right state. Mum went mad at me, she thought I'd stuck it in there myself.'

'I'm sorry, but you were being mean,' Darcy giggled.

'I love that you two have this history together,' Libby said. 'And these photos are amazing. George, you were such a cute child.'

They turned the page and there were a few of George and Darcy happily building a sandcastle together, clearly either before or after the row about mermaids. But in the background Darcy spotted a younger Ginny, taking a photo of the lighthouse. Her hair was blowing in the wind, her favourite emerald scarf was flying behind her. She looked content and happy.

'Your mum said she loved the lighthouse.'

George nodded. 'There's an art shop in the town. It sells lots of different art from local artists. Your aunt had loads of paintings in there of the beach and the lighthouse. Everyone loved them. I think most of the originals have been sold but the shop still sells the prints.'

'I've seen a few of them over the years but I'd love to see the rest. I wonder why it meant so much to her,' Darcy said, as she looked at the picture and then out at the real thing as it stood sentinel over the town. 'There's a plan to try and save it. I'm not sure what good it will do, but I've been chatting to your mum. We're going to try to get it listed and get the press involved too.'

George chuckled. 'Mum loves to get behind a good campaign. If she's not trying to save people, she's jumping on some political bandwagon. You'll be in safe hands with her. And we'll help in any way we can.'

Libby nodded. 'We could chain ourselves to the lighthouse in protest.'

'Riley would love that,' Darcy laughed.

'Well, if we are going to try to save his lighthouse, he better get used to the idea of a little interference.'

Darcy nodded. Maybe now would be as good a time as any to swim out there and tell him of the plans. He couldn't possibly be angry at her, when she was trying to help him. But telling herself that was doing nothing to diminish the nerves that had now settled into her stomach and refused to go away.

Riley finished playing a song on the piano and added a few notes and comments to the musical score in front of him. Although a lot of his work as a songwriter was done on computers and with modern technology, he liked the old-school approach of playing his final pieces on a piano rather than through a computer.

He loved his work, he could get lost in the music and the lyrics for hours. His ex-girlfriend would often accuse him of shutting her out but he had never found anything he enjoyed as much as writing music, and that included spending time with her.

He stood up and stretched, wandering over to the window to look at the spectacular view of the little town.

His thoughts returned to his little mermaid, as they had done ever since he had left the pub the night before. There was something very endearing about how she had dressed in a pretty blue dress with tiny sparkly-silvery fish teamed with blue leggings and silver flip-flops. The blue had matched her dazzling eyes perfectly. The outfit wasn't fashionable or showy; it was quirky and different to what the other women in the town wore. She had been a beacon of light in the pub and, like moths to a flame, all the regulars had come over to talk to her. She had achieved in hours of being in the town what he hadn't managed in months. With her warm, bubbly personality, she had easily made friends with everyone she had spoken to.

He had been unable to stop himself listening to her talk as she sat at the next table. He had learned her name was Darcy, she was new to the town and was starting a new job soon. He had also learned, as she had helped her team to victory in the pub quiz, that she had this quiet intelligence. She didn't crow about knowing the answers and she seemed almost embarrassed that she knew them when no one else did. She knew nothing about popular culture, music, films or TV shows but she knew a lot about science, sea life, animals, history, and myths and legends. Though he'd already got that sense with that brief talk about kelpies and folklore, and from the unexpected hurt he'd seen in her eyes when he had likened her to a siren. He leaned his hands either side of the window and sighed. The last thing he wanted was to hurt her.

It was a shame that she wouldn't be swimming to his island any more. He'd have liked the chance to get to know her better. And although he'd sworn to himself when he came here that he wouldn't get involved in town life, it wouldn't hurt to spend a little bit of time in that nice pub they had both been in the night before, especially if it meant he got to see more of her.

Kelpie leapt up onto the window seat and put her front paws on the glass, her whole body wagging incessantly at whatever she could see in the waves. Riley was quite honestly surprised she could see anything from under that mass of fur, but he refused to be a man who put bows in his dog's fur to keep it off her eyes.

He peered out of the window at something moving with grace and speed towards the lighthouse. A seal perhaps, he'd seen a few out there. He wiped the window with his sleeve and saw the flash of fiery hair as it trailed behind his mermaid like scarlet ribbons.

The smile that spread across his face at seeing her again was quickly replaced by a look of concern for her safety. If she insisted on coming back, she was risking her life climbing up the rocks that made up his tiny island, and he quickly stormed downstairs to tell her so.

Darcy was pulling herself out of the water when she was momentarily distracted by the door of the lighthouse being flung open. She missed her footing and smashed her knee on the rocks. Riley rushed towards her, and she quickly scrabbled to her feet. He didn't look happy to see her. Pain seared through her leg, as she put weight on it.

'Christ, Darcy, are you OK?'

She nodded, stunned that he knew her name. Concern and anger warred in his eyes, but anger won over.

'That's exactly why I didn't want you coming out here! These rocks are so dangerous. I slipped and knocked myself out on them a few months ago. Why the hell did you come back?' he shouted.

He didn't know why she was there, so it seemed a bit unfair that he was shouting at her before she'd even got one word out. She'd only come to offer to help with the lighthouse after all. As she tried to find words to defend herself, Darcy watched as Ben disloyally bounded up to Riley, greeting him like a long-lost friend.

'Quite apart from anything else, you're trespassing on private property,' Riley said.

'Oh, for goodness' sake, these rocks are not your property. They're bloody rocks!' Darcy said, sarcastically.

'It's my garden, my property. Just because I don't have pretty flowers growing up between them doesn't stop them from being my garden.'

'Oh, well, where does your property end then? Is that your rock down there in the sea? What about that one a bit further out, and the sea, is that yours too?' yelled Darcy.

'Well, yes, actually, it is.' Riley's jaw clenched, as he knew what a ridiculous claim that was.

'Well, Mr I-Own-the-Whole-Bloody-World, I'm leaving, and you know what . . .' She glanced around her feet and grabbed a small boulder the size of a large apple. 'I'm taking this with me. Ben, come!' Darcy scrambled down the rocks with her trophy rock in her hand. She suddenly turned back. 'You know the worst thing? I'd actually come over here to offer to help you with the lighthouse, but you can stick it up your rather pompous arse now.'

She dived into the cool waters, not waiting for a response. Cursing herself for trying to make a point by stealing a rock, she let it drop to the sea floor.

She swam back to the beach, seething over his attitude, tears of anger pricking her eyes. Ben ran up to Jack, Amy and Seb's dog, as all three of them sat on the beach. When Ben showed no sign of coming back, Darcy trudged over to them, feeling sure they had witnessed the whole embarrassing debacle.

'Are you OK?' Seb asked. 'That looked like a painful fall.'

'I'm fine, thank you. Sorry about him.' Darcy gestured at Ben, who was leaping all over Jack, as if he'd found a new best friend. Jack didn't look too convinced.

'Don't worry about it,' Seb said.

'Looked like Riley was being a bit of an ass,' Amy said and Darcy smiled. They had chatted quite a bit the night before and she had quickly realised that Amy just said what she thought, holding nothing back.

'I'm not sure if it's just me he has a problem with, the people of the town or if he's just really possessive over his little rocks.'

'Probably all three,' Amy said, scowling over at the light-house on Darcy's behalf. 'Though I've never seen him get angry at anyone before.'

Darcy sighed. 'So it *is* just me.'

'Riley is a good guy,' Seb said, ignoring the pointed glare his girlfriend was giving him. 'We've chatted a bit when we've been walking our dogs in the mornings. He is a very private person, doesn't say a lot about his past, but I know he has been hurt. He might keep himself to himself, but he's never rude or aggressive. I've seen him helping the older ladies around town with their shopping on a few occasions. He broke up a row on the beach the other week, when a couple were fighting and the woman was getting upset. He seems like a really decent bloke. I don't think you should judge him so harshly when, from what I can gather, he is only concerned for your safety. And you are trespassing on his property, after all.'

Darcy felt well and truly like she'd just been told off. And annoyingly, Seb was right. Riley did only seem worried about her hurting herself on the rocks. 'I only went over there to tell him that I and some of the people in the town have a plan to try and help him save the lighthouse. We've got off on the wrong foot and I just wanted to try to rectify that.'

'Amy said she invited you to our engagement party tomorrow night. He'll be there. Why don't you try talking to him then? At least you won't be traipsing all over his property, which seems to be the thing that upsets him the most.'

'I'm sure he would appreciate your support to try to save the lighthouse,' Amy said, encouragingly. 'You just need to catch him on neutral territory.'

Darcy nodded, reluctantly.

'Come to the pub tonight,' Seb said, obviously sensing that he might have upset her with his support for Riley. 'It's curry night and my chef, Gavril, makes the nicest curries for miles around.'

'I do love a good curry. I'll pop by later,' Darcy said, and smiling sadly she called for Ben, waved goodbye and headed back to her flat.

CHAPTER 4

Riley was standing on the beach watching Kelpie jumping in and out of the waves early the next morning when Seb joined him. He liked Seb. He didn't ask too many questions and the ones he did ask were never prying. He didn't judge him, try to change him or pressure him to become more involved in the town like his grandmother had. Seb accepted Riley for who he was.

He couldn't say they were friends – he didn't really have any of those, which was fine by him. But he enjoyed chatting to Seb for the hour or so they walked their dogs together in the morning. Occasionally they talked about serious things, but mostly the chat was about nothing more profound than the weather, what Riley was doing with the renovations of the lighthouse or what was going on in the town. So the topic Seb led with when they started talking surprised him.

'What's going on with you and Darcy?'

Riley had no words for a few moments. Admittedly, he hadn't been able to stop thinking about her since she'd first shown up on his island a few days before, but he sort of assumed that his attraction to her was a private thing. He didn't expect to be questioned about her, and least of all by Seb.

'Nothing is going on.'

'Really? Because from what I understand you've shouted at the poor girl twice now, the first time within hours of her arriving in the town and yesterday when she came over to offer to help you save the lighthouse.'

'I didn't know that's why she was there . . .' Riley started to defend himself. He felt horribly guilty about the hurt he'd seen in Darcy's eyes just before she'd jumped back into the sea, taking one of his rocks with her.

'With all the women in the town that have thrown themselves at you over the last few months, you've never shouted at one of them. Even the really pushy ones. You've been polite and respectful to them all. So what did Darcy do to deserve your anger? From what I can tell, she's lovely and she seems really upset by the whole thing.'

Damn it, Riley hadn't wanted to upset her. He'd only shouted at her the first time because she couldn't hear him over the wind and the waves, and both times he had been concerned for her safety, not wanting her to fall and hurt herself like he had. Riley looked out over the sea. He had been an ass and she hadn't deserved it.

'From what I can gather, Darcy's aunt died recently, someone she was really close to. She's moved away from all her friends and family to a strange town, so go easy on her, eh?'

Seb turned and walked down the beach, leaving Riley alone with his thoughts. Seb was right: he shouldn't have shouted at her. He felt awful. Another thought struck him and he felt even worse. He also shouldn't have called the police about her trespassing either.

Darcy looked up from her laptop over at Rose Island Lighthouse. Momentarily, the morning sun came out from behind a cloud, hit the glass at the top and the reflection sent a glare straight through her window. She quickly shielded her eyes from it.

She'd been down to the pub the night before with George and Libby, and she'd ended up chatting to a few of the locals.

Inevitably, the conversation had turned to the lighthouse and how they'd all be sad to see it go. Listening to their stories, she was even more determined now to try to save it, not for Riley but for the people of the town.

She had spent the morning researching Rose Island Lighthouse and found all the little historic snippets about the place incredibly fascinating. As she had found old photographs of the interior, stories from old lighthouse keepers and stumbled across an old campaign to keep the lighthouse painted red and white, she'd started to fall a little bit in love with the place. It had seen so much over the years, and by the looks of it, the lighthouse had been in Riley's family for several generations. How utterly heartbreaking for Riley to be forced to leave and see this piece of his history just destroyed, never mind that he had spent thousands of pounds doing it up. She had found herself looking into building regulations and planning laws. There were appeals that could be undertaken to try to stop the compulsory purchase order on the lighthouse. She wondered if Riley knew about these things. Being American he might not. There was also a chance they could get the building listed. He might not know about that either.

Anyone could apply for a building to be listed; she didn't need to own the place to do it. She opened up the form and filled it in, giving as much detail as she possibly could about the history of the lighthouse and why she thought it should be protected as part of the town's heritage and legacy. She finished the application and pressed 'send', feeling happier already that she was at least doing something to try to save it.

Next, she would create a petition and make multiple copies to distribute in shops across the town. If she could get enough signatures, she could present it to the town council and maybe they would reconsider their plans.

She paused for a second. Was it some kind of conflict of interest to do all of this to try and save the lighthouse when she would be working for the council? No, she wouldn't be working for the buildings or planning department, she would be in a completely different section working on community development projects. Helping to save the lighthouse was being a part of the community, so they couldn't be angry about it.

She opened up a blank petition template she had found online and started adding the details about the campaign to save the lighthouse. A knock on the door distracted her. She went to answer it, only to find an embarrassed George and a policeman standing next to him.

'Hi Darcy, this is my uncle Bob, erm . . . PC Donaldson,' George said awkwardly. 'He would like a word with you.'

'I'll take it from here, son,' Bob said, very seriously.

George nodded, though he didn't seem keen to leave.

What on earth was all this about? An unpaid parking ticket perhaps, or an overdue library book? Darcy didn't do 'getting into trouble with the police'. She had never even had a speeding ticket.

'Can I come in, Miss Davenport?' Bob said.

Darcy stepped back to let him in and he moved into her lounge.

'What's this about?' she whispered to George.

'I'm not sure. Don't worry about it. Just ply Bob with tea and biscuits and he'll be putty in your hands.'

Darcy nodded as she closed the door, her heart strumming nervously.

She turned to face Bob, who was standing waiting for her. 'Can I get you a cup of tea?'

Bob's face lit up. 'Oh, yes please, love. Three sugars.'

Darcy busied herself in the kitchen for a few minutes and then brought out a huge mug of tea and a packet of her finest biscuits.

'Here you go,' Darcy said.

'Now, Miss Davenport, I had a complaint yesterday afternoon about you trespassing on private property.' Bob dunked his chocolate biscuit in the tea and took a big bite.

'Riley Eddison and his precious rocks?' Darcy said, through gritted teeth.

'I wouldn't normally get involved in something which is quite obviously a lover's tiff—' Bob started to say.

'It most certainly IS NOT!' Darcy stood up, finding herself folding her arms across her chest.

'Oh sorry, I must have misunderstood. I got the impression from Riley there was something between you two.' His eyes glinted with amusement, as he took another bite of his biscuit. 'Look, whatever it is between the pair of you – sworn enemies, friends, something more – the man has a point. Rose Island Lighthouse is his property and therefore the land it is on, albeit a few rocks, also belongs to him. Now, I've taken the liberty of researching the land boundaries . . .' Bob pulled out a rather old map of White Cliff Bay. 'Originally—'

'Oh, wow! Is that White Cliff Bay?' Darcy marvelled, momentarily forgetting her outrage, and sat back down to take a closer look. She looked at the date. 'In 1889. Wow, it's so tiny.' She traced her finger along her road. 'This house wasn't even here then, and Rose Island Lighthouse was already built.' She touched the square with a circle in the middle on a small island and looked at the map with great interest, taking in all the differences between then and now.

'Yes, but you're kind of missing the point. Riley's great-great-grandfather bought Rose Island over a hundred and forty years ago and built the lighthouse himself. Originally, when the lighthouse was built, Rose Island was much bigger. The lighthouse had clear boundary lines, as there was a garden fence built around the property.' Bob pointed out the square perimeter surrounding the building. 'Over the years, the waves eroded the land and much of the island was lost; unfortunately, much of the garden was also washed away over time, leaving just the rocks that are there today. Now, the boundary lines have not been updated in the last hundred years since it was built, so officially his land is approximately twenty by twenty metres squared, with the light-house in the middle. Well, I say metres, back then everything was measured in yards, so—'

'Hang on, Bob, there are just a few rocks there now, nowhere near twenty metres . . .'

'Yes, but his property is technically still twenty by twenty metres squared – well, actually a lot more, if you include the original dimensions of Rose Island, but that was never recorded and—'

'Are you seriously telling me, then, that he owns the sea surrounding the lighthouse?' she seethed. Had Riley been right when he'd said that the sea was his? This was impossible, surely?

'Well, no, not the actual sea, but the land under the sea. It just so happens that his land is waterlogged; it doesn't stop it from being his land, though,' Bob explained patiently.

'I don't believe this,' Darcy groaned.

'Yes, and yesterday you were technically trespassing on private property,' Bob said, looking slightly embarrassed now.

'Are you kidding me? Riley phoned you about this? Riley complained I was trespassing on private property?' She stood back up again.

'Yes, Miss Davenport. Calm down. It's not like I'm arresting you or anything, you didn't know about the land boundaries and now you do. I'm sure you will respect Mr Eddison's property . . .'

'That man! That obnoxious, arrogant, egotistical little sh—'

'Now, Darcy,' Bob interrupted, kindly. 'Am I to understand that this is going to be a problem for you?'

She stood in silence for a moment.

'Because trespassing is a civil case, not a criminal case, so the police will not get involved unless criminal damage has occurred. I'm only here because, well, I like to help the people in my town and because it's a quiet day at the office,' he shrugged apologetically.

'Are you saying that if I was to trespass on his property, you wouldn't, you couldn't arrest me?' Darcy said, carefully.

Bob sucked the air through his teeth. 'I couldn't say something like that, Darcy, that would sound like I'm encouraging you to trespass. But something like that would be unlikely to go to court, especially if the person was soliciting.'

'What!' she shrieked, imagining herself standing on the rocks with high heels, fish-net stockings, a short leather skirt and a low-cut top.

'No, not that kind of soliciting,' he explained calmly. 'Sales, distributing leaflets, religious persuasion, that kind of thing. There is a sort of implied licence where these kinds of people are more or less allowed to go on someone's property to solicit their wares. You would only be technically trespassing if they asked you to leave and you refused to do so. However, even in this case it would still be a civil matter.' Bob carefully folded the map and walked towards the door. 'Now, do we have an understanding?' Bob opened the flat door and stepped into the foyer.

'Yes, Bob,' Darcy said, carefully, 'I understand.'

'In my day, if we liked someone, we just told them.' Bob smiled, knowingly.

'It's not like that, Bob, really it's not,' she protested.

'OK, I believe you,' he nodded, looking like he didn't.

'I just don't want him to win,' Darcy said quietly, realising how silly that sounded.

'And have you thought about why this is so important to you, him not winning? After all, he is only doing this to protect you. I'm just saying there might be other ways to woo him than this confrontational way you seem so keen on. Think about it.'

Darcy closed the door behind him, smiling, as much at the use of the word 'woo' as the fact that Bob was probably right. The thought of getting one over on Riley filled her with giddy excitement – not the kind of feeling she normally associated with someone she hated.

She smiled, as she looked over at the lighthouse. She wasn't going to let Riley get away with this.

After printing off thirty copies of the petition, Darcy strolled into town to distribute them around the shops and restaurants. The day was another blazing hot one and she was suddenly regretting wearing a strappy summer dress, as her back and neck were starting to burn already.

She wanted some way of getting Riley back for calling the police, so after she had finished the petition she had even spent half an hour googling rather childish practical jokes she could play on him as revenge. And although she probably wouldn't carry any of them out, it was fun to imagine Riley's face if she had somehow managed to swap his salt for his sugar or put cling film over his front door. However, she strongly suspected she would just end up having a go at him at the engagement party that evening. It was unlikely there would be much chance for a civilised conversation.

She walked into the White Cliff Bay furniture shop and was pleased to see that Maggie was working there that day.

'Hello, again,' Maggie said, coming round the counter. 'Did you change your mind about the love seat?'

Darcy laughed. 'I wish I could afford it. No, I was wondering if you would mind keeping one of these petitions in your shop and asking people to sign it?'

Maggie took one. 'I'd be happy to. I'm not here for the rest of the week, but I'll leave a note telling the others to ask the customers too. I know many of the townspeople will be happy to sign it. Though I honestly don't know if it will do any good.'

'It's worth a try, though.'

'Why don't you ask in Beside the Seaside?' Maggie gestured to the shop up the street that was painted in the bright clashing colours of a beach hut. 'That's the art gallery that sells paintings, sculptures and other art. A lot of the work they sell is influenced by the lighthouse and the tourists love the stuff in there – you might get a few tourist signatures, too.'

'Good idea.'

Darcy waved goodbye and trotted over the road, pushing open the door with a tiny jingle.

There was a young girl working behind the counter who looked to be about seventeen years old. She smiled at Darcy when she walked in and Darcy noticed she was wearing a badge saying she was called Ulrika.

'Hello, I'm doing a petition to try to save the lighthouse and I was wondering if you would mind keeping a copy in your shop and if you might ask customers to sign it?' Darcy rattled off her prepared speech.

'Of course,' Ulrika said. 'It's such a shame that they plan to pull it down. So many of our artists use the lighthouse for their inspiration.' She gestured around the shop. There were clay models, wooden carvings, fabric wall hangings, glass-blown ornaments and lots of paintings that were all influenced by the lighthouse. It would be weird to think that these things might not be here in a few months' time once the lighthouse had gone. Might it even affect the trade and sales of the shop or would the artists of the town find new things to inspire them?

She looked around the other side of the shop and stopped when she saw the brightly coloured jaunty prints of the town and the lighthouse that she knew her aunt had painted. She had only seen a few of her paintings over the years but there was no mistaking her particular style and brand.

She stepped closer to admire one in particular. It wasn't an original; as Verity had said, most if not all of those had already been sold. There was something so cheerful and whimsical about the painting. It wasn't really a true depiction of the town, lots of features had been exaggerated or moved for convenience, but it was still obviously White Cliff Bay in all its cute and laidback splendour.

'That's a Ginny Andrews print. They are probably our most popular paintings, everyone loves them,' Ulrika explained.

'Do you have more?'

Ulrika pointed to two large boxes that were filled with other prints. 'Those are all we have.'

Darcy moved to look through them, inspecting each one carefully, admiring the differences and little quirks of the town that Ginny had captured beautifully. There were easily over a hundred different prints here and Darcy wanted to buy them all and decorate every wall of her flat with them.

'Do you have any of her originals?' Darcy asked.

Ulrika shook her head. 'No, they were always snapped up really quickly, especially by the tourists . . . Oh wait, we do have one! It's different from all the rest, though.'

Ulrika hurried into the back of the shop and a few minutes later she returned carrying a large black plastic folder.

'It's not framed. We can do that for you, if you want. We never put it out, as Ginny asked that we didn't sell it, at least not until she died.'

Ulrika carefully pulled the painting out and laid it flat on top of the folder, unwrapping the tissue paper from the top. It was a painting of a man laughing; he was lying in bed, naked except for a sheet wrapped round his bottom half. He was looking out at whoever had painted this with complete love in his eyes. He was ridiculously good looking and it was somehow obvious that whoever painted this was in love with him too – each stroke of the brush was delivered with passion and care. Behind the man's head was a window and Darcy could see an expanse of blue and the tiny houses of the town in the distance. It was incredible, but nothing like the other paintings of the town and lighthouse at all. It wasn't even the same style.

'Are you sure this is a Ginny Andrews?' Darcy asked.

Ulrika nodded confidently. 'She came in about a year ago and asked to see it. She stood there and stared at it for a long time and then told us to put it back. It's got her signature on it too.'

Darcy recognised the scrawl at the bottom, the same one that was on each and every other painting.

Who was the man in the painting? Clearly, someone who had meant a lot to Ginny. But in all the years that Darcy had known and visited Ginny, she had never seen her with a man. He looked oddly familiar, as if she had seen him somewhere before, though she couldn't place where. Dark green eyes sparkled from the painting as the man laughed, his dark hair a rumpled mess.

Darcy felt a pang of guilt. She had never really spoken to Ginny about her life, about why she had come to White Cliff Bay, about the men she had dated or the places she had visited. Ginny had spent the whole of Darcy's life living in White Cliff Bay and, though Darcy knew she had been a solicitor in London before that, she didn't know much else about her aunt's life prior to coming to here. Obviously, in her younger years this man played a key role. Ginny had been in love with him, though she had never spoken about him.

She swallowed. 'How much for the painting?'

'Oh, I don't know. Most of our originals of this size go for about a hundred to two hundred pounds, it depends on the artist.'

Darcy felt her shoulders sink in disappointment.

'But I asked Gail, the shop owner, about this the other day and what we were going to do with it, now Ginny has died. Gail said that no one would be interested in it, as it wasn't a typical Ginny Andrews piece and she didn't think people would want a strange man hanging up in their homes.'

Darcy stared at her incredulously. Even without the connection that Darcy had to Ginny, it was still an incredible painting. She imagined a lot of people would be more than happy to have this piece in their homes, regardless of the fact that they didn't know who the man was.

'I'll let you have it for twenty pounds,' Ulrika said. 'I think Gail would be glad to be rid of it, to be honest.'

Darcy fished some money out of her purse and thrust it towards Ulrika before she changed her mind. 'Look, I've got a few more shops and restaurants to take these petitions to – can I come back in about an hour to collect it on my way home?'

Ulrika nodded, clearly stunned that she had managed to sell it.

Darcy stayed to watch her ring up the sale and carefully pack the painting away, and then she left the shop.

There was a little mystery there and she hoped to be able to solve it.

☀   ☀   ☀

There was another knock on her door later that night and, wondering if PC Bob had come back with more complaints, perhaps this time for stealing one of Riley's rocks, Darcy answered it. Libby was standing on her doorstep hand in hand with George; they really were the cutest couple.

'Are you coming to Amy and Seb's engagement party?' Libby asked.

'Oh, I don't know. I know I met them and they're lovely, but I don't really know them. Might be a bit cheeky to pitch up to their party just a few days after being introduced.'

'No, of course it isn't cheeky. It's a beach barbecue, everyone is invited. It's a very casual thing and Amy did invite you herself, so she obviously wants you there. Come on, get your shoes on. Bring Ben, too.'

Darcy smiled at Libby's insistence, as she slipped her feet into her sandals, grabbed her bag and whistled for Ben. Ben hauled himself off the sofa, eager to go out again.

She closed the door behind her and walked out onto the street with them. Up on the beach there was already a crowd forming, enjoying the festivities. The evening still held the warmth of the day. Stars had started to pepper the scarlet sky and the moon was out, shining brightly on the party.

'Riley will probably be there, too,' Libby said, nudging Darcy.

Seb had said the same thing, though Darcy wasn't sure if it would be a good or bad thing to see him again.

'I thought you said he was antisocial. Why would he come to a party when he isn't friends with anyone?'

'Because Riley walks Kelpie on the beach every morning and he has met Seb most days, walking Jack. I think to say they've become good friends would be an overstatement, but Seb is certainly the closest thing Riley has to a friend in White Cliff Bay.'

Something pulled at Darcy's heart on hearing this. Despite their silly row the day before, she hated the thought of Riley all alone with no friends to talk to.

They crossed the road to the beach and Darcy let Ben run on ahead. She watched him as he joined Jack, Seb's dog, in the surf and then her heart leapt as she saw Kelpie run over to join them. It seemed that Libby had been right.

Spotting Amy standing next to her fiancé at the barbecue, Darcy joined Libby and George to go and say hello.

'Congratulations,' Darcy said.

Amy greeted her with a kiss on her cheek, which made Darcy smile. 'Thank you for coming.'

'Oh, thank you for inviting me. I don't have a gift for you, I'm afraid,' Darcy realised, rather belatedly. She looked around for a present table, but there wasn't one.

'Oh, we're not expecting gifts from anyone, it's not that kind of party. It's just a gathering of our friends and family to celebrate Seb finally asking me to marry him!' Amy said, and Seb laughed.

'We've been together for six months. It's not like I made you wait for ten years.' He looked at George for back-up.

'Sorry, mate, don't look at me. I married my best friend ten days after we got together. It would have been sooner if I'd had my way, but everywhere was either booked up over Christmas or closed.'

'You were married after ten days?' Darcy asked, incredulously.

'We'd been friends for six months,' Libby said, leaning into George's side. 'He was in love with me from the moment we met. I'm ashamed to admit that it took me a bit longer to realise it. But when you know you've found your soulmate, there isn't any point in waiting around.'

Amy nudged Seb good-naturedly and he groaned. 'You give us normal men a bad name,' he laughed.

George shrugged and kissed Libby's head with a smile.

Amy turned her attention back to Darcy. 'Would you like a drink?'

'Oh, a red wine would be lovely.'

Amy went to a drinks table and poured a glass of wine, and as Giselle, Noah and a few more guests arrived to talk to Amy and Seb, Darcy moved off out of the way.

It was then that she saw Riley. He was sitting on a garden chair a little way out of the rest of the party. He was wearing his cowboy hat, sipping a bottle of beer. To the casual observer, he was part of the party, but although his chair was facing towards her and the rest of the people from the town, he was looking off towards the sea, watching the dogs playing. It was quite obvious he didn't want to be there.

He wasn't going to get away with calling the police on her, though, and she marched over to tell him so. As she got close, she saw his attention snap to her, his face lighting up into a smile just as her sandal got caught on a rock and she went flying through the air and landed face down on the semi-shingle part of the beach. As she crashed into the ground, she saw the red wine she had been carrying splatter all over Riley.

Crap.

Immediately, Riley was on his feet, strong, gentle hands around her arms as he pulled her up. When she looked up, instead of seeing anger in his eyes, she only saw concern.

'Darcy, are you OK? You came down so hard,' Riley said, wine dripping off his face and off his shirt. His shirt was soaked and his faded blue jeans had an unsightly wet patch.

'I'm so sorry, I just . . .'

'Lost your balance.' His mouth quirked up into that gorgeous half smile, as he echoed her words from the other night – though this time the fall had been genuine and not helped by her mischievous matchmaking neighbour.

'I really am sorry.' She instinctively attempted to wipe the wine off his shirt and stopped when she felt a wall of solid muscle underneath her fingers. What was she doing? What would he think of her? She quickly withdrew her hand, but he caught it in his own.

'You've cut yourself.' He frowned and she looked down to see the tiny graze on her hand.

'It's nothing.'

He bent down and snagged a bottle of water, flipped the lid and poured a little bit onto her hand, washing away the tiny stones, then he dabbed at the cut gently with the bottom of his shirt.

'You'll get blood on your shirt.'

He shrugged. 'I think the wine has probably already ruined it. Don't worry, it's very old.'

'I'm sorry.'

'Stop apologising, it's just a bit of wine. And it's probably what I deserve after calling the police on you.' He finished bathing her hand but his hand remained on hers. 'Are you hurt anywhere else?'

She shook her head.

'Did you have something you wanted to say to me, Darcy Davenport? It looked like you were on a mission when you came marching over here.'

'It's not important.'

He smiled, slightly. 'Oh, I imagine everything you have to say is important and worth listening to.'

She stared at him, wondering if he was mocking, her but she could only see sincerity shining from his eyes.

For the first time in a long time, she had nothing to say. Telling him off for calling the police seemed silly, now he was being so kind.

As he continued to stare down at her, a woman wearing a very low-cut top suddenly stepped up to them. 'Riley, how lovely to see you here,' she said, thrusting her breasts in his direction. She was beautiful in that seemingly effortless way, with long chestnut-brown hair that came down past her bum and was silky smooth, not frizzy and curly like Darcy's own hair. Flawless make-up and a perfect smile made up the stunning package.

Riley tore his eyes away from Darcy and touched his hat, as he addressed the woman. 'Ma'am.'

'Riley,' the woman giggled. 'How many times do I need to tell you? Call me Charlotte.'

'Charlotte, my apologies, I'm not good with names.'

Darcy suspected this was a lie, as he'd known her name without her even giving it to him.

'When are you going to take me out again, Riley? I had such a wonderful time the other night.'

Darcy took a step back out of the weird little Riley appreciation triangle, feeling, for some reason, a little jealous about the revelation that he had taken this vision of perfection out. But then why shouldn't he? He was a free agent and he had given Darcy no signal at all that he had any interest in her. He wasn't obligated to her and could go out with anyone he wanted.

Riley glanced at her and frowned slightly as she backed up, but he made no move to stop her leaving and when he returned his attention back to Charlotte, who was still talking, Darcy turned and walked away.

She re-joined George and Libby, feeling safe in their company. She flopped down on a chair and Libby handed her another glass of wine.

'I saw you lost the last one,' Libby said.

'I'm such an idiot! I'm so clumsy and accident-prone. I have a catalogue of disasters a mile long. Throwing wine over somebody I like has got to be up there in my top ten.'

'You like him?'

'No.'

'You just said you did.'

'No, I meant . . . It doesn't matter anyway. He is busy talking to White Cliff Bay's Beauty Queen over there. I suspect she doesn't throw wine over people.'

'Oh, I shouldn't worry about Charlotte. I'll give it thirty seconds before he shuts her out. He has no interest in the women of this town or any woman, well . . . apart from you.'

'He is not interested in me,' Darcy said.

'Sure he is, he couldn't take his eyes off you.'

'Those same eyes are now feasting on those huge boobs.'

'Twenty seconds – and he is most definitely looking at her face, not her boobs.'

'They went out together the other night.'

'She joined him in the booth he was sitting in at the pub, quietly reading his book. He was too polite to tell her to sod off. They talked for about five minutes and when she showed no sign of leaving, Riley got up and went home, leaving his pint of beer untouched. She's been telling everybody ever since that she had been on a date with him. Five seconds.'

Darcy looked back over at Riley and sure enough he touched his hat to say goodbye, untangled his arm from Charlotte's hand and walked away from her down to the shoreline to check on Kelpie. She smiled at this. Charlotte stood there waiting for him to come back, but Riley didn't and eventually she walked away.

'How did you know?' Darcy asked.

'Me and Amy timed him once. He has it down to a fine art. The women come up to him, he is polite and respectful but within one minute he makes some excuse and leaves. I think five minutes with Charlotte the other night was his record, but only because he was sitting enjoying his beer and he couldn't exactly get up and move to another table.'

As Darcy watched him, Riley looked around and locked eyes with her. He stared at her for a few moments before he looked away. She didn't dare go back up to him again, in case he shut her out too.

She looked around and noticed Maggie sitting with her husband, Daniel, and two boys fairly close to where Riley had been sitting. A baby was in her arms. Maggie and Daniel were chatting to another couple and the youngest boy ran off to join another child playing nearby, while the older boy was reading a shark book and seemed quite angry about being there.

Darcy stood up and walked over to them. 'Hi, Maggie.'

'Hello, Darcy,' Maggie smiled, warmly. 'Did you have luck with the petitions?'

'Yes, everywhere I asked was happy to take them. Let's hope it makes a difference.'

Darcy turned her attention to the boy who was wearing a shark T-shirt and clutching his shark book like it was a lifeline. 'Hello, you must be Ryan, right?'

The boy looked over the top of his book in surprise, but he nodded.

'So, you like sharks? Which one is your favourite?' Darcy asked.

He scowled at her, obviously thinking she couldn't possibly know anything about sharks.

'My favourite is the angel shark,' Darcy prompted. 'Sadly, we don't get too many round here any more, but that makes it all the more special when you do see them. I love them because they are sort of half-ray, half-shark, as if they haven't yet made their minds up which species they want to be. What about you, what's your favourite?'

She expected him to say the great white. That was everyone's favourite – or at least the one that everyone knew.

'The goblin shark.'

'That's such a cool choice,' Darcy said, sitting down next to Ryan. 'Why is that your favourite?'

'Because of their transparent skin: they look pink but actually their skin is see-through and you can see all their blood moving around the capillaries.'

Darcy blinked in surprise at his knowledge and use of the correct terminology.

'That's right, a lot of people just assume they are pink but they have no pink pigment in their skin.'

Ryan looked at her in wonder. 'And their mouth has sort of another mouth inside and it sticks out when they attack. Their mouth opens and the teeth from the second mouth shoot out like this.' He mimed one hand opening and then the other hand shot out from the palm of the first hand. The goblin shark always reminded Darcy of that scene from *Alien* when the alien's mouth opens and another mouth comes out. She often wondered if Ridley Scott had based that on the goblin shark.

'It's not really another mouth – it has a protruding jaw that shoots out kind of like a chameleon's tongue, but obviously not as far. Would you like to see a video of the goblin shark and its protruding jaw? It's quite short, but pretty amazing,' Darcy said, digging her phone out of her pocket, swiping across the screen and showing Ryan. 'See how it is slowed down? You can see that it is part of his mouth: it just shoots out, not a separate mouth. They are the most wonderful creatures.'

Ryan watched the video as if Darcy had just given him the best Christmas present ever. She hit replay and let him watch it again, his eyes lighting up in fascination.

'Why are their jaws like that?'

'It's evolution, I guess. Their bodies have adapted. Their snouts are so long they wouldn't be able to eat without it. Look . . .' She picked up Ryan's plate with a hot dog on it, which he had been astutely ignoring in favour of his shark book. 'OK, can you take a bite of this with no hands?'

Ryan held the plate and ducked his head down and with some difficulty he managed to get a bite off, giggling slightly at his efforts.

'OK, now give yourself a really long nose, put your hand over your nose as if it's a big horn, now try to eat your sausage.'

Ryan ducked his head down again but with his hand protruding from his face his mouth couldn't get anywhere near it. He laughed loudly as he tried again and again.

'You see, you need that jaw to extend from your mouth so you stand any chance of eating.'

'I'm going to always eat like a goblin shark from now on,' Ryan laughed.

'No, silly,' Darcy nudged him. 'You haven't got the protruding jaw. You have to eat like a human with a knife and fork.' Then she whispered loudly to him, 'At least when your parents are looking.'

Ryan laughed loudly and Darcy looked over at Maggie to see if she minded her talking to her son. Maggie had the biggest smile on her face. 'Thank you,' she whispered.

Darcy smiled. She looked around at the people milling about on the beach, enjoying the party, and at some of the wonderful people who were becoming her friends. She glanced over at Riley, sitting not very far away, watching her with a small smile on his lips. She was going to be very happy here, she could feel it.

CHAPTER 5

Darcy walked into town again the next day, enjoying the warm summer breeze. She was meeting Verity for lunch in The Crab-shack to talk a bit more about the angle she wanted to pursue with the national press and maybe get the names and details of a few more of the couples who had proposed to each other in the lighthouse.

She wanted to get Libby a cake first. She had seemed a bit down that morning, though, knowing Libby and her over-emotional baby hormones, she was probably upset because she'd burnt her toast or some other silly reason.

She opened the door to Sugar and Spice, the warmth and sweet smells of the bakery wrapping themselves around her, pulling her in and making her feel as if she had just walked into someone's home. Not that her home had ever smelled that way. Her mum and dad never did any baking.

She eyed the delicious delights in the glass cabinet and looked up into the smiling eyes of a middle-aged woman.

'Darcy Davenport, we were wondering when we would get to meet you.'

Darcy blinked. Everyone seemed to know her name.

'I'm Linda and this is my daughter, Polly.' The lady gestured to a pretty red-head who looked to be in her late twenties. 'I hear you've come down here for work. Is the job in the town?'

'No, it's at the council offices in Apple Hill. I start there on Monday, a week today.'

Linda nodded and Darcy guessed that the enquiry about her job was just the polite introductory chit-chat that was deemed socially necessary before Linda launched into what she really wanted to say.

'Everyone has been talking about you and Riley Eddison! It seems you've certainly captured his attention.'

'If by captured his attention you mean he called the police on me for trespassing on his island, and I threw wine over him when I tripped over last night, then yes, I've certainly done that.'

Linda smiled. 'Polly was at the party last night, she said Riley couldn't take his eyes off you.'

Darcy looked over at Polly, who smiled apologetically. 'Sorry, gossip is thin on the ground in these parts and, as Riley has shunned every single woman who has made advances on him since he arrived, the fact that he seems very interested in you is hot news.'

Darcy sighed. 'I think I irritate him more than interest him.'

'Not from where I was standing,' Polly giggled.

Darcy was about to protest when Polly carried on talking. 'Don't be upset. He is such a loner in this town and we're all worried that he hasn't made friends or seemingly has any interest in doing so. He stays in that lighthouse every day, only venturing into town to get food or groceries. We all need friends and company. I think it's lovely that he is coming out of his shell a bit and that you're the one making him do it. With all this business with the lighthouse, he'll need someone he can talk to and I think you're just the person.'

They had high hopes for her and Riley, and Darcy didn't want to let them down. Telling them they had it all wrong would be a disappointment to them, and she would hate to do that.

'I hear you're trying to save the lighthouse, too. I've seen the petition, I think it's a wonderful idea,' Linda said. 'And Verity said you're going to get a story in the national papers. I think that will really help.'

'I'm going to try, Linda, I can't promise anything,' Darcy said, hoping that she wouldn't be causing even more disappointment in the town.

Darcy ordered a cream doughnut for Libby and left the shop. She saw a girl of about her age walking towards the bakery. The girl suddenly stopped, closed her eyes and went white as a sheet. She wobbled and Darcy suddenly found herself running forward, throwing the cake to the ground as the girl crumpled to the pavement as if she were a puppet with her strings cut. Luckily, Darcy managed to catch her before she hit the ground, but she stumbled under the girl's dead weight and fell to the cobbles herself with the girl on top of her.

People rushed to help very quickly, pulling the girl gently off Darcy and carrying her into the baker's. If Darcy thought she could slink away, there was no chance of that, as she was pulled to her feet and hauled back into the bakery too.

They laid the girl on the sofa and Linda came rushing round, dabbing the girl's face with a wet dishcloth.

'Penny, lovely, can you hear me? Penny?'

If Penny had been able to hear her, Darcy thought she would probably tell Linda to stop wiping her face with a cloth used to clean dirty dishes.

'Someone needs to get Henry,' Linda said.

Feeling utterly useless as she watched Penny lying still, Darcy called out, 'I'll go. Where will he be?'

'In the factory – take the street by the side of here and the factory is just behind us. Ask for Henry Travis.'

Darcy set off at a run, tearing through the factory gates a moment later. She burst through the front entrance to the surprised gaze of the receptionist.

'I need to see Henry Travis, it's an emergency.'

The receptionist scuttled off and returned in record time with the biggest man in the world.

'Henry?'

He nodded.

'It's Penny, she's just passed out, she's in the bakery, she—'

Henry didn't wait to hear any further explanation; he raced out the door and was tearing along the street a second later. Darcy ran after him, but by the time she burst back into the bakery, Penny was already sitting up, eating a cake. The colour had returned to her cheeks and Henry was kneeling down in front of her.

'Are you OK?' Henry said, looking as pale as Penny had gone.

'I'm fine, Henry. I just felt a bit dizzy.'

Henry's hand went to her belly. 'Are you sure everything is OK?'

People started murmuring about Penny being pregnant and there were little gasps of delight.

Linda, finally realising that Penny having an audience probably wasn't the best thing for her, started shooing everyone out. Darcy turned to go, but Linda snagged her arm.

'Not you, everybody else can get out.'

People left reluctantly, taking their little piece of gossip with them. Something told Darcy that the whole town would know within ten minutes.

'You saved her, I saw you throw yourself on the ground to catch her,' Linda said.

'No, it wasn't like that, I—'

'Polly, fill a cake box for me,' Linda called to her daughter.

'Thank you,' Penny said. 'I saw you running towards me, but I don't remember a lot after that.'

'I didn't do anything, not really,' Darcy said, feeling embarrassed by the attention. She wasn't brave or heroic, but they were making out that she had saved Penny's life.

Linda pressed a huge box of cakes into Darcy's hands.

'I think I better take you to hospital,' Henry said to Penny.

'I'm fine.'

'Just to be on the safe side.'

He scooped her up as if she weighed nothing and carried her out of the shop. 'Thank you for helping,' Henry said as he passed her.

Darcy walked out of the shop with her huge box of cakes and, trying to ignore the smiles of gratitude from the people of the town who had already heard the news of how Darcy had risked her life to save Penny, she headed towards The Crabshack.

It seemed the people of White Cliff Bay were determined to raise her as a hero, either because she had saved Penny or made Riley come out of his shell. But either way, she didn't want to let them down. Even if he wasn't interested in her, she could help him get to know the people in the town and make some friends.

She pushed open the door to The Crabshack to see that Verity was already waiting for her.

'Sorry, I'm late,' Darcy said, heaving her big box onto the floor. 'I was delayed—'

'I know all about it, my dear. I just heard how you saved Penny. Give it a few days and I'm sure you'll be knighted by the town mayor for your heroic deeds,' Verity chuckled.

Darcy laughed, somewhat astounded that news had reached the far side of the town already.

The waitress came and took their order. Verity highly recommended the crab platter, so she ordered that.

'So, you wanted to talk to me a bit more about this newspaper article you're planning on doing,' Verity said, sipping her tea.

'Yes, I just need to get an idea of the angle and a few more details before I contact my friend, but actually I have something else I wanted to talk to you about first.'

Verity leaned forward, her eyes sparkling. 'I'm intrigued.'

'I wondered if Ginny ever had any boyfriends or someone she might have been seeing for a while?'

Verity looked thoughtful. 'I only became friends with her when she moved down here, and as far as I'm aware there was no one in all the time she lived here. The town is very small and gossip spreads quickly around here.'

'I know!' Darcy laughed.

'If she had been seeing someone from the town, then I think we would all have known about it. She might have been seeing someone outside the town, but she didn't venture far from her little caravan. She'd come into the town to get groceries or sell her paintings; other than that she was pretty much in her caravan all the time. You always knew where to find her, so if she was seeing someone she was very secretive about it. Why do you ask?'

'I've found a painting she did, not of the town but of a man. He was naked in bed. I thought perhaps he meant something to her.'

'Could have just been a model, posing nude. Jackson Cartwright had Amy pose nude for him last year and painted her. I can assure you that there definitely wasn't any kind of relationship between them. In fact, I think he is marrying his boyfriend later this year.'

Darcy shook her head. 'There was something about the painting that suggested she really cared for him. I think he might have been her boyfriend. The weird thing is the town is in the background, so she must have met him here.'

Verity thought for a moment. 'She did come to White Cliff Bay on holiday for a few weeks before she moved here. From what I understand, she came down for three weeks, fell in love with the place, went back to her life in London and missed White Cliff Bay too much so she packed in her job, sold her house and moved back here for good.'

'Maybe it was a man she fell in love with, that's why she came back?' Darcy said.

'It might have been, but she certainly wasn't with him after she moved here, so that must have ended badly for her. If I saw the painting I might recognise him, but I don't think I can be more help. She never mentioned him, if there was someone.'

'There was someone,' said an elderly lady from the next table. She was tiny, a shrunken version of her former self. Her hair was in a headscarf and she looked very pale.

Darcy turned to listen, eagerly.

'I can't remember who, though. John somebody, or was it Tom? Tall boy, had a motorbike. I caught them going at it like rabbits in the caves. I was walking my Billy down the beach when I heard the screams. Of course I went to see if everything was OK and he was taking her against the wall of the cave. She certainly seemed to be enjoying herself, so I left them to it. She went back to London after that but when she came back he had gone.'

'Gone?' Darcy prompted. 'He'd died?'

'No, he moved to Australia . . . or was it Austria? I saw her after she had come back, she was heartbroken.'

'And you don't know who he was?'

The old lady shook her head. 'He did have a motorbike, though. I remember that. And a dog.'

The old lady turned back to the crossword puzzle she was doing and Darcy sensed the conversation was over.

'A tall lad called John or Tom who rode a motorbike and had a dog and moved to Australia or Austria over thirty years ago, before Ginny moved here for good,' Verity muttered. 'Well, that narrows it down.'

Darcy smiled. It was something.

Darcy looked over at the lighthouse as she walked back towards her home. She wasn't sure if she was hoping to see Riley or whether she just felt some kind of affinity with the place, now she was trying to save it.

The meeting with Verity had gone very well and they'd both agreed that they were going to go down the romance and proposal angle to get people behind the fight to save the lighthouse. Everyone enjoyed a good love story. They would mention the history and the legacy of the place but that would be secondary.

She shifted the box of cakes to one arm and fished her phone out of her bag, then dialled Carmel's number.

She answered immediately. 'Hello sexy, how you doing?'

'Hey you, are you free to talk?'

'Sure, I've always got time for you,' Carmel said, though Darcy could hear the busy noises of the office in the background. 'Have you seen any more naked men?'

'Sadly not.'

'Any hot single men taken your fancy?'

'No,' Darcy said rather too quickly.

Carmel laughed. 'Ah, there is someone. Is he a surfer – no, wait, a lifeguard in those sexy red shorts?'

'No, there isn't anyone. There's a man who is arrogant and rude and . . .'

'Sexy as hell?' Carmel said.

'No, Riley isn't sexy. Quite ugly really,' Darcy lied. 'I mean, sure he is really tall and muscular with strong arms. And he has black, just-got-out-of-bed hair and beautiful dark green eyes that some women would like. He has the most incredible American accent and when he isn't shouting at me he has a lovely smile but, no, he definitely isn't sexy. I'm not attracted to him at all.'

'Sounds like it,' Carmel laughed.

Darcy stopped to look over at the lighthouse again. Immediately, someone bumped into her from behind. She quickly looked around to find Riley, who touched his hat by way of apology as he walked off towards the jetty.

She stared after him in shock. How much had he heard? She felt awful. It was one thing denying that she was attracted to him to her friend, but no one wanted to hear that they were arrogant, rude and even ugly. Though she had said some nice things too – maybe that would outweigh the bad. She back-tracked over what she had said: muscular arms, beautiful eyes, lovely smile. Her breath caught in her throat. Oh God. She could feel her cheeks burning with mortification. He would know she had feelings for him. Although it was already pretty clear – she had literally thrown herself at him twice now. How embarrassing. She really was just like the other women in the town, swarming around him like bees to a honey pot. She considered running after him to apologise or explain, but he might not have heard anything.

She sighed. She wasn't that lucky.

'Are you still there?' Carmel said.

Darcy waited for Riley to be far enough away so he definitely couldn't hear her. 'Yeah, I'm still here, but I think the sexy American just heard every word I just said.'

Carmel snorted with laughter. 'You certainly know how to make a good impression.'

Darcy winced. 'Listen, I might have a story for your paper, if you're interested.'

'Is it a story about a cow escaping from his field, because I'm not sure even *The Headline* would be interested in that kind of story?'

Darcy laughed and explained about Rose Island Lighthouse and how it was being threatened with demolition, telling Carmel about the history of the place and how it was probably the most romantic lighthouse in England, with all the people who had proposed there. Her friend listened, asking questions and clearly taking notes. As the news editor for one of the big national papers, she knew what worked as a great story and what wouldn't hit the mark. It was a local story, really, not national-news worthy, but Carmel might see potential in it.

'I like it and quite honestly, apart from Wimbledon, there is nothing else going on in the world at the moment. We ran a story on a skateboarding dog last week. It was almost front-page news. Look, providing that no one dies in the next twenty-four hours, no politicians lie and no footballers or actors have affairs, I'll send someone down tomorrow to do some interviews and take pictures. Can you line up a few people for the reporter to talk to, some of the artists maybe, those that have been proposed to in the lighthouse too?'

'Yes, I'll speak to Verity. I'm sure she would know a few people who would be happy to tell their stories,' Darcy said, excitedly. Rose Island was going to have its story told.

'The guy who lives in the lighthouse too, we'll definitely need to speak to him.'

Darcy felt her bubble of happiness pop.

'I don't think he'll agree to that.'

'We need him, Darcy. He's the human element to this. He is going to lose his home, something that's been in his family for generations. We need his take on this or there is no story.'

Darcy closed her eyes, imagining how that conversation would play out. 'OK, he'll be there.'

'Good, anywhere we could meet that has good views over the lighthouse?'

Darcy thought. 'Yes, the Bubble and Froth. It's a pub on the beach. There would be great photo opportunities from there. I'll speak to Amy and Seb to see if they are OK with it, but I'm sure they wouldn't mind. I'll ask them, then email you the details.'

'That's great. Let's say 3 p.m.' Carmel paused. 'Is your sexy American friend the man in the lighthouse?'

'Yes.' Darcy sighed.

'Then you might have a bit of grovelling to do.'

Riley poured his hot soup into a bowl and took it over to the small dining table to eat. He sat down and stirred it, watching the red ripples move around the bowl just like the red hair of his favourite mermaid.

He hadn't been able to stop thinking about Darcy. She had been angry about him going to the police and rightly so. It had been an overreaction, he knew that. But he'd wanted to do something that showed Darcy he meant business. She'd hurt herself on the rocks when she'd banged her knee and the last thing he wanted was for her to hurt herself more seriously the next time she came. But now he had probably annoyed her so much the chance of starting up any kind of friendship with her was non-existent. She would never come out there again and he had no right to be disappointed by that fact.

He lifted the spoon to his mouth just as there was a loud knock on the door. He let the spoon drop back into the bowl and sighed. There was only one person it could be – the only person who'd ever been out to Rose Island other than the builders and decorators. He was torn whether to be delighted by her return or incredibly frustrated that she wouldn't listen to his requests to stay away. Staring at his dinner, which was surely going to grow cold, he settled on frustrated.

He marched down the stairs and flung open the door. Sure enough, his mermaid was standing there, soaking wet with a huge grin on her face. There was something so endearing and charming about her. The last time she had been here he had shouted at her and she was still standing there smiling.

'I used the steps at the back of the island, so you can't get mad about me trampling over your precious rocks.'

'I told you not to come back, that you're trespassing on private property,' Riley said, though a smile tugged on his lips at her audacity.

'I'm not actually, I'm soliciting,' Darcy said, proudly.

The last thing Riley expected was Darcy to declare she was soliciting and to start to unzip her wetsuit. He saw her pull a bag from her wetsuit. She unwrapped it and pulled out a soggy piece of paper.

The bag had clearly been meant to protect the paper from the water but had failed miserably, something that Darcy was quite obviously disappointed with, but it wasn't going to keep her down.

'I'm just letting you know about the Save the Lighthouse meeting in the town hall on Saturday. I thought it might be something you would be interested in,' Darcy said cheerily, as she passed him the piece of paper.

Riley took the limp, soggy piece of paper and peered at it, stunned by this new tactic. As he held it, the paper broke apart in his hands. He tried to put it back together but the paper was beyond repair and it flopped uselessly over his fingers.

'You came here to bring me a leaflet?' Riley said, confused. Then the comment about soliciting began to make more sense. Well, much more sense than Darcy coming here to offer herself to him, although he still remembered the offer of 'great sex' she had made him the first time they'd met.

'Yep, so I'm entitled to be here if I come for business purposes,' Darcy smiled at him triumphantly.

Riley's heart missed a beat as he took in that smile. He suddenly wanted to keep that smile on her face; he wanted her to win this fight.

'Well, Darcy, thank you for bringing this to my attention. I will be sure to review the information in this leaflet.' He held up the soggy remains. 'And give it some serious consideration.'

Riley's mouth twitched at the corners, as he barely contained a smirk. He had no intention of going to the meeting, but he still liked that she had used that excuse to come over there.

'Er, right.' Darcy was clearly thrown, not expecting him to be nice. She hovered for a moment, obviously wanting to say something else. 'Actually, I need your help.'

'You want me to help you? After you called me ugly, arrogant and rude?'

Her whole face fell and he felt guilty for bringing it up. He'd also heard the words 'beautiful eyes' and 'lovely smile', so he hadn't been too bothered by her talking about him. Besides, he probably deserved the 'arrogant' and 'rude' comments.

'I'm so sorry. Carmel, my friend, would marry me off to the first man who smiled at me. I was just . . . I didn't mean . . .'

'What do you need?' he said, quickly hoping to change the subject and excuse her from her obvious torment.

'I've got a reporter from one of the national papers to come and do an article about the lighthouse in an attempt to save it from demolition and they want to speak to you too.'

The happiness that had started to bubble up at seeing her quickly vanished.

'No, I'm not being interviewed.'

'But this could really help add weight to the Save the Light-house campaign. It would only be ten minutes of your time.'

'I'm not getting involved with the town, I'm not joining a protest rally, holding placards saying "Save Our Lighthouse" and I'm not being interviewed for the papers.'

He moved to shut the door, but she stopped him. '3 p.m. in the Bubble and Froth, tomorrow. No actually, come for 3.30 and the reporter should have done all the other interviews by then. I'll buy you a drink.'

'No.'

'I'll do something for you, anything you want. Please, it's important.'

'To who? The people in the town who are all shaking their heads sympathetically at poor Riley Eddison who is about to lose his home? Who does it really affect? Who could possibly care about this lighthouse?'

'Me. I care. It's important to me.'

He felt the anger deflate out of him. The last thing he wanted was to join forces with the people of the town to fight a hopeless battle against the powers that wanted to destroy his home. He just wanted to stay in his lighthouse, for as long as they would let him, and be left alone. But there was something about Darcy Davenport that made him want to change all that. Her smile, her sweet nature. Like a siren, she called to him and he wanted to follow.

'I'll think about it,' he said, closing the door firmly before she persuaded him to do anything else he really didn't want to do.

He leaned his head against the door and tried to shut out her hopeful blue eyes and the passion and determination he had seen in them. She did care and he had no idea why.

He stomped back upstairs to his now cold soup.

He wasn't going to go and no beautiful smile in the world was going to change that.

Darcy knocked on George and Libby's door a while later, hoping that her incessant demands on their time weren't annoying them.

Libby opened the door and smiled a huge smile when she saw her. Darcy felt mildly better.

'Hello, I was just going to come round and see if you wanted to come for dinner tonight,' Libby said.

'Oh thank you, but I wouldn't want to intrude.'

'Don't be silly. We'd be happy to have you. Besides, George always makes too much food. He says it's because I'm eating for two but I'm sure he thinks I'm eating for three or four.'

Darcy smiled as Libby stepped back to let her in.

George was lying on the recliner and he waved and sat up as Darcy stepped into the lounge.

Darcy sat down on the sofa and Libby sat next to her. 'I, erm . . . George, I need a favour.'

She sighed, wishing that the last favour she'd asked of Riley hadn't ended so spectacularly badly.

'What's up?' George said, flicking the recliner back into a seated position.

Darcy took a deep breath. 'Are you any good with accents?'

George stared at her in confusion for a second. 'My Australian isn't bad,' he drawled in a bad Australian accent.

'Can you do American?'

Libby giggled. 'Darcy, just spit it out.'

'So, I've got a reporter to come out to do an article on the demolition of the lighthouse and she's going to interview some of the people who proposed out there and a few others that the demolition will affect, but they need to speak to Riley. Without him, there is no story. I've just been out there and he won't do it.'

George and Libby stared at her in confusion for a moment before realisation dawned on Libby. 'You want George to pretend to be Riley?'

'Yes.'

George laughed, loudly.

'I know, I know, it's a ridiculous idea, but I have no clue what else I can do. I need Riley, and if he won't do it, I need a fake Riley to take his place.'

'But I look nothing like him,' George protested, still laughing.

'The reporter has no idea what Riley looks like. I've told Carmel, the news editor, that he is American, so you need to try to pull that off, but other than that the reporter won't care.'

George's smile fell from his face. 'You're serious?'

'Yes,' Darcy laughed, but she was getting desperate, clutching at paper-thin straws.

'What on earth would I say?'

'Just moan about your lighthouse getting pulled down and how sad it is. The interview won't be very long.'

Libby was still giggling about the whole thing. 'Oh, go on, George, it'll be a laugh.'

'What if she wants to take my picture? Everyone in the town will know that it's me and not Riley.'

'Yes, but the rest of the UK won't. Besides, we can say you don't want your photo taken and if she insists we'll just hide your face under a big cowboy hat.'

'I really don't think I can pull this off,' George said.

'Sure you can,' Libby said. 'You've watched every Cary Grant movie a hundred times over – you can just be him.'

George looked thoughtful. 'Cary Grant was British. He just put on the American accent. And he never wore a cowboy hat.'

'He was a Hollywood hero. And the cowboy hat is just an accessory. You can still emulate him, but him with a cowboy hat. Cary Grant would never leave a damsel in distress, would he? This is your chance to be a hero too,' Libby cajoled.

George smiled. 'I'll do it. Though you do realise that means we have to watch a Cary Grant film tonight, so I can get into character.'

'I'll watch every movie he has ever made, if you agree to do it,' Darcy said.

Libby groaned. 'Don't say that.'

George laughed and stood up. 'I'll make a start on dinner. I'll let you guys choose which one we'll watch.'

Darcy sighed with relief. She felt bad about asking George to do it, and for setting up a fake interview for Carmel's paper, but desperate times called for desperate measures. And what could possibly go wrong?

CHAPTER 6

There was a knock on Darcy's door the next afternoon, and when she answered it she burst out laughing as she took in what George was wearing.

He was dressed in black with cowboy boots, complete with spurs, but to top it all he was wearing a green and orange striped giant sombrero on his head.

'The costume shop didn't have a cowboy hat – well, they did, but it was a pink glittery one – so I thought this might do,' George said.

Libby was almost in hysterics standing next to her husband, wiping away tears of laughter.

Darcy found her voice. 'It's a bit big, and Riley doesn't wear spurs.'

'I'm keeping the spurs,' George said, defiantly. 'I've never worn them before but I think this might be a new look for me. Besides, you said we needed to do something to hide my face in the photos. This is perfect.'

Darcy couldn't even argue. It was nice enough for George to agree to do this in the first place. Maybe the reporter would just think that Riley was a slightly eccentric American.

She grabbed her bag, called goodbye to Ben, who was snoring on the sofa, and walked out, still trying not to laugh.

George, she noted, was walking with a cowboy swagger, clearly getting into character. Libby was still giggling by his side.

'Libby wouldn't let me wear the gun and holster,' George said grumpily, as they descended the steps.

'It was a plastic gun,' Libby said. 'It would have been too much.'

Darcy eyed Libby behind George's back. 'And the sombrero isn't?'

Libby laughed.

Darcy attempted to change the subject slightly away from the disastrous interview ahead of them. 'I spoke to Seb yesterday and he said we can use the back room in the pub so we can have some peace and quiet away from the customers. The reporter is meeting us there.'

They pushed open the door of the pub and for a moment everyone stopped talking, as they looked at George in a sombrero. There were a few laughs and someone even whistled, but George was clearly enjoying himself as he swaggered his way past the locals towards the back room.

Verity, Charles, the elderly man she had met in the furniture shop, and a few other people from the town were already in there, talking to each other, and she guessed that the tall blonde woman with her back to her was the reporter, as she was writing everything down that an elderly couple were telling her. Darcy felt guilty that she hadn't been there to greet the reporter when she had deliberately arrived early to do just that. It seemed the reporter and the townspeople were even more efficient.

Verity came over to say hello and eyed George suspiciously.

'What's going on?' Verity said in an undertone.

'Erm, the reporter wanted to talk to Riley, so, erm . . . here he is,' Darcy said, knowing that between her and George they were turning the whole thing into a farce, which was the last thing she wanted.

'Howdy, little lady.' George touched the rim of his sombrero, giving his mum his best Cary Grant smile.

Verity stared at him in shock for a moment and then back at Darcy.

'Riley wouldn't do it?'

'He said he'd think about it, but he was pretty definite before then that he wouldn't. He practically slammed the door in my face, so I think that's a no. My friend said that there's no story without Riley, so . . .' Darcy gestured lamely at George. It was a terrible idea and they all knew it.

Verity looked back at George. 'OK, then. We'll run with this Riley, but for God's sake, George, lose the sombrero.'

'It's too late for that, Mum, she's already seen it.' George touched his hat and nodded in the reporter's direction.

'That's Annabel McHugh,' Verity said. 'She seems nice enough.'

'I'm so sorry I wasn't here when she arrived. Carmel did say three and it's not even quarter to yet.'

'It's not a problem. I was here. She's already interviewed everyone else, so once she's done with Elsie and Arthur she'll probably want to talk to you and, erm . . . Riley.'

Darcy turned round just as Annabel finished with the couple and came over to talk to her. Annabel was beautiful, probably the most beautiful woman in the world. She belonged on a catwalk dressed in the finest clothes. Her blonde hair sat in effortless waves; she had big, red pouty lips that Angelina Jolie would be jealous of, and long, long legs that seemed to go on forever. In a beautiful red summer dress she looked like a glamorous celebrity and Darcy secretly thanked her lucky stars that Riley wasn't going to be coming and talking to her. She towered over Darcy, which was no mean feat, considering how tall Darcy was, but it helped her supermodel status even more.

'I'm Annabel McHugh.' She said the name as if Darcy should know who she was.

Darcy shook her perfectly manicured outstretched hand. 'I'm Darcy, thank you for coming.'

Annabel nodded. 'It's lovely to be here,' she said, not sound-ing like it was lovely at all. 'I've chatted to quite a few of these wonderful people already but I need to talk to Riley Eddison and I'd love to get your take on this. Why are you so keen to save the lighthouse when you've only just moved to the town?'

'Well, I—'

Just then the door opened and Riley walked in. His eyes found hers straight away and she felt that familiar kick to her stomach at seeing him. For a second, it seemed like there was no one else in the room. He only had eyes for her, despite the fact that she was standing next to the most beautiful woman in the world.

Annabel soon put an end to that, though, as she left Darcy's side and stepped in front of her to greet Riley herself.

'Annabel McHugh, reporter for *The Headline.*'

'Riley Eddison, I live in the lighthouse,' he said, shaking her hand.

Annabel stared at him with undisguised desire and Darcy didn't know whether to be delighted that he had come when he really didn't want to be there or disappointed that he would get to chat to the supermodel.

Riley stepped further into the room, somehow commanding it without saying a word. He glanced at George, his eyes travel-ling down to his spurs and cowboy boots, and then back up to the ridiculous sombrero.

'Nice hat, George.'

George quickly yanked it off in embarrassment. 'Erm, thanks, I have a fancy dress thing to go to later so, erm . . .'

Riley nodded knowingly, as his eyes returned to Darcy's. He bent down and whispered in her ear, his hot breath on her neck making her heart gallop.

'You didn't think I was coming, did you?'

'It didn't look good.'

'So you made alternative arrangements?' He gestured at George, his eyes unable to disguise his amusement.

'It seemed like a good idea at the time.'

He nodded, his eyes lingering on hers for a moment before he turned back to Annabel.

'Did you want to interview me over here?' He gestured at the table.

'Actually, it would be fabulous to see the inside of the lighthouse,' Annabel said, resting her hand on his arm.

Darcy felt terrible about putting Riley in that position. He was such a private person, the last thing he wanted was someone traipsing all over his home and taking pictures.

'Oh, I don't think that's necessary,' Darcy said. 'The story is the romance and the proposals that have happened there, how sad the townspeople will be to see the lighthouse go. I don't think seeing the inside of the lighthouse will help the story.'

Annabel narrowed her eyes at Darcy. 'I disagree. The lighthouse is the story. People will want to see the inside to see it's not just a lighthouse but someone's home.'

Darcy opened her mouth to protest some more, but Riley interrupted. 'That's OK, I don't mind. I can take you over whenever you're ready.'

'Oh, we can go now, if it's not too much trouble,' Annabel breathed. 'I'm done here with all the interviews. We can just take a photo of all of these people on the beach in front of the lighthouse and then I'm all yours. We can talk while you show me round.'

Darcy's interview had clearly been forgotten, though she was secretly quite pleased.

Verity took charge of the situation, quickly shepherding people outside onto the beach, where they all lined up in front of the lighthouse. Thankfully, George declined to be in it, as Annabel called out various instructions to get them to line up.

They all shuffled around to get in the best position and Darcy found herself in front of Riley. As Verity and Charles shuffled in tighter, Darcy suddenly could feel Riley's hand on her hip in a gesture that was sweet and protective. Annabel moved around a bit to get the best angle, firing off instructions to look miserable.

'Thank you for coming,' Darcy said, quietly, finding her voice, though her tongue was stuck to the roof of her mouth at his close proximity. He had the most wonderful scent . . . the sweetness of toffee apples and the tang of the sea.

'You said it was important,' Riley said, his breath tickling the back of her neck.

'You don't have to take her over to the lighthouse.'

'It's fine.'

'I really appreciate you doing this. Can I do something to repay the favour, can I take you out for a drink some time?'

'That's not necessary.'

Darcy felt her cheeks burn red at the rejection. He thought she was asking him out when she absolutely wasn't. How utterly mortifying.

'Bunch in a bit more,' Annabel called and Riley added his hand to her other hip, shifting her completely in front of him.

'You could come for dinner?' Riley said, so quietly she barely heard him.

Before she could reply Annabel finished taking the photos and moved through the small crowd, thanking them all for their time before she took Riley's arm, almost shoving Darcy to one side.

'Let's go see that lighthouse of yours.'

Riley flashed Darcy a look of concern before allowing himself to be escorted away.

Darcy thanked everyone else for coming. Verity hung back, but the rest of the townspeople made their way towards the main town, and George and Libby headed back to the flats, George still swaggering along the road, making Libby laugh.

Darcy turned to Verity, trying to distract herself from the fact that Riley was going to be alone in his lighthouse with the supermodel. 'Were the interviews OK? Do you think we'll get the romance angle we were looking for?'

Verity nodded. 'She was very good, she was asking loads of details about the different proposals and why they chose to do it there. She said it's going to be a nice, sweet story that people will get behind.'

'I hope so. I don't know if it will do any good, but it's worth a try.'

'We need all the help we can get. Any luck identifying Ginny's mystery man?'

Darcy shook her head. 'No, I need to take a photo of the painting and show it around town. I don't know why I want to find out who he is, it's just Ginny was always alone and I like the idea that she had love at least once in her life, even if it didn't turn out as well as she hoped.'

'We're a close town, someone will recognise him.'

'Did she have any other friends?'

Verity shook her head. 'She really did like to keep herself to herself.'

That made Darcy feel even sadder, that after over thirty years in the town her aunt didn't really have anyone that she could call a friend.

'You might want to speak to Suzanna, Riley's grandmother – she might know something. They seemed to be quite friendly. She works at the chemist.'

'Thank you, I will.'

Verity looked over at the jetty at the far side of the beach, and Darcy followed her gaze, seeing Riley helping Annabel into his boat.

'I'll wait for her to come back, make sure she has everything she needs for the story,' Darcy said. 'Thank you for looking after everything else today.'

Verity smiled. 'My pleasure.'

Darcy waved goodbye to her and sauntered down towards the jetty, half watching as Riley and Annabel arrived on Rose Island and then disappeared inside the lighthouse. She checked her watch and then sat down on the side of the jetty to wait for Annabel to come back. It wouldn't take that long surely. She'd have a quick chat with him, take some photos and come back to the beach. Annabel would probably want to go back home tonight, so she wouldn't want to hang around.

Doubt nagged at her insides. Annabel had looked at Riley with obvious interest and she was certainly someone that Riley would be keen on.

Her phone beeped in her bag and she fished it out to see she had a text from Carmel.

How's the interview going, everything OK?

Darcy quickly typed a reply.

Everything is fine but did you have to send the most beautiful reporter in the world?

The phone rang a second later.

'I know you're going through a bit of a dry patch with men, but Frank isn't someone who I'd call beautiful. He's a nice enough bloke, but he's fifty-nine, bald and has that fetching wart on his chin,' Carmel said.

'Who's Frank?'

'The reporter I sent to cover your story. He has a soft, genteel approach to the older generation, I thought he would be perfect for it. Don't tell me you've gone and fallen in love with him. I suppose that the older man, twinkle in his eyes, appeals to some. I just didn't think it would be you.'

'The reporter that turned up was Annabel McHugh,' Darcy corrected. 'But Frank sounds much more up my street.'

There was silence from Carmel for a second. 'Ah crap, they must have swapped. The reporters do that sometimes. Doesn't bother me, as long as the story gets written, but she's the last person I would want around your sexy American boyfriend.'

'He's not my boyfriend. And why not, she seems professional enough? Beautiful in that annoying way but she seems to have handled the interviews well.'

'Because she has a reputation for shagging anything that moves. She's slept with most of the male journalists here, all of the photographers, other journalists from other papers when she's reported on a big story, and several of the people she has been sent to interview. It's become a bit of a running joke now, every time she comes back from a story we ask if she shagged someone. Most times it's a yes. The girl is a bloody nympho-maniac. She isn't fussy either, young, old, married, single, big, small. She's like a dog on heat. And no one hardly ever turns her down. I've seen her in action, she doesn't take no for an answer. I'd be almost impressed with her tenacity if her list of sexual conquests wasn't so repulsively long. Just don't leave them alone together.'

Darcy looked over to the lighthouse, her heart inexplicably sinking into her stomach.

'It's a bit too late for that. She wanted to see the inside of the lighthouse and Riley agreed to take her over there.'

'Of course he did,' Carmel sighed. 'You can't blame him re-ally. I'm sure she gives off these pheromones that leave any man powerless to resist. Oh well. I'm sure there are plenty of other hot single men in the town.'

Darcy was silent. She had no right to be jealous or upset, though that didn't help to get rid of those feelings.

Carmel clearly registered her silence. 'Oh, you really liked him, didn't you?'

'No, he's rude, as I said. He is free to sleep with every woman in the town if he wants. It doesn't bother me.'

But Riley wasn't rude, not really. He had only shouted at her because he was scared she would fall on the rocks. He had come to be interviewed that day purely because she'd said it was important to her. She did like him.

'Ah honey, I'm sorry. Who knows, the American might be impervious to her charms.' Carmel didn't sound convinced.

'It doesn't matter.' Darcy stared at the sea beneath her feet, watching the fish dart in and out of the shadows. 'The interview is the most important thing.'

'Well, she will write a good story. I can't fault her on that.'

'Well, that's all that matters.'

'I better go, I've got a meeting to go to. I'll chat to you soon and let you know when the piece will run. Miss you, babe.'

'Miss you, too.'

Carmel rang off and Darcy looked over to the lighthouse again. What would be a realistic time to expect Annabel to come back? Ten or fifteen minutes for the interview, probably the same for taking photos? She should be done in half an hour. Any longer than that and Riley had clearly succumbed to her charms. Not that she cared. At all.

She cast her eyes back down to her phone while she was waiting and decided to give her brother a call.

He answered straight away. 'Hey, Turnip Head.'

She laughed. 'Hey, Toad Face, any lifesaving surgery today?'

'Not today. I have the day off. Tabitha and I are spending the day together.'

'Oh, cool, you guys doing anything nice?'

'Well, we were just about to have sex.'

'Toby! That's too much detail.'

'What?' He laughed. 'At least I'm honest.'

'Well, I won't keep you. I just phoned for a chat.'

'You OK?' His voice grew serious for a moment.

'Of course, things are great,' Darcy answered, brightly.

'I was going to ring you tonight actually to warn you. Mum and Dad are going to come down to visit you next week. Not sure what day. I told them to leave you to get settled for a few weeks but they want to come down.'

'Wow, you really know how to cheer a girl up. You know they're only coming down so they can pick holes in where I live?'

'Yes, I know. Just tell them you have some rare White Cliff Bay tropical disease and that they shouldn't come.'

Darcy laughed. 'I might do that, actually. It'd be nice to have some kind of reprieve from them for a few weeks until I'm settled in.'

'Look, I should go, Tabitha is getting impatient. Why don't I see if I can rearrange things at work so that I can come down with them? Might soften the blow a bit if I'm there to protect you.'

'That'd be great.'

'OK, I'll see what I can do. Can't promise anything, depends what the situation is at work, but I'll let you know.'

Darcy said her goodbyes and then resumed her wait.

It was nearly an hour and a half after Annabel had disappeared into the lighthouse that the door opened and they both came out. To Darcy's surprise, Riley wasn't wearing a shirt.

It was like a punch to the gut, although with the amount of time that had passed it was quite obvious what they had been doing.

Annabel was clearly taking photos of Riley as he manoeuvred the boat across the waves towards the jetty. He was still wearing his faithful cowboy hat and he looked every inch the sexy cowboy. With the sun glinting off his strong arms, his toned stomach and broad shoulders, he was a glorious sight to behold. And it didn't matter that nothing was going to happen between them: Darcy could still take a moment to enjoy the view.

She stood up as the boat approached, unable to take her eyes off the magnificent sight.

Riley threw the rope around a pole and secured the boat, before stepping up onto the jetty and helping Annabel up too.

'Thank you so much for a very entertaining afternoon,' Annabel said, suggestively.

Urgh.

'It was my pleasure,' Riley said.

'I think the article will be very popular.'

Riley smiled, though Darcy could tell he was embarrassed.

'And here is my card. If you're ever in London, look me up.'

Riley took the card and Annabel walked down the jetty towards Darcy.

'Thank you for coming down here today, did you get everything you needed?' Darcy said, forcing a professional smile on her face and fighting the urge to push Annabel in the sea.

Annabel glanced back at Riley. 'Oh, I got everything I needed.'

She sauntered off, her hips swaying as she walked back onto the road towards her car.

Darcy turned back to face Riley as he watched her curiously, her cheeks heated under his gaze.

'Well, thank you for giving up your time this afternoon, though it seems it wasn't a complete hardship for you.'

He frowned in confusion.

'There was me trying to think of some way to repay you for doing something you really didn't want to do. I was stupidly thinking I'd bake you a cake, but it seems that Annabel has probably paid all my debts for me.'

She turned to walk away, but he gently snagged her arm and pulled her back.

'I'm not sure what you're implying, but if you're suggesting that I slept with Annabel I can assure you absolutely nothing happened.'

'So your shirt just fell off on its own, did it?'

Darcy stopped herself from saying any more. She wasn't with Riley, he didn't owe her any loyalty. He had simply done her a favour. He was free to sleep with anyone he wanted to. It didn't matter that he had invited her round for dinner a few hours before. It could have just been a 'come round for dinner and we can discuss the lighthouse' type date, not a date-date. She had no right to feel upset or disappointed. She took a step back. 'I'm sorry, it's absolutely none of my business.'

'No, it isn't.' He looked pissed off and she didn't blame him.

She nodded and turned away.

'She came on to me and I made it very clear that I wasn't interested,' Riley called after her. 'I told her if that was what she came over to the lighthouse for, then I would just bring her straight back to the beach.'

Darcy paused and turned back.

'She apologised. After that she was a model reporter. I showed her around all the rooms and she took lots of pictures and then we had a long chat about the history of the place, what I had done to renovate it and what it would mean to me to lose it.'

He took his hat off, running his hand through his hair, nervously.

'She then discussed with me a slightly different angle we could take to run the article. She told me all about the proposals that had happened there and suggested that we could run the angle of me moving here in the hope that I would meet my future wife, just like my father did. That I hoped to raise my children here and that if we were to run the article with me being single and looking for love it might get more interest from the public and, coupled with the "Romance on Rose Island" angle and interviews, she said it should be really successful. She suggested that the last few photos should be me on the boat with the lighthouse in the background, with no shirt on, as that would grab the interest of all the single ladies and bored housewives too. I told her I didn't want to do it, but she assured me that she had been in this job long enough to know how to write a story that the public would fall in love with. I was reluctant about it, but I knew that if taking a few photos without my shirt on would help to save the lighthouse, then I had to do it.'

Darcy swallowed uncomfortably, embarrassment burning her cheeks. 'I'm sorry. She has a terrible reputation with men and I thought . . . I'm sorry.'

Riley stared at her for a moment. 'It's OK. Though if I'd known it would have been this much hassle to do you a favour, I don't think I would have bothered.'

He got back in his boat, unhooked the rope and chugged across the bay towards the lighthouse without a single glance back.

Riley leaned back in his chair, pulling his hat further down his forehead to shield his eyes from the early evening sun. The water was getting choppy and it was likely they would have rain later but for now he could enjoy the last of the day's heat. He propped his fishing rod back in the stand and watched the tiny float bobbing about in the water.

He sighed as his thoughts returned to Darcy. He liked her, far more than he should considering his plans for the future. It was obvious that she liked him too, especially after her little spark of jealousy earlier, but they seemed to clash horns more than anything else. He didn't have a vast experience of women to draw on, but surely he and Darcy shouldn't be winding each other up the wrong way already? But despite everything he still wanted to take the time to get to know her better. Out of all the women he'd met since his arrival in England, no one had captured his interest the way Darcy had. Annabel was incredibly beautiful, any fool could see that, but even with her offering herself to him on a plate he hadn't been remotely tempted and he knew it was simply because she wasn't Darcy. He was drawn to her and he was getting tired of fighting it.

Movement out of the corner of his eye caught his attention and words failed him as he watched Darcy swim round the lighthouse towards the steps where he was now sitting.

He stood up, in shock. After the way they had parted earlier, he hadn't thought she would swim out to the island again, but it seemed she was drawn to him too.

As Ben pulled himself onto the steps and launched himself at Riley with joyous abandon, Riley ran down to the bottom and offered her a hand to help her. She took it with surprise and climbed out onto the stairs. She was carrying a small drawstring backpack on her back, which intrigued him. Her wetsuit clung to every gorgeous curve, her tangle of red wet curls cascaded and dripped over one shoulder. There wasn't a scrap of make-up on her face, just a smattering of freckles over her nose, and he'd never seen anyone so adorable and sexy in his life.

'I just came to say thank you again and to say sorry for judging you and to give you this.' She took her bag off her shoulders and delved inside. She brought out a sealed Tupperware container with what looked like chocolate brownies inside and passed it to him. 'I kept thinking what could I do for you to say thank you for your time today, and then I realised that the thing you want most is just to be left alone. I don't want things to be weird between us. We'll see each other around town and I don't want you avoiding me because you think I'm some crazy nut job who won't leave you alone. So I've also come to give you a promise. This is the last time I'll come out to the island. You like your solitude and I get that. And you don't want to be sitting out here fishing, dreading the possibility of me turning up to wreak havoc over your life again. So, hand on heart, pinky promise, scout's honour or whatever it is you Americans might say, I won't come back here again. I'll find somewhere else to swim in the future.'

Disappointment washed over him in a great wave. He was growing to love these daily visits. He cleared his throat. 'I don't think a pinky promise will stand up in a court of law.'

She laughed. 'Probably not.'

'So I reject your gift.'

Her face fell. 'You don't want the brownies.'

'Oh, I'm keeping the brownies. I don't want your promise.'

She stared at him in confusion.

'I like you coming out here.'

Her mouth fell open in shock.

'So why don't you stay for dinner?' He picked up his chair in one hand and the bucket holding his haul of fish in the other and quickly turned back to the lighthouse so Darcy wouldn't see his smirk at her completely stunned face. He dumped the stuff inside the lighthouse and turned back to face her. 'And you can come up with a new way to thank me.'

As soon as he'd said the words, he realised how they sounded. She obviously thought the same too, as her eyes flashed with fire.

'I'm not sleeping with you.'

'Christ, Darcy, the thought never even crossed my mind. I just want to have dinner with you. No obligations, no sex, we'll have dinner, we'll talk and then I'll take you back home before midnight. Pinky promise.'

The anger faded from her face. 'I'm not exactly dressed for dinner.'

'I can give you something to change into,' he said.

'I have Ben with me and he's soaking wet.'

'I have a towel and he can keep Kelpie out of mischief while we talk.'

He moved back down the steps to collect the rest of his fishing gear. Darcy still hadn't moved. 'Are you coming or do you have any other excuses?'

He moved back to the lighthouse and smiled when he saw her hesitate and then follow him, stepping up into the lighthouse beside him.

Ben bounded in and ran up the stairs ahead of them.

Riley leaned out and closed the door, the huge boom echoing around the lighthouse and momentarily plunging them into darkness.

She was standing very close, he could feel the heat of her right in front of him. Her breathing was heavy, nervous, but she didn't step back away from him. He was glad of that because her scent was wonderful. There was the tangy smell of seawater, that was unmistakable, but underneath was something sweeter that reminded him of cotton candy and hot chocolate.

Their eyes became accustomed to the muted light filtering down from the windows on the stairs and she blinked in front of him, staring straight up into his eyes.

'Welcome to my home.'

CHAPTER 7

Darcy watched Riley turn and walk up the stairs. She blinked as her eyes became more accustomed to the limited light. There wasn't much in the foot of the tower, a few sets of waterproofs, coats, hats, some fishing gear. There was a closed door, but Riley had already disappeared up the stairs so she quickly followed him.

The stairs swept round the walls of the lighthouse and as she ran up them she passed two closed doors, which presumably led to the first and second floor. The heavy footsteps continued on the stairs above her, so she ignored these doors and her curiosity for now, and ran on to catch up with him.

The third door was open and movement inside suggested that this was where Riley had gone. She peered round to see a huge bed dominating the small room. It was well lit by four large windows spaced at equal intervals in the round walls. The bedding and carpet was a royal blue, the only slash of colour in the otherwise hugely white room. It was smart, masculine and was filled with his wonderful toffee apple scent. For reasons she couldn't describe, seeing where he slept every night suddenly had her stomach clench with feelings that went way beyond the curiosity and annoyance she had been feeling for the last few days.

'Darcy,' Riley called from another room off the bedroom.

She slipped off her waterproof trainers and padded barefoot across the soft carpet into a bathroom. It was quite big, considering the lack of space, a large walk-in shower taking up one wall, with the toilet, sink, smart wood panelling and stone-tiled floor making up the rest of the room.

Riley looked up from the shower controls, as he turned them on. 'You can have a shower to warm up, if you want. I'll put some clothes out for you to change into.'

'Do you have a lot of female guests here then, that you have spare clothes to cater for them?'

Riley half smiled again. 'You're the first. You can wear something of mine, hopefully it won't be too big for you. I'm going to get dinner started. You can join me in the living room once you're ready. Next door up the stairs.'

He walked out without another word, closing the bathroom door behind him.

She stared at it for a few moments.

How was this normal? She had known this man for only a few days and she was just about to get naked and use his shower. Though she could hardly sit down to dinner with him in a wetsuit. The summer days were hot but it was relatively cool inside the thick stone walls of the lighthouse.

Darcy unzipped the wetsuit, letting it and her bikini fall to the floor, hoping that Riley was the gentlemanly sort and wouldn't suddenly find an excuse to come back into the bathroom.

She stepped into the shower and was surprised to see that it was a power shower. It seemed a bit odd, given the age of the building, to have such modern conveniences, but then what did she expect? Riley to be having a wash in an old tin bath in front of the fireplace?

She quickly showered, washed her hair and then put it up into a quick plait piled on top of her head.

She dried herself with one of the thick towels and poked her head round the bathroom door to find the bedroom empty and the bedroom door closed, protecting her privacy. On the bed was a pair of boxer briefs, which she pulled on before she turned her attention to the rest of the clothes he had left out for her. She picked up what looked like a pair of black leggings but she quickly discovered it was a pair of thermal long johns. She pulled them on and one of his shirts. No bra, obviously he didn't have those kinds of things lying around. Her breasts were quite large and there was no way she could let them hang loose and fancy free, especially as the white shirt she was wearing was somewhat see-through, but the alternative was wearing her wet, bright pink bikini top. She looked around and tentatively opened his wardrobe. Inside were several more shirts and jumpers, so she grabbed one of the thick black jumpers and pulled that on over the shirt, hoping to preserve some of her modesty.

She surveyed herself in the mirror. There was nothing sexy about what she was wearing – the jumper was huge, the leggings were baggy. It was safe to say, there would be no ravishing taking place tonight. Still, if she had wanted to impress him with her sex appeal, turning up continually to his lighthouse dressed in a skin-tight wetsuit had not been the way to do it.

She opened the door and ran up the stairs to the next floor. Wonderful sweet smells were already drifting out the door and Riley was whistling softly to some classical music. Still feeling a bit awkward about just waltzing into his home, she hovered near the door and looked around. There was a brown leather corner sofa that swept around one side of the round room, facing a large flat-screen TV that hung on the wall. The windows were much bigger up here, letting the pinkish glow of the setting sun fill the room with a near panoramic view of the town and the sea. A small dining room table and two chairs filled one window overlooking the theatrical waves below. In one part of the room was the kitchen, where Riley now stood, with his back to her as he chopped and prepared the dinner. His back was broad and strong, something she only just appreciated now. His shirt sleeves were rolled back, exposing strong, tanned arms. He was no longer wearing his cowboy hat and the dark shaggy mop of hair looked ruffled and unkempt.

He turned round and his eyes found hers. He frowned slightly.

'I hope you don't mind me wearing one of your jumpers.'

'Jumpers,' he echoed. 'I don't think I'll ever get used to you English folk calling a sweater a jumper. You can wear whatever you want, but you might get a bit hot in here, it gets very warm once the door is closed.'

'I didn't really have a choice, your shirt is a bit see-through and you didn't have a spare bra . . .'

His eyes bulged in shock, as did hers, when she realised she had pretty much drawn attention to her breasts.

'My apologies, I should have given more thought to the clothes I laid out for you. I can find you something more suitable if you want,' Riley said, blushing as he pushed his hand through his hair.

'It's fine. Don't apologise, you've been very gracious.'

Riley nodded and then looked around for something else to focus on. 'Can I get you a glass of wine? Is red OK?'

'Red is perfect.'

He grabbed the bottle and poured a large glass of red and passed it over to her, gesturing for her to come and sit at the breakfast bar. She pulled herself up onto one of the bar stools, sitting opposite where he stood.

He took a sip from his own glass, his eyes never leaving hers. 'I want to say sorry for shouting at you the first few times we met. Please know it was only out of concern for your safety. If you wish to come back, can I ask that you always use the steps at the back of the lighthouse, as you are less likely to slip and fall on those?'

She nodded. She could do that and it sounded like he wouldn't be opposed to her coming back again.

'Or I have a second boat for visitors to use, it's tethered to the jetty near Main Street. It's the blue one called *Trident*. You are welcome to use that any time you want to come over, if you don't want to swim.'

'Thank you, I'll bear that in mind.'

He stared at her a bit longer before he turned back to the dinner. She took another glance around the room and noticed Ben and Kelpie cuddled up together in a huge dog basket near the fire. She smiled at the ease with which they had made friends already. Though Riley was polite, protective and respectful, they had a long way to go before they could be called friends. She turned back to find his green eyes on her again. Something about the way he looked at her suddenly made her think he wanted to skip the friendship stage altogether and move straight onto the next phase.

Feeling suddenly nervous, she got up and moved around the room. She gasped when she saw what he had next to the fireplace.

'You've got an ammonite,' she nearly shrieked with delight. 'Please tell me it's real and not fake.'

She ran over and as she touched the swirls of the fossilised shell that was so reminiscent of a snail, she instantly realised it was real. It was bigger than her head and beautifully preserved. It was one of the finest specimens of the fossil that she had ever seen. It was a dark chestnut brown with slashes of pearl, gold and red along the ridges of the creature's chambers. It almost sparkled in the sunlight.

'Where did you get it from? Ones this size are very rare.'

'It was my dad's. I have no idea where he got it from. It was always something I admired when I was growing up, but I don't know much about it. Is it a fossilised snail?'

'It's from the mollusc family but it's closer to the squid or octopus rather than the gastropods, which are the snails. I think this one is an Asteroceras from the Jurassic or Triassic period, which would make it around a hundred and fifty million years old.'

His eyes bulged. 'Are you serious? I knew it was old but . . . shouldn't it be in a museum then, not sitting on my fireplace?'

'I think the museums of the world would gladly take it off your hands, it's very well preserved, but trust me they have hundreds of the things. The ammonites seemingly bred faster than rabbits. There are hundreds on the beach here, some are encased in rocks but some are just loose and it always amazes me when I see them lying there on the beach. This tiny piece of history that has survived millions of years – it's survived storms, tides, waves pounding on it – and it's still there. By rights they are so tough they shouldn't have been extinct at all, but something wiped them out.

'One of my favourite shark species, the angel shark, is nearing extinction now and I do wonder if in years to come the only thing left of them will be their skeletons, fossilised in the seabed as a testament to show they were once here and then the humans wiped them out.' She ran her fingers over the lumps and bumps of the ammonite before she realised she had let her geeky side have full rein there for a few minutes and Riley would no doubt be thinking about how quickly he could get her out of here. 'Sorry, this kind of stuff fascinates me. I forget that it doesn't interest most people.'

'It interests me,' he said, quietly.

She looked over at him, as he leaned over the breakfast bar watching her. She didn't know what to make of his intense gaze; no man had ever looked at her like that before. She'd had one or two men look at her as if she was a piece of steak they wanted to eat, but no man had ever looked at her as if they found her completely fascinating. She moved away to the window, looking out at the view of the beach and her flat at the bottom of

Sea View Court. There were some binoculars on the windowsill, so she picked them up and looked over at the row of rocks that jutted out of the beach and the swirl of water and the waves that crashed against the gullies in between the rocks. She moved the binoculars further down the beach towards the glass building she had seen a few days before.

'Do you know what that weird glass building is on the far side of Silver Cove beach?' Darcy asked.

'Yes,' came Riley's voice from very close behind her. She whirled around to find him so close that she could feel the warmth from his body. 'Sorry, I didn't mean to startle you. I was just going to point out where I see the seals sometimes.' He cleared his throat and stepped back a few inches, though he was still too close. His sweet smell was wonderful and heady at the same time. 'The glass building is the new aquarium, which I presume is where your new job is.'

She frowned in confusion. 'I'm not working in the aquarium, what makes you think that?'

'Because you have all this knowledge about sea creatures, and sharks especially. I heard you talking to Ryan about them at the engagement party. I know the aquarium has a shark exhibit, or it will have. I thought perhaps that's what brought you here.'

'Sadly, no. I would love to work there but . . .'

It was very unlikely that the aquarium would let her work there after her past record. Killing a whole tank of rare fish was not one of her finest moments.

He stared at her for a few seconds, as if she were a puzzle he was trying to work out. Eventually he stepped back out of her body space.

'Dinner is nearly ready. Would you like it at the breakfast bar or at the table?'

She glanced over to the table, seated in front of that spectacular view. There was no choice.

He smiled as she turned back to answer. 'Here, take the wine and silverware to the table and I'll bring the food over in just a moment.'

'Silverware?' Darcy looked around for the silver candlesticks. That was a bit more formal than she was expecting.

'The knives and forks.'

'Oh, the cutlery. You call it silverware? That's very posh.'

'Even plastic knives and forks at a barbecue are called silverware.'

Darcy smiled, loving that little nugget of information. She did as she was asked, marvelling over the normalcy of their new relationship when only a few days before they'd both been shouting at each other.

Darcy sat down and looked out over the view. From up here on the top floor she could see all the way down the coast, every little inlet and curve of the shoreline. Her eyes rested for a moment on a tall, thin black tower on the opposite headland some five hundred yards away from where they were now. This was sure to be the new lighthouse, not yet in operation but a constant reminder for Riley that his time here was short.

He joined her at the table, passing her a plate of fish and potatoes. The fish was covered in a sticky brown glaze that looked disgusting but smelled amazing.

'Hope you like maple syrup,' Riley said.

'I've never had it.'

Riley stared at her in surprise.

'It really is more of an American thing, but I'm sure it will be lovely.'

He took a sip of the wine and watched her, waiting for her to eat.

She took a forkful of the fish, which was oozing with the brown sticky sauce, and popped it in her mouth. The fish melted on her tongue, so moist and fresh, and the maple syrup was warm and sweet.

'Riley, this is delicious.'

He smiled before tucking into his own dinner.

'So tell me about Rose Island Lighthouse,' Darcy said. 'Bob – PC Donaldson – said your great-great-grandfather built it.'

Riley watched her carefully, clearly wondering if she was going to say anything about her visit from the police, but any annoyance she had felt towards him had vanished. She still felt like she needed to keep up her guard around him, but she could no longer be angry.

He opened his mouth to speak, then obviously changed his mind about what he was going to say. 'I'm sorry about that too. I did assure him that I didn't want to press charges but I just . . .'

'You don't need to apologise. I know it came from a good place.'

Riley continued staring at her for a moment before returning his attention to his dinner.

The air seemed thick between them, that tense nervous energy just before a storm. He couldn't fail to notice it too.

'From what I can glean from history books, the internet and my great-great-grandfather's journals, the villagers petitioned the Lighthouse Trust, that's the company in charge of building lighthouses, for years to build a lighthouse here in White Cliff Bay. There had been two big accidents where boats had crashed on the rocks, but fortunately loss of life was quite minimal. The people of the town thought it was only a matter of time before a bigger accident happened. The Lighthouse Trust didn't see the need for one and repeatedly turned the town's application down. In 1870 there was a terrible boat accident in a storm. The boat crashed into the rocks and sank, killing all fifty-six people on board. So many people of the town died, so many of the ones left behind lost their fathers, brothers and uncles. Matthew Eddison, my great-great-grandfather, lost his sixteen-year-old son.'

He paused while he took another sip of his wine and Darcy stared at him, her heart bleeding for poor Matthew Eddison, whom neither she nor Riley had ever met. Riley looked across the table at her and cocked his head slightly at her expression. She flushed with embarrassment. It was silly to feel sympathy for someone who had died nearly a hundred and fifty years before, but she couldn't help feeling sad.

She quickly looked down, concentrating on her food.

Riley cleared his throat. 'He swore then that no one else would lose loved ones because of the rocks. He bought Rose Island and spent five years building a lighthouse on it with the help of the people in the town. He lived here with his wife and remaining children, and when he died they carried on his legacy. There has always been an Eddison living here. When the Lighthouse Trust took over the running of Rose Island Lighthouse in the eighties and modernised it so it could be automated, my father ensured that the house part remained under the Eddison name. The Lighthouse Trust could come and go as they needed to repair or tend to the maintenance of the light, but the house is still ours, which they agreed to.'

He looked out the window for a moment. 'The Lighthouse Trust have recently worked out that the lighthouse is in the wrong place. Apparently the headland over there,' he pointed out the window, 'blocks a lot of the light from being seen further down the coast. Never mind that there has never been an accident in these waters since this lighthouse was built. The Lighthouse Trust has built a new one, a better one, apparently. I have just over a week until the light that has burned for the last one hundred and forty years is turned off for good.'

Darcy looked out the window at the fading light, silhouetting the new tower against the blueberry and scarlet sky. Without the light at the top, it looked almost foreboding. There was certainly no character or personality to the place.

'I understand decommissioning it . . .' she said carefully, but trailed off when Riley's eyes hardened at her comment.

'You do?'

'When your great-great-grandfather built the place, I imagine very little maths or logistics went into deciding where he built it. There is another lighthouse near Port Cardinal that is also being decommissioned. The beam from the new lighthouse will be strong enough to cover both areas. It's more cost-effective to run one modern lighthouse than try to maintain two older ones.'

Riley clearly thought about this. 'I didn't realise there was another lighthouse being decommissioned too.'

'I found that out while I was researching the plans for the new tower.'

He glared out at the new tower. He didn't like it, but she could see that he knew it made sense.

He stood to clear away the empty plates and Darcy felt horribly guilty. She stood up and followed him to the kitchen.

'I'm sorry.'

Riley turned to face her. He wasn't angry – well, not at her, just at the hopelessness of the situation.

'There is nothing we can do to stop the new one being activated. What I don't understand is the need to demolish your home because of it. This place has so much history; it survived two world wars and saved thousands of lives. It's the tower we need to save, not the light.'

'If I save the light, I save the tower too.'

'You need to learn which battles to fight. They have spent thousands building the new lighthouse. There is no way they are not going to use it. We can save the tower, I'm sure of it. There are several decommissioned lighthouses around the UK – most of them are not demolished because of it. Is the lighthouse structurally sound? Is it that the island is eroding that is making it unsafe?'

'No, the lighthouse is built into the seabed. They drilled a massive bore hole into the island, the foundations are deep. If every single one of these rocks were washed away, the lighthouse would still be standing. Back then, things were built to last. I've had it surveyed too. Structurally, it's safe.'

'You can file a petition against the compulsory purchase order. It will go to court and we can hire a solicitor and . . .' she trailed off as he shook his head.

'We're too late for that. The notice of the compulsory purchase order was given last year some time. Of course no one was here to receive it, which was very convenient for them. I had three months to file a protest; after that no further appeals would be accepted. It has all been done very secretly. I had no idea what was going on when I first came over here, neither did anyone in the town. I spent months and thousands of dollars doing up the place and then a month ago I was served with a notice informing me I had six weeks to leave. I've protested but apparently there's nothing that can be done.'

'I've applied to get the building listed. If they agree, no one can touch it.'

'Listed?'

'Protected because of its heritage.'

'And you've applied already?'

'Yes. I hope you don't mind . . .'

'Of course I don't mind. Why are you so invested in trying to stop the lighthouse being pulled down?'

'The lighthouse means so much to the people of the town. I want to help them.' She paused. 'My aunt Ginny used to live here and this place meant something to her, though I don't know why she loved it so much. She created hundreds of paintings of the place and I suppose I want to honour her too.'

'Well, thank you. I really appreciate your help.'

'And there's the meeting on Saturday at the town hall. We should go along and see what ideas the townspeople have. They care about this place, too.'

'I'm not going along to any meeting.'

'Why not?'

'I'm not getting involved in the life of a small town again. The gossip, the nosiness. It's not for me. I'm happy out here on my own. I don't want to be part of the town.'

'You are part of the town, whether you like it or not. They are fighting to save your home, you owe it to them to actually turn up and fight for it too.'

'I don't owe anyone anything. If they want to waste their time fighting for it, that's down to them. I haven't asked them to do it.'

'You've given up already.'

He slammed his hand down on the unit. 'No, I just don't see how arranging a cake sale or a car wash is going to achieve anything. Suzanna has the old ladies knitting red and white striped hats, for goodness' sake, how is that going to help?'

Silence descended on them.

He cared, she could see that. It wasn't just his home he was angry about losing, it was the history, his family's heritage too. Riley was polite and respectful, but it seemed when he really cared about something he got passionate and she really liked that about him.

'I'm sorry,' he said, softly. 'I know I seem to be saying that a lot tonight, but I am.'

'It's OK.'

'It's not. Thirty-two years of my life and I've never once raised my voice to a woman before. You evoke in me feelings . . .'

He didn't finish the sentence and Darcy shifted awkwardly in the void that he had left.

He stared at the floor by her feet, running his hand through his shaggy hair.

'Maybe I should go,' Darcy said and his head snapped up.

'That's the last thing I want. But if I've made you feel uncomfortable, I'll take you home.'

Her heart melted for him, suddenly wanting to hug him so much.

'Are you not at least going to offer me dessert first?'

His face softened and he smiled. 'I have ice cream. We can have it with the brownies.'

'That sounds perfect.'

She grabbed two spoons from the drawer, and snagged the two wine glasses from the table and went to sit on the sofa. It was too formal at the table and she wanted him to relax around her and not worry so much about offending her.

She curled her legs up under her but winced when the knee she had banged a few days before protested at the movement.

She tried to hide the discomfort but Riley had already seen it. 'Does your leg hurt?'

'It's fine.'

He scowled as he turned round and rooted around in his freezer. He came back to the sofa with a tub of Ben & Jerry's, the tub of brownies and a packet of peas, which he wrapped in a towel.

'Here, scoot back into the corner,' Riley said and she did as she was told.

He sat down next to her, scooping her legs into his lap. Her heart leapt at the intimacy of it, but then froze altogether when he carefully rolled the leg of her leggings up over her knee. His hands on her skin made goosebumps erupt on her body, desire and need crashing through her simultaneously. She quickly focussed on what he was doing, as he very gently applied the peas to her bruise. She gasped at the cold and he sent her an apologetic look.

'I have cookies and cream, but it's not Blue Bell ice cream . . . you guys don't have that over here.' Riley grabbed the tub and rested it on a cushion between them.

'No, but I love Ben & Jerry's.'

'Blue Bell is the king of ice cream. Once you've tried that there is no alternative.'

He flipped open the lid with his hand, still holding her leg with the other, and she passed him a spoon. She watched him dig in, turning the spoon upside down as he popped it in his mouth, sucking the creamy mixture off like it was a lollipop.

She took her own spoonful and, still trying not to focus on the feel of his thumb ever so slightly stroking just behind her knee, she turned her attention back to Riley.

'So, tell me more about you. Is there a reason you live out here in the lighthouse all alone? Why did you come to England?'

The smile fell off his face. Instantly, she could see his relaxed attitude vanish, the shutters coming up. He swallowed his mouthful of ice cream, clearly choosing which words to use.

'There's not much to tell. My dad is English, lived right here in this lighthouse. My mom is American. She was over here on holiday, they met, fell in love, one of those whirlwind-type affairs. She went back to Texas and as the lighthouse was already automated by then, he followed her. They married and nine months after their wedding day I was born. A year after I was born my brother Max arrived and a year after that my sister Megan completed our little family. We lived in the same town all our lives. My mom died a few years ago and Dad died a few months later. They always talked about taking us back to White Cliff Bay, so I thought I'd come and see what all the fuss was about.'

'I'm so sorry,' Darcy said, reaching over and taking his hand before she'd even thought about the intimacy of that act.

He stared at her. 'Thank you. We were incredibly close. I still miss them. It still hurts but it's getting easier.'

'Is that why you came here, because being around all those memories was too painful?'

He nodded. 'You're very insightful. Partly it was that, but I ran into a few problems with the people of the town and it seemed easier to have a clean break from there.'

Darcy wondered if those problems involved women. Was he leaving behind a trail of broken hearts too? But she didn't dare ask him that. Whatever it was that made him leave Texas was not good and probably had something to do with why he didn't want to get involved with town life.

'And what is it you do?' she asked, hoping that was an easier question for him to answer.

He smiled. 'I'm a songwriter. I write for all the big artists.'

'Wow, that's cool. Who have you written for?'

'Oh, too many to name them all. Bobby Lou, Vince Browne, Lois Johnson, The Beautiful Eight, Blue Diamond, Left Hand Turn, Sea and Stone.' Riley reeled off an impressive list of hugely famous stars and bands that ranged from pop, rock, country and even a rap star known to mix his raps with ballads.

'That's amazing! And you've met all these people?'

'Sadly, not. Most of the communication comes through emails and most of it doesn't even come from them but their manager or assistants. I've met Lois Johnson though, she was a joy to work with. But I generally don't work directly with the acts. I prefer to work remotely. I love my job. I generally write all those cheesy love songs that I never listen to myself, but it's good fun and pays well. What about you, why did you move to White Cliff Bay if it wasn't for the new aquarium?'

That wasn't really easy to discuss either. 'I came down here a lot as a child, staying with my aunt Ginny. I always said I'd live here one day. So, after my last job went wrong and I saw a job advertised down here, I applied and here I am.'

'You're alone? Any friends or family nearby?'

She shook her head, feeling her own defences coming up. 'I guess I needed a break from them too. There are only so many times you can see the looks of disappointment and shame from your parents before you don't want to see it any more.'

Riley paused with the job of digging out more ice cream. 'I can't believe that your parents feel anything but pride when they look at you.'

Darcy smiled weakly as she focussed her attention on her spoon, twisting it in her hands. 'If you ever meet them, you can remind them of that. I think a person has a set quota of pride and all of my parents' allocation is reserved for my brother. When my parents' friends ask about their children, they talk about Toby, they never mention me. I'm the disappointment.'

'What could you have possibly done to disappoint them?'

Darcy sighed and Riley offered her more ice cream as encouragement. She took a big spoonful and let it rest on her tongue, the heat melting it as it slid down her throat.

'I think the biggest disappointment was my chosen career. My parents and my brother are all very well-respected doctors. It was kind of expected that I would follow them into that field.'

'And you didn't want to?'

'I am a doctor, but not in medicine. My doctorate is in marine biology.'

'You're a marine biologist. Now, that's interesting. That explains your passion for sharks.'

'Sharks are my specialist area. I love the sea and have a huge interest in the varied life that populates our oceans, but sharks are my favourites. I think, whenever we got together and they were sharing their amazing stories of saving people's lives, and I was sharing photos of sharks I had swum with, they just didn't get it. A large part of the research for my dissertation involved scuba diving with sharks, which was the most amazing experience of my life, but they just saw it as a nonsense degree and thought that I got a qualification for messing around in the water. I was just a big let-down for them.'

'I'm sorry that you were made to feel that way for pursuing your dreams.'

'Oh, I'm used to it now. I've always been a huge disappointment to them. When I was young, they took me to ballet lessons, tap dancing, piano and flute lessons but the pressure was too much. I worked so hard and after every lesson they would spend hours telling me what I had done wrong. I gave up everything apart from the piano in the end. It was easier to deal with their disappointment for not going than deal with their excessive criticism three or four times a week. I soared through my piano grades very quickly but stopped when I'd passed my grade six and they told me their friends' children had already passed grade eight years before and that I was to start practising for grade seven immediately. No congratulations or words of pride. I started to realise then that no matter what I did it would never ever be good enough for them, so what was the point in trying.'

Darcy took another mouthful of ice cream.

'School bored me. This will sound so arrogant, but as a child the lessons just came too easy and so I just didn't bother trying. Toby was so good and quiet and got ten out of ten in every piece of homework he did. I was a dreamer. I wrote stories about a fantasy underwater world where I was the queen and that underwater world I escaped to was far more interesting than the lessons. I would spend most of my time drifting off into my own little dream world. My parents told me repeatedly that I was a disappointment to them and how I'd never amount to anything. They asked why I couldn't be more like Toby, though ironically Toby always told me he wanted to be more like me and do the things he wanted to do rather than do the things our parents wanted him to do.'

'I can imagine spending time in your fantasy world was much better than the real world, if your parents treated you so badly.'

Darcy nodded. 'But I've always had an unhealthy obsession with the sea. When I was in my early teens, my aunt took me to one side and asked what I wanted to do with my life. I told her my dream of working with sharks and she didn't laugh like my parents did. She told me I was clever and could be whatever I wanted to be, but I had to work at it. So I knuckled down, worked hard at school, got good grades. I thought my parents would be happy but when they found out that I was doing it to become a marine biologist, they were disappointed that I didn't want to be a "real" doctor like them. When I applied to university, they told me that they wouldn't pay for me to mess around on a worthless degree so I had to pay for it all myself. They didn't even come to my graduation.'

'That's terrible. What's that famous quote, something like "go proudly in the direction of your dreams". I hope you didn't let their small-mindedness impact on your passion.'

She shook her head. 'I didn't. I threw myself into it with everything I had. I had the best job in the world. I worked in the Marine Biology and Ecology Centre in Southend, studying sharks and working on conservation projects. I also worked a lot with the public, school kids and group tours. I loved that part of my job too, teaching them stuff about sharks or sea life that they wouldn't have known. Part of my work was about educating people about the different species to help raise awareness of the different threats faced by sharks and other marine life. We did a lot of research into the animals we had there, which gave us a better understanding of how they live and we had our own captive breeding programme for some of our rarer species. It was probably one of the most respected marine centres in the world but it still wasn't enough for my parents. They said that I didn't have the commitment and dedication to make it in my profession. That I was too much of a dreamer. And sadly they were right.'

'What happened?'

'When the Marine Biology Centre took delivery of a new fish I asked an intern to put it in one of the tanks. I was busy overseeing the birth of some shark pups, which was so exciting for me. Unfortunately the intern misunderstood which tank I meant and put it into the wrong one. By morning the new fish had eaten every single other fish in the tank. We had some of the rarest fish in the world in that tank and they were all eaten in less than twenty-four hours.'

'How is that your fault?'

'The intern was my responsibility and I should have taken charge of something that important myself. I was sacked on the spot. I was gutted. My job history is now as varied as the sea life that I studied for so many years. I haven't felt like I belonged anywhere ever since. I seem to attract disaster and, as my dad so eloquently put it, I career from one cock-up to the next. I leave behind me numerous jobs I have been fired from . . . It has become a running joke with my parents now, how long I can keep a job before I cock it up.'

'Wow, your parents sound delightful,' Riley said, dryly. 'You need to stand up for yourself more and tell them if it upsets you. You should never let someone make you feel inadequate or small, even if it is your own family.'

Darcy shrugged. 'Some of it is justified, my clumsiness or mistakes I've made. A lot of it wasn't my fault. I've had a string of jobs that only lasted a few months or sometimes even a few weeks. I crashed my boss' car when I worked as a PA, I've poisoned an important client by inadvertently giving her food she was allergic to when I worked at a bank, my computer got some kind of virus and somehow I sent porn to some of the most important people in the company . . . the list is endless. I often wonder if my fear of disappointing my parents affected my other relationships too. After losing my last job I had to move back in with my parents because my boyfriend, who I was living with, dumped me. He said I never let him in. Moving back in with my parents was very embarrassing, more so because they were equally embarrassed about my return home. I had to get out. And it doesn't matter that the flat I'm living in now is tiny, it's mine and I've got my own place without any help from my parents.'

'So what's the new job?'

'Community Development Liaison Manager for Apple Hill Council. I start on Monday. I don't know a lot about the job, to be honest, but I'm very excited about working with the public again. That part of being a marine biologist was always good fun. I'm going to show my parents I can make a success of my life. My new job is so important. I want to show them that all of those cock-ups are behind me. I feel I have something to prove to them.'

'You have nothing to prove to them. You haven't let them down, they've let you down by making you feel inadequate, as if how you choose to live your life isn't good enough for them. If I ever have children, I would make sure they knew how proud of them I was, no matter which path they chose.'

Darcy stared at him. She had never thought of it like that before. They *had* let her down by not supporting her with her decisions in life. She would never move back in with her parents again, even if she had to live on baked beans and cook her meals over a candle. She was over a hundred miles away from them now, they would never find out how she did at her job unless she told them. She would do a good job in her new position, but not for them, for her.

☀ ☀ ☀

Riley watched Darcy as she talked. She had the sort of personality that shone from her, something about her that made her so watchable, so interesting to talk to. And when she smiled her whole face lit up.

It was pitch black outside now, rain lashing against the windows. He hadn't dared look at his watch, not wanting to break the spell between them, but he knew it must be after midnight. They had talked non-stop for hours. She had told him some of the funnier job disasters she had been part of, her love for sharks and more about her brother, who she clearly adored. She had also told him a little bit about her new job working for the council. He had told her about his life in Texas, the people he grew up with. He hadn't quite managed to tell her the reason why he'd felt compelled to leave his home, but everything else had come spilling out. He just hoped she wouldn't notice the time so they could keep talking all night.

But suddenly she yawned and stretched, her legs sliding on top of his as she extended her limbs out over the sofa. She glanced at the clock on the wall.

'Oh God, it's so late, I'm so sorry. You should have kicked me out hours ago. When I start talking, I could go on all night.'

'It's been wonderful talking to you.'

She smiled and he felt his heart fill for her.

'I'll take you home.' Riley lifted her legs off his lap and stood up. He held out a hand for her and he pulled her gently to her feet.

'That's not necessary, I can swim home.'

'I'm not letting you swim in the dark. Come on, it won't take me a few minutes.'

He walked to the door and she reluctantly followed him – was she sad about the night ending too?

Riley moved down the stairs as he heard Darcy whistle for Ben. He stopped and waited, hearing Darcy trying to coax Ben away from the warmth of the fire.

'Come on, you lazy thing, I know you've made friends with Kelpie but we'll come back, I promise.'

Riley smiled at this, really hoping it was a promise she would keep.

She appeared on the stairs and Ben sleepily followed her.

They walked down the stairs in silence. It was such a stark contrast to a few moments before when they hadn't been able to stop talking.

They reached the bottom and Riley handed her a waterproof coat. 'It's coming down hard out there – we might not be able to use the boat at all, but I'll do my best.'

He opened the door and immediately a wave crashed through the door and over his feet. Riley peered out into the darkness at the huge waves that were consuming the tiny island and the swells of the sea between there and the mainland. He would be taking their lives in his hands using the boat in this weather and, while it might be something he would occasionally risk himself if he needed to get to the mainland, he wasn't prepared to endanger Darcy's life to get her home. Riley quickly shut the door.

'Looks like you're staying here tonight.'

CHAPTER 8

Darcy watched Riley go back up the stairs in shock. There was one bed, she knew that. There was a part of her that wanted to share the bed with Riley, maybe even cuddle up to him as they had almost been doing on the sofa. But the sensible part of her brain knew it was too soon to get that close to him. She liked him. A lot. And talking to him over the last few hours had made it very apparent that they had a connection. She wanted to take things slow with him and jumping into bed with him, even if they were just sleeping, suddenly seemed like a big step.

She quickly shrugged off the waterproof coat, and chased Ben back up the stairs. She reached the bedroom and peered round the door, wondering if Riley was already getting changed for bed. But he was getting sheets, blankets and pillows out from the ottoman at the foot of the bed.

Of course, he would want her to sleep on the sofa. He had been very friendly and chatty all night, but he had given her no sign that he wanted to take their friendship any further than that. He smiled at her as he walked past her back up to the lounge and she was annoyed with herself for the sense of disappointment that suddenly flooded through her.

She walked back into the lounge and smiled when she saw that Ben was cuddled up with Kelpie again.

Riley was busy making a bed up on the sofa, putting sheets down and arranging the blankets and pillows so it looked very comfy.

He turned round to face her once it was finished.

'Thank you for letting me stay.'

'It's no bother.'

He didn't make a move to leave as she stepped closer to the sofa. Closer to him. He watched her carefully.

'Can I get you anything, pyjamas or . . .' He trailed off as she shook her head. He still didn't move. What was he waiting for?

Maybe he wanted her to get into her makeshift bed before he turned all the lights out. She inched closer to her bed, moving to step past him.

'Well, goodnight then,' she said.

She froze as he bent his head down slightly and kissed her softly on the cheek. It was so tender, so gentle and so not what she was expecting to happen.

Not really knowing what to do other than grab him and kiss him properly, she slid past him to the sofa and sat down.

He watched her in confusion. 'Darcy, what are you doing?'

'Going to bed.'

'You're sleeping in my bedroom tonight. I'm sleeping here.'

'Oh.' That was why he hadn't made a move to leave, he'd been waiting for her to leave and all the time she'd been moving closer to him. He had felt compelled to kiss her because he thought that was what she wanted. 'Oh, I see, I thought . . .' She trailed off, embarrassed. 'I thought I was sleeping here, I was wondering why you weren't leaving.'

She stood up and hurried out the room, not daring to look at him on the way out.

Riley woke with a start, the muted grey light of morning before the sun had risen filtering through the windows. He glanced at the clock to see it was just coming up to four in the morning.

He'd had the weirdest dream about Darcy. In the dream she had really been a mermaid, and was trying to tempt him to come and live with her beneath the waves.

He had been reading *The Sea Lady* by H. G. Wells before he went to sleep, which told the story of a mermaid who comes to a seaside town. It had clearly been playing on his mind.

He stretched out on the sofa, trying to rid his mind of the fear he had felt as he trailed after her under the sea, knowing he was following her to his death.

Now he was awake, he really needed to go to the bathroom and that was a bit of a problem as the only bathroom in the lighthouse was the en-suite in his bedroom. He didn't want to wake her but he knew he couldn't wait another four hours until she woke up.

Maybe she would be awake too. And if she was, maybe they could go up to the roof of the lighthouse together and watch the sunrise. It was one of his favourite things to do whenever he woke early, and he was sure she would appreciate it too. And if she wasn't awake, he was sure he could sneak in quietly and use the bathroom without waking her.

He got up and padded quietly down the stairs to his bedroom.

He pushed the door open and peered inside. She was lying, clearly fast asleep, sprawled out on top of the bed, almost completely naked apart from the pair of boxer briefs he had given her to wear. He quickly looked away. She was lying face down so he couldn't see anything, but it still felt sordid and wrong to look at her without her knowing.

Maybe he should leave going to the bathroom. He was really tired, still half asleep, and he knew that once he got back to the sofa he would fall asleep again very quickly. But he was here now and he would go quickly.

Clamping his hand over his eyes, leaving just a tiny gap so he could guide himself across the room, he slowly manoeuvred across the floor, deliberately not looking at her. He reached the bed and shuffled round the side of it to get to the bathroom. She had no idea he was there. As he took his hand off his eyes to find the door handle, he noticed a large purple bruise on her thigh. It was huge, easily bigger than his hand. He wondered if she had done that on the rocks when she slipped and he didn't realise it.

He quickly went into the bathroom and when he had finished he slipped quietly back into the bedroom again.

She hadn't moved. She was so incredibly beautiful, and so much like the mermaid he had imagined in the story he had been reading, with her long red hair cascading down her back in loose curls and waves.

He looked away again, but his eyes fell back to the bruise. In the muted light from the windows, it looked odd and he couldn't help inching closer to look at it. It was blue and purple and green, almost iridescent. There seemed to be layers to it too. It was the oddest bruise he had ever seen. He moved closer, feeling perverted and terribly guilty, but he couldn't escape the cold dread that was starting to creep into his heart as he could clearly see that it wasn't a bruise at all.

They were scales.

He gasped, clamping his hand over his mouth in shock, but Darcy had already woken up at the noise. She screamed at the sight of him leaning over her. Holding the sheet to her chest, she moved away as quickly as possible, fell off the bed and shuffled into the corner.

'Darcy, shit, I'm so sorry. I was just going to the bathroom, I didn't mean to wake you.'

'You were watching me sleep. I'm naked and you were watching me, you pervert.'

'No, I wasn't. I'm really sorry.'

She didn't move from the corner and when he moved towards her she shuffled further away from him. He had never had a woman be scared of him before but waking up to find a man leaning over her in bed must have been terrifying. What was worse was that he was standing only in his boxer briefs too.

'I'm really sorry.'

'I'd like to go home.'

'Of course, I'm sorry. I'll just throw some clothes on and I'll take you. The storm seems to have passed so it'll be safer now.'

She nodded and he quickly left the room, cursing himself for his stupidity. Scales. What was he thinking? Of course they weren't scales.

He ran back up to the living room, snapped the light on and threw his clothes back on. A noise behind him made him turn. Darcy was standing there, fully dressed, her arms folded over her chest. She didn't look at him.

He didn't want things to end like this. They'd had a wonderful evening and now she was leaving thinking he was a pervert.

He moved back towards her and she stiffened. 'I'm really sorry. I went to the bathroom and I swear I didn't look at you, I kept my hand over my eyes the whole time. But as I came out I noticed the bruise, the one on your thigh. I had been reading a story about mermaids before I went to sleep and I had a dream about mermaids and I swear just for a second I thought the bruise was scales. I know it sounds crazy, I knew it was crazy as soon as I thought it, but in the limited light down there, I couldn't stop staring at it, trying to see if I was wrong. I'm so sorry. I wasn't perving over you. I was just . . . I was half asleep and . . . I'm really sorry.'

To his surprise, her face softened. She believed him. His explanation was the most ludicrous reason in the world. If he had made up a sleepwalking condition or a story about aliens it would have been more believable than the ridiculous story he had just come out with. But he wanted to be honest with her, regardless of the fact he was still questioning his own sanity round about now.

'They are scales.'

His heart stopped.

She turned sideways slightly and, using one finger, she dragged part of the leggings down her thigh to show him, his shirt and the boxer briefs she had been wearing protecting her modesty.

In the bright light of the living room the blue and green scales were clear to see, shimmering as if they were wet. But after a second or two of his heart not beating at all, he realised he was looking at a very beautiful, very skilful tattoo.

'I was obsessed with mermaids as a child. I read every single story about them, watched *The Little Mermaid* a million times. Watched *Splash*. Every time I came on holiday down here I would swim in the sea, hoping and praying that I would see one. At one point I even thought I might be one – that I had been taken away by humans and raised as one of them instead. It would explain why my parents loved my brother more than they loved me. I thought if I stayed in the sea long enough I would turn back into one and I could go back home to my real family. I had pictures all over my walls and whenever I wrote stories as a child they always included mermaids. As I grew up my obsession waned only slightly. There are so many accounts, so many sightings of them; some of these reports are hundreds of years old. I've read every report over and over again, the details are almost always the same. And I know this sounds silly and whimsical, but there's a tiny part of me that wonders if they do exist. So much of the sea remains unexplored, there are new sea creatures being discovered all the time. There is a certain amount of fact in many myths and I do wonder where all the tales come from. I got this tattoo when I qualified as a marine biologist as a reminder that, just because we haven't seen it, doesn't mean it's not there. It's a reminder to always keep an open mind.'

Without thinking, he reached out a finger to touch it. Although the scales looked hard, he could only feel her silky smooth skin. A jolt of electricity shot through him as he touched her. Her eyes snapped to his and he quickly withdrew his finger.

'It's silly, I know,' Darcy said, pulling her leggings back up.

'I think it's beautiful,' he said, softly.

'You do?'

He nodded.

'I had one boyfriend dump me over it, he said it freaked him out too much.'

'Well, he sounds like an idiot.'

She smiled. 'Did it scare you?'

He shook his head, then remembered he was going to be honest with her. 'For a second, yes.'

'Sorry.'

'I'm sorry that I scared you too, so I think we are even. I'll take you home, if that's what you want, but I'd love it if you stayed for breakfast?'

She nodded and he sighed with relief. 'I thought perhaps you might want to eat it on the roof, the view is spectacular up there.'

Her eyes lit up. 'I'd love that.'

He moved into the kitchen area, wishing he had known before that she had been going to stay the night; he would have made sure he had a better breakfast to offer her. As it was, he had cereal or toast.

'Is toast OK?'

'Toast sounds perfect.'

He smiled at how easy-going she was and at how easily she had forgiven him.

'Go and get a sweater on, it'll be chilly at this time in the morning.'

She left the room while he quickly toasted four pieces of bread. He wrapped them in foil and popped them in a bag with a jar of jam and a knife. He shoved a carton of orange juice and a couple of glasses in there and grabbed the brownies that they hadn't got round to eating the night before. It wasn't anything special but he hoped the sunrise would more than make up for it.

She returned to the room and he handed her the bag while he grabbed the blankets and pillows from the sofa, bundling them all together into a makeshift knapsack.

He ushered her back out onto the stairs and they walked up together. They passed the door to the lantern room and, shortly after, the stairs stopped, with a ladder leading straight upwards.

'The hatch at the top is quite heavy, so I'll go first,' Riley said.

He slung the knapsack over his shoulder and pulled himself up the ladder with ease. He unbolted the hatch, pushed it open and stepped out onto the roof.

He turned back for Darcy, but she was already hurriedly climbing up the steps of the ladder. As she reached the top, he leaned down and offered her his hand, which she took and he pulled her out onto the roof beside him.

She looked around. He hoped she loved the view as much as he did, but one look on her face showed she was in complete awe.

The wind whipped around them, causing her hair to fly out like a scarlet banner, and he smiled as she tried unsuccessfully to tame it.

A feeling so strong surged through him. He immediately tried to squash it down as soon as he recognised it. It was stupid and even more ridiculous than thinking she was a real mermaid a few minutes before, but he couldn't escape the feeling that he was falling for Darcy Davenport.

Darcy helped Riley spread the blanket and pillows on top of the roof, the wind making it more difficult than it should have been, but they quickly sat on the pillows and weighed them down. The sky had a slight pink tinge to it, as the sun would soon rise above the horizon. The sea was flat calm now, a completely different story to the night before. Although they were well into summer now, the chill of the night was still present without the sun to warm up the day. Riley wrapped the second huge blanket round them both, as they faced the direction of the oncoming sun.

'This is incredible, Riley.'

'I love it up here, I feel so removed from everything.'

'Well, thank you for sharing it with me.'

She looked over at the town, still fast asleep at this hour of the day. Not a soul moved along the shore or through the shops, not one single light glowed from the houses or shop windows. They were the only ones awake and it somehow made it all the more magical.

She turned her attention back to Riley, who opened up the tub of brownies, and she took one and bit into it. He did the same.

'These are really good,' he said. 'They taste like the ones my dad used to make.'

'Really? These are my aunt Ginny's recipe. She uses tea, it's her secret ingredient.'

Riley laughed. 'My dad used tea in his brownies, too.'

'Oh. Maybe it wasn't such a big secret, maybe everyone knows this recipe.'

He unwrapped the toast from the foil. He offered her a piece and she took it and spread a thick layer of jam over the top. As she took a bite, she noticed Riley was smiling at her.

'What?'

'You. Something as simple as a piece of toast and a great view and you're as happy as if I'd presented you with a three-course meal and a bottle of champagne in an expensive restaurant.'

She looked at him: his soft green eyes, his wonderful warm smile. 'It's the person that you choose to share those things with that's the most important, not the trimmings. Being with you is what makes me smile.'

He looked away and she felt suddenly very awkward. He was sending some very confusing messages. She really liked him, but she had no idea if he felt the same way.

A flash of gold lit up the sky out across the sea, as the sun made its first appearance above the horizon.

They watched it in silence, as the fingers of sunlight stretched out and touched the edges of the coast, sending a warm pink glow across the sleepy houses and fluffy clouds. They watched it until it became unbearable to look at, the sun shining too brightly for their eyes.

Riley turned back to her, smiling.

'I should go, Ben needs a walk,' Darcy said, still feeling awkward from before.

His face fell a little, but he nodded. She helped him pack everything up and he went down the ladder ahead of her, so he could help her down.

She grabbed her bag with the wetsuit inside, where she'd left it in the lounge, and they went down the stairs in silence. The atmosphere between them had suddenly changed, and Darcy wondered if he was as sad to see her go as she was to leave.

She called Ben and he followed her down the stairs.

Riley handed her a waterproof coat and pulled on a knee-length woollen coat himself. As they stepped out of the light-house, she noticed he was scowling.

He got in his boat, lifted Ben in safely, then helped her in too.

She sat down, holding Ben tightly as Riley started the outboard motor and they chugged across the bay to the jetty at the far side of Silver Cove. The sea was flat calm, the boat creating tiny ripples as it moved across the water. No one was up yet, the day only just beginning.

She glanced down into the water and was surprised she could see the seabed below and several fish.

'I'd love to scuba dive around here, the water is so clear. I used to dive around Britain all the time and I still have all the gear, though I haven't dived for a long time. Have you dived before?'

He tore his attention from where they were going to look at her. She hated that she suddenly felt like she had to fill the silence with inane chatter when she hadn't felt like that with him before, but something had changed between them.

'Once or twice, but in much warmer climates than this.'

'Diving in a dry suit is very different to diving with a wetsuit, but it's great fun. I'd love to take you one day.'

Quickly diverting his attention back to the jetty that was fast approaching, Riley slowed the engine and then cut it completely as they pulled in alongside it. He tied the boat to it. He helped Ben out, who immediately jumped down onto the beach and ran across the sand chasing the birds. Riley held out a hand for Darcy and helped her up onto the jetty.

He didn't say anything, so she knew she had to fill the silence again.

'Thank you for last night, for dinner and breakfast. I had a wonderful time.'

He nodded.

She stepped back away from him, hoping he would say something, ask her to come back again some time, or just anything to confirm that he'd had a good time too.

But he didn't.

She gave him a small wave, disappointment crashing through her as she turned away. If he didn't say anything, then it wouldn't feel right going back to the lighthouse again.

She walked to the end of the jetty, each step away from him becoming more painful as she realised he had no intention of asking her to come back to the lighthouse. Had the night before meant nothing to him? Had his good manners meant he'd sat through hours of her talking just to be polite? He couldn't escape her like he had when he had left Charlotte in the pub – he was in his own home.

'Darcy, wait,' Riley called.

She turned back as he walked slowly, cautiously towards her.

He hopped down onto the beach in front of her, shoving his hand through his hair awkwardly. He stared down at the stones underneath their feet and then bent down to pick something up, though she couldn't see what it was.

He stood back up. 'Last night was great for me too and I'd love to do it again. Can I take you out tonight?'

Her heart leapt, but she did her best to keep her face straight. She didn't want any further confusion. 'Like a date?'

He hesitated and then nodded.

This time she couldn't help the smile spreading on her face. 'I'd love that.'

Riley stared at her in shock for a moment. 'Really? I haven't scared you off? You don't think I'm a weirdo?'

'Oh no, I definitely think you're a weirdo. You live in a lighthouse on your own, you don't want to mix with other people, you read stories about mermaids. But I'm weird too, so we can be weird together.'

He grinned. 'I like that. Shall I pick you up at seven? We'll go somewhere that's not the lighthouse, prove to you that I'm not completely antisocial.'

'OK.'

She turned away again, but he caught her hand and pulled her back. The wind raced across the beach and her hair flew up around her.

'Tonight is too far away to wait for this, though,' Riley said, and taking her face in his hands, he bent his head down and kissed her softly.

The taste of him, sweet and tangy, slammed into her with a punch of desire that was so hard and the kiss very quickly escalated from something soft and sweet to something more, a kiss that was passionate and urgent. The wind whipped around them both and Riley wrapped his coat around her back, cocooning her against his warm body. She ran one hand through his hair at the back of his neck, it was silky and soft and he let out a moan of need at her touch. His tongue slid against hers and she pulled herself tighter against him. The kiss continued and Darcy knew if they had been somewhere a bit more private it would have led to a lot more than kissing.

Ben barking nearby made them break apart, but Riley held her tight in his arms so they were still wrapped up together in his coat.

'I've been wanting to do that since you first arrived on my island, my little mermaid.'

Darcy smiled. 'Well, there'll definitely be more of that tonight.'

'I hope so.' He kissed her briefly on the lips and reluctantly stepped back away from her, pressing something into her hand. 'I'll see you tonight.'

Darcy watched him go and then opened her hand to see a tiny jade green ammonite in her hand. A smile burst on her face as she put the ammonite in her pocket. As she turned away, it took every ounce of control not to run whooping with delight, do cartwheels of joy across the sand.

CHAPTER 9

After walking Ben for an hour across the beach, Darcy let herself back into the flats just as Libby was walking out of hers.

'Oh Darcy, I'm glad I bumped into you. I'm just heading out to the town. It's George's birthday soon and I want to get him something really special. Will you come with me? You can help me choose.'

After the small amount of sleep she'd had the night before, Darcy had been looking forward to having a small nap, but she really liked Libby and after Libby had helped her persuade George to pretend to be Riley she owed them both a favour.

'Sure, let me just get Ben settled and fed and I'll get changed and I'll be right with you.'

Libby's eyes cast down Darcy's clothing, obviously noticing that they were a bit big for her. She waggled her eyebrows mischievously.

'So, did you stay with Riley last night?'

Darcy stared at her in shock; how could she possibly know that?

'I saw you swim out there, but I didn't see you come back. And George said Seb told him he saw you two kissing on the jetty earlier this morning while he was walking his dog on the beach,' Libby said, clearly pleased with her detective work.

Was nothing private in this town?

Darcy cleared her throat. 'I did stay but nothing happened. He made me dinner, we talked, when I went to leave, it was raining and the waves were too high so I stayed the night.'

'Where did you sleep?'

'In his bed but . . .'

Libby's face lit up with this news.

'But he slept on the sofa, he was the perfect gentleman,' Darcy insisted.

'Until he grabbed you and snogged you on the beach this morning. Apparently the kiss was very heated.'

Darcy had no words. The thought of everyone in the town knowing her business was mortifying.

'It was just a kiss.'

'Of course it was. Are you seeing him again?'

Darcy nodded reluctantly. 'Yes, tonight.'

Libby was grinning from ear to ear. 'The women of the town have been after him for months and I love that you've been here five minutes and knocked him off his feet already. He had no interest in any of them and we all wondered why he seemed to be so anti-dating, but it seems he was waiting for the perfect woman to come along and he found that with you.'

'I like him, but he's clearly scared about getting involved with someone again, so I think we're just going to take it really slow. We've had one night together, one kiss – can we just figure it all out ourselves and see where it's going before the town starts planning the wedding?'

Libby smiled. 'OK, I won't say anything, but nothing stays secret in this place for long. If you want your affairs private, then you've picked the wrong town to live in.'

Darcy sighed.

'Look, people are nosy here, but it's only out of concern. They all want Riley to be happy, especially with all the horrible lighthouse business, and once they get to know you they'll only want the best for you too. Get changed and then I'll take you into town and introduce you to a few more people. Everyone is so friendly, I'm sure you'll love them.'

Darcy nodded.

'Knock for me when you're ready to go,' Libby said, returning to her flat.

Darcy let herself into her flat.

She loved working with people, talking to them, meeting new friends – that was partly why she had moved to the area – but she still hoped for a little bit of privacy. The thought of people talking about her and Riley was not good, especially if Riley found out, with his fear of getting involved in small-town life. He would drop her like a hot potato before they had even properly started.

She quickly showered and changed, put some food down for Ben, who was already snoring loudly on the sofa, and was just about to head out when she received a text from Carmel.

Just to let you know the article will run in tomorrow's paper. The story is great, I think you'll like it.

Darcy smiled and typed back.

Did Annabel use the photo of Riley in the boat?

The reply came back immediately.

Yes, and I think you might have been telling me little fibs about your ugly American friend. He's yummy.

Darcy hesitated. She wanted to tell Carmel all about her wonderful evening with her yummy American, but she knew Carmel would want all the details and, with Libby waiting, she didn't have time to get into it now.

Yes he is.

She slipped her phone into her bag and headed out. She knocked on Libby's door and they left the flats together.

With the sun well in the sky, the day was warming up nicely again. Darcy couldn't help looking over at the lighthouse as they walked along the road running parallel to the beach and up over the headland.

'Have you met Suzanna yet, Riley's grandmother?' Libby asked.

'No, we're not quite at the stage of meeting family members yet. As I said, we've had one kiss.'

Libby giggled. 'One amazing kiss.'

Darcy couldn't help but smile and Libby nudged her when she saw it.

'What did you have in mind for George's present?'

Libby clearly noted the subject change but didn't pursue it.

'Oh, I have a very specific idea. I've already bought him a ton of silly presents, which I know he will love, but I wanted something in particular for tomorrow night.' Libby linked arms with her and Darcy smiled at the simplicity of that gesture.

As the shops started popping up along the road, Libby walked with purpose through the town square and up the hill, obviously knowing exactly where she was going. So Darcy was surprised when they walked straight into a women's lingerie shop.

'Oh, so George's main present he'll get to unwrap is you?'

Libby laughed. 'Yes, that's about right. I never really had a proper boyfriend before George. I had men that I went on the odd date with, but nothing serious, and George fell in love with me when I was just wearing jeans and a hoodie, so I've never done the dressing-to-impress-sex-kitten thing for him before. We have a great sex life but I thought I might . . . spice things up a little for him.'

Darcy blinked at her candour. 'OK, so what are we looking for? Something slutty or romantic, lacy or satin?'

Libby shrugged. 'That's why you're here, you can help me choose. Maybe something green. George loves green. A lot of his clothes are green.'

'Because of your eyes,' Darcy said, noting how vivid they were. They reminded her of Riley's eyes, although his were darker, and something suddenly clenched in her stomach at the thought of him.

Libby smiled and held out her hand. 'My engagement ring has twenty shades of green in it, because George says it matches my eyes.'

Darcy smiled. 'Green it is.'

'Although George loves the sea, so maybe something blue, or gold like the sun.'

'OK, we can try a few options. Why don't we split up and grab a few things and then we can compare. In a former life, I used to have a job as a personal shopper, so I have some idea what suits people.'

'Brilliant, you can always come shopping with me in the future. I'm rubbish at buying clothes for myself, especially if they aren't jeans or T-shirts.'

Libby walked off to one side of the shop and Darcy moved to the other. She didn't know Libby very well, but she knew she wasn't the slutty, peep-hole-bra-type of person. She glanced over at her. Libby was tiny in every way, the true meaning of the word petite. Even with her tiny baby bump she was still small. She noted that the things that Libby was picking out for herself were camisole tops, not just bras. Maybe she was self-conscious about her little bump. Taking her lead, Darcy picked out several sets of camisole tops with matching knickers or shorts, some with sexy lace and spaghetti-thin straps, some more demure.

She moved round the very front of the shop near the open entrance to look at some of the more risqué items that were made with leather or fur and included corsets and lots of black or red. Libby came to join her, giggling to herself at some of the more outlandish outfits.

'You should get something for Riley,' Libby said, her eyebrows waggling again.

Darcy grabbed an outfit that looked like a black leather low-cut swimsuit with nipple tassels. 'Something like this perhaps?'

Libby burst out laughing and then quickly stifled it at a sharp look from the shop owner. Clearly, for the owner to put these weird outfits right at the front of the shop next to the open door, she was very proud of that particular collection. Darcy would never have been seen dead in anything like that.

Darcy held up another strange-looking thing that looked like Borat's famous green mankini, only this one was in red leather. 'Do you think Riley would like me in this?' she teased.

Libby looked up and laughed again, but then her smile fell off her face at something over Darcy's shoulder. Darcy knew without looking that it was Riley. Her luck of blundering from one disaster to the next had struck again.

She turned round to find Riley standing in the open doorway, examining the mankini she was holding with evident amusement. He had obviously been passing and saw her, maybe he'd come over to say hello. She heard Libby stifle her laughter.

'I might go and try a few things on,' Libby said, leaving Darcy to her awkward encounter alone.

He couldn't possibly think Darcy was serious about the mankini or that she was really shopping for sexy underwear for him after just one kiss. She also really hoped that this sort of kinky fetish stuff wasn't what he was into either.

'We were just being silly,' Darcy said.

'It's nice,' Riley said and her heart fell. He looked up from the mankini, his mouth twitching with amusement. 'But it's not really you.'

'It's not?'

He shook his head. 'You have this soft natural beauty that just shines from you. You don't need anything to make you sexier than you already are.'

Darcy swallowed, trying to take her eyes off his but she couldn't. 'What would you choose for me then?'

Riley stared at her for a moment and then lowered his head to whisper in her ear. 'There was nothing sexier than you wearing my shirt this morning, only I'd prefer it without the thermal leggings.'

Oh God. Things had suddenly got a lot more intimate.

'So you wouldn't choose anything in here?'

He tore his eyes from her to look around. He moved over towards the changing room and she followed him. She watched him as he plucked a mid-length greeny-blue negligee off the hanger and held it up to her. It came to just above her knee and sparkled with turquoise sequins around the breast. It was simple and beautiful and exactly the sort of thing she would have chosen for herself.

'It matches your scales,' he said, softly.

She stared at him. She had to put a stop to this. If he was expecting her to pitch up to their first date tonight wearing the negligee or the mankini and jump straight into bed with him, he could think again.

'We were shopping for Libby, hence the ridiculously small clothes I picked out for her. I wouldn't fit an arm into most of these things.' She held up the items she had chosen.

'They're not really designed for arms,' he said, his mouth pulling up into a small half smile.

She had to explain herself further. She didn't want him to be under any illusions about what the night would hold.

'I don't sleep with men on the first date,' she blurted out, and then felt her cheeks burn red under his steady gaze. Shit, she could have been more subtle than that.

'I didn't think for one minute that you were the sort of girl who would do that. I'm happy to wait until you're ready, but I'm much more interested in having a repeat performance of last night where we talked all night but hopefully with more kissing.'

'Me, too,' Darcy sighed with relief.

He smiled. 'But you should know that tonight would probably count as a third date, as we already had dinner and breakfast. Just in case you have any rules about sleeping with men on a third date?'

Darcy felt her mouth fall open, but then realised he was teasing her. She nudged him and he laughed. Suddenly she heard quiet sobs coming from the changing room and her smile fell from her face. Riley had heard it too. As he quickly rushed over to the cubicle, Darcy managed to catch up with him and stop him. She didn't know what state of undress Libby was in.

'Libby?' Darcy called through the curtain.

There was no answer, just a few sniffles. Darcy peeled back the curtain and slipped inside, shutting the curtain behind her.

Libby was sitting on the bench, looking very forlorn, tears flowing down her cheeks as if she'd had the worst news in the world. She was dressed in one of the pretty camisole tops and shorts.

Darcy quickly knelt down in front of her. 'What's wrong?'

'I wanted to do this for George. I'm scared he might not find me sexy any more since I've put on a few pounds of baby weight, but I'm too fat to be sexy.' Libby ran her hand over her baby bump.

Darcy knew this was just baby hormones making Libby feel vulnerable, especially as George had told her that Libby had cried when he'd found a stone on the beach shaped like a cat; her emotions were all over the place.

'Libby, George loves you and he would love you if you were twenty stone heavier. Besides, you're not fat, you're carrying his child.'

'Libby,' Riley said, softly through the curtain. 'When a couple first get married, the man will lie awake for many nights next to his bride, watching her sleep and knowing that no woman could ever be more beautiful than the woman he married. I guarantee you every married man has had those feelings. Then when the woman becomes pregnant with his child, something changes. The beautiful woman he had lain next to for all those months as husband and wife becomes even more beautiful and as she grows bigger with his child she becomes sexier and infinitely more desirable than she ever was before. If at all possible, the man loves his wife even more when she is pregnant with his child.'

Libby's tears seemed to dry up altogether as she stared at the shadow on the other side of the curtain.

Darcy quickly picked up where Riley had left off. 'I bet George hasn't been able to keep his hands off you since you've become pregnant, has he?'

Libby nodded. 'It's true. He wants to have sex all day, every day. But what if it doesn't last?'

'You know he loves you, I've never seen a man look at a woman with as much love as as when George looks at you.'

Libby smiled. 'The boy is crazy in love with me, isn't he?'

Darcy nodded.

'I've just spotted George in the street, I'll go get him,' Riley said and the shadow disappeared.

'No, wait. Crap,' Libby said, quickly wiping the tears off her face. 'I don't want him to see me like this.'

Darcy stood up to get Riley to come back, but when she peeled back the curtain an inch she could see Riley already out on the street talking to a worried-looking George. For someone who didn't want to get involved in town life, Riley was doing a bad job at staying out of other people's business.

George came rushing into the shop and Darcy turned back to face Libby. 'He's here.'

George opened the curtain and squeezed himself into the cubicle with Darcy and Libby.

'Libby, what's wrong?'

Libby stood up. 'Nothing, just silly baby hormones getting the better of me.'

George quickly held her in his arms. 'Riley said you were worried I wouldn't find you attractive any more . . .'

Darcy discreetly slipped out.

'Do you have any idea how much you turn me on when I see you walk around the flat naked, with our baby growing inside you?' George whispered.

Darcy snagged Riley's sleeve and pulled him away from the cubicle.

'That was a very nice thing you said to Libby,' Darcy said, her heart filling a little bit because of the beautiful way he'd dealt with Libby's insecurities, though doubt had worked its way into her brain too. What Riley had said had come from experience.

Riley shrugged, clearly embarrassed. 'I should go, I have some work I need to do before we go out tonight. Can I pick you up earlier, say six? I've found somewhere for our date, but it's out of town and it might take a while to get there.'

Darcy nodded just as Libby and George came out of the cubicle. Libby hugged Darcy on her way past, whispering in her ear, 'George is taking me home to prove how much he loves me. I was going to tell him that it's not necessary but if he feels he has something to prove in the bedroom . . . I'm not going to stop him.' She pulled back and addressed both Darcy and Riley. 'Thank you for putting up with me. I'm not normally like this, I promise.'

George shook Riley's hand and gave Darcy a hug too, then they left, almost breaking into a run as they made their way back to Silver Cove.

Riley turned his attention back to Darcy. 'See you later.'

It was clear he wanted to kiss her but wasn't entirely comfortable doing that in public, so he gave her a quick peck on the cheek and walked out of the shop.

She watched him leave, then chased after him. The underwear she had been holding for Libby suddenly set off the shop alarm, the incessant, unbearably loud wailing catching the attention of every single person in the street as they all stopped to look at the shoplifter. Riley stood staring at her in shock, as she looked at the stolen goods in her hand.

'Thief, THIEF!' screamed the shop owner.

Darcy quickly turned round to face her. 'I'm so sorry, I wasn't stealing them, I just forgot I was holding them . . .'

'THIEF!' the shop owner continued to yell.

'No, look, I'm sorry, I just wanted to say something to Riley, I didn't realise I still had them.'

'THIEF!'

What the hell was wrong with this woman? The items Darcy was holding were quite clearly too small for her, so why she would be stealing them was a mystery. Darcy tried to give them back but the shop owner was having none of it. A crowd had started to gather now and she wondered if they would all make some kind of citizen's arrest or drag her off to the town square to be put into stocks and have rotten vegetables thrown at her.

Riley suddenly snatched the items from Darcy's hands, marched back into the shop and hung them on the nearest rail, then turned, grabbed Darcy's hand and ran down the street. No one tried to stop them, even though the shop owner was still screaming after them.

They ran down twisting roads, round corners and through tiny alleyways until the shop owner's cries for help could no longer be heard. Riley pulled her under an archway into a tiny public garden that had flowers of every colour cascading down the walls, sheltering them from view.

He stared at her. 'Being with you is going to get me in a whole heap load of trouble, isn't it?'

'I'm so sorry, I didn't realise . . .' Darcy panted.

'I shouldn't worry. It was quite obvious to anyone watching that you hadn't really stolen those things. The woman is clearly bat-shit crazy.'

'You'll get into trouble for assisting a fugitive.'

'At least we'll both go down together.' He brushed her hair gently off her face. 'What did you want to say to me?'

There had been something she had wanted to say but it seemed childish to bring it up now, after risking a criminal record for it. But Riley was waiting for her patiently.

'What you said to Libby sounded like it came from the heart. Have you been married before? Not that it matters, not that it's any of my business. I just wondered if you had children of your own back in Texas . . .' She trailed off, cursing herself. If he had wanted to tell her about that part of his life in Texas, he would have done so the night before.

'No. That stuff came from Max, my brother. He got a bit drunk one night and told me how much he loved his wife, even more so after she got pregnant. There was a lot more to it than what I said but I just adapted it to give the general gist. I've never been married and I don't have children . . . I was engaged, though.'

'Was?'

'She dumped me. But looking back now, I never had the kind of love that Max described, I never watched her sleep counting my lucky stars that she came into my life. So I imagine it was for the best. And if she hadn't dumped me I would never have come here and I'd never have met you, so I suppose I should be grateful to her too.'

Her heart stuttered against her chest at the soft look in his eyes.

'Why did she dump you?'

He took a sharp intake of breath and looked over her head at the lilac that was tumbling down the walls from the twisted tree. She had pushed him too far.

'It seemed that reputation was more important to Cassidy than anything else. With my connections as a songwriter, I was useful to her. But after . . . when things went wrong in the town and it started to get unpleasant, my usefulness suddenly came to an end. It didn't help that I flat refused to use my contacts with people in the music industry to secure her a recording deal. I didn't want to be that person. People respect me in my line of work and I didn't want to lose that respect by using my influence to get my girlfriend a recording contract. Sadly, she had no singing talent at all and, though I tried to encourage her, apparently me paying for singing lessons for her was not appreciated.'

'Oh Riley, she was using you?' Her heart ached for him.

He stared at her. 'You wear your heart on your sleeve, don't you? You feel so much empathy for other people. Most people just nod and say the right words, but you genuinely feel the pain of others.'

Darcy blushed. 'Oh, I know. I always get too involved in people's lives. I'm sorry, I shouldn't have asked . . .'

Riley ran a finger down her cheek to her lips. 'It's a very attractive quality.' He bent his head down and kissed her softly, briefly on the lips. 'And you can ask me anything.'

'Oh . . . well, you can ask me anything as well.'

He stared at her for a moment. 'I'd like to know about your past relationships too.'

Darcy looked down. 'There's not a lot to tell. There've been four relationships, none of them have been what I would call serious.'

'Didn't you live with one? That sounds pretty serious.'

'I was his lodger. I rented a room in his house, that's how we met. I don't think it was ever serious.'

'What about the others?'

'The first one was disappointed when I wouldn't sleep with him when I was seventeen, the second one was disappointed when I did. I was so terrified that I would be rubbish that when it actually came to the main event I just sort of froze. The other two men said I never gave myself to them emotionally and I suppose they were right. I was always fearful of doing something wrong or letting them down, so maybe I held myself back. But ultimately my unwillingness to connect with them was the thing that split us up.'

'I would disagree.'

Darcy looked up.

'I've seen the sort of person you are, kind, compassionate, fiery. You're friendly and warm. You've made friends in the last few days, which is more than I've done since I've been here. You don't have trouble connecting with people, but I think you held yourself back because you knew these men weren't right for you. The right man would wait for you to be ready to sleep with him, not get angry because you made him wait. The right man would make your first time special, not pound away at you when you're lying there scared to death. And the right man would be patient enough to work through the barriers you've made to protect yourself, even if that meant pulling your walls down slowly brick by brick because they can see that the girl on the other side is worth the wait.'

She stared at him.

'You connected with me in more ways in the last few days than anyone in this town has in the last few months. I don't feel that you are holding back.'

'I'm not holding back with you, I feel like I can really be myself for the first time in a long time. You've seen my geeky side and you haven't run away.'

'I happen to like your geeky side.'

She smiled.

'I want you to be yourself with me, I want to know the real Darcy, the good, the bad, the beautiful.'

He kissed her softly, running his hands through her hair as he pulled her towards him. He tasted sweet and smelled so good. This connection between them felt so right, she knew there was never going to be any holding back with him.

Eventually, he pulled away.

'I really have to go. Wear something warm tonight.' He kissed her on the forehead and left her alone standing among the flowers.

CHAPTER 10

There was a knock on Darcy's door later that evening. Giving up trying to do something sexy and alluring with her tangle of red curls, she ran to answer it. Riley was dressed in his dark jeans, long wool coat, and a woolly hat had replaced the cowboy hat.

'You look lovely,' he said, casting his eyes down her leggings and turquoise sea-coloured knitted jumper dress. 'But you'll need a coat too.'

The day had been deliciously warm, White Cliff Bay basking in the summer sun, but the nights were a bit chilly and wherever they were going, it seemed they would be outside. Darcy grabbed her coat, scarf and – grateful for the excuse to hide her messy curls – she grabbed her favourite blue-sequinned beanie hat too.

'I bought you something for our date.' Riley dug in his coat pocket and pulled out a chalky grey ammonite, still encased in a small rock. 'I just saw it on the beach.'

Darcy laughed. 'Is this going to be our thing?'

He moved his hands to her waist, pressing his lips to her forehead. 'I like that we have a thing.'

'I do too. I will treasure it.'

She moved back into the flat and placed it in the glass bowl with the jade green one he had given her just after their first kiss.

'Where are we going?' Darcy moved back to the door and closed it behind her, noticing for the first time that Libby was taking her time to clean her front door . . . with a tissue. Libby glanced over at them casually, as she polished the handle. Darcy smiled to herself.

'It's a surprise.'

'I love surprises.'

'I thought you might.'

With his hand gently in the small of her back, he escorted her down the steps onto the street.

She was pleased to see that Riley's car was a simple black Peugeot. She got the sense he had money and she didn't want to feel inadequate around him, what with her barely being able to scrape together enough to pay the rent. She hoped wherever they were going wasn't somewhere flash and expensive.

He opened the door for her and she smiled at his impeccable manners. She slid into the warm interior and noticed that it was an automatic.

'Didn't fancy the complicated gears of the English cars, then?' she said as Riley climbed into the driver's seat.

'Why choose the harder option?'

She smiled. He had a point.

Riley started driving through the tiny winding lanes of White Cliff Bay and every now and again Darcy caught glimpses of the sun setting over the waves between the whitewashed houses.

'It's so pretty here. It feels nicer – the atmosphere just feels so friendly. Everyone is so unhurried and laidback. I've been here only a short time but I feel calmer already. Do you like it here?'

'I love the view. I've not been anywhere in the world that has a better view.'

Darcy felt her bubble of happiness pop slightly. 'But you don't love the town?'

'I just prefer to keep myself to myself.'

She watched him as he kept his eyes on the road, as they slowly left the town of White Cliff Bay behind.

'Something bad happened to you in Texas, didn't it, something that made you leave?'

'I was betrayed and not just by my fiancée. By my friends, too. I don't want to put myself in that position again.'

He clearly didn't want to talk about what had actually happened and Darcy didn't want to push him. 'What will you do if you lose the lighthouse? Will you leave White Cliff Bay?'

He sighed. 'I hope it doesn't come to that, but yes, that was the plan. I was thinking I might go back to America. I have an apartment in New York that I use from time to time when I have to travel there with work. I'd probably move in there. I wouldn't go back to Texas, though. That chapter of my life is done.'

'You wouldn't just move to somewhere else in England?'

'I haven't felt at home here. With all the hassle with the lighthouse and the council trying to take away my family home, I'm feeling even less of an affinity with the place. I haven't connected with England. Well, at least not until now.'

She stared at him and smiled slightly. He reached over and took her hand, holding it tight all the way to their destination.

If she couldn't help him with the lighthouse, would she be enough to make him want to stay? White Cliff Bay was a wonderful place. After Riley had left her earlier in the day, she had used the time to explore the town and talk to more people. They were friendly, caring and looked out for one another. She really liked it here and if she could persuade Riley to open up his heart to get to know the people of the town more, she knew he would fall in love with the place too.

'What did you love about Texas? What do you miss the most? I bet we could recreate it here.'

He was silent as he tried really hard to think of something. Whatever had happened there had tainted Texas for him.

'Ice hockey,' he finally said. 'The Dallas Demons are the most incredible team. Harrison Flynn, Nate Johansson – just the most brilliant line. I watched every game, even went to the stadium a few times too. I can't watch it over here and I miss that.'

'Well, we have ice hockey here too. It's not as big but we have it. Maybe you could find a new team to love, not as a replacement for the Demons but as an addition.'

'Maybe.' He smiled at her, which showed her he didn't hate the idea, so she pushed it a little more.

'And I've never seen an ice hockey game before. You could take me and talk me through the ins and outs?'

'I'd like that.'

'What else do you miss?'

'Blue Bell ice cream.'

She laughed. 'What is it with this ice cream?'

'It's the best in the world.'

'Have you tried Rookbeare Farm? Their Devon fudge or Swiss truffle flavour is to die for. I bet I could convert you, or at least give you a very good substitute.'

'I'll try it. But I'm not making any promises.' He smiled and she felt a jolt to her heart. She was falling for him and she couldn't bear the thought of losing him when she was only just getting to know him.

Maybe the possibility of him leaving wouldn't happen. She had already sent off the application to have the lighthouse listed. She knew they would move quite quickly with a decision once a building was under threat from demolition. She could only hope that the right decision was made. Plus there was the article coming out tomorrow. That might help too.

They pulled into a field that was already filled with cars. People were making their way down the bank towards another field. Most were carrying chairs, blankets and bags of food and drink.

She got out the car and followed Riley round to the boot. He pulled out a picnic hamper, a large picnic blanket and what looked like a large sleeping bag. Slightly confused, she looked down into the other field and saw a huge cinema screen.

'Oh, an outdoor cinema, how exciting! Watching a film under the stars, now that's romantic. Which film are we going to see?'

Riley arched an eyebrow and she laughed, knowing he wasn't going to tell her.

Taking her hand, he led her over to the ticket booth, where they were told to help themselves to free popcorn and big squashy beanbags.

They found a space in front of the screen and spread out the blanket, then she helped Riley to unpack the contents of the hamper. Pâté, bread, cheese and chutneys came out, along with a bottle of champagne and two glasses. Darcy looked out over the field, the gentle breeze blowing her hair from her face as the sun sank below the horizon. Nothing could be more romantic than a picnic beneath a blanket of stars. She just hoped the film was something sweepingly romantic too and not some big action film with explosions and people dying. She enjoyed those films but she wanted to complete the evening with something gooey and heartwarming. As she tucked into the wonderful food that Riley had provided, she noticed there were quite a lot of children in the audience, which seemed odd for some of the romance films she loved so much.

They chatted, ate and drank and, as day turned to night, the cinema screen flickered into life, much to the appreciation of the audience.

Riley packed away the remains of the picnic and then pulled out the sleeping bag from its holder. It was huge.

'Is that a double sleeping bag?'

'King-size actually. The best way to keep warm on chilly nights like this is to cuddle.'

She laughed at the innocent look on his face. He slipped off his shoes, climbed into the oversized bag and lay down, sprawling out on the two large beanbags.

Darcy pulled on her hat and scarf, kicked off her shoes and slipped into the sleeping bag with him, sitting as far away as she could from him, leaving a huge gap in between them.

'It really is roomy, isn't it? We could fit the whole of White Cliff Bay rugby team in here with us.'

Riley scowled at her and she giggled. 'I think you're missing the point of the king-sized sleeping bag. Why don't you shuffle a bit closer? I promise to be completely respectable.'

She shuffled over and he watched her. Feeling mischievous, she sat on his lap, stretching her legs out between his and resting her head on his chest. 'How's that, is this close enough?'

Riley folded the edges of the sleeping bag over them both and wrapped his arms around her, holding her tight. 'This is perfect.'

She felt the smile spread across her face at the sudden co-siness of their relationship. She snuggled into his arms as the film started and the famous opening credits of the fairy tale castle that marked the start of all Disney movies appeared on the screen. As she watched dolphins swim and dive through the sea, her heart leapt with recognition before the title of the film even appeared.

She swivelled slightly so she could see his face. '*The Little Mermaid*?'

He smiled. 'It seemed appropriate.'

She knew her grin couldn't possibly get any wider. 'Surely it's not your thing?'

'I watched this several times with my nieces. My favourite song is "Part of Your World".'

She gasped at his knowledge of her favourite film.

'What's your favourite song?' he asked.

'"Kiss the Girl".'

He laughed as he bent his head to kiss her and she found herself smiling against his lips. She hoped he would want to be a part of her world but that meant opening himself up to the people of White Cliff Bay too. She had to find a way to persuade him to stay because there was no way she was letting him go now.

＊＊＊

Darcy couldn't help but smile as she watched Riley manoeuvre the boat across the silver-dappled bay. It had been a wonderful night. They had stopped at her flat to collect Ben and now they were heading back to the lighthouse for coffee. It had been Riley's suggestion to collect Ben, and Darcy couldn't help wonder about his motives. As much as she liked Riley, she had meant it earlier that day when she said she wouldn't be jumping into bed with him on the first date.

As Riley pulled the boat closer, slinging a rope around a post, Ben leapt ashore and ran up the steps excitedly. Obviously, he was happy about seeing Kelpie again.

Riley stepped onto the rocks and held his hand out to help her ashore.

'I had a wonderful time tonight, thank you so much for taking me to see it. I've never been to an outdoor cinema before and watching my favourite film, cuddled up with you under the canopy of stars, was just magical.'

He pulled her close, kissing her forehead as the gentle waves lapped against the rocks. 'I had a great time too. I never thought for one second I would ever take a date to see *The Little Mermaid* but I thoroughly enjoyed myself too. But then I've done quite a few things recently that I never thought I'd do.' He stared down at her, as if he held her responsible for that.

She leaned her head on his chest, listening to his heart. 'You need to open your mind to different possibilities and adventures. You're in England now and it's one of the most wonderful places in the world. Eat bacon sandwiches, drive a manual car, have a 99 ice cream, eat Marmite on toast, ride a double-decker bus, watch *Coronation Street* or *Ant and Dec*, go to a football match, eat a crisp butty.'

He pulled back slightly to look at her in confusion. 'I don't understand half of what you just said. A crisp butty? What on earth is that?'

'It's a sandwich: two slices of bread filled with crisps, or potato chips, as you call them.'

'That's disgusting.'

'No, it's amazing.'

'We have football in the States, you know.'

'No, you have American football, we have soccer.'

'Oh yes, we have that too, although it's not really big over there.'

'Chocolate Hobnobs, HP brown sauce, afternoon tea, sticks of rocks.' Darcy could feel herself getting excited about all the wonders of England. 'You lock yourself away in the lighthouse, refusing to get involved in the town, you stick to your American foods like Ben & Jerry's and maple syrup, but you are missing out on so much. I am going to make it my mission to educate you in the ways of England over the next few days. You don't want to get involved in town life because you were hurt in the past, and I won't push you on that, but you still need to experience everything England has to offer. At least then, if you do lose the lighthouse, you might want to stay here a bit longer.'

He stared down at her, his eyes almost bottle green in the moonlight. 'OK.'

She smiled. 'Tomorrow, I'll take you somewhere, my choice.'

'I have to do a few hours' work tomorrow, but we could do something tomorrow afternoon or in the evening.'

She nodded.

He took her hand and led her up the steps to the lighthouse. He opened the door and Ben ran inside and up the stairs. Riley switched on the light and closed the door behind them.

'Do you have slumber parties over here?' Riley asked, his attention on her hand, as his thumb ran small circles over her palm.

'We call them sleepovers, why?'

He looked up, his eyes holding hers. 'Do you want to have a sleepover tonight?'

CHAPTER 11

Darcy had no words, which made a change for her.

'No, I don't mean that – unless you want to, of course,' Riley said. 'I just meant to sleep. I've had a lovely night with you and I don't want it to end. If you want, you can sleep in my bed again and I'll sleep on the sofa, but I'd really like to hold you while we sleep. I absolutely promise I won't do anything untoward.'

She smiled at Riley fumbling over his words and she reached out to touch his cheek. 'I'd like to stay.'

Riley let out a laugh of relief. 'I've never had any guests in the lighthouse before apart from Annabel and she definitely didn't count. I've never had anyone else stay over either. So that's new too.'

'Really? You've not had your grandmother over here?'

His face clouded slightly. 'We're not really close.'

'Oh.' Darcy felt a bit sad about that, despite not knowing the woman herself.

'It's nothing to be sad about, I just don't know her. When my dad moved to America thirty-three years ago, Suzanna was, I guess, distraught, and she blamed my mother totally for taking her son away from her. It caused a big rift in the family and they barely spoke after that. I grew up never meeting her or talking to her. We have met a few times since I've come here, but she's a stranger to me. As much as it would be lovely to build a relationship with her and have this wonderful grandmotherly bond, it's a bit hard to conjure that with a woman I spoke to for the first time six months ago. Maybe that will change over time, but . . .'

'Maybe you should invite her over for dinner one night?'

He frowned. 'Maybe,' he said, though he didn't sound too convinced.

'Well, as the first guest in Rose Island Lighthouse, do you want to give me the grand tour? I've only seen the lounge and bedroom. There are other rooms.'

'There's not really a lot to see beyond that. But I'm happy to show you round. The basement is probably the best thing to show you.'

'You have a basement? In a lighthouse?'

'Originally, when the lighthouse was first built, when the tide went out you could walk across the beach to the lighthouse. There were two entrances, one at the very bottom of the lighthouse at the back of the island and this one. But something they've done further down the coast has created a bit of a natural ledge along here and this has made the sea level higher here and the tide never fully goes out any more. It means the bottom entrance is always covered in water. So . . .'

He took her hand and led her to the door in the bottom of the stairs. He switched on a light and went ahead down a very steep ladder. She followed him down and turned around to face the room she was in and gasped.

'These were double doors they fitted to get all the equipment in, so I replaced the doors with glass. Most expensive thing I've had done in the lighthouse because the glass had to be special glass that could withstand the pressure of the sea, but in the daylight the view down here is spectacular, you can see all the fish and . . .' He trailed off as he saw Darcy's expression.

She walked closer to the glass, pressing her face and hands up against it. The water was clear and up above them she could see the moonlit surface shimmering in the darkness. She couldn't see anything else beyond the darkness, but she knew in the daylight it would be a completely different story.

She swallowed down the unexpected emotion that had suddenly hit her like a bus. Riley was looking at her with concern.

'When I was a child, I dreamed that one day I would live in a glass house under the sea. I obviously hadn't figured out the logistics of that, but I envisaged that my bedroom would have this glass roof and I'd lie in my bed and watch the sharks and other animals swimming above my head. I imagined that I would come out every day to feed all the sea creatures and then I'd swim with them all. I drew endless pictures of my dream house until my dad got impatient with my childish dreams and explained how I could never live in a house under the sea.'

She sighed.

'He bluntly told me about the air locks I'd have to have every time I came out the house or my home would flood, that I'd need breathing apparatus to feed and swim with the fish, that no glass would ever be strong enough to support the weight of the sea. He told me about the issues of having electricity and toilets there and everything else I hadn't considered about my dream home under the waves. He basically crushed my dream. I remember feeling worse about that than finding out Santa Claus didn't exist a few years later. And yet you've done it. You're living my dream. I mean, sure it's not a house under the sea, it's just a glass wall but . . . If I lived here, I don't think I'd ever leave this room.'

Riley came to her side. 'I'm sorry that you had your dreams ruined and at such a young age too.'

'He was just being practical.'

'But still . . .'

They stared out at the sparkly blackness for a few minutes as Darcy craned her eyes at possible movement beyond the glass.

'I come here to think a lot. It's very peaceful and you never ever see the same view twice. I was thinking of putting a bed in here, have it as a second bedroom, but I thought that I would miss waking up to daylight. Even when the sun is out it's still quite dark, but maybe I could look at getting a sofa bed in here and we could sleep down here occasionally.'

Darcy looked at him, a smile spreading on her face. They had been on one date and he was already planning their future. But she had felt the connection between them too. There was something between them that was so strong it scared her. It wasn't natural to feel this way about someone she had known for such a short amount of time, but she felt more for him than she had for any of her previous boyfriends. As ridiculous as it was, she could see this man in her future and, judging from the way he had just spoken, he could see that too.

'We'll come back down here tomorrow morning, have breakfast with the fish. We can't feed them, but it's close enough.'

'I'd love that.'

He encouraged her to climb back up the ladder and then he followed her. Holding her hand, he led the way upstairs to the door on the first floor.

'This room belongs to the Lighthouse Trust, it has all the radar equipment and power generators and all the computers and things that help communicate with the main headquarters and keeps everything running smoothly. I don't technically have a key for it.'

'Technically?'

He reached up to a key on a hook above the door. 'The first few times the engineers were called out, they didn't have a key either, so in the end the engineers left the key here in case they had to come back. I'm under strict instructions never to go in here, though.'

He unlocked the door and stepped inside a room filled with electric panels all flashing with little lights as the Lighthouse Trust monitored the workings of the lighthouse.

'Do you know what each panel is for?'

Riley shrugged. 'No idea. From the limited photos I've seen of this place before it was automated, it was very different to all of this.'

She stepped out of his way as he closed and locked the door, returning the key to the hook. He moved on up the stairs and opened the next door.

Inside was a grand piano and a few computers that were lined up next to each other. There were also a few squashy chairs.

'How did you get a piano in here?'

'Like a lot of the furniture, it was delivered in pieces and then put back together once it was in the room. This is just where I work. I like to keep it separate to the rest of my home. No distractions. Well, that's until I see a beautiful mermaid pitch up on my island. That was one pretty fine distraction.'

Darcy blushed.

He closed the door and took her hand. Leading her up the stairs, he stopped outside the bedroom. 'That's the tour, really. You've seen the bedroom and the living room and kitchen. The only other room is the lantern room, which I can't take you to at night. We'd get in the way of the light beam and quite honestly we'd probably blind ourselves.'

'You have a beautiful home. I'm going to do everything I can to help you save it.'

Riley stared at her as if he was trying to work her out. Finally, he looked away.

'So I was going to offer you a coffee, but I'm more inclined to skip straight to the going to bed part. I haven't kissed you anywhere near enough tonight and I'd like to rectify that.'

Her heart leapt at the promise and she nodded.

She followed him into the bedroom, suddenly feeling very nervous. 'Do you have a T-shirt I can change into?'

He nodded and moved to some drawers. He grabbed a black one and gave it to her.

She hesitated, not sure whether to get changed in front of him or not. They were about to sleep in the same bed together and probably kiss until the early hours in the morning; that was probably more intimate than getting undressed in front of him.

Feeling shy, she moved into the bathroom to get changed. She pulled her jumper dress off and the T-shirt on. She debated whether to leave her leggings on, but she knew she would get hot in them, so they came off too. She returned to the room and saw Riley was lying in bed, either naked or at least topless. His eyes swung to her as she walked in and immediately cast down to her bare legs. He quickly looked away, as if he was embarrassed to see her half undressed. She dumped her clothes on top of the drawers, turned out the light so the room was bathed only in the moonlight streaming in through the four windows, and slipped into the bed. Knowing Riley was there next to her was weird and wonderful and terrifying all at once. She heard him roll over towards her and when his hands moved to her waist she realised he was nervous too. She shifted onto her side, wrapping her arms round his neck as he kissed her. It was soft and gentle at first, but very quickly turned to that heated, passionate kiss they had shared on the beach earlier that day. As he pulled her tighter against him, she knew that if he wanted to make love to her there was not a single bone in her body that would try to stop it.

Riley woke up to the early morning sunshine streaming in through the windows and his beautiful mermaid in his arms. She was facing away from him and he was curled round her back. Her gorgeous fiery red curls cascaded over the pillow. His T-shirt had slipped off her shoulder during the night, leaving her pale skin exposed. He tried to ignore how hard he already was for her. It had taken every ounce of willpower the

night before not to take their relationship to the next level.
He wanted to respect her no-sex-on-the-first-date rule. Hell,
he had waited six months for his first girlfriend to be ready to
sleep with him. He had been the perfect gentleman with Sadie,
never pressurising her for more, never even bringing it up until
she was ready. With Cassidy, his ex-fiancée, the physical side
of their relationship had happened very quickly and, looking
back now, the sex had been the only thing that kept them together for so long.

He didn't want his relationship with Darcy to be defined by
sex. He wanted the time to get to know her more. He wanted to
talk to her all day until the sun set and the moon came back out
and then hold her in bed again and talk and kiss some more. But
the more and more time he spent with her, the more attracted
to her he was becoming. She was beautiful, there was no doubt
about that, but she was endlessly fascinating too, intelligent and
funny, kind, sweet, empathic. Lying next to her now but not being able to take it further was driving him insane.

He reached over and kissed her shoulder gently and she
stirred in his arms. Darcy turned over and smiled at him sleepily, her hair falling over her face. She looked dishevelled and
gorgeous and unbelievably desirable.

'Good morning.' He kissed her on the forehead. The forehead was a safe place to kiss her.

'Morning.' She kissed him on the mouth. She was warm
with sleep, and not even fully awake. If he let her, she would go
back to sleep again very quickly, though now he was kissing her,
he had no intention of doing that.

As his tongue slid into her mouth, Riley pulled her closer
against him. He had spent hours kissing her the night before
and it wasn't enough. It would never be enough. She moaned
softly against his lips and the sound of it nearly sent him over
the edge.

He pulled back abruptly and she frowned slightly at his sudden change of mind. Riley prided himself on being a gentleman and being respectful to women. But five seconds' kissing Darcy and all of that went straight out the window. He knew if he didn't stop kissing her right now, his thin grasp on his control would snap.

Riley climbed out of bed and pulled his jeans on. 'Why don't I make some breakfast for us, just come on up when you're ready.'

He bent over and kissed her on the head to take the sting out of his switch in mood and quickly headed upstairs to the living room.

He leaned against the breakfast bar, trying to cool his thoughts. Hearing a noise behind him, he turned to see Darcy there, dressed in just his T-shirt. He had hoped she would be in more clothes by the time she came up for breakfast. She looked incredible and he wasn't sure why the sight of her in just his T-shirt turned him on so much but it did.

She moved closer, a shy smile on her face. 'I missed you.'

Oh God, she was going to be the undoing of him. She ran her hand up his arm and he cupped her face and kissed her. All sense and reasoning went straight out of his mind, the sweet cotton candy taste of her was too much. Riley lifted her and she wrapped her arms and legs around him.

Without taking his lips from hers, he quickly carried her to his recliner, lowering her to it and moving on top of her. With a quick press of the button, he quickly flicked the recliner into the horizontal position. As the chair flipped back, Darcy gave a little shriek and then giggled against his lips. The sound was wonderful.

Riley kissed her again, his hands wandering down her sides and over her hips until he reached the bottom of the T-shirt. As he slid his hand underneath, caressing her silky soft skin, he dragged the T-shirt back up her body and then over her head.

Suddenly he caught himself. She hadn't expressed any wish to make love to him. She was obviously enjoying the kissing, but they hadn't talked about taking it any further. Mortified, he quickly tried to pull the T-shirt back on, but it was balled up in his hand. He quickly shook it out, trying to find the bottom.

'I'm so sorry, I just . . . I'm sorry, I got carried away. I'm such an ass. There's me telling you I would wait until you're ready to make love and here I am ripping your clothes off after only one date. I'm so sorry.'

The T-shirt still wasn't playing ball, as he fumbled to put it back on her; she took it off him and tossed it across the room. Riley stared at her as she reached up and stroked his face.

'I want to make love to you too. I would never have let you get this far unless I wanted that too, so don't even think for one second that you've forced me into doing something I don't want to do. I want this as much as you do.' She ran her fingers down his chest towards the top of his jeans. 'Do you know how much of a turn-on it is to see you so reserved in your normal day-to-day life, but with me you are passionate, impetuous and reckless?'

'It seems I have no control when it comes to you.'

'I love that about you.' She popped open the button at the top of his jeans.

'Are you sure? We can wait. I don't want to rush things.'

'There is nothing I want more right now.'

Riley kissed her softly. Staring into her eyes, a look of understanding passed between them. She wanted this too. Darcy nodded and that was the only other encouragement he needed.

The taste of her, the feel of her skin against his was too much. Darcy was already wriggling out of the rest of her clothes, clearly intent on moving things along too. He wanted to take his time, explore her body, kiss her everywhere, but her frantic movements showed she was as desperate for this as he was.

He grabbed a condom from his jeans pocket and then knelt up to slide it on but caught his first glimpse of her lying beneath him completely naked, her wonderful hair splayed out across the chair, her pale skin almost shimmering in the gold light of the early morning sun. If there was a more beautiful sight in the world than this wonderful woman lying waiting for him, he didn't think he had seen it.

Riley quickly manoeuvred himself on top of her, taking the weight of his body on his forearms as he moved slowly and carefully inside her.

She moaned and he captured the sound of it with his mouth. She felt indescribably good as he thrust inside her again and again. Riley stared into her eyes, feeling the bond between them solidify to something almost tangible. There was never any coming back from this. He was lost to her and it scared the crap out of him.

Darcy woke again later on the sofa with a huge smile on her face. They'd had breakfast together but then Riley had reluctantly needed to get on with some work. He'd asked if she wanted to be taken home or if she would prefer to stay for lunch, if she could occupy herself for a few hours, and she had opted to stay. Darcy had selected one of his books from his bookshelf, curled up on the sofa and fell promptly asleep, clearly worn out from spending half the night kissing and the morning's vigorous antics.

She stretched and padded into the kitchen. It was already lunchtime, so Darcy looked in the fridge for something she could make. There was an abundance of fresh vegetables, so she decided to make a soup. She sung quietly to herself as she cut, diced, boiled and mashed, adding some herbs that she could find in his cupboard and even adding a dash of his favourite maple syrup. But as it slowly simmered on the stove, there was still no sign of him. She cut some bread and laid it on a plate and then went off in search of him.

Darcy went down to the music room and knocked on the door. There was no answer. She didn't want to disturb his work, but he must be getting hungry by now.

She opened the door slightly and poked her head round. He was sitting next to the piano with his headphones on staring at the computer. He didn't seem to be doing a lot of work, though.

She walked over to him and he looked up at her as she approached, his face lighting up into a huge grin. He yanked his headphones off.

'I did knock.'

'Sorry, I didn't hear you with these things on.'

Riley pulled her down into his lap as he nuzzled into her neck.

'You're a sight for sore eyes. Just when I think I might throw my computer through the window out of frustration, you walk in here wearing just my T-shirt and suddenly everything becomes right with the world.'

'You having problems with your work?' Darcy looked at the computer screen at what looked like a very complicated program.

'Yes, I haven't done any all morning. I might have to take you home after lunch. It's too much temptation having you here. All I've thought about is coming upstairs and making love to you again, and when I'm not thinking about that, I'm thinking of how wonderful it was to make love to you this morning.'

He kissed her neck, running his hands over her stomach.

'Are you saying that I'm a distraction?'

'Oh yes, of the very best kind.' He kissed the back of her head. 'I have a song in my head that I want to write, but it's not one I'm contracted to do, so I'm trying to concentrate on the things I'm being paid to do today, though I'm not having much success. My head is all over the place and I'm not sure whether I'm just tired or distracted or something else. I get days like this though, where no matter how hard I try, the words and the music just don't seem to flow together.'

'I read an interview with one of my favourite authors once and she said whenever she got stuck with her own writing, she would read the stories from her favourite authors and be reminded of how beautiful writing could be. Maybe you should listen or play your favourite songs to get you in the mood.'

'That's a good idea.' Riley swivelled the chair they were in to face the piano.

She pressed a few keys on the piano and it made her fingers itch to play again. She had always loved playing it when she was a child and had only given up out of principle, but she still practised it when her parents weren't around to hear her.

'What's your favourite love song?' he asked.

'"Bohemian Rhapsody",' Darcy teased and giggled as Riley played the first few lines of the song with his hands either side of her.

'As much as I love Queen, this song is not particularly romantic.'

'OK, how about "Thinking Out Loud" by Ed Sheeran?'

'Good choice.'

He started playing, the notes flawlessly flowing from his fingers as he started to sing. She smiled as she listened to his wonderful deep baritone voice that had that rich velvety feel to it.

She leaned her head against his shoulder as he came to the end of the song, though the music carried on.

'That was lovely, what's your favourite?' Darcy said.

Without taking his fingers off the keys, the music flowed faultlessly from Ed Sheeran's song into the utterly beautiful 'Songbird' by Eva Cassidy. It was wonderful, and as he sang each line of the song with feeling and passion, she felt tears spring to her eyes. It felt like he was singing it to her.

Eventually, he came to an end.

'That was beautiful.' She turned to look at him and he kissed her softly on the head. 'Has it helped?'

'You know what, I think it might have done. But there are other ways you could help too.'

Darcy looked up at him and saw the dark look of intent in his eyes.

She moved round on his lap so she was straddling him and undid the buttons on his shirt. 'I'm not sure more sex is a good idea when it's distracting you from your work.'

He pulled her T-shirt off and placed a kiss on her shoulder. 'Believe me, it will help.'

She peeled his shirt off his shoulders, caressing his arms and chest. Darcy knelt up so he could wriggle out of his jeans.

'I made soup.'

'You did?'

'I thought you might be hungry.'

He fixed her with a sultry gaze. 'Oh, I am.'

She laughed. 'It will get cold.'

His hands moved to her hips, guiding her down on top of him as he moved inside her. 'We can reheat it.'

Darcy kissed him as he pulled her tighter against him. As they moved slowly against each other she knew she was falling for him. It was the most wonderful feeling in the world and nothing could take that away from her.

Darcy looked at Riley over the dining table. Something had happened after they had made love in the music room, though she wasn't sure what. She had retraced every comment she had made and found nothing untoward, but he had barely spoken over lunch; the affectionate side of him had vanished.

'Are you OK?'

He nodded, absently, not even glancing up from his bowl of soup, which he had barely touched.

A million doubts suddenly ran through her mind. What if he had lost respect for her for sleeping with him on what was technically their first date? What if he had changed his mind about wanting to be with her? She was pushing him too much and he didn't like it. What if the sex was rubbish for him?

As she sat there hoping for some kind of affirmation from him, something that would tell her he wasn't upset with her, every insecurity she'd ever felt suddenly resurfaced. The men in her life never stayed long. She'd never been too upset when relationships had ended in the past because she had never felt a real connection. But she had started to worry that there was something wrong with her, a fear that had been confirmed when her last boyfriend told her sex with her was like making love to a robot. She did all the right moves but there was no emotion there. He'd even called her cold.

Riley had been so completely different, that connection had been there from the first moment they had met. At least it had been for her. If it was over between them already, she would be crushed.

She turned away to face the view so he wouldn't see the tears that had suddenly sprung to her eyes with these thoughts.

'If you've finished, I'll take you home.'

He was being polite and friendly but only an idiot would fail to notice the change between them. Darcy followed him down to the bedroom and quickly got dressed, wanting to escape from the suddenly cold atmosphere. He was waiting for her on the stairs and as soon as she came out of the bedroom, he went on ahead of her. Darcy whistled for Ben and heard a scrabbling of feet on the stairs above.

By the time she got down to the bottom of the lighthouse, Riley was already standing in the boat waiting for her. The waves

were quite choppy today, but there was no question of her staying in the lighthouse until it calmed down. Riley had already
started the engine. As she approached the side, he rushed over
to help her and Ben in. She sat down and watched him negoti-
ate the short distance across the bay with ease, his eyes on the
horizon and not on her.

They pulled alongside the jetty and he stepped up to help
her ashore.

She looked up at him, wondering if this was goodbye.

'Have I done something wrong?'

He shook his head. 'No, sorry, I was just thinking about
work.'

'Can I see you tonight?'

He hesitated just long enough for Darcy to think that he
didn't want to see her. Then he nodded reluctantly. 'I'll meet you
at the pub at seven.'

He kissed her briefly on the forehead and he gave her that
gorgeous half smile before getting back in the boat and heading
back to the lighthouse.

She watched him for a few moments, but he didn't look back.

Darcy hadn't been back in her flat long after walking Ben when
there was a heavy knocking on the door. When she answered
it, George and Libby were both standing there, looking very
excited.

'The article is in the paper. Mum just called, she's in the Bubble and Froth and wants you to come down to see it,' George
said.

With everything that had happened the night before and
that morning, Darcy had almost forgotten about the article.
She still couldn't shake off the feeling that something had gone
wrong between her and Riley, but this would be a good distrac-

tion until she saw him again later that night. She grabbed her bag and followed George and Libby out of the flats.

'Is it good?' Darcy asked. Carmel had said it would be but she really hoped that it would have the desired effect. After all, if Annabel somehow painted Riley, the lighthouse or the town in a bad light, then it would be Darcy's fault for arranging it all.

'Mum didn't say, but she sounded pretty happy.'

They pushed open the door of the pub and Darcy was surprised to see how crowded it was.

'Here she is, the woman behind the article. It wouldn't have happened if it wasn't for our Darcy Davenport,' Verity called and the pub cheered.

Darcy blushed with the attention, as a few people clapped her on the back or shook her hand. When the crowd had calmed down a bit, she approached Verity. 'Is it OK?'

'It's a wonderful article,' Verity said, excitedly. 'There's all the history of the place, presumably from Riley or she's spent her time doing her research, there's all the stuff about the proposals and then there's our hero, Riley, being all rugged and manly and looking for love. Have a look yourself.' Verity handed her a copy of the paper. 'Page five.'

Darcy flicked through and was delighted to see it was a double-page spread. The photo of Riley half naked on the boat with the sun and lighthouse behind him took up half of one page. He looked dramatic and sexy as hell. There was also another photo of one of the elderly couples who were at the interview and then one of them all together looking sad. She started reading and, credit where it was due, Annabel had painted a wonderful story, delivering it with heart and warmth. A large part of the article was about Riley and how he hoped he could find love in the lighthouse just like his dad had. She didn't know if it would make any difference but it was a great article. She just hoped that Riley wouldn't mind the coverage.

Maggie was standing nearby. 'It's great, isn't it? But you should see the comments on the article online, there were over three thousand the last time I looked. A lot of them are from women offering to help Riley out if he is lonely and some saying how hot he is, but many of the comments are getting behind the campaign to save the lighthouse.'

Amy came over and offered Darcy a glass of red wine. '*The Headline* have even set up their own online petition for people to sign to try to save the lighthouse. It's had over a thousand signatures so far.'

'It's got quite a following on Twitter too,' Linda from the bakery said, swiping through her phone. 'The original article has had over seven hundred retweets, loads of people are commenting and tagging Apple Hill Council into the conversation. People are demanding that the council change their mind. "Save Rose Island Lighthouse" is even trending.'

It was like a foreign language. Darcy was obviously aware of Twitter but she'd never been on it. She wasn't sure what retweets, tagging and trending even meant, but it all sounded good.

'The comments on Facebook are quite interesting too,' said a man she had seen in the pub before.

'Have the council said anything?' Darcy said, wondering, not for the first time, if she was going to get into some kind of trouble for this. She started her new job in four days, but surely her involvement in the community would be a good thing, as that was what her job would probably be about.

'No word yet, but I bet they'll change their mind after this. They won't like the spotlight being turned on them in this way,' Verity said.

'Where's Riley?' Libby asked, after reading the article for herself. 'He should be here for this.'

'He's working this afternoon, but he's coming over to the pub later,' Darcy explained, though he certainly wouldn't want all this attention if he did come over.

'We'll have to start the celebrations without him then,' Amy said. 'I'll get more wine.'

Darcy bit her lip nervously. He wouldn't like this one bit.

As it happened, Darcy needn't have worried. Seven o'clock came and went and Riley didn't show. The celebrations had carried on throughout the afternoon and the early evening, with people sharing the comments that were posted on Twitter or Facebook. It was creating quite a movement in the online world but there had been no sign of Riley. She didn't know whether he'd seen the article and regretted exploiting himself in that way, or he had seen the furore erupting on social media and didn't want to face the townspeople, or maybe it had been nothing to do with the article and he just didn't want to see her, but his lack of presence was certainly some kind of message.

It was now past eight o'clock, Riley was an hour late and stupidly they hadn't exchanged numbers yet so she couldn't even call him.

It was possible he had got caught up with work and forgotten what time it was, but now, being over an hour late, it was quite obvious he wasn't coming at all.

Luckily she had been sitting with George, Libby, Verity and a few others for the rest of the afternoon, watching all the excitement playing out online. No one had really noticed that he wasn't there or knew that she had been stood up.

She had been torn with her emotions all afternoon. She was really pleased with the success of the article, and the new friendships that she was making in the town had started to flourish – in just a week she really felt like she belonged there – but the celebrations had been overshadowed by Riley not turning up.

She hadn't moved to White Cliff Bay to look for love, she'd moved because she had always loved the town and she wanted to be close to the sea, to swim and dive in it again. She wanted to make friends and finally build a home for herself, and all that was happening, but now it wasn't enough because Riley wasn't here to enjoy it with her. She hated that he had this effect on her already; that it could hurt when he let her down.

Getting tired of holding the mask on her face, she finished her wine, slung her bag over her shoulder and said her goodbyes.

She left the pub and looked over at the lighthouse. Riley's boat was still bobbing around outside at the back, but there were no lights on inside apart from the lighthouse beam that was diligently keeping watch over the sea.

She thought about going over there to have it out with him, but she decided against it. If he'd wanted to see her, he would have shown up at the pub.

Turning her back on Rose Island, she headed for home.

CHAPTER 12

The next evening Darcy lay on the sofa staring out at the sea. Ben lay next to her, his nose pressed into her armpit as he snored loudly, causing the whole of her body to vibrate.

It had been a weird day. She had unpacked the last of her boxes and then, feeling at a loss about what to do, she had gone into town to buy some paints and ended up painting a terrible mural on the wall of her bedroom. She had envisaged a wall of sea creatures all gliding through the crystal blue waves and multi-coloured seaweed. What she had achieved looked like something a six year old had painted. In fact, a six year old would probably have done a better job. She'd given up after her beloved angel shark had ended up looking like an abnormal potato swimming through a bunch of cherries. She had moved her chest of drawers in front of it and put the paints away in case she was tempted to be creative again in the future. Art had never been her strong point. In fact, nothing seemed to be Darcy's strong point apart from marine biology. She missed that.

She had even walked down to the new aquarium and tried to peer through the windows. Most of it was closed off and not open to public viewing, but she had managed to see a few tanks, glistening in the darkness, waiting for their new inhabitants. She'd felt a pang so strong standing there next to the aquarium, which in a few weeks would be teeming with all that incredible sea life. And right on her doorstep too. She knew that the first thing she would buy with her wages was an annual pass so she could come there every day after work and just sit among the sharks and fish.

She glanced over at the lighthouse feeling completely fed up. How could her spectacular date have ended so badly? She had tried to tell herself all day that she was being irrational, that Riley had said nothing to indicate he didn't want to see her any more or that he was angry with her. She had told herself repeatedly that he was just busy or stressed out with work and had forgotten their date. Maybe his attitude the day before had nothing to do with her. But she couldn't escape the difference in him from the morning before, when he had held her hand almost constantly, when he couldn't keep his hands off her, when kissing her had long become the norm. They had grown so close, so quickly, and she'd thought this thing between them actually meant something. But his distance after they had made love showed that it didn't mean the same to him as it did to her.

She glared at the lighthouse. She had done nothing wrong and if he had changed his mind about being together or if he had an issue with her, then at the very least she deserved to be told that.

There was a knock on her door. She hoped it was Libby, come to take her down to the pub or pop round for a chat; she needed something to cheer her up tonight.

She plastered on a smile and went to answer the door.

Riley was standing there looking every inch the sexy cowboy in worn jeans, black shirt and his faithful hat, but although her heart leapt at the sight of him she couldn't help the smile from falling off her face at his arrival. He was carrying a bunch of flowers though, a tumbling bouquet of blue and purple blooms.

'I am sorry I missed our date last night,' Riley said, softly, taking his hat off.

'Missing our date was bad enough, but what about the way you treated me yesterday afternoon? You barely spoke to me after we made love.'

He frowned. 'I didn't realise . . .'

'You didn't realise? You behaved like an ass farmer – do you have that expression in Texas?'

He nodded.

'We made love and you barely talked to me or looked at me afterwards. I kept thinking maybe I wasn't good enough, maybe you didn't enjoy yourself. A million doubts ran through my head. My parents give me enough reason to doubt myself, I don't need that from you.'

He looked around to see if anyone was nearby, then stepped forward. 'Believe me when I say that making love to you yesterday was the best sex I've ever had. I mean you were good at what you did, Christ you were so good. But it was much more than that. We just . . . sort of . . . fitted. Like we were two pieces of a whole reconnecting. Didn't you feel that?'

She nodded, staring at him in shock before she remembered it was his job to be poetic. But she had felt that connection between them, which made what happened afterwards so confusing.

'So what was it then? Was it me you were pissed off with? Was it something I said or did or were you just being an ass to me because of work or something else that had nothing to do with me?'

'I wasn't . . . pissed. Can I come in?'

'Not really, I was on my way out.' Darcy grabbed her handbag and slung it over her shoulder, then stepped out and closed the door behind her. There was no way she was going to let him think she was sitting around the flat feeling sorry for herself.

'You're going out in your pyjamas?'

She glanced down at her *Finding Nemo* pyjamas that she had changed into after her trip to the aquarium and her heart sank. So much for proving a point.

'These aren't pyjamas. They are the latest fashion in Britain. You've been stuck in that lighthouse for too long. If you came out once in a while, you'd see lots of people wearing them. But I've just realised I've forgotten my purse, so excuse me.'

She grabbed the handle but the door didn't give. She rummaged around in what was obviously an empty handbag to find the keys but there was nothing in there.

'Is there a problem?'

The fight went out of her. 'I'm locked out.'

'Does anyone have a spare key?'

She shook her head. 'My landlord, but he doesn't live in White Cliff Bay.'

'Do you have any windows open?'

She thought for a second. 'Yes, the lounge window is open, but it's too high off the ground.'

'Let me see if I can get in,' Riley said. He handed her the bunch of flowers and walked out the main front door. Darcy found herself glaring after him, annoyed that he was having to come to her rescue.

She followed him out and watched as he pulled himself with ease to the top of the flat part of the banister, which lined the stairs. He stepped across to her windowsill and she let out an involuntary gasp as he wobbled for a second. He looked back and gave her a wink and then, with as much grace as a tightrope walker, he manoeuvred himself round the bay window to the open window on the other side. A second later he had slipped inside her home.

She quickly went back to her front door and Riley opened it from the inside to let her in.

'Thank you,' she muttered, grudgingly.

'Is it possible I can have five minutes of your time before you go out, as reward for my brave deeds?'

He wasn't taking this remotely seriously and that infuriated her, but he was already standing in her flat so telling him to get out and going back in and slamming the door in his face would be stupidly childish, even if that's what she wanted to do. She didn't want to be in a relationship that blew hot, then cold, then hot again. She deserved better than that. She would let him say what he'd come to say and then she would tell him that.

She walked into her flat and resisted the polite British urge to make a cup of tea for her guest. She put the flowers down and wondered if she could play for time by putting them in a vase.

He gestured for her to sit down on the sofa and, when she did, he sat down next to her. 'I'm so sorry about yesterday. I wasn't well. As soon as I got back to the lighthouse, I threw up and then . . .' he trailed off, clearly embarrassed.

'Then?' Darcy prompted. He wasn't being completely truthful and she hated that.

'Then . . . It was coming out of both ends. At the same time.'

Darcy stared at him. He was so embarrassed and clearly telling the truth. She couldn't suppress the smirk on her face at that disgusting image, but partly she was smiling out of relief too. Her mind had conjured a million possibilities of why he didn't want to be with her any more.

He laughed at her reaction. 'It's not funny. I couldn't get off the toilet for hours. I—'

'Stop talking, I don't need to know the details. Wow, Riley, let me share a tip with you for when you are dating a woman. Don't ever share details like that. We like to think of our men as strong and heroic, not sitting on the toilet.'

'I don't want to lie to you, Darcy, ever. I won't share any more details, but I spent almost the whole night in the bathroom. I'm so sorry. I didn't even have your number to call you to cancel. I went to lie down and passed out. When I woke, it was the early hours in the morning so I couldn't even call the pub to let you know either.'

'Why didn't you tell me you weren't feeling well? I would have stayed to look after you.'

'I didn't tell you for that exact reason. I knew you would stay with me and I didn't want you there to witness that. All through lunch I could feel my stomach churning and I knew I was going to be sick. It came on so fast and I just wanted you out of there as quickly as possible so I didn't throw up in front of you. I hoped once I was sick that I would feel better, but I didn't recover until this morning. I stayed in the lighthouse all day just in case it came back but I've been fine, although a little tired. I really am sorry.'

She leaned her head against him, smiling with relief.

'I had a wonderful time on our date and yesterday morning. I don't want to do anything to ruin that.' He dug in his pocket and pulled out another ammonite, a creamy coloured one, encased in its rocky grave.

She smiled. 'I have a first-kiss ammonite, our first-date ammonite and now our first-toilet-incident ammonite.'

'How about our first-apology ammonite, if we're to give it a label. We don't need to taint it with its sordid details.'

She took it and ran her fingers over the lumps and bumps. 'I hope there won't be lots of these.'

'I imagine there will be many. Relationships are a bumpy road and it won't always be plain sailing for us. But these ammonites have survived millions of years, as you said, they've survived storms and tides and waves. If they can survive that, then they can be a reminder for us that we can survive a few bumps in the road along the way.'

'So we're OK? You're not having second thoughts about us?'

He kissed her on the head. 'A girlfriend was the last thing I wanted when I came here. I never wanted to put my trust in anyone again in case it was betrayed. I wanted to come to this lighthouse, write my songs all day and speak to the least amount of people possible. Then this mermaid comes crashing into my life and everything changes.'

Darcy swallowed. 'Good change or bad change?'

'The best change.'

She found herself smiling slightly.

'You're the best thing that has happened to me in the last few months. Hell, you're the best thing that has happened to me in the last few years and I'm not going to throw it away. I promise that me being quiet yesterday was only because I was sick, there is no other reason.'

She cuddled into him and he put his arm around her.

'Did you see the article?'

'I saw it today. It's nicely written. Very embarrassing, though. I started reading the comments and so many women were proposing to me. They've never even met me and they just see me half naked in the boat and they decide they want to marry me. It's the strangest thing.'

'Well, you can have your pick of beautiful women now.'

'There's only one beautiful woman I want and she's right here next to me.'

Darcy smiled. 'I don't know if the article will do anything to help, but public interest is a wonderful thing in these cases. I hope you're not finding the attention too overwhelming.'

He shrugged. 'Whatever is hot news today will be lining the cat litter trays tomorrow. Me sailing my little boat will be almost forgotten in a day or two. I do appreciate your help, though. I love how much you care.'

He kissed the top of her head.

'Did you work today?' she asked.

'Not really. When I write a new song, I kind of have a tendency to close in on myself to be able to concentrate on the notes, the lyrics, the tempo. I am very good at shutting out all distractions, focussing solely on my music for those hours of the day that I'm working on it. In Texas, I would see Cassidy most nights. I would look forward to seeing her, but when I was working on my music she didn't even enter my head. The last few days I have barely got any work done and it's driving me insane. I can't think straight, the words don't fit. If there is such a thing as a mojo, I've well and truly lost it.'

Darcy looked up at him with concern. 'Because you're worried about the lighthouse?'

He stared at her. 'Because every time I close my eyes to imagine the notes, the cadence, the rhythm, I can only see you, your smile, your eyes, your lips. If you're not with me, I actually miss you. I want to talk to you, hear you laugh, listen to your stories.'

Riley fished his phone out of his pocket. 'I've had this song in my head for the last few days, not one that I can ever do anything with, but I couldn't stop thinking about it. I wanted some time to get it down and out of my head today. I thought once I had written it, I could put it away and get on with the stuff I'm being paid to do. What I thought would take me an hour has ended up taking all day. I wanted to make it better, I wanted it to be perfect and quite honestly it's probably the best song I've ever written. Would you like to hear it?'

Darcy nodded.

Riley swiped the screen on his phone. 'I saved it on here. It's not the best quality, the cell doesn't have the best speakers, but I'll play it for you properly when you come back to the lighthouse.'

He pressed a button and Darcy could hear the beautiful chords of the piano, which sounded like the big intro of a typical romantic movie score. And then through the phone's speakers, Riley started singing in that deep, rich baritone voice that sent goosebumps down her body and made her smile straight away.

'Don't laugh,' Riley said, smiling. 'My voice is awful. I don't write the songs for me, I write them for other people.'

'I love it, it's wonderful.'

Riley shook his head. She tuned back into the song again and the smile fell from her face as she listened to the lyrics. The song was about a beautiful mermaid who bewitched a man who lived on an island and all the tiny things that the man liked about her. Some parts were funny, gently mocking the English ways of the mermaid, but mostly it was beautiful, and although love was not mentioned at all throughout the song, it was clear the man on the island was completely smitten with his mermaid.

The song came to an end and Riley stared at her.

Eventually he spoke. 'So I hope . . .' The rest of his words were lost when Darcy leaned forward and kissed him.

Immediately his hands went to the back of her head, his fingers tangling with her curls as his tongue slid into her mouth. He tasted so good. He moved his hands down her back, pulling her against him as he sank back into the sofa, taking her with him.

Eventually she pulled back from him slightly. 'I can't believe you wrote a song about me.'

'I write songs about anything that touches me – an overheard conversation, an elderly couple walking along the beach, a summer's day – but you are the most beautiful, most interesting inspiration I've had for a very long time.'

She smiled and kissed him again. It was silly to have those doubts, but whereas previously she hadn't really cared when men had lost interest in her, with Riley it mattered. For the first time, she wanted this relationship to work, but they had to be honest with each other if that was going to happen.

She pulled back slightly and snuggled into his side, interlocking her fingers with his. 'What happened in Texas that caused you to run? How were you betrayed?'

He frowned and shook his head. 'I'd rather not talk about it.'

'I know we've only been on one date but I feel closer to you than anyone I've ever been involved with before. You know so much about me, but I know so little about you. I want this to work. I know that whatever happened has made you fear getting hurt again, but if I don't know what that is, I can't be sure not to hurt you in the same way.'

He stared down at her and sighed. 'As you know, I lived in a very small town in Texas – there were probably no more than two hundred people who lived there. I was born and raised there and everyone knew everyone else. Not just as acquaintances either, real friends. If someone had a barbecue, almost the whole town would come. Everyone knew everyone's business. If someone was in trouble, the whole town would come to help.'

'Sounds wonderful.'

Riley pulled a face. 'Cal Grayson was my next-door neighbour's kid. Eighteen years old and the most promising football talent you've ever seen. This kid was incredible on the field and you just knew he was going to be this huge professional star. He got a football scholarship to go to college and everyone in the town couldn't be prouder and more excited for him. One night, just before he was due to start college, I was driving back to my house and Cal's car smashed straight into mine.'

'Oh God, was he killed?'

'No, he was fine, we both were, thankfully. It wasn't a bad smash and although my car was badly damaged, neither of us was injured. But when I got out to see if Cal was OK, it was very clear the kid was drunk. I'm not talking a bit tipsy, I'm talking couldn't-stand-couldn't-walk-was-barely-conscious kind of drunk.'

'Oh no.'

'Cal immediately told me not to say anything to anyone and went to get back in the car to drive home. I tried to stop him, but he took a swing for me and pushed me down into the dirt. The next thing, he gets back in the car and drives off, despite my best efforts to stop him. The worst thing was Jenny, my fiancée's kid sister, was passed out in the car with him. They had been seeing each other for a while. I knew that if he was arrested for DUI he could lose his scholarship for college, but it was better that than lose his life or kill Jenny or anyone else on the road. It took me about five seconds to decide and I called the police. They caught up with him up the road and arrested him, miraculously before he managed to do any real damage to anyone. But he lost his scholarship and probably his dream of ever playing professional football, and the whole town turned against me because of it.'

'No! But you did the right thing. You probably saved his life and Jenny's.'

'I know I did the right thing, and faced with that decision again I wouldn't change a single thing. But the rest of the town, including my fiancée, her parents, Cal's parents and even my sister's husband, didn't see it that way. Apparently I should have handled it myself, I should have called Cal's parents. I should have kept it quiet. They said I was mad about my car and that Cal had pushed me over and that's why I called the police. Cal was driving his car like a maniac and it was only a miracle that stopped Cal killing himself or someone else before the police caught up with him.'

She squeezed his hand to show him she understood.

'My friends, my teachers, my doctor, my neighbours, people I had grown up with my whole life suddenly started treating me like I was a convicted rapist or murderer. I was the scum of the earth and the people in the shops and restaurants even stopped serving me. The only person who stood by me was my brother, Max. Even my sister became distant, as she was married to Cal's older brother. I was betrayed by every single person I had ever known and loved. I put up with it for a couple of months, but it never got any better. So after spending Christmas utterly alone because no one wanted anything to do with me, I packed up my bags and moved here.'

'I'm so sorry you went through that. I understand now why you don't want anything to do with the people in the town. You don't want to make friendships in case you're betrayed again.'

'I know it's silly. I know nothing like that will happen again here but I never thought a whole town of my friends, and even my family, would turn against me for trying to save a kid's life. It hurt, more so than my fiancée suddenly wanting nothing more to do with me, and I swore I'd never let anyone get that close to me again. Though I'm re-evaluating that promise.'

She smiled. 'You are?'

'Some people are worth the risk.'

She leaned up and kissed him briefly on the lips. 'I totally understand how utterly hurt and disappointed you must have been, but you are missing out by closing yourself off to friendships and relationships. We need other people in our life. My aunt Ginny lived here for over thirty years and she never really had anyone she could call a friend. That makes me so sad to think of her alone for all that time.'

'I have you. I don't need anyone else.'

She didn't know whether to be flattered or saddened by that, but she wasn't going to push it for now.

'I'm still going to try to anglicise you. If you lose the lighthouse, I want you to stay here, even if you do want to be an antisocial git.'

He smiled. 'I'm happy to try these things, but I'm still not going to eat a crisp butty.'

'We'll see.' She rolled off him, pulled a hair tie off her wrist and tied up her hair in a loose bun. 'I'm going to make you an English tea.'

'I've had English tea, PG Tips or Tetley. It's nice.'

Darcy laughed. 'Tea as in dinner, not tea as in a cup of tea. It's slang. I'm going to make you a meal consisting of all things

British. I haven't got a lot in but I certainly can make a start on your English lessons.'

Riley sat up. 'I'm having tea for my dinner? I think that's enough of a change to start with.'

'You don't get out of it that easily.' She moved to a cupboard and pulled out a picnic blanket and spread it on the lounge floor. 'We're going to have a picnic.'

'We have those in Texas, you know, although normally it's outdoors.'

'Indoor picnics are much better, no bugs landing on the food, no rain spoiling all the fun. We used to do this a lot when we were kids because the British weather is so unpredictable. My aunt always used to have us round her house and we'd have picnics in her lounge.'

'Why don't we just sit at the table?' Riley looked confused and utterly adorable.

'Because this is fun, I promise.'

She ran into the kitchen and put two crumpets and one piece of bread under the grill to make toast. She opened up a can of baked beans and poured the contents into a saucepan. She grabbed a few other things and put them on several plates. It was going to be a mishmash of different foods but it would be fun to see Riley try everything. As the toast and crumpets cooked, she took the rest of the plates out to the blanket, much to Riley's amusement. She lit some candles and placed them around the room and drew the curtains to make it cosier.

She ran to the bedroom, grabbed a few things and then went back to the kitchen to dish up the beans on toast and crumpets before taking them back to the lounge as well.

As she knelt on the blanket, Riley shifted off the sofa onto the blanket too. She smiled, loving that he was humouring her.

'OK first up, this is Cornish cider.' She passed him a can of her favourite drink.

He cracked the ring pull and took a long swig. 'Very nice.'

Darcy laughed. 'Well, that might be the only thing you like tonight. As your starter for this evening we have crumpets. You can spread whatever you like on these, jam, peanut butter, cheese, but traditionally we British like to smother them in butter.'

Riley, taking it all very seriously, picked up the crumpet and examined it, then he scooped up a knob of butter and went to spread it on the brown side.

'No, the other side, that's the bottom,' Darcy laughed.

Riley flipped it over and spread the butter over the top. He offered it out for her approval and when she nodded he took a big bite out of it, frowning slightly as he ran the crumpet over his tongue and rolled it round his mouth.

'The texture is weird.'

Darcy giggled as he finally chewed it and swallowed. He obviously didn't hate it as he took another bite, though he still didn't look entirely convinced.

'OK, for the main course, this is beans on toast.'

'What? Baked beans on toast? That's disgusting.'

'No, it's a big thing here. It's wonderful.'

'Doesn't the toast go all soggy?'

'Well, yes, but that's kind of the point.' She cut the piece of bread in half and handed him a plate with his half on, covered in beans.

She tucked into her own piece as Riley examined his with a look of horror and disgust.

'Just try it, it won't kill you.'

'You don't know that.'

Finally, he took his knife and fork, cut a small piece off and popped it in his mouth. She could see that he liked this even less than the crumpets.

'You might want to try your next bite with some brown sauce.'

'What's brown sauce?'

'HP sauce.'

'But what flavour is it?'

Darcy shrugged and giggled. 'It's just brown.'

'Brown flavoured?'

'Yes, that's right.'

His mouth pulled up into that gorgeous half smile. He squirted the tiniest blob of sauce on top of the beans.

'You don't do anything with gay abandon, do you? Everything is controlled and reserved.'

He shrugged, still chuckling over the brown sauce as he popped it into his mouth. His eyebrows shot up in pleasant surprise. He chewed it for a few seconds. 'Oh, that isn't so bad. I'm not overly impressed with the soggy toast with beans, but it doesn't taste too bad with the brown-flavoured sauce.'

'OK, now for a crisp butty.'

'No. No way. I draw the line at that.'

'It's nice. I made you a cheese and onion one.' She passed him the plate and he shook his head.

'It's a potato chip sandwich. That's just weird.'

'OK, leave it for now. We'll move on to dessert.'

'Is that what's under the mystery bowl?' Riley's hand went to the upside down bowl mischievously.

'No, that's for later. Hands off. I wanted to give you spotted dick for pudding but I'll have to take you to the Bubble and Froth for that. I've seen it on the menu and they serve it with custard, so I'm sure it's gorgeous.'

'Spotted dick? Are you kidding me?'

'No, it's a suet-spongey-type pudding with fruit. It's very nice, anyway we don't have that, we have chocolate Hobnobs and . . .' She trailed off as Riley burst out laughing.

'Hobnobs and spotted dick, what kind of weird ass country have I moved to?'

'Hobnobs are a biscuit – a cookie, as you guys call it. And we have a Mr Kipling's Bakewell tart and a Curly Wurly.'

'Oh, Cadbury's. We have that in the States. It's cool. I like their chocolate. Don't think I've had a Curly Wurly before, though.' He unwrapped the bar of chocolate and took a big bite. His face contorted in confusion, as he chewed his way through the sticky toffee. Eventually, he swallowed it. 'Probably the best thing I've tasted all night.' He picked up the Hobnob and took a bite of that and again he nodded his approval. Finally, he picked up the Bakewell tart, peeled back the silver wrapper and took a bite of that too. 'That's nice, a bit sweet, but nice. Now do I get to see what's under the bowl?'

'Only if you finish your crisp butty.'

Riley laughed. 'I need to see what is at stake first. I'm not eating a crisp butty to win another crisp butty.'

'No, I think you'll like the prize.'

Riley didn't look too sure and he tried to take a sneaky peek under the bowl, but Darcy swiped his hand away.

Sighing theatrically, he picked up the sandwich and took a bite. It crunched in his mouth and his face screwed up with another look of disgust. Darcy pulled the hair tie out of her hair, shaking out her long curls, and Riley stopped chewing midmouthful as he stared at her. He quickly swallowed and tentatively took another bite, not taking his eyes off hers. To reward him for his efforts she pulled her pyjama top off and his eyes bulged. He took another big bite and she stood up, taking a step towards him and sliding down her pyjama bottoms. He shoved the rest of the sandwich in his mouth, so his cheeks bulged like a hamster's and she slid her knickers down too, trying her best to be seductive. Completely naked, she knelt next to him as he desperately tried to finish his sandwich. Slowly, she undid the buttons on his shirt and as he swallowed down the last mouthful he helped her by shrugging out of it. He took a big swig of cider to help wash down the rest of the sandwich as she tackled the buttons of his jeans.

He cupped her face, kissing her hard and making desire crash through her. His hands cradled her as he lowered her to the floor, moving on top of her as the kiss continued.

He pulled away slightly. 'If you're the prize for eating a crisp butty, what's underneath the bowl?'

She leaned over slightly to lift the bowl up, revealing three condoms. He laughed and quickly grabbed one. 'I've changed my mind. I love indoor picnics.'

CHAPTER 13

Darcy woke in the middle of the night lying on Riley's chest with his arms tight around her as if he never wanted to let her go. Moonlight streamed in through the window, painting Riley's bare chest and face with a silvery glow. He was fast asleep.

Everything had happened so quickly between them, she'd barely had a chance to draw breath. He meant so much to her already. She'd never believed in love at first sight, and she had never been in love before, but with Riley her feelings were so strong that it was hard to define them as anything else. It was ridiculous. Her parents always said she was a dreamer, living her life with her head in the clouds. If she told them now that she had fallen in love with the lighthouse keeper just days after meeting him, they would laugh so loud she would probably hear them all the way down in White Cliff Bay. But she couldn't escape the feeling that this thing between them was something beyond lust and sex, it was something serious and life-changing. They talked and laughed together about anything and everything. It had taken a lot for him to tell her about his problems in Texas and it felt like they had moved forward now. She just hoped that he felt the same way as her.

She pressed her mouth gently to his chest, kissing where his heart was. He didn't stir.

'You're the best thing that has happened to me too,' Darcy whispered.

A smile spread across his beautiful face and her heart leapt, knowing he had heard it. He opened his eyes and smiled at her, stroking his hand through her hair.

'Did I wake you?' she asked.

'I was awake, thinking about you, about us.'

She shifted up so she was face to face with him and he rolled onto his side, taking her with him.

'I was thinking about us too. I've never had a relationship like this before. The boys I've been with, it started off nice and then sometimes it developed into something nicer but it's never been like this. This feels like everything all at once . . .' She trailed off, knowing she sounded like a crazy person. How to scare off the man you were falling for in one easy lesson. All she had to do now was start talking about marriage and babies and there would be a Riley-shaped hole in her bedroom wall. Although surprisingly Riley didn't seem perturbed by her words.

Instead, he leaned forward and kissed her gently. There was no urgency from him as there was usually; it was soft, tender and languid. But it didn't lessen the desire she felt for him. As he ran his hand slowly down her side to her waist, the feel of his fingers caressing her skin was like velvet. He traced his hand down the back of her leg towards her knee and then hooked her leg over the top of his hip. He shifted himself closer and, without taking his mouth from hers, he slid carefully and gently inside her. He hardly moved at all as he kissed her, almost as if he just wanted to be connected to her in every possible way. She pulled him closer with her leg, needing to feel him against her. He moaned softly against her mouth as he finally started to move against her, rolling gently on top of her. She stared into his eyes as he continued in his slow, unhurried love-making.

He was right. They did fit together. In every possible way.

'So this is . . .what? A bacon sandwich?' Riley asked, poking at it suspiciously, and Darcy giggled.

'Just eat it.'

She watched as he tried to suppress a smile as he tucked into the sandwich. He loved winding her up.

'Try it with brown sauce.'

'The brown-flavoured sauce?'

'Yes, that's right.'

He shook his head in disbelief and she snorted.

'What do you have planned today? Do you wish to continue with your English lessons or have I put you off with crumpets and crisp butties?'

'Sadly, the English lessons will have to wait, I really do have work to do. And that's not me pushing you away or not wanting to be with you, it genuinely is a need to work.'

She smiled. 'It's OK. I understand.'

'And it's a shame because I was really looking forward to trying this disgusting Marmite stuff you've been telling me about. But sadly there is no time.'

Darcy laughed. She didn't blame him; she couldn't stand the stuff either.

'Why don't I come over later this afternoon and we can do something English then?' Riley said. 'Something that hopefully doesn't involve Marmite.'

'That would be great. I have just the plan too.'

'I look forward to it.'

He finished off the last bite of his sandwich and stood up.

He stopped as he noticed the painting of the man Ginny had painted propped up against the wall. He stared at it.

'My aunt painted him. I think it was someone she was in love with once, someone that lived round here.' She gestured to the tiny White Cliff Bay that could be seen through the window in the painting. 'Though I have no idea who it is. If the little old lady I met in The Crabshack is to believed, he's called Tom or John, used to ride a motorbike and moved to Australia or Austria. It's not a lot to go on. I keep meaning to take a photo of it and ask around town.'

He swallowed. 'I know who it is.'

'You do?'

'That's my dad.'

'What?' She glanced up at him in shock. 'Are you sure?'

'Very sure. This was him a lot younger than I remember him, maybe thirty years ago, but it's definitely him. I've seen photos of him at my parents' wedding, he doesn't look much older than he does here.'

She stared back at the painting. 'What was his name?'

'Thomas. Everyone called him Tom.'

'And he moved to America not Australia.'

Riley nodded. 'He also used to have a motorbike.'

'Your dad had an affair with my aunt,' Darcy said.

'In the lighthouse, too. That's the view from my bedroom window.'

She looked at the man who had broken her aunt's heart. 'I think she was in love with him. She packed up her whole life and came to live here, but he'd already gone. Did he speak of her at all?'

'Not by name. There was someone who broke his heart. He only said that they fell in love and she chose her job over him. He said it was his fault too, he let her go and never went after her. When he met my mom and fell in love with her, he said he knew that he wasn't going to make the same mistake twice. When she went back to Texas, he went with her.'

'He never knew that Ginny came back for him.'

'I guess not. Or maybe he did but he was already happily married to my mom by that point. They got married very quickly once he moved to Texas and she got pregnant with me straight away. There was no coming back after that.'

'It's so sad, it could have ended very differently.'

'Maybe. But if it had and I was the son of Dad and Ginny instead of Dad and Mom, then we'd be cousins and I'm pretty sure what we did in bed this morning would be illegal.'

Darcy laughed. 'It is a bit weird, though. Two generations of my family dating the lighthouse keeper.'

'It is. But there's one notable difference between this generation and theirs. I have no intention of letting you go.'

She smiled and leaned up to kiss him.

He kissed her briefly on the lips and placed a lingering kiss on her forehead. 'I should go.'

She followed him to the door and he gave her another brief, sweet kiss on the lips before putting his hat on and walking out the flat.

She watched him go, and he got as far as the top stair outside the flat before she ran after him. 'Riley.'

He turned and caught her as she threw herself into his arms, kissing him hard. He hauled her tight against him, kissing her back with equal fervour and not caring who saw. Eventually, he pulled away.

'Something to think about while you work.'

He pretended to scowl at her, straightened his hat on his head and walked away, giving her a wink over his shoulder as he did.

She couldn't help smiling as she watched him disappear towards the jetty. Everything was perfect. Moving to White Cliff Bay had been the best decision she had ever made.

Strolling through the town later, Darcy couldn't help the huge smile spreading on her face. The sun was shining and the gentle clink of boats out in the bay and the call of the seagulls filled the air. As it was Saturday, children ran around chasing each other with water pistols, while others sat on the sea wall with ice cream round their faces. People smiled at her as she walked past and a few of them she had chatted to before waved at her and called out their hellos. She was starting a new job on Monday. Working within this community was going to be wonderful. Everything was perfect and the cherry on top of the really big fat cake was being completely in love with the lighthouse keeper. And, although he hadn't said anything yet, she was pretty sure Riley felt the same. He had let her in and explained his fears and she knew they had moved past that now.

'Excuse me!' A round old lady called from the doorway of the chemist, waving her hands frantically in Darcy's direction.

Darcy looked around to see if she was waving at anyone else, but as no one was close she guessed the lady was waving at her. She jogged over the road towards her.

'Hello, are you OK?'

'Darcy Davenport, I presume?' The old lady looked her up and down.

Darcy jolted a bit that she knew her name, but she nodded.

'And is it true that you are sleeping with my grandson?'

Darcy felt her mouth fall open. This must be Suzanna, Riley's grandmother. But how could she possibly know that they were sleeping together? The town grapevine was one thing, but unless Suzanna had cameras in Riley's bedroom or hers, there was no way she could know. And knowing how private Riley was about his life, Darcy wasn't going to talk about it either.

'Riley and I are friends,' Darcy tried.

Suzanna scoffed. 'Friends with benefits, from what I've heard.'

Darcy really didn't like the thought of people discussing her sex life, especially as the townspeople had obviously been filling in the gaps of their knowledge with their own embellishments. Riley would be mortified too. How could she encourage him to embrace town life if they were all gossiping about them behind his back?

'And what have you heard, Mrs Eddison? I didn't realise that Riley and I had been so indiscreet as to shag each other in the middle of the street.'

Suzanna's eyes bulged and then she hooted with laughter. 'I like you. I think you'll be perfect to bring my straight-laced grandson out of his shell. Why don't you come in for a bit and we can have a chat over a cup of tea and a slice of cake?'

'I'd be happy to come and chat to you for a bit, but I'm not discussing my relationship with Riley.'

'Of course not, dear.' Suzanna grabbed her firmly by the arm and frogmarched her into the shop. 'Cathy dear, can you watch the shop for me for a while?' she shouted across to a near identical old lady, who nodded.

Still holding her arm, Suzanna pushed a door open at the back of the shop and escorted Darcy along a narrow corridor and into a warm lounge. Despite the warmth of the day, the lounge obviously had all the radiators or heating turned up and it was like walking into an oven. Darcy immediately shrugged out of her tiny cardigan, but Suzanna didn't seem to notice anything was amiss. There was a red velvet sofa that filled one side of the room and two small red velvet armchairs on either side, but everywhere was covered in lace doilies. The arms and the backs of the sofa and chairs, the coffee table had three large ones, and all the shelves had them positioned underneath tiny cottages in all shapes and sizes, which Darcy recognised were from the Lilliput Lane collection. There were even doilies on top of the TV. And there was an extra-large doily that served as a lace rug in the middle of the room.

'Tea, coffee?' Suzanna asked, practically bursting with excitement at having Darcy there.

'Tea, please.'

'Banana cake?'

'Yes, that would be lovely.'

'Please sit down,' Suzanna said and Darcy was surprised she wasn't given her own personal doily to sit on. Suzanna bustled off towards the kitchen and she could hear clanking of cups and plates from the room next door.

Darcy looked around nervously. What were they going to talk about that would be appropriate, considering she was sleeping with Suzanna's grandson?

Suzanna came back out with a banana cake that was bigger than Darcy's head. It was topped with white icing and even had a tiny marzipan banana sitting on the top. 'I made it fresh today, dear, help yourself to a slice and I'll be back in a moment with the tea.'

Darcy cut two large slices and dished them out onto the two china plates as Suzanna came back in with a tray holding two china cups and saucers, a bright red teapot, and even a sugar bowl with silver tongs and a small jug of milk. It made Darcy smile, but this was obviously the norm for Suzanna.

Suzanna sat down and served two cups of tea, passing one to Darcy before sitting back in her armchair and eyeing her speculatively.

Neither said anything for a moment and the gold carriage clock on the mantelpiece ticked loudly between them.

Suddenly, Darcy had an idea. 'Verity mentioned that you knew my aunt Ginny?'

Suzanna's face fell a little. 'I did.'

'I know she was seeing Riley's dad for a while, but I don't know any of the details.'

'He broke her heart.'

'I gathered that. Though I don't think she was entirely blameless. Do you know what happened?'

'I don't know a lot, but I'll tell you what I know. She came down here on holiday and met Tom on her first day. They fell madly in love and she spent a lot of time over at the lighthouse with him. I think she was here for three weeks and then she went back to her life in London. He begged her to stay but she said she couldn't leave her job. She had a high-powered job in London, I think.'

'She was a solicitor.'

'Yes. She had spent years working her way up the law firm she worked for and she didn't want to just throw it all away. She left and Tom had no way of contacting her. He moped around for a month and then Claudia turned up in the town. It was quite obvious she was just rebound sex for Tom. Someone to distract him from losing Ginny. They were into each other, but it wasn't love. When she went back to America, he went with her. I was furious that he would walk away from his life here for something that I thought was nothing more than a fling. I said some really hurtful things about Claudia and we had a big row about it. She got pregnant, and they married as soon as he found out. We had another row and we hardly ever spoke again. Then Ginny showed up just a few weeks after he'd left. She'd packed up her job, sold her house and moved down here to be with Tom, but he was already gone. She never saw him again either.'

It was a slightly different story to the one that Riley had told her about his parents. But then Suzanna obviously didn't like Claudia, so her version of events would be slightly skewed.

'Riley says his parents were very much in love.'

'I imagine that they were eventually. They stayed married until they died and had three children together. But the way he was with Claudia was so different to how he was with Ginny. What he had with Ginny was the real thing, I'm sure of it. With Claudia it was lust that grew into fondness and love over the years they were together, but it certainly didn't start that way. When I told him Ginny had come back for him, he went all quiet and said he had to think. I think he was thinking of coming back.

Next thing I heard was that Claudia was pregnant and they were getting married. I don't know if she trapped him into staying by getting pregnant or whether it was an accident, but he never came home. He was loyal and I brought him up to always do the right thing. I just never imagined that the right thing would be breaking Ginny's heart. That he'd choose Claudia over Ginny.'

Darcy sipped her tea and broke off a large piece of the cake and nibbled at it. It must have hurt Ginny to know that Tom had moved on so quickly, having the marriage and children that she never had.

'And Ginny never went back to London once she realised that Tom wasn't coming home?'

'She was waiting for him. She wasted her whole life waiting and hoping he'd come home for her. There was never anyone else for her after that. I worry that the same thing will happen with you and Riley.'

Darcy's head snapped up. 'What do you mean?'

'I don't think he has any intention of staying. He hasn't made any friends, he keeps himself to himself. Now, with all the business of the lighthouse being pulled down, there's no reason for him to stay. I asked him about it a few weeks ago and he said he'd be going back to America once the lighthouse gets pulled down. I worry that you'll be left with a broken heart just like your Ginny.'

Darcy shifted awkwardly. 'I hope I'm enough to make him want to stay.'

'Oh, don't mind me. I'm sure it's very different for you two. From what I hear, he's completely smitten.' She paused while she took a sip of tea herself. 'Will you tell me about him?'

Darcy opened her mouth to protest, but Suzanna held up her hand to stop her.

'I don't want to know about your sex life. Normally I'd love to hear all the saucy details of a new couple in the town, but even I draw the line at listening to stories about my own grand-son. I don't even want to know about your relationship. If you wish to keep that private, then I respect that. I just want to know about him. He is thirty-two years old, my own grandson, and I know nothing about him. And I know that's my fault, silly bitter old fool, and it's probably too late to start a relation-ship with him now – Lord knows I've tried – but I'd just like to know what he is like. What kind of things interest him, what makes him tick. We've talked four times since he moved here six months ago, and while he is very polite he's a stranger to me and I don't want him to be.'

Darcy's heart ached for her, for the lost relationship with Su-zanna's son and three grandchildren and probably great-grand-children that she would never get to meet.

'Riley is a wonderful man. Kind, respectful, a real gentleman,' Darcy said. 'He is a musician, he writes songs for other artists. He is hugely talented and very passionate about his music.'

Suzanna nodded, leaning forward in her chair, drinking in all the details. As Darcy continued to talk, the tea grew cold on the table between them.

Riley could see Darcy was standing on the jetty waiting for him as his boat chugged across the bay towards her. The warm sum-mer breeze flew around her, causing her dress to blow and her hair to cascade out like a fiery red banner. And for Riley there was no finer sight than that. Well, apart from that hair cascading over the floor or the bed when she lay naked underneath him. That was the best thing he had ever seen. He hoped she would come back with him to the lighthouse that night and recreate that image several times over.

He had been much better focussing on his work that day. Knowing he was going to be seeing her that afternoon had at least made him stop thinking about her every second, though he couldn't banish thoughts of her entirely. She made him smile so much, and it had been a long time since he had smiled or laughed. Her attempts to anglicise him were funny, sweet and in many cases downright disgusting, but he wouldn't change a single moment. And regardless of the taste and texture, crisp butties were now his new favourite thing ever.

Darcy was wearing a sea-blue dress with white flowers around the hem and her futile attempts to tame her hair in the wind just made him smile even more. She still reminded him of a mermaid, her hair making her look wild and dangerous, as if it were caught in the waves. She was dangerous too, but mainly because he knew he was falling for her and he was still a bit fearful of that.

He drew alongside the jetty, threw a rope around one of the poles and turned off the engine. He secured the rope and looked up to see Darcy holding out her hand to help him out. He smiled at the cheeky grin on her face as he took her hand and pulled himself up onto the jetty.

'Hello, Miss Davenport.' He touched the rim of his hat and watched her blush with delight at his gesture.

'Hello there, yourself.' She leaned up and kissed him. She tasted so sweet and her cotton candy scent wrapped around him. He was tempted to bundle her back in the boat and whisk her back to the lighthouse now. She pulled away before he could get too carried away with the kiss. 'Are you ready for more English lessons?'

'Yes, what do you have planned for me this afternoon?'

She linked arms with him and they walked along the beach towards the main town.

'We are riding on a double-decker bus and going to see something that is entirely British.'

'I look forward to it. And then will you accompany me back to the lighthouse afterwards?'

'I'm going to the Save the Lighthouse meeting at the town hall tonight, but I'll come by after.'

He'd forgotten about the meeting. He waited for her to try to persuade him to come, but the words never came.

'I saw your grandmother today.'

He frowned. 'What did she say?'

'Well, she knew who I was before I knew who she was. She knew about us. She invited me in for a cup of tea and cake.'

'I hope you said no.'

'Riley! Why would I say no? I said yes and we had a lovely chat.'

He didn't like the sound of that. 'What did you talk about?'

'You mostly. Don't look like that,' Darcy said, seeing his frown deepen.

'Why are you talking about me? I prefer my business to stay private.'

'I didn't tell her anything private, like what happened in Texas to bring you over here or what happened with your fiancée. I just told her what a wonderful person you are, kind, respectful, not at all grumpy.' She looked at him pointedly and he tried to rearrange his features so he wasn't scowling. 'She just wants to know more about you. She doesn't know you and I can tell it's something she really regrets. Maybe you should invite her round for dinner one night, I'm sure she'd be delighted to see the lighthouse, and if you thought it might be awkward I could be there to act as an intermediary.'

'Maybe.'

Riley didn't like that she was trying to get him to change. He was happy in the lighthouse not having to deal with anyone. He didn't want to form a relationship with the people of the town, least of all his grandmother. Darcy had already pushed his walls down, and although he wouldn't change or regret his relationship with her, it didn't mean that he wanted to open himself up to anyone else.

'Don't let what happened between her and your parents affect your relationship with her. You said you weren't bitter.'

'I'm not. I just don't know her.'

'And that's not going to change with you hiding in your lighthouse and barely talking to her. She's lovely. She knows a lot about Rose Island Lighthouse too, she lived in it for a few years. I'm sure you would get lots of interesting stories out of her if you were just to talk to her for a while. I don't expect you to be sitting on her knee while she knits you a jumper but you could at least be friends with her.'

Darcy stepped up onto the side of the road as a big red double-decker bus trundled towards them. She waved her hand out to catch the driver's attention and then turned back to face him.

'Just think about it.'

He nodded, though he wasn't sure thinking about it would give him a different feeling about it.

As the bus stopped in front of them and opened its doors, Darcy stepped up and paid for both of them. Then she took his hand and led him up the stairs. There was an old man sitting in the corner downstairs, but no one else was on the upper deck but them.

Darcy pulled him down the aisle to the very back seat, as Riley looked out the windows at the view of the town below them.

'This is really cool,' Riley said, seeing White Cliff Bay from a completely different perspective. He sat down in the window seat and Darcy sat next to him, leaning into him.

'Riding at the top of a double-decker bus is a rite of passage for all British kids and teenagers. As a child I'd sit at the front and pretend I was driving the bus; you get such a great view from the front. But as a teenager I always wanted to sit at the back.'

'Why, if the view is better at the front?'

Darcy leaned in and he wrapped his arm round her shoulders. She nipped his bottom lip and gazed up at him, her blue eyes suddenly darkening.

'Because the back seat was always the best place to make out.'

He smiled against her lips as he kissed her. Opening himself up to a relationship with her really was the best thing that had ever happened to him. So maybe he could open himself up to the people of the town too.

Riley stood in the middle of the park and stared around him in shock. There were teams of mostly old, slightly overweight men, predominantly dressed in white, dancing around each other in some kind of choreographed routine that involved lots of clapping, hitting sticks or waving handkerchiefs. They had bells and ribbons attached to their shins, thighs and elbows, wore multicoloured braces across their bodies and some men had huge hats with flowers attached all round the sides. Some even had pompoms on their shoes. There was a lot of singing, fiddle-playing and some men playing small drums or accordions.

It was ridiculous, farcical and wonderful all at once, and Riley had never seen something so brilliant and ludicrous in his life.

'What is this?' he asked, unable to keep the smile from his face.

'The Southwest championship of Morris dancing.'

'Morris dancing?'

'That's what it's called, though no one really knows why. It dates back to the fifteenth century and was often entertainment in royal households or out on the village greens.'

'Is there some meaning behind the dances?'

'Ha, I don't think even they know that.'

'But all the dances are different and they all know the steps.'

'They practise for hours and hours, especially for a championship like this.'

'I think it's wonderful.'

Darcy smiled up at him. 'I knew you'd like it.'

She took his hand and slowly steered him around the different dance teams, all of them dressed in slightly different ways.

'Why is that man wearing a dress?' Riley asked.

'A lot of dance teams will have someone who plays the fool, he will dance the opposite way to the rest of the team or dance in between them. They are often dressed in weird costumes – well, weirder than everyone else – and some dress as women or babies. There is also Molly dancing, which is a dance where one of the men will play the part of a woman.'

'Why not just get a woman to play that part?'

'I think traditionally Morris dancing was just for men and any team that had women in it wasn't even allowed in the Morris dancing league.'

'There's a league?'

Darcy laughed and nodded. 'Now they have women's teams and mixed teams, though there are still the all-male teams.'

'Bit sexist.'

'A bit, but then traditionally in Shakespeare's time women weren't allowed to be actors and all plays were performed by an all-male cast, so I guess the tradition of all-male dancers comes from that era.'

'You've done your research on this.'

'I knew you would have questions. Besides, research is what I do best. I love finding out little facts and gems.'

He smiled. She had such a nerdy side and he loved that about her.

'These guys are different.' Riley pointed to a team of dancers dressed entirely in black. Black ribbons spilled from all over their bodies, making them look like oversized ravens. They had big black bowler hats with long black feathers coming out in a plume at the top. Even their faces were black.

'These are Border Morris dancers, from the English–Welsh border. It is said that traditionally farmers would often go out dancing in the winter to supplement their income but this was classed as begging, which was illegal, so they dressed in over-sized tatty costumes and blackened their faces so they couldn't be recognised.'

He stopped her and kissed her briefly on the lips. 'I love that you know this stuff.'

She smiled. 'I'm such a geek.'

'I love that you're a geek. Don't knock it. The women of my town knew what every celebrity was wearing, who they were dating or marrying, the names of the celebrity children, who had been caught kissing who, who had been caught staggering drunkenly out of a nightclub, and the British women seem to enjoy the same pursuits. It holds no interest to me and I can't see how the lives of the rich and famous could possibly be so interesting. Then there's you, who loves sharks, ammonites and sea life. Who has an endless knowledge of mermaids, who loves history and stuff about science. It's very refreshing. I love that about you. I could listen to you talk forever.'

She blushed, as she looked away, and they carried on walking around the festivities for a few minutes.

'None of my previous boyfriends ever appreciated my geeky side. I learned to play it down quite quickly, as you can tell fairly easily when you are boring people.'

'But it's something you are passionate about. What do you talk about on your dates if you can't talk about your passions?'

Darcy shrugged. 'Football, cars, their work.'

'The stuff they care about?'

'The stuff I care about is boring, for most people. I can't expect everyone to be interested in what I love.'

'If you love someone, then you are interested in what they have to say.'

'Oh, none of my boyfriends loved me.'

This bothered Riley more than it should. Why had Darcy dated these jerks who hadn't appreciated how wonderful she was?

'Were you in love with any of them?'

She shook her head straight away, no hesitation. 'The relationships never got that far. Love is not something that appears overnight. It's something that builds over time. Well, that's what I always believed. Maybe there are some exceptions to that rule.' She looked up at him and he felt a kick to the stomach as her eyes locked on his. 'I was never with my boyfriends long enough for it to develop into love. I never ever felt what I'm feeling . . . what I imagine love feels like, with them. What about you, have you been in love? Though I imagine that's a stupid question – you were engaged. You must have loved your fiancée at some point to ask her to marry you.'

He noticed the conversation had quickly been diverted back to him to cover over that little stumble in her sentence. She felt something for him and it went way beyond what it should be after such a short amount of time. She didn't want to tell him in case it freaked him out, but he could suddenly find no fear in that any more. He had feelings for her too.

'Cassidy asked me to marry her. There was no grand gesture of a proposal from me. I liked her, the sex was good and I kind of assumed that the big all-singing-all-dancing-type love that happens in movies was a farce. People didn't feel that in real life. We got on OK, most of the time, so I presumed that I loved her. She asked me to marry her and . . .'

'You were too polite to say no?'

He laughed. 'Something like that. I didn't want to hurt her, and I didn't really want to break up with her, so it seemed the natural conclusion to our relationship.'

'You should never settle, Riley. When you get married, it needs to be to someone who makes your heart thunder and sing. She should be your most favourite person in the whole world. Spending time with her should be your favourite thing. If you're not with her, you should miss her. She should make you smile every day. When you make love to her, you should be able to look into her eyes and know that it will never ever get better than that. All that stuff that Max said to you that night about how he feels about his wife. It should be like that. Always.'

He turned her towards him, moving his hands to her waist. He leaned his forehead against hers. 'I want all that and actually now, more recently, I have a better understanding of what it means. My expectation of what love means has been raised and there is no way I'd settle for anything less again.'

She moved back slightly to look at him and she knew he was talking about her. They both knew this was something special that went beyond the normal dating and having fun stage they should be at. She pressed her hand against his heart and a look of understanding passed between them. They were in way too deep here and there was nothing Riley could or would do to change that.

There was a cheer from a nearby group of people as one dance came to an end and Darcy stepped back away from him, blinking as if she had forgotten that they weren't alone.

'Shall we go and have some lunch? I've booked us a table in the marquee. We'll still have a great view of the dancing. We're having afternoon tea.'

'Tea as in a cup of tea or tea as in dinner?'

'Neither, this tea comes with cakes, scones and tiny sandwiches all served on pretty china plates. There is tea served, of course, or coffee if that's what you prefer, but the whole thing is called afternoon tea.'

'This is getting very confusing.'

Darcy laughed. 'That's why I booked it.'

She escorted him over to a large white marquee on the edge of the dancing area and he was surprised to see tables covered in white tablecloths with pretty silver candelabras in the middle. There were even chandeliers in the arches of the marquee. Everything looked very posh and sophisticated, like something out of *Downton Abbey*. There was a man in tails who looked like a butler standing at the entrance and there were proper waiters and waitresses serving the cakes and sandwiches.

This wasn't his scene at all. He was dressed in jeans and a cowboy hat, and he always felt out of place in restaurants like this.

But Darcy was grinning hugely. 'This is a rite of passage, too. Everyone likes to go for afternoon tea so they can pretend, just for a few hours, they are secretly far posher than they are.'

Riley looked around and, sure enough, all the customers were dressed in jeans or shorts and T-shirts. No one looked like they were really a lord or lady, and no one cared what anyone else was wearing either.

Darcy approached the butler and gave her name.

'Of course, Madam, Sir. I have your table over here, if you'd like to follow me.'

The butler trotted off and, giggling, Darcy followed him, still holding Riley's hand so there was no chance of escape.

They sat down right near an open side, where they could look out at all the dancing that was going on. The butler presented them with a gold inlaid menu with a royal-blue tassel before leaving them alone.

Riley scanned down the menu briefly, not recognising any of the words on the page in front of him. This was not a good sign.

'What's this?'

'It's a tea menu. You get to choose which tea you want.'

'Can I not just have that normal stuff, Tetley or PG Tips?'

'You can have English Breakfast tea, which is the same thing, or you could be a bit more daring and try something different. Open your mind. You might like Assam or Darjeeling, but I think you'll like Lapsang Souchong. It has a slight smoky taste to it that reminds me of you.'

He arched an eyebrow. 'This tea reminds you of me? OK, I better have that.'

One of the waitresses came over and took their tea order. Darcy ordered a mango one and the waitress left.

She reached over to take his hand and he wrapped his fingers around hers.

'You're very sweet humouring me with all this. I know a lot of what we have done is not your thing.'

'If this is important to you, then it's important to me too. I love spending time with you. Let's just say it's my new favourite thing.'

Her breath caught in her throat as he stared at her across the table. She only tore her eyes away when a three-tiered cake stand was placed on the table between them, with all manner of delights.

All the walls he had built to protect himself were tumbling down and for the first time he didn't care.

CHAPTER 14

Darcy leaned into Riley's side as they looked over the bay at Rose Island. The sun was just starting to set and the lantern at the top of the lighthouse had just come on, sending its golden arc of light across the water.

She stared down at the email that had just come through on her phone. The application to have the lighthouse listed had been rejected. She was gutted. There was nothing special about Rose Island Lighthouse that would deem it worth saving. The email said it wasn't rare or technologically innovative enough and, though it was regrettable, there was nothing they could do.

In a few days the light would go out. Although that would be sad, it would be even worse to look out and not see the lighthouse at all.

'We'll figure something out,' Darcy said. 'I haven't given up hope yet.'

Riley smiled and kissed her on the forehead, but she knew he was sad about the rejection too.

She looked at her watch. The meeting at the town hall was due to start soon and she hoped they might have some suggestions about how to save it because now the lighthouse wasn't going to be listed Darcy was fresh out of ideas.

She leaned up and kissed Riley on the cheek.

'Go back to the lighthouse, you don't need to wait for me. I'll take your other boat over as soon as the meeting is finished.'

'I'll wait. It's choppy out there today and I don't want you having to drive the boat on your own.' Riley wrapped his arms round her, leaning his head on top of hers.

'Well, why don't you go and wait in my flat? It's warmer and Ben will appreciate the company. I can't imagine the meeting will take longer than an hour. I'll meet you back there as soon as it's finished.'

Darcy dug in her bag and fished out her keys. She handed them to him and then, giving him a little wave, she turned and walked away.

Suzanna had asked her to try to persuade Riley to come to the meeting, but she wouldn't do that. After all his friends, family and neighbours betrayed him back in Texas, it was hard for him to trust anyone again. It was surprising enough that he was willing to trust her. She was already trying to push him to embrace England a bit more and sample new things, and she was pushing him into having some kind of relationship with his grandmother; she wouldn't push him into being part of the town, too. Maybe that would come over time, and maybe it wouldn't, but Riley had to make his own mind up on that one.

She walked into the entrance of the town hall and a woman Darcy recognised as Cathy, Suzanna's friend from the chemist, was sitting in the foyer selling knitted red and white striped hats to show support for the Save the Lighthouse scheme. Darcy picked one up. It was tall like a lighthouse and even had a yellow top, which was obviously supposed to represent the light. Darcy smiled as she dug in her purse and bought two. She didn't know if Riley would appreciate the hat, but she sure would get a kick out of making him wear it, even if it were only for a few seconds.

She pulled her hat on, walked into the town hall and gasped. It was full to the brim with people. By the looks of it, every single person in the town had come, every seat was taken and some people were standing at the back. The best part was they were all wearing the stupid stripy hats, making it look like a 'Where's Wally?' convention. Darcy had a lump in her throat as she looked around. People really cared here. If the lighthouse was pulled down, it wouldn't impact on any of these people's lives, not really, but yet here they all were, trying to save it. It made her more determined than ever to do something to help. She wanted to be part of this community of wonderful people, and she wanted to save the place where she had met the man she was falling in love with.

Suzanna spotted her and waved her down to the front. She walked down the aisle and saw George, Libby, Verity and Maggie, waving at them as she made her way down to the front. Suzanna greeted her with a huge hug.

'I've saved you two seats, I wasn't sure if . . .' Suzanna trailed off. 'He isn't coming, is he?'

'No, but it's not because of you, he is just a very private person. He likes to keep himself to himself and this isn't his sort of thing.'

Suzanna nodded sadly as she walked off to go and talk to someone else, her shoulders slumping in disappointment. Darcy felt awful. All these people were here fighting to save Riley's home and Riley wasn't even here himself.

She turned to sit down and realised that she was sitting next to Penny, the girl who had passed out the other day, and her boyfriend Henry.

'Hello,' Darcy said. 'Lovely to see you again.'

Penny smiled warmly at her. 'Hello, thank you again for your help the other day.'

'Oh no problem, how are you feeling now?'

'Fine, I was just a little dizzy.'

Penny unconsciously stroked her belly and Darcy smiled at the reason why she had felt dizzy.

'I heard you had some trouble at Silk & Lace the other day,' Penny said.

'I didn't steal anything, if that's what you heard. That was a complete misunderstanding . . .'

Penny laughed. 'Don't worry. Phoebe, who owns the shop, is madder than a box of frogs. It was quite obvious what had happened. I don't think you'll be arrested any time soon. By the way, I think you met Henry the other day, and this is our daughter, Daisy.'

Darcy gave them all a little wave, noticing Daisy, who must have been about sixteen, suddenly smiling hugely over what Penny had just said.

'I'm Darcy,' she said, just in case Penny didn't know her name. 'I've just moved here. I live down in Silver Cove. I can't believe the turnout tonight, it's incredible.'

'The great thing about White Cliff Bay is at events like this everyone will turn out to help. It was the same for the Christmas Ball last year. We had bad snow and the whole town came out to make sure the ball went ahead. Rose Island Lighthouse is part of our history, we'd all be sad to see it go,' Penny said.

Daisy nodded. 'It's one of the things the tourists come to see as well. It brings money to the town. When people talk about White Cliff Bay, that image of the lighthouse is synonymous with our town. It's one of those classic pictures – on all the boxes of fudge, the postcards, mugs and souvenirs that they sell in the gift shops in the town. I'm not sure what the focal point of the town would be without it. I imagine the tourist numbers would drop significantly,' she said, surprising Darcy with her insightful intelligence.

'You're seeing Riley Eddison, aren't you?' Penny said. 'The lighthouse keeper?'

Darcy nodded, still not entirely comfortable with the fact that the whole town knew her business.

'And he isn't coming tonight?' Henry said.

Darcy blushed. 'He couldn't make it.'

Henry didn't seem too impressed with that but he didn't say anything. She wondered if everyone was thinking Riley should be here too. She didn't want people to think badly of him. He was a wonderful man.

There was suddenly a hum of excitement from the people of the town – something had piqued their interest. Darcy turned round to see Riley walking down the aisle towards her and, to her utmost surprise, he was wearing one of the stripy lighthouse hats. Her heart filled with love for him. He had come and he had done it for her.

He was scanning the rows for her and she gave him a wave so he would see her. He hurried over, as every eye in the room followed him. He sat down next to her, kissing her on the cheek. She couldn't stop the smile from spreading on her face.

'I didn't expect to see you here,' Darcy said, quietly so no one else could hear.

'Couldn't let you have all the fun,' Riley whispered back.

He pressed a chalky ammonite into her hand that was about the size of a fifty-pence piece. She smiled. 'What's this one for?'

'Another apology one. You're fighting to save my home and I should be too. I shouldn't be letting you do all the work, while I do nothing. I know this meeting is important to you, and I want you to know that what's important to you is important to me too. Even if it does mean wearing a silly lighthouse hat.'

Darcy leaned into him and he kissed her on the head.

Suzanna came bustling over and, like the perfect gentleman, Riley stood up to talk to her. Darcy's heart swelled even more when Riley kissed Suzanna on the cheek to say hello.

Suzanna blushed with happiness at the gesture. 'Riley, I'm so glad you could make it, it's wonderful to see you again.'

'It's nice to see you again too. I'm sorry I haven't been around a lot lately. I've been very busy redecorating the lighthouse and with work. But maybe you'd like to come over for dinner one night?'

Darcy nearly cried at this sign of friendship from Riley.

'I'm not a great cook, but my fish is pretty decent. And Darcy here makes a fab dessert.' Riley glanced back at Darcy, his eyes alight with mischief.

Darcy's cheeks heated as she remembered the kind of dessert they had shared the night before. The one after the Curly Wurly and the Bakewell tart.

'I would love that, thank you so much,' Suzanna said.

Riley gave her a little hug before she hurried off again with a huge smile on her face.

He sat back down again and Darcy took his hand. She loved this wonderful, polite, reserved, kind man. She loved him so much her heart felt like it was going to burst. She wanted to tell him – hell, she wanted to get up on the stage and shout it out across the room. She was sure he felt the same way too. It was too soon, though. She'd only known him a week. Although he was opening up to her and the town, a declaration of love might be the thing that sent him scuttling back into his shell again. She would tread gently where that possibility was concerned.

There was a little stage erected at the front and as Suzanna mounted the steps people started to quieten down. She turned on the mic and the room went quiet.

'Thank you all for coming tonight. As many of you know, Rose Island Lighthouse was built in 1875 by my granddad. I never met him. As the youngest of twelve children, by the time I came along he was long gone, but he left behind a legacy that saved hundreds of thousands of lives.'

There was a cheer from the crowd and Darcy found herself clapping along with them.

'On Thursday next week, the light that has burned for over one hundred and forty years will go out and the light will be turned on in the new lighthouse,' Suzanna said.

There were some boos from the crowd and Darcy smiled, feeling like she was in a panto. In a minute someone would shout, 'He's behind you', and the night would be complete.

'There is little we can do to save the light at this stage. We might be able to get it reinstated in the future, but right now it is more important that we focus on saving the tower. Thanks to the newest member of the town, Darcy Davenport,' Suzanna gestured at Darcy, 'the lighthouse was in the national papers this week, which helped to build a lot of interest from people outside the town. Thousands of people have signed the petition to save it. Apparently the petition has now been delivered to the council, courtesy of the paper, and we wait to see if this will make any difference.'

There was some clapping and a few cheers.

'However, we have recently uncovered plans which explains why they are so keen to pull the lighthouse down. Plans I am sure the council would prefer for us not to know about. A foreign investor has bought the rights to build a hotel exactly in the place where Rose Island Lighthouse is.'

There were gasps of shock and horror from the audience and Darcy looked at Riley.

'Did you know this?'

He shook his head.

'It seems, as they have no further use for the lighthouse now that the Lighthouse Trust has built a new one further down the bay, Rose Island Lighthouse has had a compulsory purchase order placed on it. They plan to demolish it and the land has been bought from the council to build this development. The hotel will be twenty storeys high and will be an exclusive spa resort that will only be accessible by boat or helicopter. I may be alone in thinking this, but I believe that is exactly the kind of hotel we do not want in White Cliff Bay. It will be an eyesore on our beautiful landscape. We have always been a tiny town and this has always been part of our charm, as far as the tourists are concerned. There are plenty of other towns or cities that offer this kind of facility, and I don't think we want to become like them.'

There were murmurs of agreement from the people in the hall.

'It is, therefore, of vital importance that we save the tower, to protect our heritage and to avoid having that blight on our landscape. We are going to hire a solicitor who is willing to take our case to court and fight for the lighthouse, but we have to cover the legal fees, which could be thousands of pounds, depending on how long the court case goes on for. So we need to raise some money and fast. The Women's Institute has arranged a cake sale for tomorrow's fete and the head of White Cliff Bay primary has arranged for a car wash at the school and all the children are going to help. We are also doing an auction and many of you have been kind enough to donate wonderful prizes to be auctioned off at the summer fete tomorrow. Does anyone else have any ideas for how we could raise some money?'

Riley sighed quietly, his shoulders slumping in defeat. Darcy knew he had hoped that something could be done to save the lighthouse. Clearly, his last hope had been to come and see what the people of the town had come up with. She knew from her many conversations with Riley about the lighthouse that the time for appeals and court cases had come and gone. It had been ruled that Rose Island Lighthouse would be demolished and it was doubtful or near impossible that any solicitor in the land would take on the case, or that they could do anything about it if they did. It was only a matter of time now before Riley received the final eviction notice and he would have to leave so they could pull it down. She looked over at him and saw that the happy, mischievous demeanour he'd had when he came in had now gone. He pulled the hat off his head and ran his fingers through his hair. She wished she had never mentioned the meeting to him; he had got his hopes up and now they had been dashed. She hated to see him so disappointed.

People started shouting out suggestions and things they would donate, and several old ladies at the front were writing all the ideas down. Penny offered an ice carving as a prize and Henry offered some handmade wooden furniture. Everyone wanted to help in some small – or sometimes big – way, but it was all for nothing and Riley clearly knew that. Darcy guessed he probably had enough money to hire the best solicitor in the land and it seemed that he had already tried all that. Once the council had decreed that the compulsory purchase order would go ahead, there was nothing that could be done.

Darcy watched Riley as he looked up at his grandmother on the stage, her face filled with hope as all the suggestions came in thick and fast, and he stood up. Darcy's heart leapt. If he was to say what a waste of time it all was, the people of the town would be crushed and he would most likely be lynched.

'I can offer paid tours around the lighthouse if you think anyone would be interested. It's completely renovated now and very different to how it was inside when it was first built. I could do small boat tours across to the island and I could print out old photos of the lighthouse for people to look at before they go on the tour. If we wait until after the light is turned off, I can show them the lantern room and the radar room too.'

There were excited murmurs of interest around the room. People would pay good money for that.

Riley sat back down again and Darcy took his hand, squeezing it tight. He knew it was useless but the most private person she knew had just opened his home up to be looked at by the whole town purely to support his grandmother. It wasn't possible to love him more right then.

Several more ideas and suggestions were bandied about and eventually the well grew dry.

'Well, that was great, I can't thank you all enough for your help with this,' Suzanna said. 'Now, on Tuesday we have a visit from someone from the council who is going to come here and answer all our questions so we want to come up with some questions that might be able to help us in our quest, something that might uncover some loophole, but we also want to give them as hard a time as possible. We want them scuttling out of here with their tail between their legs, knowing that they can't take the people of White Cliff Bay on and win without a fight.'

There were cheers from the crowd and not for the first time Darcy felt suddenly uneasy about her new job with the council, starting on Monday. She was sure it would be a completely different department to hers that would be dealing with all of this, but she was currently sitting on the side that wanted to stand against the council. But maybe she could use her connections at the council to help fight the decision. Maybe there was someone she could talk to who could help. She wouldn't say anything to Riley or Suzanna yet because it could be a shot in the dark, but if the council knew how upset the people of the town were about the plans maybe they would be willing to listen and do something about it.

'We also have the opening ceremony of the new lighthouse on Thursday night, with fireworks and other entertainment, which we would ask you to boycott to show how strongly we feel about this decision. There are a few of us who plan to hold a peaceful protest rally, which we hope will overshadow their celebrations. If you'd like to come along to this, please do, but remember it will be a peaceful rally, there will be no violence or swearing and no throwing eggs. We don't want to do anything that could affect our chances of having this decision changed.'

Darcy had to smile at the thought of any of the residents of White Cliff Bay getting angry and violent – they were all too laidback for that.

A few more words and messages of appreciation were said and suddenly the meeting was over and people were getting up to leave. Riley stood up and moved quickly to help his grandmother off the stage. Suzanna smiled up at him, as they said a few words. He bent to kiss her on the cheek again and then came back for Darcy. He took her hand and led her out. Darcy waved goodbye to Penny and Henry, and followed Riley onto the street.

People were saying their goodbyes as Riley weaved his way through the crowds and up the road towards the headland that would lead them down onto Silver Cove beach. Finally, when they were alone, she pulled him to a stop.

'Are you angry?'

He frowned and shook his head. 'Why would I be angry?'

'Because I coerced you into coming and it was all for nothing.'

He took a step closer to her, running the back of his finger gently down her cheek.

'You've been in this town just over a week. If the lighthouse goes, it wouldn't make any difference to you. You probably wouldn't miss it like some of the older generation. In reality it's not going to make any difference to any person in the town. The only people it will affect are me and Suzanna. Yet you want to fight for it. You applied for it to be listed, you've done hours of research into possible loopholes. You've gone to meetings and bought stupid hats. How could I possibly be angry about that? You care and that means the world to me. And you've opened my eyes to how much the people of this town care as well.'

'But we're still no better off. We're going to lose it.'

'I know.'

'You must be so disappointed. I told you I was going to do everything I could to save it and I've let you down.'

His eyebrows slashed down into a frown. 'You could never let me down or disappoint me. Ever. I didn't come tonight because I thought there was some miracle fix. The time for that has come and gone. I came because it was important to you.'

'But you were disappointed in there, I saw it. When they started talking about hiring a solicitor and you realised that was all they had, you were upset.'

'No. I feel bad for them, for Suzanna. All this time and effort they are putting into this, it'll be for nothing and I have no idea how to tell them. If I had tried harder at having a proper relationship with Suzanna, if we had sat down and talked about all of this lighthouse business, I could have told her that raising money to hire a solicitor was a waste of time and she wouldn't be hell-bent on this fool's errand.'

'That's why you offered tours of your lighthouse – because you feel guilty?'

He nodded. 'Though I doubt it will come to that. With the light going out on Thursday and the new lighthouse being switched on, there is no need to wait around. The foreign investors will be eager to start and I imagine the date for the demolition will be set very quickly.'

'But you knew all this. The date the light gets switched off has been set for a while.'

'Yes.'

'So you knew you would have to leave the lighthouse soon.'

'I was hoping something would come up, but yes, I knew that the chance of me staying was almost non-existent.'

Pain slammed into her chest. 'And you'll go back to the States?'

He looked away over the sea.

'You never had any intention of staying, did you? You knew the first time we made love that you were going to leave. You knew when you held me in your arms this morning and made love to me so beautifully that this was never going to last.'

'I told you I don't want to do anything to ruin what we have, but . . .'

'But then you thought, sod it, I can get sex out of her for a good few weeks before I leave so let's go for it. God, I am such an idiot. Suzanna warned me that you wouldn't stay and I stupidly thought that maybe I was enough to change that. All that stuff that you've been feeding me about what I mean to you and how you love listening to me talk and that spending time with me was your favourite thing – it was all bullshit, wasn't it? Just lines to guarantee that I would continue to jump into bed with you.'

Darcy groaned in disgust at Riley and at herself. She had never been the sort of woman to jump into bed with a stranger before. A sexy accent, a gorgeous smile and she'd been putty in his hands. He'd known every step of the way the right words to use, the little gestures that would get her to keep coming back. It had all been an act.

She turned away, but he snagged her arm. She pushed him off her. 'Don't touch me, you don't ever get to touch me again.'

Immediately he dropped her arm and she hurried down the headland towards the beach away from him, but he continued to follow her.

'How can you possibly think that you mean that little to me after everything we shared? I know we have only known each other a week but it was special to me too.' He hurried ahead of her to block her path and she flinched away from him, but he moved in front of her again. 'I'm not going to touch you but you will listen to my side before you throw all this away.'

A shadow loomed from behind them, making Darcy realise they weren't alone. She turned to see Seb and Amy from the Bubble and Froth. They were obviously on their way back from the meeting too.

'Hey, is everything OK?' Seb said, his eyes flicking between Darcy and Riley, and then resting on Darcy with concern.

Darcy nodded. Whatever was going to happen between her and Riley, she knew Riley wouldn't hurt her.

'Are you sure?' Amy asked. 'You can come back to the pub with us if you need some . . . space.'

'No, it's fine. Thank you.'

Seb and Amy hesitated for a moment or two before they walked off, Seb looking over his shoulder as they left.

A couple of other people who obviously lived down this part of the town were walking towards them too. Not keen to give the townspeople more gossip to talk about, she marched past Riley.

'We'll talk about this back in my flat.'

He followed her but kept his distance and didn't utter a word. She stormed back into her flat and as he closed the flat door behind him she rounded on him.

She caught sight of her reflection in the mirror and, realising that she still had the stupid lighthouse hat on, quickly tore it off. But Riley spoke before she had a chance to say anything.

'When all this lighthouse business reared its ugly head, I knew that if I lost it I would go back to America,' Riley said. He wasn't shouting but she could tell he was angry and upset. 'As I said, I have an apartment in New York and I have a lot of clients there. The week before I met you I was told about the switching-off date, and although I've not been given an eviction notice yet or a date to leave I knew it wouldn't be long. I spoke to a friend who works at a recording studio in New York and he said that he could get me a job there, working directly with the artists to create songs. There are quite a few clients there that want to work with me directly. It's not how I like to work, but it looks better for the artists if they collaborated on a song and, although the profits are split, the initial fee is much bigger, so I agreed. There was no point in staying, there was nothing for me here.'

He moved closer.

'Then, as I said, everything changed. What I thought I wanted, my plans, everything. When I came over here yesterday afternoon, I told you I wanted to give things a go between us. Neither of us knows how long this is going to last, but I wanted to stay here to see what happens. I've been looking at houses to rent around here. But now I wonder what was the point. You don't know me at all, if you think I'm the sort of person to use you for sex before I ditch you and go back to America. You clearly don't trust me and this thing between us obviously doesn't mean as much to you as I thought if you are willing to throw it away so readily. So let's just call a halt to it now.'

He walked to the door and Darcy watched him in horror. What had she done? She quickly moved to block his path, standing right in front of the door. There was a tiny part of her that expected him to move her out the way or barge past her, but she knew he wouldn't. His manners were too good for that.

'Please don't go. Let's talk this through sensibly. We're both being rash, I storm off, you storm off. We're only getting so upset because we both care so much. If you want to be mad, I get it, but stay and we can sit at opposite ends of the sofa and be mad with each other.'

He sighed and shook his head. 'I have to get back for Kelpie.'

'If you leave, I'm just going to have to come after you to apologise properly and I've not driven that boat before and you already said that it's rough out there and you don't want me to go on the water on my own,' Darcy said and the tiniest hint of a smile crossed his face. 'I'm sorry, I just panicked when I thought I was going to lose you. I've had boyfriends before and they all finished with me after a few dates or a few weeks. Some found me boring or . . .'

'Or they were intimidated by how clever you are.'

'I don't think that was it.'

'I do.'

She stared at him. God, she wanted to kiss him right now. She wanted to drag him back to the bedroom and show him how sorry she was . . . but first she needed to explain why she overreacted.

'A lot of my relationships finished because the men said I was emotionally unavailable, that we didn't connect. And they were right: for whatever reason, these men meant nothing to me. I liked them. But when it came to an end, apart from a bit of wounded pride, I didn't care. I care about you. I care a lot. It scares me how much I feel for you already. I have never felt like this before and I know I'm not handling this at all well. Maybe we do need some space from each other. Everything is so intense between us. We haven't really been apart since we met. I'm starting my new job on Monday and I'll be busy with that and I know you're busy with work, so maybe we take a few days off from each other and meet up for dinner one night during the week . . .' She was utterly horrified to find a huge lump in her throat at the thought of not seeing him.

'Is that what you want?' Riley asked, softly.

She shook her head.

'I don't want that either. I don't want to see you once a week. I love spending time with you, chatting to you, listening to you laugh. You mean the world to me and I don't want to lose you.'

She wrapped her arms round his neck. 'You've really been looking at houses?'

'I can show you the ones I have saved.'

She leaned against him. 'I'm sorry.'

He kissed her on the forehead. 'I'm scared too. It's happening so fast. But I'm enjoying the ride immensely and right now there is nowhere else I'd rather be than here with you.'

He bent his head down to kiss her. As she kissed him back, he lifted her and she instinctively wrapped her legs round his hips.

He pulled back slightly to look at her. 'You're about to start your new important job, so let's make the most of the time we have together now and save the arguing for another time.'

She nodded and then giggled as he walked off towards the bedroom with her body still wrapped around him.

CHAPTER 15

Riley woke the next day to the sun streaming through the windows, the sea outside a slice of pure gold. The bed next to him was empty and Darcy was moving around the room, stark naked apart from a pair of tiny denim shorts.

It was later in the day than Riley would have liked but after making love for hours the night before and then nipping back to the lighthouse to collect Kelpie once Darcy had fallen asleep, he hadn't fallen asleep himself until the very early hours in the morning. It was no wonder he had slept in.

'What are you doing?'

'I'm getting ready for the fete. I told your grandmother I'd help out.'

'The fete to raise money for the lighthouse?'

'Yes, I know it's useless, but I still want to be part of this town. I want to make friends and feel like I'm doing something to contribute. Don't forget my new job is the Community Development Liaison Manager. I'll probably be arranging events like this in the town all the time so it will give me a good idea of what people like and dislike. What they'd like to see more of. It will be useful to make some good contacts too, chat to people. I can gently tell them that trying to hire a solicitor to save the lighthouse probably isn't going to work. At the moment they are all pinning their hopes on that, but if I casually tell them that it's probably too late they might start to think about other ideas to help.'

She still hadn't given up, while he had given up weeks before. He had to admire her spirit. His eyes cast down to her bum as she turned away to carry on getting dressed. He could admire that as well.

'I'll come with you.'

'You have work to do, come by later, it's on all day. Oh God, I'm so late. I have to walk Ben and you kept me awake most of the night and I'm probably going to fall asleep at the fete and that's not a good impression . . .'

'I didn't hear any complaints from you last night. In fact I'm pretty sure it was you that kept me awake, not the other way round.'

Darcy giggled. 'What can I say? I'm addicted to Riley sex. It's a problem, I'm trying to deal with it.'

He smirked. 'Well, we will have to abstain tonight. The best way to deal with an addiction is to go cold turkey.'

The look of horror on her face made him laugh.

'I'll walk Ben. I have to take Kelpie out anyway and I'll meet you at the fete later.'

'Oh, that would be great.' She leaned over the bed to give him a quick kiss. 'Help yourself to a bacon sandwich if you like, brown sauce is in the fridge, I know how you love it.'

He laughed again as she stood up to slip her feet into a pair of gold sparkly sandals, gave him a little wave and left him lying in her bed. A second later he heard the front door close.

He loved the closeness they had, the ease with each other, the fact that she had just left him alone in her home, the light-hearted banter. It was as if they had known each other for years, not days. Of course there had been a few hiccups along the way, but that was only to be expected at the start of a relationship and, as she had pointed out, it was only because they cared so much. Everything was perfect between them and he couldn't wait to see what would happen next.

There was a queue a mile long for the food tent, where Darcy was frantically cooking and serving customers at the same time. Thankfully there were a few others helping, but they had been so busy. The bacon and sausage sandwiches had been popular all morning and now at lunchtime the burgers were growing in popularity instead.

The smell from the uncooked meat was vile. She wasn't sure whether it was the bacon, the burgers or all of it. Evidently, the meat had been delivered to the school the day before and had been accidentally left overnight in a cardboard box outside. As far as Darcy could tell the meat had gone off. She had told the other people who were serving and Suzanna that they shouldn't be selling it but her concerns had been waved away, so she had just carried on with her given role. The smell was sickening, though: it was enough to put Darcy off eating any food that day.

To make matters worse, one of the teachers, Mr Quentin, had been coming up with excuses to come and talk to her all day. He was young and good looking, but he had been staring at her like he wanted to eat her and it was giving her the creeps.

Darcy flipped a burger, put an overcooked sausage into a bun and handed it to George, who smiled at her sympathetically, before shoving the money into her money belt.

She'd had no time to chat either. Her carefully constructed plan of gently telling people that raising money for a solicitor wouldn't be any good had failed. There had been no time to talk to anyone about anything.

She looked up into the creepy eyes of Mr Quentin again and forced a smile on her face.

'How you doing here?' he asked, smiling at her as his eyes cast down for the hundredth time to her breasts.

'Actually, the smell of the meat is making me feel quite queasy. Is there any chance you could swap with me for a little while and I'll go and see Suzanna and ask if there is another job she would like me to do instead? The cake stand looks quite busy, I'm sure they could do with another pair of hands over there.'

'Oh, I'm not supposed to be on a stand, I'm supposed to be circulating and talking to parents,' Mr Quentin said.

That was a pathetic excuse for not digging in and helping. She fixed him with her best puppy dog eyes. 'Please, just for half an hour, I could really do with a break.'

The puppy dog eyes worked and Mr Quentin immediately came round to where she was, taking the spatula from her hand and deliberately brushing his fingers over hers as he did so.

'Go and take a break, you've worked so hard all morning. I can man the battle stations for a little while.'

Darcy flashed him with a brilliant smile and walked off, vowing that he could man the table for a lot longer than a little while if she had anything to do with it.

She immediately found Suzanna, who was directing operations in the middle of the field, a clipboard in one hand and a megaphone in the other.

'Hello, my lovely,' Suzanna said. 'How's it going over there?'

'I really do think the meat is off, the smell is awful. I've persuaded Mr Quentin to cover for me for a while, would it be OK if I did something else instead?'

Suzanna frowned slightly as she looked down at her clipboard, obviously not happy about the change of plans.

'Yes, if you wouldn't mind helping on the cake stand, they're a bit busy too.'

Happy that she would be surrounded by sweet smells instead of rotting meat, Darcy jogged over quickly, leaving Suzanna before she changed her mind.

There were three stands in the cake tent. One for big cakes that people were having slices of, one for fairy cakes and one for cookies, biscuits, fudge and gingerbread men. There were two elderly ladies manning the tables and they looked as stressed as Darcy had felt running the food tent.

'Hello, I'm Darcy. I've been sent over to help you.'

The ladies smiled with relief, though the queue was dying off a little bit now; Darcy had just heard Suzanna announce there was to be a 'dunk the head teacher' event shortly and everyone was keen to watch that.

'That would be lovely, dear. I'm Geri and this is Anne,' said one lady, who was wearing a thick blue cardigan despite the heat of the day. 'Why don't you be in charge of the big cakes? Charge one pound fifty for a slice about this thick.' She showed her with her fingers what looked like an overly large slice.

Darcy nodded and moved behind the table, as the ladies served the last customer.

'So, you're dating the lovely Riley, aren't you?' Anne said, taking her glasses off and peering over at Darcy. She was a tiny, frail-looking thing, with her hair in curlers and still wearing her slippers. She looked to be over a hundred years old.

'Yes.' There was no point denying it, but she would try to keep the details to a minimum.

'He is a fine bit of stuff, isn't he?' Anne said. 'I did ask him if he wanted to be my toy boy, I've never had one of those and thought it might be fun. He politely declined. He seemed to think my husband would be upset by it. I told him Frank is deaf as a post and certainly wouldn't hear us if we were going at it like rabbits upstairs. Riley still wasn't keen, though. I don't know why. I was sure I could break him down eventually, but, now he is dating you, I think that ship has sailed. Unless of course you're interested in a threesome?'

Darcy had never found herself speechless in her life before, but there were no words at all that she could find to convey her shock over that offer, or the right words to politely decline either.

Anne stared at her, waiting for her to reply. Even Geri seemed to be waiting for the answer.

'I, erm . . . group sex isn't really my thing, I'm afraid.'

'Pity. You've never had a threesome then?'

'No, normally just one man.'

'Oh, you don't know what you're missing,' Anne said. 'It's the most wonderful thing. Admittedly I've never had a threesome with a girl before, but I once had one with two men. I was about your age too. Two sailors. Both of them kissing me and touching me at the same time and then we had sex all at once. Best sex I've ever had. Shame Frank wasn't really into that scene, but I'd love to do it again one day.'

'I'm sure there are websites for that sort of thing,' Geri said, knowledgeably, clearly not perturbed at all by her friend's revelations. 'There seems to be websites for all sorts of things these days. I bet you could find somewhere that did threesomes.'

Geri pulled out her iPhone from her pocket and started swiping at the screen.

Darcy looked away and smiled. Although Geri was probably right and threesome websites would probably be quite easy to find, Darcy wondered if having a threesome with a centenarian would be quite a niche market.

'You know what else I'd like to try?' Anne said. 'Dogging.'

'With a dog? Isn't that illegal?' Geri asked, finally shocked over at least one of the revelations from Anne.

'No, you silly thing. It's when people drive to car parks and have sex in the car and other people watch. I tell you, if I could persuade that young Riley to have sex with me in the back of his car, I'd invite the whole town to watch. I'd put it out on the emergency text number and tell them where and when it was going down.'

'Oh look, there are dogging websites,' Geri said. 'Come Dogging with Me dot com. Like *Come Dine with Me*, but a naughty version.'

Anne hooted as she looked at Geri's phone. 'I wonder if they give each other points for starters, main course and dessert.'

Geri howled with laughter.

'Hello,' said a small voice and Darcy whirled round to see Ryan standing on the other side of the cake table, wearing a shark jumper.

'Hello, Ryan, how are you?' Darcy smiled, relieved to be excused from the conversation, though Geri and Anne were both now looking at Geri's phone and giggling at whatever saucy sex act they had stumbled against.

'I found a new shark species the other day and I wanted to tell you about it,' Ryan said, as Geri's giggling got louder.

'Which one did you find? There are hundreds.'

'It's called the frilled shark.'

'Oh, that's a cool species. They don't even look like sharks, they look like giant eels.'

'Yes,' Ryan said, getting excited. 'And their heads are so big they look like those Chinese dragons you see at the Chinese New Year celebrations. They have these huge mouths and massive eyes and they move like this.' He started moving his arms and body in a snake-like gesture but, as he wiggled around, his hip banged into the cake table and one of the legs of the trestle table collapsed. Everything happened in slow motion . . . six cakes slid down the table and plopped onto the floor, one on top of the other. Darcy made a grab for the sixth one and managed to hold it aloft before it hit the floor with the others, but the first five were a lost cause.

Ryan stared at the mess in horror, and then turned and ran out of the tent. Darcy looked around at Geri and Anne, who were staring at Darcy in shock.

'Did Ryan do that? I'll have a word with his mum about this,' Geri said, finally recovering.

'No, no, it wasn't Ryan, it was me. I must have kicked one of the legs by mistake. I'm so sorry.'

She looked up as a shadow fell over the tent entrance and saw Suzanna staring in horror at the mess. Darcy's heart sank. She wanted to stay in White Cliff Bay; it was the first time she'd felt like she belonged anywhere since losing her job as a marine biologist. She wanted to be a valued member of the community and make a good impression on the people of the town, especially Suzanna, though she didn't know why exactly she wanted Suzanna to have a good opinion of her when Riley barely had a relationship with her himself.

'I just came to see how things were going . . .' she trailed off, clearly at a loss for what to say.

'I'm so sorry, it just sort of happened. But look, the cakes aren't wasted, there are lots of the cakes that aren't touching the floor. We can scoop them up and serve mixed cake in a bowl for a pound. I'm sure people will love it.'

Darcy grabbed a bowl and spoon and scooped up some of the broken pieces of cake that hadn't landed on the grass. She didn't dare look at Suzanna to see if this was a good or bad thing. But, to Darcy's utmost relief, Anne and Geri came rushing to help, spooning up a small portion of each broken cake into a bowl. After a few minutes of salvaging as much cake as possible, Darcy glanced up to see Suzanna still watching her. She wasn't angry, more bemused, probably wondering what on earth Riley saw in her.

'Why don't you come and man the bouncy castle for a bit, Darcy dear, maybe you and food are not a good mix. You can't go too far wrong with the bouncy castle.'

Darcy sighed, sadly. She waved goodbye to Anne and Geri, who at least looked sad to see her go, though that might be to do with Anne wanting Darcy to stay so she could persuade her to have a threesome.

Darcy followed Suzanna past the roped-off paddock, where they were giving pony rides to the kids on some very fat ponies, and across the field towards the bouncy castle.

Suzanna's friend Cathy was manning the payment table, still wearing her red-and-white-striped lighthouse hat and frantically knitting another one, though surely there could be no one left in the town who hadn't yet bought one. Her fingers and hands were moving so fast, Darcy suspected that Cathy would have finished the extra-tall hat before the day was out.

'Cathy dear, go and take a break, Darcy is going to man the castle for a while.'

Darcy didn't dare mention that she would love a break too. Cathy nodded gratefully, as if sitting and knitting all morning had been an arduous task.

Cathy stood up and Darcy took her place.

'How much are we charging?'

'Just a pound, dear, and make sure they take their shoes off.'

Darcy nodded and Cathy joined Suzanna, and they left her alone.

To her disappointment, she had only been there for five minutes when the creepy Mr Quentin spotted her and came over to talk to her again. Clearly, he hadn't spent very long manning the burger tent.

'Hello again, we will have to stop meeting like this! People will think something is going on between us,' he laughed.

Darcy forced a smile onto her face. She was glad of the distraction when a couple of kids with their warm coins pressed into their hands came and paid and jumped onto the bouncy castle with gay abandon.

'You're working so hard today, it's very much appreciated,' Mr Quentin said. 'We haven't properly been introduced, I'm Christopher Quentin, I teach Year Five.'

'Darcy, nice to meet you.' She offered out her hand, and to her disgust he bent down and kissed it.

She was delighted when Ryan came to talk to her then. She held up her hand, so Ryan could give her a high-five. 'Hello again.'

She could see that Christopher was confused by their easy relationship, as Ryan slapped her hand a little too hard.

'Do you two know each other?'

'Ryan has been telling me all about sharks,' Darcy said.

To her annoyance, Christopher rolled his eyes slightly. 'Ryan loves sharks, it's all he ever talks about.'

'Well, it's lucky that I absolutely love sharks too. I used to be a marine biologist and sharks were my speciality.'

'Oh, I love sharks too,' Christopher said.

'Really, which one is your favourite?'

'The, erm . . . great white, obviously.'

Ryan rolled his eyes and Darcy smirked.

'Obviously.' She turned her attention back to Ryan. 'I have a video of a frilled shark if you want to see one.'

Ryan nodded keenly and Darcy pulled out her phone. As she swiped at the screen, she was vaguely aware of three immaculate blonde girls about her age coming to talk to Christopher.

'Hi, Mr Quentin,' purred one of them, sexily.

'Hi Jade.' Christopher diverted his creepy gaze to them. They were all wearing tiny skirts and even tinier tops. Admittedly, it was a hot day, but it didn't quite warrant the small amount of clothing they were all wearing.

'Do you think they are actually part of the eel family?' Ryan asked, interrupting Darcy's thoughts on the girls' lack of clothing.

'No, they are definitely sharks, they just have a very unusual long shape.'

Darcy was vaguely aware of the blondes paying Christopher and going on the castle. As they walked past, Darcy caught a whiff of alcohol from all of them. It was lunchtime at a summer fete held at a school and they were quite obviously a bit drunk. She shouldn't be so judgemental, but she found herself a bit appalled by that. If it had been down to Darcy, she wouldn't have allowed them on the castle, but Christopher had let them on, so she wasn't going to argue. Though she was saddened slightly to see the little kids who had paid to go on minutes before come scurrying off the castle, obviously to get out of the way of the adults who shouldn't have even been on there.

She looked back at Ryan, as he played the video clip for the tenth time. 'They were thought to be extinct until very recently,' Darcy said and Ryan nodded, taking it all in.

She noticed Christopher leaving and sighed with relief. Ryan watched him go too.

'Am I going to get into trouble because of what happened in the cake tent? I didn't mean to knock the table, it was an accident,' Ryan said, fearfully.

'No, I told them it was me who did it, don't worry. No one saw it was you.'

Ryan stared at her. 'Why did you do that?'

'I didn't want you to get into trouble.'

'But didn't you get into trouble?'

'No, well yes, but it doesn't matter. They're not going to shout at me.'

'Thank you.'

There were shrieks of laughter coming from inside the bouncy castle and Darcy peered round to check what they were doing and noticed the three blondes staggering around, bouncing off the walls and each other. As she watched she realised that all three of them were still wearing their high-heel shoes. She realised that the one Christopher had called Jade had particularly sharp stilettos on and as she jumped on the castle she was leaving tiny puncture holes everywhere she went.

'Girls, sorry, you need to take your shoes off, you're damaging the bouncy castle,' Darcy said. How on earth had Christopher not noticed they still had their shoes on when he let them in? Although she was in charge of the bouncy castle, not him – it was her responsibility.

The girls glanced in her direction, obviously having heard Darcy but choosing to deliberately ignore her as they carried on jumping around, giggling like teenagers. Darcy knew she was going to have to get strict, but she didn't handle confrontation very well.

'Excuse me, you need to take your shoes off . . .'

They didn't even look at her this time.

Remembering what Riley said about standing up for herself, she stepped closer and cupped her hands.

'Oi, get off the bouncy castle right now,' Darcy yelled and the girls at least stopped bouncing this time to look at her.

'Or what?' challenged Jade.

Anger boiled inside her. They were deliberately damaging property that didn't belong to them and it wasn't fair.

Kicking her shoes off, she climbed on the bouncy castle. The girls scarpered, clearly not wanting to get into a fight, though Darcy doubted she had it in her to start one.

They leapt off the bouncy castle and ran, but not before Darcy heard Jade mutter, 'Stupid fat bitch.'

Darcy sighed as she looked down at her wobbly bits, and then around at the tiny puncture holes all over the castle, all of them emitting little puffs of air.

If today was about making a good impression, she had failed miserably.

CHAPTER 16

As Riley walked into the grounds of White Cliff Bay primary school, he looked around with a smile. It seemed like the whole town had come out to support the fete and the lighthouse. Apparently every year they raised funds for local charities or good causes with their fete and this year the school had unanimously voted to support the lighthouse. It simultaneously made him feel warm inside, guilty that they were all going to this much trouble for what was already a lost cause and a bit fearful that he was getting involved in town life again.

He had arrived at the fete a bit later than he had planned. With his late start to work, he hadn't had time to do all the things he had wanted to do. The fete seemed to be slowing down, with several families leaving with the obligatory goldfish in one hand and oversized, deranged-looking bear they had won in the other. Pony rides had evidently been running all day, but now the ponies had had their saddles removed and were just grazing in a roped-off paddock. There was a small paddock of rabbits, pigs and goats too. One large goat, with a red shiny harness that declared he was called Lucky, was being fed sweets by some of the smaller children. Every time he ate one, he gave a high-pitched bleat, which made the children giggle endlessly and then try to feed him more. It probably wasn't good for the goat, but the children were having too much fun and it wasn't his responsibility to be the party pooper and tell them to stop.

The bouncy castle seemed to be looking a bit deflated, the first-aid tent seemed to be a bit crowded and several small children were running around with really bad face paints. Wonky butterflies, inane-looking squashed spiders, and several animals that were completely indiscernible were chasing each other around the field. Maybe the face painter had had too many ciders?

He moved through the crowds of people and smiled when he saw that it was Darcy doing the face painting. He stood and watched her for a minute, her tongue out slightly as she concentrated on doing something arty on some poor kid's face.

He stepped closer to go and talk to her, but Suzanna stepped in his way. She was with a good-looking young man who seemed to ooze charm and charisma. Riley disliked him immediately.

'Riley, how lovely to see you here.'

He kissed her on the cheek. 'How's it all going?'

'Good, really good, we've raised so much money. I mean, there's been a few hiccups but . . .' She eyed Darcy over her shoulder.

He suddenly felt insanely protective of Darcy. He didn't want anyone to say anything bad about her, not when she was trying so hard to be a member of this town.

'What happened?'

'Nothing, Darcy's wonderful, but . . . she's like a whirlwind, isn't she, leaving behind a trail of devastation in her wake? We put her on the burger stand this morning and . . . well, the first-aid tent has been full for most of the afternoon with people complaining of sickness and stomach pains. Darcy said the burgers smelled funny and she thought they might be off, but I wonder if she cooked them properly. She looked after the cake stand for ten minutes and one of the tables collapsed and a few of the cakes were broken. While she was in charge of the bouncy castle, she got talking to one of the kids and didn't notice when some people who'd had a bit too much to drink decided to get on in their high heels and there are puncture holes in the castle now. Then she took part in the sack race and ripped the sack and she's now in charge of face painting and, well, I'm sure you've seen the children who have had their faces painted by her. I'm not sure if that boy over there is supposed to be a lizard or the Incredible Hulk.'

Before Riley could leap to Darcy's defence, the other man spoke. 'I think she's wonderful. So do most of the parents here today. I've never seen one person work so hard at a fete before. She has worked her arse off for the whole day. And none of those things were actually her fault. And you should have seen her with Ryan, the kid she was talking to when she was supposed to be watching the bouncy castle. He has . . . a few issues and isn't good with people. The only thing he is interested in at school is sharks and she noticed he had a shark jumper on and just started talking to him about them. I have never seen him so engaged, so interested in anything before as he was when she was talking to him. His whole face just lit up in excitement. In fact, she's been like the Pied Piper all day, with the kids following her around and talking to her – she's so good with them all and Ryan hasn't left her side all day. The kid is smitten with her and I can see why.'

Riley smiled tightly. 'Sorry, we haven't met.'

'Oh, I'm Christopher Quentin, I'm a teacher at the school.'

Riley stared at him; he didn't look any older than twelve.

Suzanna waved at someone across the field and excused herself from them as she went to greet her friend. Christopher watched her go.

'Between you and me, I'm hoping she will agree to go out with me tonight.'

'Suzanna? Go for it, ask her out, I'm sure she'll be delighted.'

Christopher laughed. 'I meant Darcy. Hot piece of ass like that. I bet she's amazing in bed.'

Riley's manners prevented him from punching Christopher in the face. Instead, he clapped him on the back. 'Believe me, she is.'

He stepped forward to greet Darcy and her whole face lit up as soon as she spotted him. The kid she had finished painting ran off with blobs of pink and white across his face. Darcy stood up and ran straight into Riley's arms, as if she hadn't seen him in weeks.

She pressed her head against his chest and he held her tight.

'I have had the worst day in the history of worst days. It can't possibly get any worse.'

'I've heard, but it seems that you have yourself a fan.'

'Urgh, the creepy Mr Quentin, who has been staring at me all day.'

Riley laughed, somewhat in relief. 'No, I meant Ryan.'

'Oh, he is adorable. We've been sharing our mutual love of sharks. He just went home about ten minutes ago.'

'I think it's time for you to come home too.'

She smiled up at him. 'I'd like that. I want to have dinner with my favourite person in the world and then spend the night wrapped in his arms.'

'That can be arranged.'

Suddenly a shout rang out across the field and Riley turned around to see that Lucky, the fat goat who had been fed all the sweets, had broken free from his paddock and was charging across the grass towards Libby, who was lying on the grass, her eyes closed, enjoying the sun, completely unaware that she was about to be trampled. Before he could even make a move, Darcy was already running across the field to intercept Lucky's path. He ran after her, not sure if she could restrain a goat on her own, especially as he was so big.

She reached him, grabbed his harness and eased him to a stop. She moved to his head, stroking him soothingly to get him to calm down, and then Lucky threw up all over her, bright green, projectile vomit, the hundreds of sweets the poor goat had been fed clearly taking their toll.

Darcy stood there in shock, dripping from head to toe with thick pea-green vomit, and Riley cringed. It was safe to say her day had just got a whole lot worse.

*   *   *

Riley tried to suppress the smile as he watched Darcy shake the vomit from her clothes. As she looked up at him, he quickly looked away, as he manoeuvred his boat towards the rocks surrounding the lighthouse.

'Do you think this is funny?' Darcy asked.

He shook his head. 'Not at all.'

Suzanna was right, she was like a whirlwind, but for some reason he found it utterly adorable.

He threw the rope around the pole and stepped out onto the island, offering his hand for Darcy to take.

She took it and stepped up in front of him. 'I think you are smirking, Riley Eddison.'

'Of course not.' He struggled to keep the smile from his face.

'Do you still find me sexy when I'm dripping in vomit?'

He leaned down to kiss her. 'I'll always find you sexy. Always.'

She smiled and cheekily wrapped her arms around him, pressing her body against his. He winced a little as he felt the vomit squish into his clothes.

'Even now?'

He laughed. 'Yes. Nothing could change the way I feel about you. But maybe I'd like you a tiny bit more after you've had a shower.'

He took her hand and let them into the lighthouse. He heard footsteps from upstairs as Ben came down to greet them. No sign of Kelpie though, she was too lazy for that. Ben ran towards Darcy and then whimpered and backed away as he caught the smell of the sick.

'Ha, even he doesn't love me when I'm covered in sick.'

'What does that tell you about my feelings for you?'

Darcy leaned up to kiss him again. 'That you're a good, kind, patient man who just wants to get me in the shower so you can have your wicked way with me – which I am totally on board with, by the way.'

He smiled and took her hand, leading her up the stairs and straight into the bathroom. He turned on the water, stepped into the shower fully clothed and pulled her in with him.

She gasped as the water hit her.

'Your clothes will get wet,' she said.

'My clothes are covered in sick so I think a little water is the least of our worries.'

He kissed her sweetly on the lips and then dragged her T-shirt off her, dumping it on the floor of the shower. He quickly removed the rest of her clothes as she helped him out of his. But as she reached up to kiss him again he gently turned her round.

'Let me wash you,' he whispered in her ear, kissing her neck.

He grabbed hold of the sponge and squeezed some shower gel onto it, then stroked it across her shoulders and down her back, caressing her skin with his other hand as he followed the trail he had made with the sponge.

'I'm pretty sure Lucky didn't throw up over my back,' Darcy said, though her voice was rough and he smiled that she was enjoying this as much as he was.

'I just want to be thorough.'

He leaned round her and ran the soapy sponge over her chest and breasts. She leaned back against his shoulder as he moved the sponge down her belly, but he stopped just before he reached her most sensitive area.

He turned her around again and smiled when she reached up to kiss him. He leaned round her to grab the shampoo.

'We need to wash your hair first.'

He laughed at the scowl. He poured the shampoo into his hand and gently lathered up her hair, watching as the scowl turned into a huge smile as he looked after her. He kissed her, shuffling her backwards under the spray of water again. He carefully rinsed the soap from her hair.

She was so beautiful, the water clumping to her eyelashes as she looked up at him, her pale skin, her flame-red hair. He was never ever going to have enough of her.

'Am I clean enough for you to ravish me now?'

'Oh, there's definitely going to be ravishing.' He kissed her hard, just as her stomach let out a loud gurgle. He paused and pulled back slightly. 'Are you hungry?'

'I'm starving, I haven't eaten all day. Those burgers absolutely stank and there wasn't time to eat anything after. But I can wait.'

He frowned but kissed her again, but her stomach gurgled loudly just to call her a liar. He leaned round her and turned off the water. 'Why don't we save the ravishing until after dinner? I promise it'll be worth the wait.'

She nodded reluctantly. 'I am hungry.'

'Don't want you passing out on me.'

He reached out and grabbed a towel. He wrapped one around her shoulders and then grabbed another and gently rubbed her hair dry. He kissed her on the head and then grabbed a towel for himself.

'I'll see you upstairs whenever you are ready. I'll make a start on dinner.'

He quickly dressed and went upstairs and threw some chicken, onions and peppers into a pan with a few herbs and spices.

A few minutes later, he laid the chicken on the table with some soft tortilla wraps and some grated cheese, just as Darcy arrived in the room wearing nothing but his robe, her hair piled on top of her head in a loose bun of sexy curls.

He poured two glasses of wine and sat down opposite her in the window.

She dug into the food with great relish.

'Are you nervous about starting your new job tomorrow?'

'Not really. I'm looking forward to seeing what the job will hold. I knew nothing about it when I applied, it was just a job that would bring me down here. I would have applied for a job as a rubbish collector if it meant getting away from my parents' house, but the job description sounded so wonderful, working with the community on new projects. It sounds exciting. I don't fully know what I'll be doing, but I know I will give it my all. I'm not going to fail at another job. And I want to stay here now. White Cliff Bay is such a lovely place, the people are wonderful and then there's you. I don't want to lose you. I have to make this work to be able to afford to stay.'

'I think you'll be great at it. Today showed what a fantastic people person you are, how easy you are to talk to, how people instantly like you and listen to you. This sounds like it will be a good fit for you.' He sipped on his wine as he thought about how to phrase what he wanted to say. 'Though I do wonder why you won't apply for a job in the aquarium, when the sea and sea life means so much to you?'

'You know why. It breaks my heart that I can never have a job like that. But why would they want me to work for them when my last marine biology job ended so badly?'

'Because you're intelligent, experienced, knowledgeable about sharks in particular, and you're passionate about all sea life too. They'd be fools not to take you on.'

She shook her head.

He decided to take another approach. 'Why sharks, why did you choose to specialise in them?'

'Because I saw one down here, on my first scuba dive, when I was twelve. An angel shark actually, they're my favourites and so rare now.'

'I've never heard of that kind of shark. I didn't know England had sharks.'

'There are lots of sharks that live around the coast of Britain. I didn't know what it was when I saw it, thought it was some kind of ray. It was only after the dive that my aunt told me it was a shark. It was so fascinating for me because I'd always thought that sharks came in a pretty standard shape. Of course I knew there were variations like the hammerhead but even those sharks still have that familiar shark shape. I started researching and found there were hundreds of different sharks. I just wanted to learn as much as I could about them, to see them and work with them. After mermaids, they became my new obsession.'

'So it was your life's dream to work with them?'

'Yes.'

'So why are you giving all that up? I know you moved down here so you could be near the sea, but it's never going to be enough for you. You'll never be truly happy and I don't want that for you.'

'It's fine. The job is working with people and I love that sort of thing. I'll just be content to go to the aquarium every week and see all the creatures.'

She wasn't going to agree, at least not yet. He would work on her over the next few weeks when the aquarium opened. He would leave it for now.

'You'll be brilliant at your new job because you want this to work and you'll do anything you can to make sure you make a success of it. I just really hope it's everything you want it to be.'

'I'm also hoping that there's someone I can talk to about the lighthouse.' Darcy quickly changed the subject away from her working for the aquarium. 'It's not my department but I'm sure the council wouldn't want to go ahead with it if they knew how upset everyone was by the prospect of having it demolished. Surely Rose Island Lighthouse and the hotel can co-exist somehow. It doesn't need one to be destroyed for the other to be built.'

He smiled at her rose-tinted view of the world. 'You're very sweet.'

She blushed. 'Naïve, you mean. I know the council have probably been offered millions of pounds for the hotel development to go ahead and they aren't just going to turn it down to keep the townspeople happy, but surely the hotel can be built anywhere out in that bay. The plan is for it to be some exclusive resort that can only be reached by boat; well, that's true of any area around White Cliff Bay, so why do they need Rose Island? Tourists come here to see the lighthouse: if that's pulled down, then how many people would come to stay in the fancy hotel? Of course, they'd get some guests, but a lot of the people that come to take pictures of the iconic lighthouse and the white cliffs wouldn't come any more. It's in the hotel's interest to keep the main tourist attraction and they can still build their hotel as well. I'll find someone to talk to and see what they say.'

'Don't go making enemies on the first day just for me. If you must talk to someone, give it a few days to get yourself settled first.'

She nodded. 'Yes, it makes sense to find my feet, but I'm not going to let this go.'

He smiled. 'I wouldn't expect you to.'

She wiped a bit of tortilla round the plate to collect the last of the sauce and popped it in her mouth. She yawned and stretched. 'Is there any dessert?'

'Well, I was kind of hoping you'd want to pick up from where we left off earlier.'

Her eyes lit up. 'Now that sounds like my idea of dessert.'

He took her hand and led her downstairs. She looked really tired now and he wondered if she would prefer to go straight to sleep instead. He walked into the bedroom and then remembered that their clothes were still lying on the floor of the shower.

'I'll just pop those clothes in the washing machine. They might start to smell otherwise.'

She nodded as she sat down on the bed. He moved into the bathroom, scooped up the clothes and went back upstairs to the washing machine. He threw them in, switched it on, put some food down for the dogs and went back downstairs to his bedroom, where he found Darcy, stark naked and curled up on his bed fast asleep.

He sighed. He got undressed, set the alarm on his phone and got into bed by her side, wrapping himself around her and pulling her into him so her back was against his chest. She didn't even stir. Life was pretty perfect right now: he didn't think it could get any better. He switched off the light and closed his eyes, drifting off to sleep with his mermaid in his arms.

CHAPTER 17

Darcy was shaken gently awake the next day. She smiled when she saw Riley standing over her. He was dressed in jeans and a shirt and looked just delicious. Her heart suddenly leapt when she saw the sun streaming in through the window.

'What time is it?'

'It's just after six. I've made you breakfast and then after I'll take you home. You've got plenty of time to get ready.'

She nodded.

'I've put some clothes out for you. I'll make you a cup of tea. I only have PG Tips though, not Lapsang Souchong, I'm afraid.'

She laughed. 'PG Tips is perfect.'

He left her alone and she heard him singing his mermaid song as he went up the stairs.

She quickly dressed in his clothes, knowing she would change once she got back home, and then ran upstairs to join him in the lounge.

She smiled at the huge breakfast he had made for her and at the champagne glasses filled with orange juice.

'You needed a good breakfast for your big day, so I looked up the full English. I think I got everything. Bacon, sausages, eggs, toast, tomatoes, mushrooms and this black stuff which apparently is pigs' blood and smells disgusting, but I'm reliably informed that you English love this on your breakfast.'

She laughed. 'Black pudding is possibly even more disgusting than Marmite, so we can let the dogs eat that, but I'll eat the rest. It looks delicious, thank you.'

'And I wanted something to toast your new job but I thought champagne might be a bit much this time of the morning, so I just went with orange juice instead.'

'That's perfect, this is so lovely, thank you.' She sat down and he offered her the glass of orange juice, taking his as he sat down opposite her.

Propped up against the butter dish was a polished ammonite necklace. Carved into the shape of a heart, it was green and gold and sparkled in the sun.

'Riley, it's beautiful.'

'I'm sorry to say I didn't find it on the beach, I bought that in a shop, but it's the real thing.'

Darcy picked it up and fastened it round her neck. 'I love it and it's perfect for my first day. Thank you.'

'If you come over tonight, we'll celebrate the first day in your new job properly. But for now . . .' He held his glass aloft. 'To you, you wonderful, clever, sweet woman who has turned my life upside down, I want to wish you all the luck in the world with your new job, but you won't need it. Go show them that Darcy brilliance and turn their world upside down too.'

She clinked her glass against his and smiled. Darcy couldn't wait to get back there that night and tell him all about her day. She was going to make a difference in her job. She was looking forward to the challenge. She would make the best Community Development Liaison Manager the council had ever had.

Darcy stared out the office window at the hustle and bustle of Apple Hill on the streets below her. Although the town was pretty, with its old town hall and bell tower, it was busier, more frenetic and chaotic than White Cliff Bay. She had only been in White Cliff Bay just over a week but she had been spoiled by the laidback, relaxed atmosphere of the town, where people stopped each other on the street to chat and everyone seemed to care about each other. Here in Apple Hill, people hurried about, intent on their own business. It was noisy and impersonal and Darcy couldn't wait to get back to her little home town.

Up here, in the council offices that overlooked the town, she was removed from all that, though. The office that looked after Apple Hill, White Cliff Bay and Port Cardinal was quiet, pristine and ultra-modern. And although it wasn't entirely to her taste, being a bit too clinical for her liking, it would still be a lovely place to come to and work in every day.

Riley had dropped her back at the jetty after breakfast. She had showered, dressed and received text messages from Toby and Carmel both wishing her good luck, which was nice, though of course nothing from her parents.

She had arrived at work ten minutes early. The receptionist had greeted her cheerfully, she'd met her boss, Marjorie, who quite frankly seemed a bit of a battle-axe but nothing she hadn't dealt with before. She had also met the people she would be working alongside every day, all with their own jobs to do but all very friendly and helpful people.

She was looking forward to starting work. Marjorie had said she had a big project for her to get her teeth into, although she hadn't seen any sign of that yet.

She'd filled in loads of new employee forms, read the health and safety manual, made several rounds of coffee and tea for everyone, but still there hadn't been any work. As she hated sitting there doing nothing, she had even offered to help type up some letters for Sarah, who was sitting at the next desk.

Marjorie's office door opened and she came out with a large black folder in her hand. Darcy hoped it was her project; she could feel brain cells dying of boredom. To her delight, Marjorie marched straight over to Darcy's desk and plonked the folder down in front of her.

'Here you go, something fun for you to do. Maxine, your predecessor, has made a really good start on this, but she moved to Australia before the project could be completed. This will be your sole responsibility for the next month or two but after that, once the building gets underway, we will have other development projects too. There is a new road which will start construction later this year and we will need you to oversee that as well. For now, Maxine has left you a list of instructions of what needs to be done over the next few weeks and, once you become more familiar with the project, you'll have your own things to do too. I'll just go and get the paperwork for this afternoon. Have a look through the instructions and then start flicking through the file so you can become familiar with the project. Maxine was very organised, so everything should be in order.'

Marjorie hurried off to a desk on the opposite side of the office and Darcy excitedly opened the file. On the very front was a brief summary of the project and a list of instructions from the ever-organised Maxine.

Darcy started reading, keen to get started on her new project.

Rose Island Lighthouse in White Cliff Bay is set to be demolished to make way for an exclusive five-star resort hotel to be built off the headland near Silver Cove. The lighthouse is currently operational but it will be decommissioned and the light will be turned off on Thursday July 14th at 7pm. The new lighthouse on Dagger's Point will be switched on at this time. There is a party planned for the switching-on ceremony, which has already been organised. Demolition of Rose Island Lighthouse is scheduled for Friday 29th July.

At present Rose Island Lighthouse is occupied by Mr Riley Eddison but he will need to be removed from the property, with force if necessary.

Here is a rough list of jobs to be undertaken in the next few weeks. This is just a guide and there will be much more involved that isn't listed here but Sarah or Marjorie will be happy to point you in the right direction, should you get stuck.

1. *Liaise with the people of White Cliff Bay at a meeting in the town hall on Tuesday 12th July, answering their questions and dealing with their complaints in a calm and efficient manner.*

2. *Continue to deal with incoming complaints over the phone and email regarding the demolition of Rose Island Lighthouse.*

3. *Oversee the smooth running of the 'switching-off and -on' ceremony on Thursday 14th July.*

4. *Ensure that Rose Island Lighthouse is evicted of all persons and property by no later than Monday 18th July*

5. *Oversee the demolition of Rose Island Lighthouse on Friday 29th July.*

6. *Organise a party to celebrate the demolition of Rose Island Lighthouse. Many of the contractors used for the switching-on party have already been booked to supply food and fireworks for this event too. Entertainment will need to be finalised.*

7. *Oversee the development of Excalibur Hotel on the existing Rose Island site and its surrounding area.*

There was a list of appendices at the bottom, detailing where Darcy could find maps, plans for the new hotel, information on the party, the demolition, the meeting at the town hall and everything else Darcy would need to know, but she couldn't focus on any of that as tears sprang to her eyes.

She felt sick. She couldn't even blame it on a dodgy burger or a piece of black pudding, as she hadn't eaten either.

She read the list of instructions again, praying that she wouldn't throw up while she went through them or that she had made a mistake.

No, there had been no mistake. It was now her responsibility to destroy the lighthouse she had been battling to save for the last week.

Marjorie came marching across the office towards her with a letter in her hand. Darcy half hoped it was a termination of employment letter, so she wouldn't have to deal with any of this.

'Sally has typed up the final eviction notice for you, you're to deliver it to Mr Edwards at Rose Island Lighthouse today. There's a fisherman called Rob Saunders who lives at number twelve on Main Street, he'll take you over for a fee. Get him to take you over to Rose Island. Make sure Mr Edwards gets the eviction notice personally and then he can't pretend he didn't get it. Tell him he has seven days to remove himself and all his belongings from the property and then you can come back here and work on the presentation for tomorrow night.'

'It's Mr Eddison, not Edwards,' Darcy said, finding her voice at last.

'What?'

'Riley Eddison.'

'I don't think it really matters what his name is as long as he gets out of the lighthouse in seven days. Stupid American. We told him he had to leave two months ago and he refused. Well, now he has a week or we will be forced to enter his property and forcibly remove him.'

'I think it does matter when we kick someone out of their home that we at least take the time to get their name right.'

Marjorie stared at her for a moment, then laughed. 'You're a sensitive little sausage, aren't you? Probably why they hired you for the job – so you can be sensitive while you're handing over the final eviction notice. Why do you care whether we get the name right? Do you know him?'

Should she say she knew him? Would that be enough to have her removed from the project and given something else to do instead?

She looked up at Marjorie. 'I'm dating him. I think me being in charge of this project would therefore be a conflict of interest.'

Marjorie didn't say anything for a few moments. 'Are you saying that your personal life is going to stop you fulfilling your job contract? Because if you are unable to perform your job, then there is no point in being here.'

Should she just walk out? Quit her job within two hours of starting it? Her parents would be mortified. It would become a new anecdote to laugh at her over. The shortest time anyone had spent in a job ever. The other jobs she had failed at had normally lasted at least a few weeks. They had told her how foolish she was to take a job she knew nothing about, to pack up all her worldly goods and travel hundreds of miles away from them, and now it seemed they were right.

But she suddenly didn't care what her parents thought. She couldn't lose Riley over this – he was the best thing that had ever happened to her. She didn't care if she embarrassed them, or even herself. Riley was more important than any of that.

She sighed. But she needed this job. She had to pay her rent, bills, food. Without it she would have to leave White Cliff Bay and then she was sure to lose Riley. She could try to get another one in the town, but she might not get anything, so she had to at least stay in her new job until she had found something else.

Darcy stared down at the huge file on her desk, the one that held all the information about the appeals that had been made and denied, the protests, the details of the demolition and letters of complaint from the people of the town, even letters from the kids in the school. She couldn't touch any of this, she couldn't make a stand against Riley and she couldn't fight against those people. How was she going to face the people in White Cliff Bay, the friends she had made through fighting to save the lighthouse?

'It's not just him, though, I've made a lot of friends in White Cliff Bay. None of them want to see the lighthouse demolished and it would be awkward for me to work on this project and live there,' Darcy tried again. Surely Marjorie would understand this. There must be something else she could do in this job that didn't involve the lighthouse. There would always be new developments to oversee; helping to develop the opening of the new aquarium would be much more up her street.

'This is an unfortunate situation, but this is all part of working for the council in a small community,' Marjorie said. 'The council's path will always cross with the locals, especially in this department, and there will always be someone that you know affected by the changes. Most jobs will upset someone or other. If you were a traffic warden or even worked for the police, you wouldn't be particularly popular either. We hired you because you seemed to be professional enough to be able to cope with that. You can either accept the pros and cons that come with this job or get another job somewhere else.'

Maybe the eviction notice would be better coming from her rather than anyone else. She could be supportive and sensitive. Riley knew this was coming, so it wouldn't be a total shock for him. Maybe he would even laugh at the irony of her being given this job.

Maybe this wouldn't be a bad thing after all. Maybe, now she was on the inside, she could use her position to find out more information, anything that could be useful in the fight to save the lighthouse. Maybe there were some loopholes that she could twist to her advantage. She could talk to people who worked in the department or the powers-that-be who had made this decision. She could convey how upset the townspeople were about losing the lighthouse. If she was going to leave the first chance she got, she was going to use the opportunity to fight from the inside while she could.

She swallowed down the lump in her throat. 'No, if you don't think it is inappropriate for me to be working on this project, then I am happy to continue to manage it.'

'We don't have anyone else to manage this project, so we will have to trust that you can carry out the job you've been hired to do professionally and without bias. Now take that notice over to your boyfriend and make sure you are back here by one.'

Darcy watched Marjorie march back across the office until she had disappeared and then let her head fall into her hands. When she had said she was looking forward to the challenge, she had never expected this. Life was so much simpler when she only had fish and sharks to deal with on a daily basis. On days like this she missed that more than anything.

On the half-hour drive from Apple Hill where the council offices were based, Darcy had been practising what she was going to say to Riley, but she had nothing good. She kept telling herself the final eviction notice would be so much better coming from her rather than some arsehole in a suit who didn't care about Riley or the lighthouse. He would appreciate that it was her delivering it. But that didn't stop her stomach churning like it was in a tumble dryer.

She had decided to use Riley's second boat, *Trident*, instead of getting this Rob Saunders to take her. Riley had already offered it to her whenever she wanted to use it and she would prefer to conduct this horrible business without a witness.

Darcy stepped down into Riley's boat, staring at the controls uselessly. She had watched Riley enough times that she should know how these things worked, but she had never really paid too much attention. His main boat was a bit different to this one. She started the engine, thankful that at least there was a steering wheel and not a rudder to control. She looked down at what probably were some gears. She wondered whether first gear was the fastest or the slowest. She unhooked the boat and watched nervously as the boat floated away from the jetty. Thankfully, there were no other boats nearby, so she couldn't cause too much damage.

Closing one eye, she moved the gear stick into first and the boat shot forward. She let out a shriek and quickly moved it back into neutral again and the boat drifted to a stop. OK, she could do this, it was only her nerves over seeing Riley that were making this worse. She put it into first again and as the boat moved forward she steered it in the direction of the lighthouse. It was quite easy when she got the hang of it, but she knew parking the boat wouldn't be that simple.

Thankfully, as she drew close, Riley came running down the steps to greet her. He had the biggest grin on his face at seeing her and it broke her heart that she would be the one to take the smile away.

'Riley, how do I park the boat without crashing into the rocks?' Darcy called.

'Just cut the engine and then throw me the rope, I'll pull you in.'

She did as she was told and he hauled the boat towards the rocks and secured it in place. She grabbed her briefcase and then took his hand as she stepped up onto the rocks in front of him.

He kissed her on the cheek. 'What a wonderful surprise, I wasn't expecting to see you until later. Were you so good at your job they've given you the rest of the day off?'

It hurt that he had such faith in her. If she did her job well, it would hurt him even more.

She took a deep breath. 'I'm here in an official capacity.'

His brow furrowed in confusion.

Like ripping a plaster off, she had to do it all in one go. She dug in her briefcase and pulled out the final eviction notice. She didn't dare look at him as she held it out. 'I'm so sorry, I didn't want to do this. I'm afraid you have seven days to leave the property and remove all your belongings too.'

He took the notice and stared at it, then looked back at her uncomprehendingly. 'Why are you giving me this?'

God, she was going to cry or throw up or maybe both. 'My new job is to oversee the demolition of the lighthouse, help to organise the celebrations for the demolition of Rose Island Lighthouse, and help with the development of the new hotel,' she said quickly, hating that her voice wobbled as she spoke.

Riley took a step back away from her, hurt and betrayal etched on his face. She took a step towards him, reaching out to touch him, but he pulled his arm from her hand.

'I'm so sorry, I know it's rubbish that I'm the one who has to tell you to leave, but if it wasn't me standing here it'd be someone else.'

'But it *is* you standing there and that makes it so much worse. You were the one who didn't give up, who gave me a glimmer of hope that something could be done. I took my shirt off and exploited myself for that article because you said it was important and I thought if you were fighting for my home that I had to fight for it too. Now you're just giving up? It's so disappointing.'

That one word hurt like he had just slapped her round the face. She had let him down.

She choked back the tears. 'I haven't given up. This is just a job.'

'Your job is to oversee the smooth demolition of my home. My family's legacy. You know how important this place is to me.'

'But you said yourself it was a lost cause. You'd given up.'

'I had given up until you came along. There was nothing that I could do, no battles left to fight, you know that. Doesn't mean that I'm not absolutely destroyed by it. And now all the anger and hatred I feel against the people who are evicting me from my home is going to be directed at you.' He ran his hands through his hair so it stuck out like he had been electrocuted.

'Nothing has to change between us. It's unfortunate that I'm in charge of this, but you knew this was coming, you knew that there was very little we could do to stop it. I understand you are upset and angry, but you have no right to direct that anger at me. It's just a job. I have bills to pay, I can't just quit, but it doesn't change who I am.'

'Do you want a job that hurts people? That's not who you are. I don't know this Darcy, the one shoving papers in my face. My Darcy would never do that.'

My Darcy. She echoed that around in her head, loving the sound of belonging to him. But he was right. This job wasn't who she was.

He suddenly took a step back, the look on his face one of utter horror. 'Unless none of it was real. That's what all this was about, wasn't it? I'm so stupid. I asked myself why you came to my island that day when no one had ever swam out here before. I asked myself who would leave their home and travel hundreds of miles to take a job they knew next to nothing about. I asked myself why someone like you would be interested in a man like me. None of it was real, was it? You were just a honey trap. You knew what your job was all along and you were sent here to get me to trust you. Christ, that's why you were so intent on getting the townspeople to like you over the last week – because you wanted them to trust you as well.'

'No, that wasn't how it was at all. How could you even begin to think that?'

Though she'd suspected he would take it badly, she had never in her wildest dreams expected this.

But before she could say anything else, Riley turned and walked back to the lighthouse. She stared after him in shock and a second later she heard the door to the lighthouse slam close.

She was frozen to the spot for a second before she marched up to the lighthouse door and banged on the door. How dare he accuse her of that?

There was no answer, so she banged again.

There was still no answer.

She leaned her head against the door, the fight going out of her as tears welled in her eyes.

'I could never do anything like that because I love you,' she told the closed door quietly. 'And it breaks my heart that I've hurt you.'

She sighed. She wasn't going to let him go without a fight but she knew she had to give him time to realise how unreasonable he was being, or at least to calm down after her shock revelation.

She got back into the boat, unhooked the rope and drove back to the mainland, hating her new job more than anything.

CHAPTER 18

Darcy sailed the boat back to Rose Island that night after work, determined to talk to Riley. The clouds were a charcoal grey and the waves were choppy, echoing her mood exactly. It had been the worst first day in a job she had ever had. Not only had she hurt Riley and potentially lost him for good, but she had spent the whole afternoon creating a presentation for her meeting in the town hall with the people of the town the next night. She had made so many friends over the last few days and now they were all about to be betrayed by her. Knowing that Suzanna had encouraged the townspeople to give whoever came from the council a hard time wasn't exactly encouraging either.

She had been so close to quitting her job that afternoon. She wasn't prepared to lose Riley over it, but if she had already lost him and he wouldn't forgive her for something which was out of her control, then there would be no point losing her job and her home too.

She approached the island and cut the engine as she had done earlier that day. The boat drifted, but it didn't get close enough to the pole for her to be able to throw the rope around it. The boat floated past, two or three metres from the steps, narrowly avoiding crashing into Riley's other boat, and so she restarted the engine and turned the boat around to make a second pass. This time she managed to get the rope around the pole and quickly cut the engine. She hopped onto the steps, walked up to the door and hammered on it.

She waited for a few minutes, knowing it could take Riley a while to get down all the stairs, especially if he was at the top, but when there was no answer she banged on the door again. There was still no answer. This was ridiculous; he was ignoring her.

Darcy moved carefully down the rock to the end of the island in the hope she could attract his attention from one of the windows.

There was no movement at any of them, but she jumped up and down, waving like crazy, in the hope he might see her. Kelpie appeared at one of the windows, wagging her whole body in excitement at seeing her, but there was no sign of Riley in the same room.

What should she do? Just keep banging on his door in the vain hope that he would get tired of the knocking and eventually let her in?

She moved forward and slipped on the ground, falling hard on her side and smacking her head on the rocks. She cried out in pain as she sat up woozily. She looked up at the lighthouse and for a moment she saw movement at a window, the floor below where Kelpie had been seconds before. If Riley had seen her fall, he would be down there in seconds to see if she was OK and, while she'd prefer not to have an argument with him while she was bruised and wet, she would take that over not talking to him at all.

She staggered to her feet and moved back to the door, feeling the sticky wetness on her head that indicated she had cut herself.

The door stayed resolutely closed. If Riley had seen her fall, he clearly didn't care. Feeling the tears threatening to come again and determined not to let him see her cry, she moved back towards her boat, only to find that it had floated away – clearly, she hadn't tied it up properly. It was over fifty metres away now and getting still further away. Just as Darcy thought it couldn't get any worse, the heavens opened and the rain came down, soaking her to the skin within seconds. She sat down on the steps and burst into tears.

※ ※ ※

Riley pulled off his headphones and stood up to stretch, peering out the window at the dark clouds outside. He had written quite possibly the worst song he had ever written. Fuelled by anger and hurt, his supposed love song had ended up being a rant about betrayal. But it had served a purpose. Getting all his angst down on paper, he was now left feeling numb. He had to talk to Darcy. If it was going to end between them, and he strongly suspected it would, then he would end things properly and not leave the words he had poured into his song left unsaid. It had been childish to ignore her when he'd stormed off earlier, but he'd been so angry that he was afraid he would say something that could never be taken back. He had needed space and, now he'd had it, he needed to talk to her. She'd be finished work by now and probably just arriving home. He would go over and talk to her calmly.

Rain suddenly lashed against the window and off in the distance thunder rumbled. He sighed. He would have a shower first and hope the weather passed later, so he could talk to her, although it really wasn't a conversation he was looking forward to.

※ ※ ※

Darcy pressed the buzzer for Libby and George's flat and shivered against the cold and the rain.

Libby's cheery voice came over the intercom. 'Hello?'

'Libby, it's me, can you let me in?' Darcy's teeth chattered as she spoke.

Libby buzzed the door and then came out as Darcy let herself in.

'Oh no, you're soaked, it looks like you've been for a swim.'

'I have and now I'm locked out, do you have some spare clothes?'

Libby's face fell. 'What do you mean, you've been for a swim? You're dressed in your clothes for the office.'

Darcy shivered and Libby quickly ushered her inside their flat.

'Here, let me get you something to wear, my clothes might be a bit small as you're so tall but I'm sure George will have something.'

George stood up as Darcy moved into the lounge, his eyes widening in horror.

'Darcy, what happened, are you OK? What happened to your face?'

'George, put the kettle on and make a cup of tea, we're just going to borrow some of your clothes,' Libby said and George nodded.

'Do you want a bath or anything?' Libby asked, ushering her into the bedroom.

'I think I'm wet enough. Just some dry clothes would be great and then I'll get out of your hair.'

Libby laid a pair of jeans, underwear and a hoodie on the bed, gave her a towel and left her alone. Darcy got changed in record time, still shivering even though she was now at least in dry clothes. She went back out into the lounge and smiled weakly when she saw that George had a fire going and Libby was waiting for her with a mug of tea.

'Come and sit down and tell us what happened,' Libby said, gently.

Darcy didn't think she had the energy to rehash it again – she had used every ounce of energy to swim across the bay in her clothes – but the fire was very tempting so she sat down right in front of it and sipped her tea. She closed her eyes for a second, letting the warmth seep into her bones. When she opened them, Libby and George were watching her with concern.

Darcy sighed and determined that she wouldn't cry again. 'So it turns out my new job is to ensure the smooth demolition of Rose Island Lighthouse, including making sure Riley leaves. I had to give him his final eviction notice today and he didn't take it too well. We had a big row and he . . .'

'Hit you?' George said, showing the first sign of anger she had seen from him.

'No!'

'Threw you in the sea?' Libby said.

'No, God no. Riley would never do anything like that. He just stormed off. I went over there to talk to him again tonight, but he wouldn't answer the door. I slipped on the rocks, banged my head. When I went to leave, I realised that I hadn't tied up his boat properly and it had floated away. His other boat needs a key, which he keeps just inside the door of the lighthouse, and he still wouldn't open the door for me, so I had to swim back. I've had to leave my bag with my keys, phone and laptop in his other boat and swim back without them, which was the hardest swim in my life in my clothes.'

'Oh, Darcy,' Libby said.

'And now I have no way to get back in my flat, I've lost a beautiful necklace he gave me and the man I was falling in love with hates me and I have to do a presentation tomorrow night to the people of White Cliff Bay to tell them when the lighthouse will be demolished and how this will be a wonderful thing for them.' It was no good – her voice had already taken on a wobble, something Libby and George were bound to notice.

They stared at her, clearly having no idea how to deal with this situation. So Libby did what any good mother would do: she got up and enveloped her in a big hug. Darcy smiled and her smile grew even bigger when George joined them for the hug too.

Eventually, they let her go.

'You guys don't hate me?'

'Why would we hate you? It sounds like that lighthouse is coming down regardless of what we do, and although I'll be gutted to see it go, we can't shoot the messenger,' Libby said.

'That's what I was trying to say to Riley . . . if it wasn't me, it would be someone else, but he is so hurt by it that there's no reasoning with him at the moment. Do you think the rest of the town will be this understanding?'

Libby nodded and George shook his head.

'George!' Libby scolded.

'Sorry, but I don't think they will. I wonder if some will think that you deliberately tried to befriend them as part of your job so it would be easier to present to them the fait accompli.'

'That's what Riley thought too, is that what you think?'

'No, but there will be some who think that. You sat with them, joked with them, and now you are going to take away the very thing they have been battling to save for months.'

'I didn't know what my job was. My job title wasn't lighthouse destroyer, it's Community Development Liaison Manager. Nowhere in my job description or my interview was there ever any mention about lighthouses or demolition or stomping all over people's hopes, dreams and the heritage of the town.' Darcy could hear her voice getting louder and she winced. 'Sorry.'

Libby shook her head. 'Don't be sorry, none of this is your fault. And if any of the small-minded people in the town give you any grief, you send them to us and we'll sort them out.'

George nodded and Darcy nearly wept again that at least she would still have two friends by the end of all this.

'I can't quit. I need the money to pay the rent and bills.'

'Why should you quit? So this first project is a shitty one, there will be other projects which you can get your teeth into. You were really looking forward to this job too, and you're perfect for it, with the way you can engage with people. You just have to get through this and move on to the next project.'

'But will any of the community want to engage with me on the next project after I let them down so badly on this one? God, I hate disappointing people. I feel like I've spent my whole life letting people down and now I've done it again.'

They were both silent. There really was nothing left to say.

'I'm sorry for interrupting your evening.'

'Don't be silly.' Libby waved away her concern.

'I need to phone the landlord to come and let me in. Though I have no idea what his number is.'

'I probably have a spare key actually,' Libby said. 'I used to live there before George swept me off my feet and I gave George a spare key back then. I don't think we ever gave it back when I moved out. Where would it be, George?'

George thought for a moment and then stood up and moved into the kitchen. Darcy could hear him rooting around for a moment or two, but then he came back holding a key and looking triumphant.

'You don't have to go now, stay for dinner. It's spaghetti Bolognese and George's Bolognese is always amazing,' Libby said.

'No, thank you, you've been very kind, but I'd rather lick my wounds on my own for a while. Besides, I have to take Ben out, he's been on his own all day.'

Libby stood up and hugged Darcy goodbye, and George passed her the key.

'That flat was very lucky for me,' Libby said. 'I found the love of my life while I was living there and it sounds like you have too. Don't give it up without a fight.'

Darcy nodded and then left them to go back to her flat.

Ben greeted her joyously as she walked in, and she bent down to bury her face in his fur.

Riley had told her off a few days before for giving up on him without a fight but that was exactly what he had done to her. He had seen her fall and hadn't come down to check on her, and even when it had started to rain he had ignored her bangs on the door – these were not the signs of someone who reciprocated the loving feelings she felt for him, or someone she was particularly keen on getting involved with.

She sighed and stood up, ready to make some dinner. She noticed that the light on her answer machine was flashing, so she hit 'play', hoping somehow that it was a message from Riley to say all was forgiven.

She listened to the message and recognised the voice straight away. The nasal tone sent ice to her heart. It seemed that her parents were coming to see her tomorrow. As Toby hadn't called to say he was coming down with them, she guessed they were coming down without him. If there was a straw that broke the camel's back, her parents visiting would be it.

CHAPTER 19

Riley watched Kelpie jump in and out of the gentle waves at the end of Silver Cove beach. For a puppy that had nearly drowned in the underwater current not far from where she was playing, she didn't seem to have any lasting effects or residual fears.

He looked back towards Sea View Court where Darcy lived, and sighed. He had spent most of his walk glancing over at her home, wanting to see her and dreading it at the same time.

Riley had found her bag in his boat that morning, though he had no idea how it had got there. Maybe she had accidentally left it there when she had been round the day before to drop the bombshell but hadn't dared come back last night to collect it. He had been round to her flat earlier to drop the bag back and she hadn't been in. It was nearly lunchtime, so she would be at work anyway and he couldn't help feeling a tiny bit disappointed about that. Riley missed her. His bed felt empty without her – hell, his whole life felt empty without her – and it annoyed him that he had fallen so hard, so fast for her. He couldn't forget how hurt she had been the day before and it gnawed at his insides, making him ache with guilt. Riley realised now that accusing her of pretending to like him just so he would be more amenable to leaving was completely not true. He didn't know her well but he knew her enough to realise that she could never be capable of something like that. He was still angry though, and although he thought he had every right to be, he was beginning to doubt that too.

Riley saw George and Libby walking hand in hand along the beach towards him and he waved. Libby waved back, George did not.

They approached and Riley smiled at them.

'Hi, Riley,' Libby said. But George looked away, clearly annoyed about something and Riley got the impression that that something was him.

'Hi . . .' He wanted to ask about Darcy, but what could he say? *Have you seen her? Was she OK? Was she angry? Am I justified in my reaction?*

In the end, Libby helped him out. 'We saw Darcy last night, she was in a bit of a bad way.'

That was the last thing he wanted to hear.

George turned to look at him. 'I think that's a bit of an understatement. I get that you are angry with her, but the way you treated her last night was out of order.'

Riley frowned. 'You mean yesterday morning. I didn't see her last night.'

'I know, she came round to see you after work and you refused to let her in. She fell on the rocks, banged her head, then it started to rain and you still wouldn't let her in. I know you are angry, but you should have checked on her, she could have been seriously hurt.'

His heart thundered against his chest. '*What?* Is she OK? I had no idea she came round. I was working on my music yesterday afternoon. I didn't hear her. Christ, is she OK?'

Libby put a hand on George's arm to stop him talking. 'She has a bad cut to the side of her head, but it didn't look like it needed stitches or anything. When Darcy couldn't get your attention, she went back to the boat, only to find that she hadn't tied it up properly and it had floated away. She tried to let you know but you still weren't answering, so she had to swim back.'

'In her clothes?'

Libby nodded and Riley groaned. This was just getting worse and worse. That at least explained why her bag had been left in his boat. 'Are you sure she's OK?'

'She was a bit cold, a bit upset by the whole thing, but physically she is fine.'

Riley sighed. 'I didn't know.' It didn't change anything between them, but if he had known he would never have left her outside.

'Are you really going to let her job come between you?' Libby said. 'From what I've seen, you two are completely head over heels in love with each other. A love like that doesn't come around very often. It seems silly to throw it away for something that is quite clearly not her fault. The lighthouse will be pulled down with or without her, so . . .'

He was so conflicted over all of this. The island and the lighthouse was a huge part of his family's history and Darcy was the person who would oversee its destruction, but Libby was right, it would happen without Darcy's help. But the last thing he needed right now was to be told he was in the wrong.

'I'm sorry, I need to go. I left Darcy's bag outside her flat door, will you make sure she gets it?'

Libby nodded.

Riley touched his hat and, whistling for Kelpie, he walked away.

Riley sat on the outdoor terrace of The Crabshack, a restaurant that served the most amazing seafood. He had agreed to meet Suzanna for lunch. He was early, so he was enjoying a glass of iced tea while Kelpie rested under the shade of the table.

Already the news that he had been given his final eviction notice had spread across the town. A lot of the people who worked in the town council office in Apple Hill had friends and relatives who lived in White Cliff Bay, so by the time that Riley walked through the town, the news had reached the ears of most people who lived there. It amazed him that in a place like this you couldn't even sneeze without the whole town knowing about it. He had been stopped several times on the way from the beach with people offering their sympathies; many of them had heard about Darcy's role in it all and he had found himself defending her on quite a few occasions.

In the gap between the houses he could see his lighthouse and it tore him apart to know it would be gone in a couple of weeks. He sighed as he looked around the terrace. It was quite busy today, just as it had been every time he had come. The demolition of the lighthouse wouldn't affect these people. Some of them might be sad to see it go, but after a few days life would continue as normal. Was he holding too much stock in what was essentially bricks and mortar? Wasn't his relationship with Darcy worth preserving more?

His ears pricked up as a middle-aged couple at the next table mentioned Darcy's name. He hadn't seen them around before and didn't think they were from the town.

'So another Darcy cock-up to add to the list,' said the man who almost looked clown-like with his crop of red curly hair and red cheeks.

'She is embarrassing us and herself by starting a job with little experience or knowledge of the role,' the woman said. She was blonde with the same sea-blue eyes as Darcy, but there was nothing pretty or sweet about this woman. Her mouth was sucked in so tight with disapproval Riley could barely see her lips. This was obviously a normal pose for the woman, as the age lines on her face suggested that she had used this look of disapproval many, many times before. 'I can't believe she has been in the job for one day and she has upset so many people in the town already. I'm embarrassed to tell people she is our daughter now, in case we get ousted from the town with pitchforks because of our association with her.'

Riley stared at the couple in shock. These were Darcy's parents. The ones solely responsible for her low self-esteem and fear of disappointing people. It was easy to see why Darcy felt like she had let them down because they made her feel that way – and seemingly deliberately so. What kind of parents would do that to their child? He had grown up with parents who told him he could be whatever he wanted to be, that if he wanted to be an astronaut or a pilot or a florist or an actor, then he could do that. They told him he was brilliant at everything he turned his hand to, that they were proud of him every single day. That's what parents were supposed to do, and he had always taken it for granted that all children had that, but clearly Darcy hadn't.

'She'll be back home again before the month is out, you mark my words. She'll be fired again or quit and have to move out of this inbred backwater,' her father said.

'And how do we explain that to our friends at the golf club? This will be the seventeenth job she will have lost. She'll be a laughing stock.'

'She already is.' Darcy's father shook his head, laughing to himself.

Riley stared at the menu but didn't see the words, suddenly losing any appetite at all. He had to say something, though he knew he had to calm down first or he would say something awful.

'And who is this Riley bloke everyone keeps referring to when they talk about her? She's sleeping with him? She's been here one week and she's sleeping with him already. I raised her better than that,' her mum said.

'He's an American apparently.'

'I don't like Americans, they're so loud and crass.'

'He's very rich too.'

'Oh well, maybe I can make an exception for him,' she guffawed and Darcy's father joined in too.

Riley stood up and approached the table before he knew what he was doing. They looked up at him and he instinctively touched the rim of his hat and then regretted it. These people didn't deserve any respect.

'I'm Riley Eddison, the rich, crass American who is sleeping with your daughter.'

Darcy's mum's jaw dropped, her eyes bulging as she looked around her to see who was listening. It seemed that everyone on the terrace had stopped talking to tune in to this piece of gossip. Well, if he was going to leave this place, if it was really over between him and Darcy, he might as well go out with a bang.

'Darcy is one of the most remarkable people I have ever met. You should be immensely proud of her, but you're not. But that's OK because she is this amazing, incredible woman in spite of you, not because of you. You crushed her dreams, mocked her life choices and mistakes, made it very clear how disappointed you were of her, laughed at her to her face and behind her back, made her feel worthless and not good enough. But despite this terrible upbringing, she is strong, determined and brave. She is gentle, funny, passionate, intelligent and one of the kindest people I know. Maybe I should say thank you because she saw what kind of people you were and either consciously or subconsciously decided that she never wanted to be like that. You want to know why she travelled hundreds of miles to take a job with no idea what was involved? Because she couldn't bear to see the looks of disappointment on your faces any more. Want to know why she is staying in a job that causes everyone in the town to hate her? Because that is preferable to coming home to live with you and, after spending five minutes listening to your conversation, I can see why.'

He turned to see Suzanna looking at him in shock. He slammed some money on his table and took her arm. 'We'll have to eat elsewhere, I'm afraid, the clientele here is not to my taste.'

He walked away with Suzanna, with Kelpie hurrying at his side. If things between him and Darcy weren't over before, they were now. Telling her parents exactly what he thought of them would be the final nail in the coffin.

Darcy stood in the little kitchen off the town hall listening to the hundreds of people make their way to their seats, ready for the meeting which she was leading. She had spent the whole day preparing for this presentation, and she knew it was going to be a disaster. There was a gentle knock on the door and Darcy turned round to see Libby, George and Verity standing in the doorway. They moved into the room and Verity immediately hugged her.

Darcy felt some of the tension seep out of her. 'Verity, I'm so sorry. I never knew this was what my job entailed. I was going to quit as soon as I found out, but I need the money and I thought maybe I might be able to use my contacts at the council to help somehow and . . .'

'It's not your fault and most of the people in the town will see that,' Verity said.

'I don't think so. They're going to hate me,' Darcy said, sadly.

'How are you doing?' Libby asked, taking her hand.

'Fine.'

'Really?'

'No, not really. I haven't seen Riley and despite the fact that the man refuses to talk to me, I still care about how much I'm hurting him. My head hasn't stopped banging all day, I'm about to do a presentation about demolishing the lighthouse and how great this is for the town when I don't honestly believe a word of what I'm going to say and, to top it all, I left work to find a furious voicemail from my parents about how disappointed they are that I've been badmouthing them to the people of White Cliff Bay. I have no idea what that's about because they won't return my calls but they've gone back home and they've made it very clear that I won't be welcome back there when I fail at this job, which they have no doubt that I will.'

'Do you think Riley said something to them?' George said.

'I doubt it. I've only seen him get angry about the things he really cares about, namely the lighthouse.'

'I think he cares about you too,' Libby said.

Darcy shook her head. 'I don't think he does and honestly, if I was in his shoes, I would hate me too.'

There was another knock on the door, and Darcy turned to see Riley standing there. Her heart skipped a beat and then thundered against her ribs. What could she say to him that hadn't already been said? The thought that she had lost him for good was completely heartbreaking.

'Suzanna sent me to come and get you. She said that we're ready for you to start now.'

Darcy couldn't move. Verity and Libby gave her a hug and George squeezed her hand and they left her alone with Riley. He stepped into the room with her, making the tiny kitchen feel even smaller all of a sudden.

He was standing close, too close, and his warm intoxicating sweet scent enveloped her.

He reached out and ever so gently touched her temple just below her wound.

'I'm sorry that you fell and banged your head. I had no idea you came round last night until George and Libby told me what happened this morning. I wouldn't have left you outside in the rain.'

Darcy swallowed. 'I'm sorry about your boat.'

'Someone found it and brought it back.'

'That's good.'

He nodded. 'I'm sorry about what I said to your parents too.'

'That was you? What did you say?'

'I told them what I thought of you and mostly what I thought of them. It wasn't very nice.'

Her heart dropped into her stomach. She imagined Riley had gone to town about how she had betrayed and deceived him and what a lowlife she was.

He dug into his pocket and pulled out the heart-shaped ammonite necklace he had given her on her first day at work.

'I found this on the rocks tonight. The chain must have broken when you fell, so I put it on a new chain.' He stared down at it for a moment, then passed it to her. 'Do you remember what I said when I gave you the apology ammonite?'

Darcy thought back, but she couldn't remember anything specific. She shook her head.

'About the ammonites surviving millions of years,' he prompted.

Something tugged at her memory, but with him staring at her so intently she couldn't think straight. What was he trying to say? He was almost being nice to her, though she didn't understand why.

He stared at her as if he was going to say something else, but after a moment he stepped to one side. 'You better go and give your speech, everyone is waiting.'

Darcy hesitated for a second, then walked past him into the hall, putting the ammonite into the pocket of her suit jacket. She walked up the aisle towards the stage and conversation quietened down. Suzanna was already up there and, as silence descended on the room, she spoke.

'Thank you again for coming. Most of you already know this, but since our last meeting there have been some very unfortunate developments. Riley has been given his final eviction notice, he has less than one week until he has to leave and the demolition date, we are told, will be very shortly after that. This is a great blow to us all – we had raised thousands of pounds for the appeal – but it seems we are now too late . . .'

There were several mutterings of discontent around the room as Riley took his seat in the front row. His eyes weren't on Suzanna though, but on Darcy, as she waited for her turn to talk.

'Many of you know Darcy Davenport, she works for the council department in charge of the demolition of the lighthouse and she is going to give a speech about the developments and then answer your questions after.'

There were gasps from some of the people in the audience who hadn't yet heard the news that she was a traitor.

Darcy took to the steps and as she swapped places with Suzanna she stared out at the crowd of people. She had talked to most of these people over the last week, joined them in the fight for the lighthouse, and now she was on the other side.

She cleared her throat. 'I know you are all very disappointed with the recent developments. Mr Eddison has been told to leave the premises by the 18th of July and the date for the demolition has been set for the 29th of July, just over two weeks from now.'

There were mutterings and angry words said and Darcy didn't know whether to go on talking or wait for them to finish. When they didn't show any signs of stopping, she decided to carry on regardless.

'We are very excited about the new plans for the town. The new hotel, Excalibur, will provide much-needed income. The town is dying, many shops and business seem to be closing, and Excalibur will bring tourists to the town who will come and spend money in your shops and restaurants—'

'What about all the guesthouses and small hotels that will go out of business because people are staying in your big posh hotel instead?' someone from the audience suddenly shouted out.

Darcy faltered, not expecting questions to be fired at her half-way through the speech. 'There is no reason why Excalibur and the guesthouses can't coexist. Excalibur will be offering day spa packages and many people will prefer to stay in slightly cheaper accommodation than in the hotel itself. There will also be many functions in Excalibur and again many people will not want to pay the extra to stay overnight there. We need to move with the times, most of the hotels here don't offer Wi-Fi. There is no pool or even a gym in the town. Tourists want those facilities as standard and Excalibur will give it to them. Some restaurants in the town stop serving food at eight, whereas Excalibur's restaurants will be open almost twenty-four hours.'

'We don't want it,' someone else shouted. 'We're happy with our town exactly how it is.'

'It's not just an upgrade in facilities,' Darcy continued smoothly, slowly feeling her integrity and pride in herself dying as she spouted the corporate crap that would change the face of the wonderful town of White Cliff Bay forever. 'Excalibur will bring jobs to the people of White Cliff Bay, Port Cardinal and the surrounding areas. The hotel will need chefs, waiters, waitresses, maintenance staff, housekeepers, receptionists and managers. We will also be employing local people for the construction of the hotel too. Excalibur comes from a successful hotel chain and the wages will be very good.'

There were more murmurs of unhappiness. They weren't buying any of this.

'This week the light will be switched off in Rose Island Lighthouse and the light in the new lighthouse at Dagger's Point will be switched on. There will be fireworks and a barbecue at Dagger's Point and you are of course welcome to come along with your families and children. We are also planning a big party for the demolition of Rose Island Lighthouse. We want to do something to celebrate its legacy for the town and I'm sure all of you will want to come to watch the spectacle of Rose Island Lighthouse being destroyed.'

'Why would we want to watch that?' someone shouted with disgust.

Why indeed. It was a terrible idea, and one that she had tried to persuade Marjorie from doing but she had insisted it was a brilliant idea.

Ryan, the boy she'd talked to about sharks, suddenly stood up. 'If the lighthouse is blown up, won't it hurt all the sharks and fishes?'

Something jolted inside Darcy at this and she was surprised that she hadn't thought of that. With all the stress of her new job it hadn't crossed her mind.

'It will be a controlled explosion, honey, and the damage and debris in the sea will be reduced to an absolute minimum.'

'So there will be some debris in the sea?' said someone else. 'A lot of the townspeople are fishermen. We can't have the fish killed, as that will damage our livelihood.'

'I'm not totally up to speed on the way the explosion will be carried out, but from what I understand there will be precautionary measures in place to reduce the impact of the explosion on the sea,' Darcy continued. 'If you come along to the demolition party you can see for yourselves. We will have fireworks and food. There will be entertainment, songs, dancers, fire breathers and acrobats. It will be a wonderful night. We are hoping that the lord mayor will press the button to initiate the demolition and—'

'I will not,' a lady called out from the audience and Darcy looked through the crowd at the chains of office around the neck of a young woman. 'I want no part of such a disgusting event. A celebration of our lighthouse being pulled down? That doesn't sound like anything to celebrate to me.'

There were cheers of agreement.

'Well, maybe the head teacher of the local school would like to—'

'Nope,' said a man from three rows back, who she guessed was the head teacher.

'Well, I guess I'll be pressing the button myself then,' Darcy said sarcastically and then instantly regretted it.

Riley suddenly got up from the front row and walked out and to her horror several other members of the audience left with him. There was silence from the audience as they registered what was going on and then all at once everyone was leaving until there was only George, Libby and Verity left.

Darcy didn't move for a moment, wondering if anyone was coming back, but as the doors closed behind the last person she stepped down from the stage.

Libby, George and Verity came over.

'It was a good speech.' Libby tried unsuccessfully to cheer Darcy up.

'It was a terrible speech. The council have no idea how upset the people of the town are by this. They don't want the hotel and I can see why. It will ruin this town. Part of its charm is its sleepy nature and laidback way of life, that's why people come here. The tourists don't want big, corporate all-exclusive hotels when they come here; they go to London or Paris or New York for that. The tourists come to see Rose Island Lighthouse and the iconic white cliffs. That's the only reason. Destroying the lighthouse will kill this town and then the final nail in the coffin will be that stupid hotel. And a demolition party? What are they thinking?'

She was suddenly aware that they weren't alone. Suzanna appeared from the back of the room.

'So you *do* care? Riley said that you did, but I wasn't so sure.'

Darcy sighed. 'I do. I will be gutted when the lighthouse is pulled down, for the town, for you and for Riley.'

'I wanted to give you a hard time tonight, but Riley forbade it, even though he is hurt by it all.'

This surprised Darcy. 'I think that's the worst part. I don't want to see him get hurt, but I know he hates me because of it.'

'I think hate is a strong word. He feels very protective over you and you should have seen him defend you against your parents.'

'Defend me? He told them what he thought of me.'

'Yes. I heard the words: remarkable, amazing, kind, passionate, strong. He obviously thinks a lot of you and he told your parents that you had become this incredible woman in spite of them, not because of them.'

Darcy had no words at all, but Libby gave a little squeak of joy.

'I told you he loved you.'

'But he walked out,' Darcy protested.

'You did say you were going to press the button to demolish the lighthouse yourself,' George said.

'I didn't mean it.'

Darcy rubbed her eyes, suddenly feeling very tired. God, it was such a mess.

'I need to talk to him.'

'He's already gone. He was heading straight for the jetty when he left.'

'There's no way past this, is there? He's too hurt. Even if I quit my job now, the damage has been done. I've betrayed him, let him down. I chose my job over him and he won't forgive that.'

She was suddenly reminded of Ginny and Riley's dad. Ginny had chosen her job over him and in the end that had been the end of their relationship. Tom had never forgiven her or come back for her.

Suzanna sighed. 'I asked him today if he was going to stay once he leaves the lighthouse. He said he wasn't sure there was anything left here for him any more.'

It shouldn't have hurt Darcy so much, but it did. It was over and it didn't seem like there was anything she could do about it.

Anger ripped through her. None of this was her fault and Riley knew that. The man was being a stubborn arse and he had no right to treat her like this. She deserved better and the next time she saw him, she would tell him that.

CHAPTER 20

Riley looked around him at the boxes filled with all his things. He had spent the whole day packing, with no idea where he was going to go. He hadn't seen Darcy since the night before at the town council meeting, and he still didn't know whether to shake or kiss her the next time he saw her.

He looked out of the lighthouse window towards her apartment, hoping to get a glimpse of her maybe taking Ben for his evening walk after she had finished her day at work. There was no movement from the house, but just as he was about to turn away he saw a flash of fire from the doorway. There was no mistaking that hair as it gleamed in the sun nor the big black dog jumping up and down at her side.

Riley picked up the binoculars he sometimes used to watch the seals and trained them on her. Darcy was dressed in her wetsuit again, obviously going out for a swim, but she was heading in the opposite direction to the lighthouse and towards the rocks on the other end of the beach.

He shifted uncomfortably. She surely wouldn't go swimming there. There were signs warning of the dangers of the underwater currents that ripped through the gaps in the rocks. He had rescued Kelpie from those exact rocks when somehow she had got caught in the current.

But as Darcy walked straight past one of the warning signs without giving it a sideways glance and then paddled out into the water right by the rocks, he threw the binoculars aside and ran down the stairs.

By the time Riley had reached the door, she was already half-way up the rocky outcrop, with Ben swimming just ahead of her. He swore under his breath, leapt in his boat and tore across the bay towards her, waving his arms and sounding his horn.

Riley slowed his boat to a stop just in front of Darcy and she stopped, treading water as she looked up at him with surprise.

'What's wrong? Don't tell me you own these rocks as well.'

'Get in.'

'What?'

'There are underwater currents and rip tides here – if you'd bothered to read the signs, you would know that. Now get in.'

She paled in the water and suddenly looked around for Ben.

'Where is he?'

Riley looked around too and saw Ben had carried on swimming around his boat. He swore again and manoeuvred the boat in between Darcy and Ben so she wouldn't go after him. He wasn't sure which rocks had the underwater current, but he parked the boat against the gully between the rocks, hoping that if this was where the currents ripped through the rocks, his boat could stop Ben from being dragged through.

'Ben, here boy, Ben!' Riley called, whistling and clapping his hands to get the dog's attention.

Ben turned and swam back towards the boat, getting too near the rocks for Riley's liking. He reached over the edge of the boat towards him, ready to grab him as soon as he could, but when Ben was only a metre away from his fingers he was suddenly snatched from above the surface and disappeared under the water.

Riley grabbed the rope he used to tie the boat up, leaping onto the rocks, ignoring Darcy's cries of panic. The gully between the rocks was deep, but if he was right the sea would drag Ben through the crack into the water on the other side, just as it had with Kelpie. Sure enough, a second later a black shadow tore past him in the water below. He reached down, grabbed Ben's collar and yanked him out onto the rocks.

Ben coughed, spluttered and looked stunned, but he was breathing and alive.

Darcy scrabbled up onto the rocks with them, threw her arms around the poor dog's neck and sobbed into his fur. Ben licked her face a few times, threw up a load of seawater, then carried on licking her and Darcy didn't bat an eyelid.

After the sobbing subsided a little, Riley knelt down by her side. 'Let's take you both home.'

She nodded and he helped her to her feet and pulled the boat in close so she could get in. Ben jumped in after her, clearly unfazed by his brush with death.

Riley climbed in, started the engine and drove back across the bay towards the lighthouse. If Darcy was confused by him taking her to his home and not hers, she didn't say anything. She was too busy hugging and squeezing Ben. Even when he cut the engine, and Ben leapt out and ran up the steps, clearly delighted to be back, she still didn't say anything as he helped her out of the boat.

She followed him up the steps and he let them into the lighthouse. She was shaking and he didn't think it was from the cold.

'Why don't you have a shower and get changed and I'll make us some dinner.'

'OK,' she said, quietly.

He followed her up the stairs and, as she went into the bedroom, he moved upstairs to the living room to start dinner.

Ben was being greeted joyously by Kelpie, and Riley wondered if he was somehow regaling her with his ordeal.

This was an unexpected turn of events. Riley had wanted to see Darcy again but not under these circumstances. But now she was here, what was he going to say to her?

He quickly made a pasta and sauce dish, and was just putting it on the table when Darcy arrived in the room wearing just his robe again.

They ate in complete silence, with Darcy barely looking at him. He was still angry, but he knew he couldn't take it out on her any longer. However, now it seemed that she was angry with him too. When she had finished, she went and sat on the sofa by the fire, watching Ben astutely.

She had her arms wrapped around her and looked so pale. She'd had such a shock that night, now would be the wrong time to talk. She shivered.

'I'll get a blanket or a sweater.'

She didn't even acknowledge that he had spoken.

He went downstairs, grabbed a woolly sweater from the closet and a fleecy warm blanket and went back up to the living room.

Darcy was leaning against the back of the sofa, fast asleep.

He lifted her feet and swung her round, catching the back of her head and lowering her down. Then he covered her with the blanket.

He stared at her for a few moments and then, not knowing why other than it felt the right thing to do, he crawled under the blanket with her and pulled her against him.

He felt his body almost sigh with relief. She was back where she belonged.

Darcy felt herself shaken awake the next day. She opened her eyes to see Riley leaning over her with a mug of tea in his hand. She sat up, noticing the blanket that he'd put over her the night before, and took the mug from him.

'I didn't want you to be late for work, thought you'd want to go home and get changed.'

'Thank you.'

'I've made you some breakfast. When you've finished, I'll take you back home.'

He was being nice to her and she had no idea why. She looked around at all the boxes and felt her throat tighten with emotion.

'So you're getting ready to leave?'

Riley stared at her for a moment before speaking. 'I didn't think it would be a good idea to still be here when you blow the place up.'

Darcy winced and Riley's face softened slightly. 'It makes sense to start packing up now, I have a lot of stuff.'

'Where will you go?'

Riley shrugged.

'I am sorry about all of this, the lighthouse, the demolition party, my job. I hate it all as much as you do.'

'I know you do.'

'I wanted this job to work so badly, to prove to my parents and to me that for once I could hold down a job, that my decision to come here was a good one. But now I wish more than anything that I hadn't taken it.'

'Do you regret coming here?'

'No, I love it here. I've looked for other jobs, anything which meant that I could quit my council job and still stay here, but there's nothing. What I said the other night at the meeting about the shops and restaurants closing down was true. Many businesses are cutting back on their staff, not taking new people on. There are no jobs in the town and even if there were no one is going to hire me now, I've made enough enemies to ensure that.'

'People are a lot more forgiving here than they were in my home town.'

She stared at him. 'Does that go for you too? Are you a forgiving sort?'

He said nothing for a while. 'You need to eat your breakfast, you'll be late.'

She nodded. There would be no forgiveness from him.

After breakfast, Riley gave her some of his clothes to wear and then took her and Ben across the bay to the jetty at the end of Silver Cove beach.

He helped her up onto the jetty and she stared up at him. If he was leaving soon, would this be the last time she saw him?

'Thank you for saving Ben, I would have been distraught if anything had happened to him.'

He nodded.

She turned and walked away, knowing this time he wouldn't be calling her back. She stopped and turned back; he was still standing there and watching her.

Darcy walked back towards him, not knowing what she was doing, but knowing she needed to do something.

She stood in front of him as he stared at her, his green eyes reflecting the colour of the sea in the early morning sunshine. She leaned up and kissed him, and though she fully expected him to push her off, she wrapped her arms round his neck and kissed him hard. It was only a second or two later when his arms slid round her and he kissed her back. She jolted with shock against him, but his arms tightened around her, refusing to let her go. God, he was kissing her goodbye. This was it. The last time she would see him and he knew it too. She kissed him with everything she had.

Eventually, they parted.

'I love you, Riley Eddison. I don't know if that makes any difference to your plans, but I love you. You asked if I regretted coming here, and I could never regret it because this is where I met you, and even if I never see you again after today, you will always be the best thing that ever happened to me.'

Riley didn't say anything, but his eyes were dark with emotion.

She pulled back out of his arms and walked away. She didn't look back and he didn't call her back either.

Darcy was quite surprised by the turnout for the switching-off ceremony that night, as she stepped out from her flat onto the beach on Silver Cove where everyone had congregated. She'd expected everyone to boycott it, but she supposed it was something interesting to watch for the locals. After all, it was the first time in a hundred and forty years that the light on Rose Island Lighthouse would go out.

Marjorie wanted to be the one to switch off the light, and Darcy was thrilled that she wouldn't be the one to do it. There was a big button rigged up like something out of one of those cheesy game shows. In reality the button didn't do anything, the light would be turned off by the Lighthouse Trust hundreds of miles away from where they were standing, but Marjorie probably didn't know that and the crowds that had come to watch wouldn't care anyway.

Darcy pulled her suit jacket tighter around her as a cool breeze swept over the beach. She had deliberated over what she should wear tonight. She had considered something black, perhaps to mark the bereavement of the town. She certainly didn't feel she could wear something bright and celebratory, like Marjorie in her bright yellow dress. She had settled in the end for a midnight-blue summer dress teamed with her suit jacket again, as she was there in a professional capacity.

Darcy moved through the crowds to get to the front. Some people smiled at her sadly, some people blanked her completely. Libby squeezed her hand as she walked past her and George. She wondered if Riley was there or whether he was inside his lighthouse, licking his wounds. But then she saw him. He was so tall and, with his cowboy hat on, he was hard to miss. He was standing a little way off from the main crowd, where there were just a few stragglers on the sides. He was staring out at the lighthouse across the waves as the sun disappeared into the scarlet sea.

She slipped her hands into her pocket and her fingers grazed against something smooth. She pulled it out and stared at the heart-shaped ammonite. She ran her finger across it, suddenly remembering what Riley had said when he had given her the apology ammonite. He'd said that if the ammonites could survive millions of years, then their relationship could survive a few bumps in the road. Was this a bump? Was that what he had been trying to say before the meeting had started, that somehow they would get through this?

Regardless of what the future held for them, she knew she wanted to be there for Riley now. There was no one he could turn to for a sympathetic ear; he was utterly alone and he would be devastated to see the light go out.

As Marjorie mounted the steps on the temporary stage, Darcy cut through the crowds to be at Riley's side. He didn't notice her. Marjorie started some big speech about Rose Island Lighthouse and what an important part it had played in the community and how the people of the town owed the Eddison family a debt of gratitude but, like putting a great racehorse out to grass, it was time to retire the lighthouse too.

Marjorie started a countdown, which she clearly hoped everyone in the town would join in with. Nobody did. Everyone was silent.

Darcy slipped her hand into Riley's and he tore his eyes from the lighthouse for a moment to look at her. He turned back to look at his home, interlacing his fingers through hers. She smiled slightly, just for a second, but as Marjorie hit number one in the countdown and slammed her hand on the red button and the arc of light from Rose Island Lighthouse went out, plunging the coastline temporarily into darkness, Darcy couldn't fight the tears that filled her eyes.

Some people booed, others just turned and walked away. A second or two later a bright white beam of light burst out from the new lighthouse on Dagger's Point. The light was infinitely brighter than the beam from Rose Island Lighthouse and seemed to reach much further out into the sea than the old light did.

Riley looked down at Darcy.

'I'm sorry,' she whispered.

He'd opened his mouth to speak just as several people came up to commiserate with him. As they gathered round him and she was jostled in the crowd, her hand came loose from his. She sighed and walked away. She had to be up at the new lighthouse in the next few minutes to oversee the celebrations and fireworks up there.

She left Silver Cove beach and followed the crowds through White Cliff Bay towards the opposite headland. She hoped that some of these people would be going to the party, that they had been persuaded by the lure of free food and fireworks. But as she walked through the town the crowd thinned out, as people either went back home or disappeared into pubs, until she was alone on the cobbled streets.

She took the steep path up to the headland and saw all the food vans that were offering a range of Chinese and Italian or the standard burgers and chips. The pyrotechnic team were at the very end of the headland and she ducked under the rope to go and talk to them.

'What's going on, love? We were told to wait for everyone to get up here, but your boss said they'd all be here by now,' said one of the team.

'I don't think anyone is coming. You might as well make a start.'

The man's shoulders slumped. 'No one? I've never done a display for no one before.'

'I think most people are still down on the beach. They'll get a much better view of the fireworks over the sea from down there,' Darcy lied, but the man visibly brightened.

'Yes, of course, I can see that. I expect they want to take photos of the fireworks over the old lighthouse and the sea.'

Darcy nodded encouragingly.

'Well, step back, love, it can get a bit dangerous unless you know what you are doing.'

Darcy walked back behind the rope, as the first explosion of silver filled the night sky. It was quickly joined by a burst of scarlet.

Marjorie suddenly puffed to Darcy's side. 'What's going on, why are they starting? We need to wait for the townspeople to get here.'

'No one is coming, Marjorie. They've all gone home. No one wants to celebrate the light going out. Everyone is so upset about all of this. People wouldn't mind the hotel so much if only the lighthouse could stay. But no one is going to support or celebrate the lighthouse's demise.'

'Nonsense, they were all upset about the new aquarium being built. That ugly monstrosity on the far side of Silver Cove! They protested that it wasn't in keeping with the landscape, but they got over it. It opens in two weeks and they've sold out of tickets for every day of the first few weeks, so the people of the town clearly are not that upset by it.'

There was some irony in there somewhere – that Darcy hadn't been put in charge of the development of the new aquarium, but instead destroying the lighthouse that she had been trying to save.

'Although they might have to delay the opening,' Marjorie went on. 'There was a small fire in there a few weeks ago and it's going to cost thousands to repair the damage . . . money they simply don't have.'

'I can see why people would be excited about an aquarium, though, it's something new and wonderful for the town. People are not going to change their mind about this.'

'We'll see,' Marjorie said. 'The hotel will be the best thing that has happened to this town.'

'No, it'll be the worst.'

Marjorie shook her head, presumably in despair, as she walked away to talk to a few more council officials.

Darcy turned her attention back to the fireworks. It was all pretty spectacular, the colours and explosions of light over the inky water.

Suddenly she felt a hand in hers, strong fingers linking with her own.

She looked up to see Riley staring at her.

'You're the last person I expected to see here.'

'I came to see you.'

She turned, giving him her full attention.

'It makes a difference,' he said.

'What does?'

He stared down at her, his face lit up by the sparkling fireworks above him, making him look even more beautiful.

'What you said this morning. It makes a difference.'

Darcy was still confused.

'Come home with me. We need to talk.'

She looked around at the celebrations, or rather the lack of them. There was nothing left for her to do. She nodded and Riley started leading her away from the headland and down the path back towards the jetty. 'I'll make sure you get up tomorrow for work, so you don't need to worry.'

'I have tomorrow off actually. I only work four and half days a week and I've worked my half a day this week by leading the meeting on Tuesday night and helping to organise tonight's fiasco . . .' she trailed off as she suddenly registered what he had said. 'Am I staying over?'

'I hope so.'

Her poor broken heart suddenly stuttered back to life again, as Riley led her out onto the jetty.

'Wait, I can't. I have to get back for Ben.'

'He's already at the lighthouse. I asked Libby and George if they would take him over.'

'What? They colluded with you in the kidnapping of my dog?'

'I told Libby I needed to talk to you, but that I needed Ben to do it and she agreed.'

'No questions asked?'

'She asked if the talking would involve making you cry and I said I hoped not.'

'Wow, security is lax around here.'

Riley hopped down into the boat and helped Darcy down with him. She sat down and watched the fireworks light up the dark sky, as Riley manoeuvred the boat across the bay. When he got to the other side, he cut the engine and helped her out onto the steps just as the fireworks reached an explosive crescendo, with bursts of colour filling up the sky.

Riley's hand went to her waist and she looked up at him as he held her close. 'What you said this morning made a difference. Because I love you, too.'

Darcy stared at him, her heart suddenly thundering against her chest. 'What? But . . .'

'I love you, my little mermaid. I'm not sure at what point I fell in love with you, whether it was the first time I saw you, or when you stood on my rocks with a triumphant smile on your face and told me you were soliciting. But I know I love you. I have never felt for anybody what I feel for you. You have filled my life with colour and laughter and you have filled my heart with your love and kindness. I simply cannot imagine my life without you in it. I have rented a house in the town and I move in tomorrow. I want to see where this goes for us.'

'But . . . you were so angry.'

'I'm still angry. I'm angry that the council are demolishing it to make room for a luxury hotel without any thought for the impact of that on the town and I'm angry that in a few weeks they will hold a demolition party to celebrate my family's legacy being destroyed and that you apparently will be the one to press the button.'

'No, I won't, I didn't mean . . .'

'I know, it's OK. All of that would have happened whether you came into my life or not and I can't lay the blame at your feet. I'm sorry that it even crossed my mind for a second that you had got involved with me purely to get me to leave the lighthouse. I was hurt and I took it out on you and I'm sorry for that. But I have missed you so much over the last few days. I don't want to lose you. If I had to choose between keeping you in my life or saving the lighthouse, I'd choose you without any hesitation. I love you, and I'm hoping we can pretend the last few days didn't happen.'

Darcy shook her head. 'I don't want to pretend they didn't happen. It's made us stronger because of it and it's made us re-alise what is important to us. I'd already decided that I would hand my notice in on Monday. I can't do this job and maintain any integrity. The town needs the lighthouse more than it needs a new fancy hotel and if working there means losing you, then I can't do it.'

'You won't lose me and I don't want you to quit your job for me. I know it's important to you and I won't stand in the way of that.'

'I don't want to hurt you either, that's the last thing I want. I love you, too.'

He bent his head down and kissed her as the last fireworks exploded in the night sky, then the silence of the sea descended on them. She kissed him, suddenly hungry for him. He tasted so good, sweet and smoky, and he loved her too. She couldn't stop the tears that filled her eyes.

'Stay with me tonight,' he whispered in her ear, before kissing her neck.

She nodded. 'I'm not going anywhere.'

He took her hand and led her back inside the lighthouse, but to her surprise they didn't stop at his bedroom or the lounge, they walked all the way to the very top, where the lantern room was.

'I've never been in here at night,' Riley said. 'I'd likely have been blinded by the light if I had. But now that's not a problem, and I imagine the view will be quite spectacular. I wanted to share my first time with you.'

He climbed up the few ladder-like stairs to the door and opened it, stepping inside. Darcy followed him up. The disused lantern was in the middle and there was a wide walkway around the outside of it. The room had windows almost all the way round, apart from the back plate, which stopped the light reaching the town. The back plate took up about a quarter of the wall space, but the rest of it was just glass and the view was incredible.

The sky was clear, a deep perfect blue, millions of stars lighting up the darkness like tiny sparkly snowflakes. The midnight-blue dress she had worn, embedded with tiny sequins, sparkled in the moonlight and up here she felt for a moment as if she was part of the endless starry sky. The room they were in was dark, but outside it was dazzling. The moon was huge tonight, casting its silvery blanket over the inky water. The world was peaceful out there and it was just the two of them up here where no one could see them.

She moved round the walkway so she could only see the sea and not the town. Nothing moved out there, no boats or lights, the twinkling sea stretching out as far as she could see in every direction.

She felt Riley behind her, his hands on her shoulders as he kissed the back of her head. She turned in his arms and looked at the lantern that stood in the darkness.

She wound her arms round his neck. 'Do you feel sad being in here?'

He shook his head. 'I thought I might, but you're here with me and that means more to me than anything else. You look incredible tonight and right now there's only one thing I want to do.'

He eased her back against the furthest edge of the back plate, so the glass window was next to her. She looked down at the silver-crested waves lapping against the rocks.

It was then she saw the bedding, the duvets, blankets and pillows on the floor. 'Oh, so I was a bit of a foregone conclusion, was I?' She smiled up at him.

He laughed. 'No, I just fancied sleeping up here myself tonight, under the stars. Thought I might need reminding that it's a big world out there and though I will be gutted to see this lighthouse destroyed, it's quite insignificant in the grand scheme of things.'

'We have each other and that's what matters.'

He nodded and kissed her, softly, sliding the jacket off her shoulders and then his hands slipped round her back to undo the zip of her dress. She ran her hands down his sides until she found the bottom of his jumper. She slipped her hands underneath that and the T-shirt he was wearing so she could feel his soft skin and that solid wall of muscle. He moaned softly against her lips at her touch. She pulled his T-shirt over his head. He let the dress pool at her feet and she relished the feel of his hot skin against hers. Without taking his mouth from hers, he managed to divest them both of the rest of their clothes. His hands caressed her all over, stroking, touching as if he wanted her all at once.

He lifted her and she quickly wrapped her legs around him, as he pinned her against the wall with his weight sliding carefully inside her. She wrapped her arms tight around him, arching back and tilting her head up so she could see the stars. Right then and there, the only thing that mattered was her and Riley. They might be insignificant in the world, but they weren't insignificant to each other. He kissed her neck as he moved inside her again and again, but with his fingers gently on her chin he brought her mouth back to his and kissed her hard, swallowing her groans of desire for him. She had been searching all her life for the perfect job, the perfect place, but here in his arms was where she belonged.

CHAPTER 21

Darcy woke next morning to a cornflower-blue sky filling the windows of the lantern room. Not a cloud was in sight. Riley wasn't in sight either. She grabbed his T-shirt and pulled it on and went off in search of him. She found him in the basement with his hands against the glass as he stared out at all the sea life that was moving serenely past the window.

He turned to face her as she came down the stairs and his face lit up in a huge smile. He pulled her into his arms in front of the window and kissed her sweetly.

'So you'll be pleased to know I have a date next week,' Riley said, peppering soft kisses down her neck.

'A date?' God, he knew the exact place to kiss her to make her go weak.

'Yes, with Seb.'

She pulled back to look at him in confusion.

'I realised you were right, that I was missing out on so much, closing myself off from forming relationships with anyone here. And if I was going to stay here, I knew I had to make friends and not just with the beautiful woman I'm dating. So yesterday, when I saw Seb walking Jack on the beach, I marched straight up to him and told him I wanted to go out with him for a drink some time.'

Darcy burst out laughing. 'You asked him out on a date?'

'Yes, I didn't realise that's how it would sound when I asked him, until the awkward silence had lasted for longer than thirty seconds. Then I quickly explained and we had a good laugh about it, but he has invited me to play golf with him and his friends next week.'

'Do you play?'

'Not really. I've played once or twice. I used to be really good at ice hockey when I was younger and I guess it's the same sort of skills. Different-shaped puck, but the stick is pretty much the same shape.'

'I think the stick is called a club in golf.'

Riley shrugged.

Darcy smiled that he was making an effort to be part of this town. She didn't want him to be alone. Everyone needed friends and it was quite a turning point for him that he was actively looking to make a connection here that was not just with her.

'I love that you have a date.'

He smiled and hugged her, leaning his head against hers.

'What were you thinking when I came in here? You looked deep in thought,' Darcy asked, her hands snaking round and giving his bum a quick squeeze.

He looked away out the window. 'I was actually thinking these poor fish are going to have the shock of their lives when this place is demolished. The explosion will scare the crap out of them.'

'I've been thinking that too, ever since Ryan mentioned it at the town council meeting. I might contact the Sea Life Conservation Society on Monday. They'll come down and make sure there are precautions in place, but you're right, no matter what measures are taken to reduce the amount of debris in the water, the explosion will scare them. Sound travels four times faster in water than in air, which means the noise will spread further too.'

He smiled at her and she laughed. 'Sorry, I'm such a geek.'

'Don't ever apologise for being you. I love you, exactly as you are.'

She moved in front of him to stare out the window at the fish. The visibility was quite spectacular, but as the sea faded into the gloom, something big moved out there just beyond where her vision couldn't reach. It was probably a seal: Riley had mentioned he had seen quite a few of them around the lighthouse. She pressed her face against the glass, but the shadow didn't become any clearer.

'What's the plan for today? Are we going to start moving your things into your new house?'

Riley kissed her neck, his hands going round her stomach. 'Well, that was my plan, but now you're here, half dressed, I think I'd quite like to make love to you in every room of the lighthouse, including the radar room, as that's no longer in action. Give the lighthouse a proper send-off. Let's start in here and give the fish something to think about.' He ran his hands under her T-shirt and across her stomach and hips. She giggled but the laugh stalled in her throat as the shadow momentarily became clear. She wriggled out of his grasp, cupping her hands against the glass so she could only see out the window. But the shadow was gone.

Had she imagined it?

'Did you see that?'

'What? The big brownish ray-type fish? Sure. They're here all the time.'

'They?' Darcy squeaked.

'I've seen two, but there could be more of them. What's wrong, you've gone so pale?'

'That was an angel shark.' She felt stupid saying it, but she knew what she had seen. 'The angel shark is very rare. It's now on the critically endangered list and is extinct in the North Sea.

The last reported sighting of one round here was a dead one they found in Plymouth three or four years ago.'

'Oh. Wow, I never knew. I've been watching them for months and didn't think they were anything special. Hang on, if they're so rare, we don't want to do anything that might hurt them or scare them off.'

Darcy smiled, hugely. 'Exactly. I need to check first. Thank God I kept my scuba-diving equipment. You can be my dive boat. I have a dive flag I think, you can attach it to the boat to warn other boats that I'm diving and then when I release my SMB – my Surface Marker Buoy – you can come and collect me. I shouldn't be too long and hopefully I won't need to go too far . . .'

'Wait. You're going diving with sharks?'

'These aren't dangerous. Well, they can be, but only if provoked and I won't get close enough for that. I've dived with sharks hundreds of times, we are not prey for sharks. We don't taste good to them, so they're just not interested, and the angel shark definitely won't eat a human, we're too big for that. I have to see for myself they are there. I can't call in the experts based on a three-second shadow.' She raced from the room before Riley could protest any more. 'Get dressed, I need you to take me home.'

Riley stood in the boat, scanning the surface of the water, not sure where Darcy would come up. He didn't like the idea of her diving on her own, let alone with sharks. She had assured him she knew what she was doing and was highly experienced and trained in diving in British waters, but he still wasn't happy. She had been gone for about twenty minutes now and that was nineteen minutes too long by his book. But what could he do? He had no diving equipment, so he could hardly go in after her and look for her, and even if he did he wouldn't know what to do with it. At what point should he start to worry . . . well, more so than he was doing now? Who should he call if there was a problem – the lifeguard, the air ambulance, the SAS?

Suddenly a bright orange sausage burst from the waves less than a hundred metres off the starboard side. He manoeuvred the boat very slowly in that direction so that he wouldn't drive over her. He watched her surface next to the buoy and she gave him the OK signal to let him know that everything was fine. Everything would be fine as soon as he got her back into the boat and she was safe from being eaten.

He manoeuvred the boat slowly to her side and he grabbed the handle at the back of her jacket and hauled her aboard. She was giggling and laughing as she offered up her fins one by one, and he removed them from her feet. She unstrapped herself from the dive jacket and leapt up, pulling her hood and gloves off too.

'That was amazing, I've missed diving so much. And the good news is it's definitely an angel shark. I only saw one, hiding in the sand, but it was unmistakable and one is all we need.'

She leapt into his arms, soaking him to the skin in seconds, shrieking and laughing with joy.

'Wait, what does it mean?'

'It means that as soon as we get back to the lighthouse I put out a call to the Sea Life Conservation Society and the Shark Trust. They will need to come out here themselves to check I am telling the truth, probably tonight because the angel shark is generally a nocturnal species, and if they find just one shark, let alone more than one, they will slap a protection order on the lighthouse so fast the council won't know what's hit them. It means that the lighthouse will be saved and that the hotel can't be built anywhere near here either.'

'No way. A shark just saved my home? How is that even possible?'

'It's critically endangered, nearing extinction. It's protected under the Wildlife and Countryside Act. They will want to do anything that is possible to protect its species, including protecting any possible nesting sites. They might need to do further studies on the area, tag the sharks to see if they are migrating or staying localised, but if what you said is true and you've been watching them for months they might not be migratory. Some of them are and some aren't, and it sounds like our sharks aren't. We may only get a temporary reprieve to start with until they have done more studies. But in most cases a temporary protection order will almost always turn into a permanent one. If they are passing through here now, they will most likely pass through here again and we don't want to do anything that would threaten that.'

'The lighthouse will stay?'

Darcy nodded. 'It looks that way. I don't want to make any false promises, but I know how seriously these guys take the protection of endangered species.'

He hugged her, barely daring to believe it. There was no way this was over and would end so easily. He would hold out a little longer before he got his hopes up.

CHAPTER 22

'Thank you all for coming to this emergency meeting,' Suzanna said, from her usual position on the stage at the town hall. 'I know it's Sunday and this was very last minute, so thank you for all your support . . .'

Darcy looked around at all the sad and angry faces. There had been many confused looks, as she had walked into the town hall hand in hand with Riley. She didn't know whether any of them would move on as easily as Riley had, but she didn't really care. She had Riley and that was all that mattered.

'There has been a new development since our last meeting, but I'm going to let our Darcy Davenport explain the details.'

Darcy stood up and climbed the steps to the stage, ignoring the stony looks on the faces of the audience. 'I actually have an assistant to help me share the news. Ryan?' She gestured for him to join her.

Ryan stood up proudly with his roll of paper and came to join her on the stage. Darcy took one edge of the paper and Ryan took a few steps back, unfurling the paper between them. Darcy hadn't seen the drawing he had done before, so she was utterly surprised to see how good it was.

'THIS IS AN ANGEL SHARK!' Ryan shouted, failing to understand the difference between speaking loudly and yelling. Darcy saw Maggie look completely shocked by this sudden new-found confidence in her son. 'My top three facts about the angel shark are: number three, they look like a ray and are a part of the ray family. Number two, they are ovoviviparous . . .'

Darcy smiled as he said the word as easily as if he was saying the word cat or dog.

'. . . which means they lay eggs in their bellies and then when the eggs hatch they give birth to the shark pups like mammals do. And number one is that they hide in the sand so the fish can't see them and when the fish swim over their heads they burst from the sand and BOOM! They eat the fish.'

Darcy smirked at his undeniable enthusiasm. She looked around the room and a lot of the people were smiling at Ryan's mini-presentation too.

Darcy cleared her throat. 'Thank you, Ryan. The reason we wanted to share with you some information about the angel shark tonight is because we thought you might want to see the reason why the lighthouse has been saved.'

There were gasps of excitement from the audience.

'Some of you may know that I used to be a marine biologist and two days ago I spotted the angel shark from Rose Island Lighthouse. The angel shark is classed as critically endangered and I knew the importance of letting the Shark Trust and the Sea Life Conservation Society know about the sighting. They have been here for the last few days and spotted and tagged three of them in this area, which they are very excited about. One we believe is pregnant and will give birth in the next few days. This is a huge discovery as far as the Shark Trust is concerned but, more importantly for the town, it means that no developments, including the demolition of the current lighthouse or the building of the new hotel, can take place, now or at any time in the future, in case the sharks are hurt and—'

The rest of her sentence was drowned out in a huge cheer from the crowd. When she had phoned Suzanna to tell her of the developments, Suzanna had insisted that Darcy be the one to tell the town the reason why. At first Darcy had protested, but Suzanna hadn't taken no for an answer. Now she was glad she hadn't. Being able to put the smiles back on the townspeople's faces was worth it.

She waited for the cheering to pass, but it didn't. She held her hand out for Ryan to high-five, but he gave her a big hug instead. She hugged him back and then went to sit down with Riley.

He kissed her on the cheek. 'Good job.'

She smiled.

Suzanna took to the stage again and she gestured for quiet, which eventually the crowd gave her.

'Yes, it's wonderful news and all thanks to Darcy here, too. There is the small matter to decide of what to do with the money we raised to help save the lighthouse. I had the idea that maybe we could donate it to the new aquarium. As many of you know, there was a small fire there a few weeks ago and there is several thousands pounds' worth of damage. It looks likely that the opening will have to be postponed. Now, as the aquarium is working closely with the Sea Life Conservation Society and the Shark Trust with marine conservation projects in the local area, I thought it was fitting that, as the angel shark saved our lighthouse, we should give something back to help continue the fight to save these animals and many others that are under threat. We could take a vote now. All those in favour of giving the money to the aquarium, please stand up and . . .'

The noise in the room was almost deafening, as every single person in the room stood up to vote yes.

Darcy couldn't help the smile from spreading on her face.

The meeting was over quite quickly after that, but as Darcy and Riley tried to leave, several people stopped her to say thank you or to give her a hug. Eventually they made it out onto the street and they headed back to the jetty to take the boat over to the lighthouse.

'You're a hero,' Riley said, giving her hand a squeeze.

Darcy laughed. 'Hardly, but it's nice to know that I'm back in the good books again, though I doubt the reception will be the same once I go back to work tomorrow.'

'Do you think they'll be mad?'

'Oh, they'll be furious. The people who had bought the land for Excalibur paid millions of pounds for it and now the council will have to give it all back. But hopefully I'll be given some new projects to get my teeth into now, ones that are not going to upset the whole of the town.'

Riley helped her down into the boat. 'Do you think Anthony would offer you a job?'

Darcy smiled hugely. The marine biologist who worked for the Shark Trust on conservation projects had hinted that he might have a job for her, but it had been mentioned in such a casual way that Darcy hadn't wanted to pin her hopes on it. He had said that the Shark Trust needed someone with her expertise and he had taken her number. Whether he was just being polite remained to be seen.

'I don't know. But I do know the aquarium is looking for staff, specifically to do talks with the public and school children. I was thinking I might apply. It might only be part time and if so the money won't be very good, but it's what I love and what I spent years training to do. I haven't decided yet, but I think I'm better suited to working there than as a Community Development Liaison Manager.'

'Oh, I don't know, you worked very well within the community before you switched sides.'

She laughed. 'I never switched sides, I was always on your side, always will be.'

She watched him smile in the moonlight. 'Well, that's good because I have an awful lot of unpacking to do.'

He helped her out onto the steps at the lighthouse. 'Didn't you promise me that you were going to make love to me in every room of the lighthouse?'

He laughed. 'I did.'

'Well, I think you better make a start.'

Riley was worried for Darcy. He knew she had been nervous going into work that morning too. She had been at work an hour now and he'd asked her to call him to let him know how it was going, but he hadn't heard a peep.

He watched Kelpie jumping all over Ben in a vain attempt to get him to play with her, but he was happy sleeping or at least pretending to.

Suddenly, there was a knock on the door and he quickly ran downstairs to answer it. Darcy was standing on his doorstep with the biggest grin on her face.

'I've got good news and good news.'

He laughed. 'Tell me the good news.'

'Thanks to the coverage in the national papers and the petition, Barry, one of the men from the planning department, said that he will make sure the compulsory purchase order is withdrawn. The council can't do anything with the lighthouse or the island now, so I guess it's in their interest to let you stay. They certainly won't want any backlash from the public for kicking you out of your home for no reason.'

'That's wonderful news. I hoped they would let me stay now they can't build the hotel. I've not accepted any money for the compulsory purchase order, so I imagine it will be quite straightforward. What's the other good news?'

'I got fired.'

His heart fell a little, but it was hard to feel too sorry for her when she was looking so euphoric.

'I'm sorry to hear that.'

'I'm not. I woke up this morning and I knew this job just isn't for me. There will always be developments in the local areas that will upset someone or other, a road that goes through someone's farm, a school that is going to close, a new supermarket that will affect the local shops, a new theme park with a rollercoaster that goes straight through the town centre. I don't want to stand for the council and tell the people of the town how wonderful these things are, I just can't do it. I trained to be a marine biologist and I'm really good at it. I want to do that again. So I went in today to tell them I was going to quit. They fired me before I got that far, but I really don't care. Anyway, I walked out of there and Anthony had left me a message on my phone. He is offering me two days a week to help with the shark conservation projects in the local area. I'm not sure what the money will be like and I have no idea how I'm going to afford the rent on my place, but he was pretty confident he'd be able to get me a day or two at the aquarium too. Maybe I can get a few bar shifts in the Bubble and Froth to help pay the rent as well . . . I don't know, I'll make it work somehow.'

'This is fantastic news, I'm so happy for you. You get to do what you love and there is nothing more wonderful than that.'

'I have to tell my parents.' She rooted in her bag for her phone.

'Do you? I don't think you owe them any kind of explanation.'

'I need to do this.'

He wanted to protest, but she had a huge smile on her face and he didn't want to do anything to take that away from her. Though he was sure her parents would do that soon enough.

He watched as she dialled the number with confidence and then put it onto loudspeaker so he could hear the conversation. The phone rang a few times and was then picked up by her mum.

'Hello?'

'Hi Mum, it's me.'

Riley could hear the coldness in Darcy's mum's voice when she spoke. 'Hello, Darcy.'

'Hi. Is Dad with you?'

'No, he's playing golf.'

Darcy hesitated for a second but clearly decided to proceed anyway. 'I'm just ringing to say I quit my job . . .'

'Darcy! This is so disappointing. I don't know what your father will say when I tell him . . .'

'You can tell him that I quit my job on moral grounds, that doing a job that upsets so many people is not who I am and I would rather live on beans on toast for the rest of my life than do a job that strips me of my integrity. I'm going to work as a marine biologist for the Shark Trust and for the local aquarium, which is what I want to do more than anything.'

Riley heard her mum sigh. Darcy smiled, which surprised him.

'And for the first time in my life I don't care what either of you think. You feel let down by me, that I'm an embarrassment, but I feel let down by you too. When I lost my job at the Marine Centre, I let your disappointment in my chosen career cloud my judgement. I should have found another marine biology job but instead almost every job I tried to get after that was a job I hoped you'd be proud of. But none of them made you proud and none of them were me. That's why I failed at them. Because I could never ever be the person you wanted me to be.'

'Darcy, I . . .'

'I love the sea and the animals in it and that is never going to change,' Darcy continued. 'I am a brilliant marine biologist and you should be proud of that. Marine biology is a hard subject to be good at, as sea life is so diverse. It takes intelligence and commitment and if you think that I got a doctorate in it by messing around in the sea then you are obviously not as clever as I think you are either. But more than that, you should be proud that I'm going to do the job of my dreams. I made my dreams a reality with hard work and dedication, despite you trying to destroy them. I am going to do something good in this town and for shark conservation in general. And if you can come here without once saying anything about how disappointed you are or looking at me with disapproval, then I'd like to see you. If not . . . well, I guess we'll see each other once a year at Christmas. I'll bring Riley, I'm sure you guys will get on like a house on fire.'

There was silence from the other end until finally her mum spoke. 'I don't think . . .'

'That's the trouble, Mum, you don't think. You don't think about how your actions or what you say impact on other people. But I'm not going to let you put me down again. Perhaps once you've relayed this conversation to Dad, you might want to give me a call back. That's if you have anything positive to say. I have to go now. Bye, Mum.'

Darcy hung up and stared at her phone for a moment before looking up at Riley. 'God, that felt so good.'

Riley laughed and hugged her. 'Will it make a difference to the way she treats you?'

'I doubt it, but at least she knows now that I'm not going to put up with it any more. And I just won't tell her how little money I'll be earning in my new jobs. She doesn't need to know that.'

'Well, I might be able to offer you a job too.'

She frowned in confusion. 'You can?'

He nodded, seriously. 'I was looking to get a live-in dog walker. Kelpie needs someone to walk her twice a day and sometimes I just don't have the time. I was going to use the basement room, put a bed in there and rent it out to the dog walker for a very reduced rent in return for a bit of dog walking.'

Darcy smiled. 'Is that right?'

'But it needs to be someone who likes fish and sea life, as that plays quite a big part of that room, someone who likes dogs and also someone who doesn't mind sharing a bathroom and even sharing a shower.'

Darcy tapped her chin thoughtfully. 'Those are quite specific requirements.'

'I know, believe me I've been looking everywhere for someone to fill the job, but when I say that I might actually be in the shower with them it just puts them off. But then it occurred to me, you like fish.'

'I do.'

'And dogs.'

'Yes. I have one myself, so I am aware of their needs.'

'And you have experience of sharing a shower with me and you haven't been put off.'

'No, definitely not.'

'So I thought, why don't I ask you?'

She looped her arms round his neck. 'Are you asking me to move in with you?'

'No, it's too soon for that. I have strong morals, you know. But I'm asking if you would like to lodge with me. Some nights I'd sleep over in your bedroom and other nights you could sleep over in mine. And you'd walk Kelpie in return for free rent, although most days I'd walk her with you, just to make sure you are doing a good enough job.'

'I'll have to think about your terms. Just how often would I be expected to share the shower with you?'

He smiled. 'Every day.'

'Hmmm, it sounds very tempting.'

He wrapped his hands round her waist and leaned his forehead against hers. 'I love you and this is your home. You belong here.'

'I belong with you and there's nowhere else I'd rather be.'

EPILOGUE

Darcy felt the warm sea breeze brush over her skin. She could hear whispering, Riley's deep voice and someone else, though she couldn't make out the words. The only thing she could see was an endless black as she stared at the inside of the blindfold.

Riley returned to her side then, putting his hand on her back and guiding her gently forward. She shivered slightly at his touch and with nervous anticipation.

'Don't be scared,' Riley whispered.

She smiled. 'I'm not scared, I'm with you.'

Riley had said he wanted to do something special to celebrate their one-year anniversary of their first date, but she'd had no idea what he had been planning.

Their footsteps echoed as they walked across the room, the slight tang of seawater hitting her nose, and she immediately knew where they were. She had worked at the aquarium for the past year and she knew the sounds and scents of the place as if they were part of her.

Riley stopped her and undid the blindfold at the back of her head. As he pulled it away from her face, she blinked and smiled at where they were. They were standing in the underwater tunnel that ran through the aquarium's shark and ray tank. The top of the enclosure had a glass roof and the moon and stars twinkled and shimmered through the water. The sharks and rays swam serenely past, always breathtaking in their beauty. She smiled when she saw the bedding on the floor.

It had been her idea to offer 'Sleep with the Fish' nights, where people would bring their own beds and bedding and sleep in the tunnel under the sharks, making her childhood dream come true for members of the town. The aquarium would offer hot chocolates and midnight snacks and different members of the team would take it in turns to give the people nocturnal tours and, in the case of the children's sleepovers, tell spooky sea-themed ghost stories. It had been hugely popular for people of all ages, and not just the residents of White Cliff Bay but people from further afield and many tourists too. It had been something that Darcy wanted to do herself one night with Riley but hadn't had the time, what with all her shifts at the aquarium and the work she did for the Shark Trust. Now Riley had made it happen.

'It's just the two of us here, no members of staff to offer us tours. I thought you could give me your own tour later, if you wanted, but for now we're alone,' Riley said.

'I love this idea, thank you . . .' She trailed off as she saw the flickering gold from the tunnel that was round the corner. That wasn't normal. She moved round the corner and gasped at all the candles that lined each side of the tunnel, sending gold elongated shadows over the glass.

Music started from a nearby stereo and the sounds of 'Kiss the Girl' from *The Little Mermaid* drifted from the speakers. She giggled as she looked round for Riley.

He held out his hand. 'May I have this dance?'

She moved into his arms as he swung her round the glass tunnel. If the sharks were surprised to see two people dancing below them, they didn't show it.

'This is beautiful, thank you,' Darcy said, laying her head on his chest as he slowed down and the music stopped.

He kissed her on the forehead. 'This past year has been the happiest of my life. Partly because toad in the hole and Marmite on toast have become my new favourite foods, partly because I have real friendships in this town now that I never thought I'd have, and a relationship with my grandmother, a woman I adore. All of that is down to you – you taught me to embrace life again, to try new things, you taught me that life is better when you let people in. I love you so much for opening my eyes to that. But mostly my life has been happy because of you. You make me laugh every single day, I love listening to you talk, I love watching you with other people, how kind and understanding you are. I love lying in bed, holding you in my arms. I love walking our dogs along the beach. My life before you feels empty and dark, and now it feels complete. You are my best friend and I thank my lucky stars every day that you swam into my life.'

She looked up at him and smiled. 'You've turned my life around too. You've made me realise that I should never settle, that I should always reach for my dreams. I wouldn't be doing a job I love if it wasn't for you. I wake up every day with the biggest smile on my face because you're lying next to me. I love you, with everything I have.'

He pulled out of her arms and went to retrieve a large square blue box, wrapped in a silver bow.

'I bought you an anniversary present.' He passed her the box.

'Oh, I bought you one too, but I didn't bring it with us tonight.'

She tugged at the ribbon and opened the lid and laughed when she saw the white cowboy hat inside. It had a silver ribbon round the middle, which finished with a silvery pearl flower in the centre of the hat.

She took it out and put it on. 'I love it so much, thank you.'

His mouth quirked up into that gorgeous half smile as he pulled it off her head. 'I thought you might want to wear it on our wedding day.'

Her heart stopped as he undid the bow just under the flower to release the ring she hadn't seen when she'd pulled the hat out of the box. He placed the hat back on her head and sank down to one knee. The ring had three small circular stones; one was a diamond, one a sapphire and, in the middle, slightly bigger than the others, was a tiny polished green ammonite. She smiled at the significance.

'I love you so much, Darcy Davenport, and I simply cannot imagine my life without you. Would you do me the honour of being my wife?'

Tears fell from her eyes, as she laughed and nodded at the same time. 'Of course I will.'

She bent down to kiss him and he slid the ring on her finger. She admired the deep blue of the sapphire, the sparkle of the diamond, and the green and gold of the ammonite as it twinkled in the glow of the candles. He stood up and hugged her, holding her tight against him. Nothing felt more right at that moment than being with him.

'I want to get married in the sea. We'll both wear mermaid costumes,' she joked.

He swung her up in his arms and planted a kiss on her lips. 'How about we get married in the lantern room, now we've had the lantern removed? We can take the love seat out temporarily and we can put chairs round the edge. We can have a blue theme.'

'Oh, I like your way better, can I have bridesmaids dressed as dolphins?'

He laughed. 'If that's what you want.'

'And sharks?'

'Sure.'

'Can we get married at night, under the stars?'

'That can be arranged. Now, tell me, do you have security cameras in the tunnel?'

'No, are you planning on doing something wicked? There are shark pups in the tank, I don't want them to be corrupted.'

'You better tell them to look away then.'

He kissed her as he carried her back towards the bed and she giggled against his lips. As he laid her down on the blankets and she looked up at the stars twinkling through the water, she knew that there in Riley's arms was exactly where she belonged.

LETTER FROM HOLLY

Thank you so much for reading *Summer at Rose Island*. I had so much fun creating this story and I hope you enjoyed reading it as much as I enjoyed writing it.

One of the best parts of writing comes from seeing the reaction from readers. Did it make you smile or laugh, did it make you cry? Hopefully happy tears! Did you fall in love with Riley and Darcy? Did you like the gorgeous town of White Cliff Bay? If you enjoyed the story, I would absolutely love it if you could leave a short review. Getting feedback from readers is amazing and it also helps to persuade other readers to pick up one of my books for the first time.

To keep up to date with the latest news on my new releases, go to the address below to sign up for a newsletter. I promise to only contact you when I have a new book out and I'll never share your email with anyone else.

www.bookouture.com/holly-martin

I have two other books set in the town of White Cliff Bay, so if you enjoyed this book and haven't read *Christmas at Lilac Cottage* or *Snowflakes on Silver Cove* yet, I hope you will love them too.

Thank you for reading.

Love,

Holly x

@hollymartin00
hollymartinauthor
www.hollymartinwriter.wordpress.com

ACKNOWLEDGEMENTS

To my family: my mom, my biggest fan, who reads every word I have written a hundred times over and loves it every single time; my dad; my brother Lee and my sister-in-law Julie, for your support, love, encouragement and endless excitement for my stories.

For my Texas twinnie, the gorgeous Aven Ellis, for just being my wonderful friend, for your endless support, for cheering me on and for keeping me entertained with wonderful stories and pictures of hot men, and for helping me ensure that all of Riley's speech and thoughts were American English and not British English. I love you dearly.

To my friends Gareth and Mandie, for your support, patience and enthusiasm. My lovely friends Jac, Verity and Jodie, who listen to me talk about my books endlessly and get excited about it every single time.

For Sharon Sant, for just being there always and your wonderful friendship.

To Emma Poulloura, for being wonderful and efficient and organising a fabulous blog tour.

To my wonderful agent Madeleine Milburn, and Cara Lee Simpson, for just being amazing and fighting my corner, and for your unending patience with my constant questions.

To my wonderful editor Claire, for putting up with all my craziness throughout the whole process, for replying to every single email and for listening to me freak out with complete and utter patience. To my editor Celine Kelly, for helping to make this book so much better; my copyeditor Rhian, for doing such a good job at spotting any issues or typos. And to Natasha Hodgson, for your help with the edits and the audiobook too. Thank you to Kim Nash for the tireless promoting, tweeting and general cheerleading. Thank you to all the other wonderful people at Bookouture: Oliver Rhodes, the editing team and the wonderful designers who created this absolutely gorgeous cover. Thank you to the team at the Audio Factory for working hard to complete the audiobook of *Summer at Rose Island*, too.

Thank you to Bruce Stokell for information on his wonderful lighthouse in New Zealand; the staff at Portland Bill Lighthouse who were very helpful and informative; Historic England, who gave me some great advice on listings, how to apply and why the lighthouse might be rejected; Rob Wassell, who gave me loads of really useful information about Beachy Head Lighthouse, sent me loads of really interesting photos and his fantastic book, *The Story of Beachy Head Lighthouse*, which proved invaluable; David Martin, for his help on marine biology; the Marine Conservation Society, for their help; and the wonderful Cat Gordon from the Shark Trust, who helped me so much with my research on angel sharks and tying them into my story. Thanks to the Shark Siders website, who have all these brilliant videos on their website that Darcy shows Ryan in the story; Elaina James, Derek Johnson, Karan Eleni, Amanda Hagel, who helped me with my questions about songwriting; Erin Lawless for her great help regarding the legal powers of a council in the case of Compulsory Purchase Orders; Carmel Harrington, for lending me her name.

To the CASG, the best writing group in the world: you wonderful, talented, supportive bunch of authors. I feel very blessed to know you all – you guys are the very best.

To the wonderful Bookouture authors, for all your encouragement and support.

To all those involved in the blog tour. To anyone who has read my book and taken the time to tell me you've enjoyed it or written a review, thank you so much.

Thank you, I love you all.

CPSIA information can be obtained at www.ICGtesting.com
Printed in the USA
LVOW10s1350310716

498494LV00018B/955/P